What the critics are saying…

GOLD STAR! "*Promises Prevail* is an emotion charged book that will test the limits of your heart. Whether this is your first or your fourth read by *Ms. McCarty,* you'll find yourself discovering that this author definitely has the Midas touch, with a *Gold Star* being the most natural reward for a spectacular piece." ~ *J.B. DuBose Just Erotic Romance Review*

GOLD STAR!! "Without a doubt, *Promises Prevail* has taken my breath away with its deeply impacting storyline and beautifully charismatic characters." ~ *Francesca Hayne Just Erotic Romance Reviews*

FIVE BLUE RIBBONS! "*PROMISES PREVAIL* is one of the most heart warming, compassionate, love stories that I have ever read. *Sarah McCarty* is a truly gifted writer." ~ *Dina Romance Junkies*

5 STARS!!! "*Sarah McCarty* delivers again with *Promises Prevail,* the newest in the *Promises* series. With her usual flair she has created a powerfully erotic, emotional, and thought provoking romance that draws you in from the first chapter and refuses to let go," ~ *Rowan Ecataromance*

Sarah McCarty

Promises Prevail

ELLORA'S CAVE
ROMANTICA PUBLISHING

An Ellora's Cave Romantica Publication

www.ellorascave.com

Promises Prevail

ISBN # 1419952447
ALL RIGHTS RESERVED.
Promises Prevail Copyright© 2005 Sarah McCarty
Edited by: Pamela Campbell
Cover art by: Syneca

Electronic book Publication: March, 2005
Trade paperback Publication: September, 2005

Warning:

The following material contains graphic sexual content meant for mature readers. *Promises Prevail* has been rated *E-rotic* by a minimum of three independent reviewers.

Ellora's Cave Publishing offers three levels of Romantica™ reading entertainment: S (S-ensuous), E (E-rotic), and X (X-treme).

S-*ensuous* love scenes are explicit and leave nothing to the imagination.

E-*rotic* love scenes are explicit, leave nothing to the imagination, and are high in volume per the overall word count. In addition, some E-rated titles might contain fantasy material that some readers find objectionable, such as bondage, submission, same sex encounters, forced seductions, etc. E-rated titles are the most graphic titles we carry; it is common, for instance, for an author to use words such as "fucking", "cock", "pussy", etc., within their work of literature.

X-*treme* titles differ from E-rated titles only in plot premise and storyline execution. Unlike E-rated titles, stories designated with the letter X tend to contain controversial subject matter not for the faint of heart.

Also by Sarah McCarty:

Mac's Law
Promises Linger
Promises Keep

Promises Prevail

Dedication

For Kimberly, who can laugh in the face of adversity and persevere despite the odds. May life reward you with your fondest dream come true.

And from the real Danny and the incredible Jebediah: Thank you Carol and Dorothy of the Bartow County Humane Society for recognizing the greatness of these phenomenal dogs despite their physical conditions. Illness can be cured, wounds can be healed, but only a family could fill the void in their devastated hearts. You made that possible. Rescue thanks you and so do their forever homes.

Trademarks Acknowledgement

The author acknowledges the trademarked status and trademark owners of the following wordmarks mentioned in this work of fiction:

Stetson: John B. Stetson, Company

Chapter One

Clint couldn't believe he was doing this again. Another Saturday, another woman. Another pointless excursion to the Sweet Thyme Bakery in search of a connection that wasn't going to happen. He'd long since given up that it ever would, so now his search for a wife was purely a matter of lining up traits and searching for a woman who fit them. The same way he selected a brood mare for his breeding program.

He glanced down at the young woman at his side. She smiled up at him, all hope and innocence. So pure she made him feel ancient. Rebecca Salisbury was his latest hopeful. She possessed all the qualities a good wife should have—good breeding, good training, and good wide hips for easy childbirth. He knew he wouldn't have with her the passionate love his cousin Cougar had with his wife, but she'd be stable and a good mother. Most importantly, she wouldn't clutter up his calm with a lot of emotion. He cupped Rebecca's elbow in his palm and helped her up the wooden steps to the walkway. Peace, he'd discovered, was a hard won commodity.

The smells from the bakery wrapped around him like a fragrant hug, soothing his senses.

Rebecca paused and waited for him to open the door. Her smile was shy as he reached over her shoulder. His response was an automatic stretch of his lips, but his attention was ahead of them, checking out the small, crowded shop and its occupants—most especially the owner.

She was just stepping out from behind the counter, her gait more awkward than usual. He ushered Rebecca in ahead of him, watching Jenna Hennesey as he did, noting the lines of strain on her face, frowning as she pulled up with a gasp, pausing, her focus turning inward. No doubt controlling the pain that all this running around was provoking in her damaged leg.

Damn it! He'd told her to hire some help.

He knew the minute she saw him. It wasn't obvious as she kept her head down and rarely met anyone's eyes, but the slight start in her body, and the blush that surged over her cheeks were dead giveaways.

"I'll be right with you," she called across the small room. Her voice, with its husky timbre, tickled his senses like a lure. He didn't like the way she could slip under his calm, yet at the same time some perverse part of him relished these little moments of connection. As if Jenna could ever be for him.

His "Take your time" coincided with Rebecca's "Thank you".

He watched as Jenna brought the tray of coffee and dessert to the older couple at the table in the far corner. Their greeting was warm. Hers was quiet and unassuming like the woman herself. Jenna Hennesey was sweet, shy and the biggest temptation he'd ever fought off in his life.

Jenna laughed at something the older couple, the Jacobsons, said. Her dimples flashed, sparking that wild core of lust inside of him that he tried to keep contained. The Jacobsons laughed back. They'd come to help their daughter through her lying-in and had stayed. That was happening more and more frequently, proving the theory of the town fathers that Cheyenne just might become civilized after all.

"Word must be out that Jenna can cook." Rebecca stepped back into him as a little boy rushed past her on his way to the counter. For one second, her rear pressed against his groin. It would have been nice if his body gave a shit. She blushed and stepped away. He merely nodded in response to her "Excuse me". She was beautiful and perfect, but she left him cold.

The boy reached the counter and proceeded to hop from one foot to the other as he waited for Jenna to notice him. Little Fred was the spitting image of his pa, and at six looked as though he'd have his father's size and build. And his lack of patience.

"That's Cyrus' boy, isn't it?" Rebecca asked.

"Yes. Once a week Gertie sends him in for cinnamon buns." Speculation was rampant as to what Cyrus did for the woman to get that boon. Gertie could pinch a penny until it screamed.

As soon as Jenna noticed the boy, she dropped everything and walked away from her customers, a smile on her full, soft lips, her dimples coming to life. Clint's cock came to life right along with them. The woman had a killer smile.

She smoothed the boy's hair, the gesture so soft and gentle that it made Clint ache. He wanted that softness for himself, and the knowledge that there wasn't much stopping him from taking it ate at his decency. Jenna was alone in the world. Fair game. And she owed him. All he had to do was say the word, and she'd be his. There was nothing stopping him but his own damned conscience. Son of a bitch, it was a pain having a conscience.

"It'd be nice if she could make a go of the place," Rebecca murmured, watching them. "My momma said she had a hard time of it after her husband died."

She'd had a harder time of it when he was alive, but Clint didn't mention that. That was Jenna's secret. A tinge of guilt hit his conscience when he caught the admiring glance Rebecca shot him. It said more clearly than words that she considered him husband material. He mentally shook his head. Some women just had no sense.

He glanced at Jenna. *She* had sense, along with the incredible strength that allowed her to endure and rebuild when others would have just given up. Problem was, she was too often done in by her big heart. He frowned as she wrapped some cookies in a napkin and slipped them to Fred. There was no way that Gertie had sent more than the cost of the rolls with the kid. Now Jenna was going to be out the cost of the cookies and the cost of the napkin. All because she was a soft touch. So damned soft that he didn't know how much longer he was going to be able to keep his hands off of her. He might be a son of a bitch, but he hoped to hell he wasn't that far gone.

* * * * *

Jenna put the tray on the counter, quelled the unease that always nibbled at her calm when she was around McKinnely, put on her most welcoming smile, and turned to face the couple standing just inside the door. They were a beautiful study in contrasts. Big Clint McKinnely with his dark skin and darker eyes, and that generous, purely masculine mouth was standing beside the tall, elegant mayor's daughter with her fair skin, smattering of freckles, and easy smile. Of the two, Rebecca was the least intimidating so Jenna focused on her.

"I'm sorry to keep you waiting but if you'll follow me, your table is ready."

Rebecca smiled and placed her hand on Clint's arm. "Thank you."

Clint didn't say anything, just followed in her wake. Jenna knew he was annoyed that she hadn't addressed him directly, but she couldn't. The man made her a bundle of nerves, always watching her. If he were a gentler kind of man, she might have hoped for his interest, but Clint was so aggressively masculine that she wondered why lawbreakers even bothered to resist when he went after them. She had only to look at him to know that he would always have his way. In everything.

She blamed him entirely when she stumbled. Anyone would be nervous to be watched so intently. Still, she would have been fine if her weight hadn't fallen on her bad leg, and it hadn't chosen that moment to collapse. Behind her, she heard someone gasp as she lurched into an empty table. For one second she caught herself on the edge, but then it skipped out from under her. One minute, she was falling and the next she was being yanked against the hard surface of a well-muscled chest. She breathed deeply as the scents of man, smoke and pine swept over her. Clint had saved her. Again.

His hand slid down her back, and she mentally moaned. Why had she chosen today of all days to not wear her best corset? At least with that corset some of her…ampleness would have been contained. His big hands spanned her waist and he set her away from him.

Heat surged to her cheeks. "I'm sorry."

"No harm done." Though he'd pushed her a foot away, he didn't release her. His hands on her waist burned like fire as he steadied her. "Are you okay?"

"I'm fine. I just stumbled."

"Maybe you should sit down for a minute?" Rebecca suggested as Clint stepped back, holding out a chair, frowning with concern.

Jenna mentally sighed. She was so tired of being pitied. "Really, I'm fine."

The glance Clint cast from under his hat brim said he had doubts. She ignored it. "If you'll take your seats, I'll be right with you. Would you like tea or coffee?"

Rebecca's request for tea was no more a surprise than Clint's request for black coffee. She glanced across the restaurant and pressed her skirt against the knot below the scar on her leg. The coffeepot was a long way away. She gritted her teeth and headed for it, doing her best to smooth her gait. She made it back to the table without incident.

Before she could set the tray down, Clint had it out of her hands and on the table.

"You need to rest."

"I'm fine."

"You are not making me happy."

A kernel of dread took root in her stomach. "I'm sorry."

She ducked her head and waited. He wasn't her husband, but he was a man and she was a woman alone. He could pretty much demand whatever he wanted and she would have to obey. She could feel Rebecca's stare as well as Clint's. Bile rose in her throat as she waited for Clint's decision.

"Could we see the menu?" Rebecca asked.

Jenna wanted to move more than anything, but the years of training froze her in place until Clint released her with a sigh. "Fetch the menus, Jenna."

Clint's black gaze followed her as she moved away. She shivered. He was such an intense man. There was no telling what he was thinking. He frowned as she neared the table, and his gaze dropped. As much as she'd like to believe that it was her rose-colored skirt cut to de-emphasize her generous hips that caught his eye, she knew differently.

She was limping. There wasn't anything she could do about that. All this extra business waiting on what used to be only occasional tables was heck on her leg. She forced a more normal stride. It was vain and pointless, but she didn't want to look weak in front of him. She struggled to keep from gasping as pain knifed up her thigh.

"Here are today's choices, Mr. McKinnely." From the way Clint's eyes narrowed, she knew he hadn't missed the breathless quality of her voice after that last step. If he knew how much pain she was in, he'd be furious. Ever since he'd saved her life, he'd been protective. If he didn't completely ignore her otherwise, she'd think he was staking a claim. But until this last week, he'd never approached her or spoken to her personally. For which she was eternally grateful.

"*Mr. McKinnely*, Jenna?" Clint asked, taking the paper menus from her hand.

Dropping her gaze at Clint's disapproving tone was as much instinct as it was upbringing. Clint had a way of speaking that demanded compliance. She barely stopped herself from apologizing.

But she did. She wasn't with her father, her husband, or their church anymore. She was an independent woman.

From beneath her lashes, she saw Rebecca shoot Clint a quick look as he read the short menu, caught a glimpse of conclusion as she looked between them, and then saw her frown of disapproval.

Jenna winced. Rebecca wasn't the first woman to assume Clint had a relationship with her. He had given her the money for her bakery and he was a frequent customer, though if they thought she was his mistress, she didn't know what they thought about him doing his courting here.

She wet her dry lips. She didn't meet Rebecca's eyes as the flush rushed over her cheeks. She struggled through her embarrassment for a business-like tone. "I'm out of chicken soup, but I have a nice beef barley all ready to go."

"That'll be fine." Clint looked around. "Business looks good."

"It is."

He leaned back in his chair. "Enough to have that leg giving you trouble?"

Heat crept into her cheeks anew. She wished he wouldn't always notice her weaknesses. "No more than usual."

"You were limping."

"I always limp."

His frown deepened. "Not that much."

She shrugged. "It can't be helped."

His black eyes cut to hers, unreadable as always, as he said in a perfectly reasonable tone of voice, "You could get off it. Put it up. Wrap a warm towel around it."

She fought down the instinctive urge to leap to do as he wanted. "I will when I close up shop."

His gaze flicked over her face, no doubt taking in every sign of the tiredness and strain she tried to hide. "That's not for four hours."

It was a reasonable observation in a reasonable tone of voice, but the underlying censure pricked her nerves.

"Clint," Rebecca interjected gently. "I'm sure Mrs. Hennesey knows when she needs to rest."

Jenna's "Thank you" coincided with Clint's "Maybe".

Rebecca shook her head, a reprimand that Jenna couldn't ever imagine giving a man. "You're embarrassing Mrs. Hennesey."

His gaze never left Jenna. "Maybe."

No maybe about it. He was. Jenna felt inferior enough in front of perfect Rebecca without him making a fuss about something that couldn't be helped.

"I can't afford to close early."

Rebecca shot Jenna a sympathetic glance. "Honestly Clint, no woman likes to have it pointed out that she's crippled."

Jenna clutched her pencil in her hand. She knew how her limp made her look to others, but she wasn't a cripple.

Clint's normally cool gaze chilled as he turned toward Rebecca. "That was a damned callous thing to say."

Rebecca flushed. "I'm sorry, I shouldn't have mentioned it."

Jenna believed her. Rebecca was enviably sheltered and sweet, but never deliberately cruel. Either Clint didn't share her opinion or he didn't care, because he didn't relax his expression. *The big bully.*

Jenna squared her shoulders and took a breath. If she was going to be an independent woman, she couldn't be afraid of taking someone's side when they were being treated unfairly in her establishment. The pencil bit into her palm as she pointed out, "You didn't mention it. Mr. McKinnely did."

Clint went very still. "Are you challenging me?"

Fear pooled in Jenna's stomach like a lead weight. Maybe taking this stand wasn't such a smart idea. She gripped the pencil between her fingers, saw the distress on Rebecca's face, and forced starch back into her knees. "I just think you're being too harsh."

Clint would have probably been more impressed with her stand if she'd been able to get her eyes higher than the open neck of his shirt. Truth was, she was impressed that she'd gotten the words out at all. She'd always been a weak woman, though she was learning to fake strength.

"I'm sure you've heard the stories of how I handle a challenge," Clint pointed out, still using that reasonable tone.

Rebecca's eyes widened as she sat back.

Jenna wished she had something against which to brace herself. She dropped her gaze to the table. Clint reached for his coffee cup. His hand dwarfed the cup. Ridges and scars marked the back. He hadn't gotten them by being soft or backing down. And she'd just told him he was wrong. Dear God, maybe she was as crazy as Jack had always said. She moistened her lips and managed to say, "I've heard."

Clint arched his brow and took a sip of his coffee. Jenna's knees shook, making her leg ache more, and a cold sweat broke out over her body. She waited for him to say something. Anything.

He just sat there drinking his coffee and watching her. Her stomach knotted. She focused on the shadowed hollow of his throat, her heartbeat thundering in her ears as she waited. On the fifth beat, she couldn't stand it anymore."I just meant, if I didn't mind maybe you shouldn't."

A strange sound rumbled in Clint's chest. Almost like a growl. The ice left his gaze to be replaced by a strange heat. Was he angry? The point of the pencil bit into her palm.

Dear God! she thought, *if you could send me some help, I'd really appreciate it.*

"But what if I do mind?" Clint asked, replacing the cup on the table.

"I don't know why you should."

Out of the corner of her eye, she glimpsed a flash of white as Rebecca covered Clint's hand with hers and said, "Clint, you're upsetting Mrs. Hennesey."

Jenna stared at the contrast, Rebecca's hand so soft and white and fragile, sitting on top of Clint's lean, powerful one. Jenna envied Rebecca the innocence that protected her from the knowledge of how fast a man could turn on a woman.

"Am I scaring you, Jenna?" Clint asked in that calm, "reveal nothing" voice.

Jenna swallowed hard, aware that everyone in the small restaurant watched the scene, witnessing her humiliation. The bell over the door jangled as it opened. She didn't look up, but she knew who, or rather what, had entered by the way the door thumped twice before closing.

God had heard her after all. He'd sent her protector. Jenna opened her hand to the warm nose that slid under her palm and sank her fingers into the black fur of the massive dog's neck. As he leaned against her a low, rumbling growl emanated from Danny's throat, clearly directed at Clint.

"What is that?" Rebecca gasped pulling back.

Clint's answer was full of dry amusement. "My dog."

"Are you sure it's not a pony?" Rebecca's hand slid from Clint's as she inched away.

"I'm sure. Threw a saddle on him once and he howled for hours. No mistaking what he was, after that."

The tension in the room eased as a couple of the men snorted with laughter. Jenna patted Danny as he sat, being careful to avoid his burn scars, knowing they were as painfully sensitive as hers. He rested his head on her chest, the slobber from his jowls soaking through the bib of her apron. She didn't mind. Danny was safety.

Clint's chair creaked as he leaned back and folded his arms across his chest. "So Jenna... Do you disapprove of my treatment of Miss Salisbury?"

She clutched Danny close and battled her cowardice. She'd started this, and she should end it with a definitive "Yes", but it wasn't that easy to get the word out. Clint could destroy her business. He could destroy her. She opened her mouth. Her lips formed the word, but nothing came out.

"What was that?" Clint asked.

She closed her eyes, humiliation washing over her at her own cowardice. Within her arms, Danny straightened and growled a long, low, warning rumble at Clint.

"Aren't you supposed to be out guarding my horse?" Clint asked the dog, the straight slash of his brow rising on the question.

Danny didn't move and he didn't shut up. Jenna leaned down and whispered in his ear. He quieted immediately.

Clint watched as Jenna bent to Danny. Her skin was whiter than white, and her eyes held that haunted look that told him how close she was to breaking. She stood there, her deliciously plump body half hidden by his dog, her pride around her toes, and he knew she reached for the strength that she relied on. Knew she'd find it, too. Goddamn it, he ought to let her humiliate herself like this simply because she would. Instead, he found himself wanting to slip between her silence and her intent, wanting to offer her a way out. The impulse faded as Jenna slowly straightened. Her bright blue eyes met his for the first time in the last five minutes, before dropping away uncomfortably.

"Danny is very sensitive," she whispered.

Clint gave the huge dog, which looked like a cross between a bear and a bloodhound, a tap on his nose. "He didn't used to be."

But he was a damned good judge of character, and he'd taken to Jenna Hennesey right off, lying beside her in that burning building, ready to die with her. Almost did when the roof of that bedraggled shack had come crashing down around them. He still didn't know how they'd gotten out of there. She'd shown incredible inner strength that night. Holding on despite the tremendous pain. Holding on when he thought she'd pass out, knowing he'd lose her if she did. Digging deep when he asked her to. He hadn't seen a lick of that incredible inner strength since, but that didn't mean it wasn't there.

Plain and simple, Jenna Hennesey was too nice for her own good. Almost a doormat. Unless she thought someone was being picked on. Then she dug in her heels and fought. Quietly, subtly, but with an iron will that didn't flinch. The hell of it was that she pulled him both ways. One way he wanted to wrap her up and cuddle all that softness close. The other he wanted to throw her to the ground and bury himself in all that lush feminine strength.

Neither was an option. Jenna Hennesey had paid enough in her life for one woman. Hooking up with him would only give her more pain. Jenna needed a man filled with ideals and hope for tomorrow. A man who could echo the optimism she wore like a banner. His had long since dried up.

"Now that we've cleared up the unpleasantness, could we have our lunch?" Rebecca asked.

Jenna flashed her a grateful look, one that showed her dimples. Clint felt the familiar twitch in his cock that he always experienced in Jenna's presence. He squashed the arousal and gave Rebecca his best smile. She blinked and caught her breath. He'd seen the reaction a thousand times from a thousand women. In his youth, he'd used it. In later years, he'd taken advantage of it, but now… Hell. He looked into Rebecca's expectant face. Hell, now he had no use for it.

"Lunch would be fine."

Clint glanced at Jenna. Her round face was drawn with tension. She was worried. He was willing to bet that the fingers buried in the dog's ruff were white-knuckled. Damn, why did he always feel compelled to push her? Was he so shallow, so empty, that he couldn't handle one woman who did not fall at his feet? The knowledge that he probably was didn't lighten his mood.

"I'll have the soup." He glanced at the smug looking dog. "And if you haven't earmarked every piece of that custard pie for Danny, I'll have a slice of that to go with it."

He could tell from the dismay flooding Jenna's expression that she had done just that.

"There's only one piece left…" her voice trailed off.

Clint would have pleaded his case, but as if sensing his pie was in danger, Danny tipped his head back and let the loose skin around his face sag, giving him a look so woeful that Clint didn't bother to compete.

"Hell."

Jenna kissed Danny's nose. "I'm sorry."

She stumbled back as Danny let his full weight lean against her.

"I should be used to it by now," Clint muttered, catching her wrist and steadying her.

"Used to what?" Rebecca asked, eyeing his fingers on Jenna's wrist.

"Being outmaneuvered by a mutt." He released Jenna, noting with interest the faint pink touching her cheeks.

"Danny is not a mutt." There was that hint of steel threading Jenna's husky voice that always triggered a purely sexual reaction in him.

"Then what is he?"

She didn't have an answer, but her soft mouth thinned with determination. Three seconds later she had one. "He's special."

He would give her that. He had yet to decide if the dog was a blessing or a curse.

"What else is on the menu?"

She shifted her feet and bit her lip, something he'd noticed she did when ill at ease. "I experimented today with a new recipe."

"Yeah?" Things were looking up. Jenna's experiments were always a jaw-dropping experience.

"Yes."

"What did you make?" Rebecca asked cautiously, sitting up and keeping her eyes on Danny the whole time.

"I tried a torte."

Clint's mouth was already watering.

"Chocolate?" he asked, hoping against hope. Used to be that Jenna always baked a chocolate dessert on Saturdays, but then someone had noted that the new desserts always coincided with his visits, and she'd stopped. He figured she didn't want him thinking she was encouraging his kind.

Her "Yes" was soft, and her gaze didn't meet his. Her bottom lip slipped between her teeth, forcing her dimples into prominence. His cock went rock-hard in a rush. Damn, the woman was too beautiful for words. Jenna might not be for him, but he'd like to sink for a week into those lush curves of hers. Bury his face in the deep cleavage between her breasts and immerse himself in her scent. He bet she'd be soft and welcoming all over. The kind of softness that took away a man's loneliness.

"That sounds delicious," Rebecca sighed.

Jenna's head came up. Clint noted that she didn't avoid Rebecca's gaze the way she did his.

"I hope so. It has a mocha walnut butter cream filling with a dark chocolate glaze. It might be too much for some."

"There can never be too much chocolate," Clint countered. At the same time Rebecca moaned and asked, "Any chance you are looking for sacrificial lambs to try out this new recipe?"

Jenna's hands twisted in Danny's fur. "I couldn't charge you for it."

Clint swore under his breath. "Like hell you couldn't."

"But it's only an experiment."

She looked genuinely distressed, as if paying for a dessert he might not like would break him. "I'll tell you what, if I don't like it, I won't pay for it."

"I'd like to try it, too," Rebecca piped up. "My momma has it in her head that chocolate is bad for the complexion, so I never get it unless I sneak it."

That cinched it, Clint knew. Jenna would bring Rebecca the torte, because the one thing Jenna loved was chocolate and being without it made her cranky. It was why he'd paid Eloise to stock it in her store and to sell it to Jenna for a quarter of the price. She'd never been anywhere to know that the price she paid was too low. And it made Clint happy to know his money gave someone pleasure.

Jenna let go of Danny, wrapped her hands in her skirt and bit her lip, flashing those dimples again. He bit back a moan. His hunger for Jenna was getting out of control.

"I'll bring it out, but only if you promise that you won't feel obligated to say you like it if you don't."

"I'm pretty sure I'm going to like it," Rebecca assured her. "It's chocolate after all."

The gentleness in her tone while talking to Jenna raised her up a notch in Clint's opinion. He made a mental note to find a way to slip Rebecca chocolate now and again.

"I'll be right back, then." Jenna turned, flinching as her weight came down on her bad leg. Danny whined and leaned against her. With a nod, she acknowledged the bum hovering by the door and rubbed her thigh.

Clint shook his head when she invited the bum in before heading to the back of the shop, Danny pressed against her side, supporting her weight. Even from this distance he could smell the sour whiskey and old sweat emanating from the drunk's dirty clothes. Any other shopkeeper wouldn't have let him in the door, but Clint knew Jenna would seat him and treat him like a king, apologizing profusely to everyone he offended, but she wouldn't send him away. He'd bet she wouldn't even charge the no-account, her heart once again getting in the way of business.

Clint made a mental note to double his tip. The woman was too soft for her own good. Too stubborn, too. He could tell from her limp as she pushed through the kitchen door that her leg was killing her. No way was she going to make it through the whole day without a disaster, which meant no way was he going to get any peace for worrying about what form it would take. No sooner had the thought formed in his mind than a crash and a scream came from behind the swinging door.

There was a moment of deafening silence, and then Danny howled.

Chapter Two

Clint was out of his chair, over the counter and through the door before the last note of the eerie howl faded to nothing. The only other time he'd heard Danny howl like that, Jenna had been trapped in that shack, fire roaring all around.

His first impression of the room was chaos. A shelf was down, the contents strewn over the stove and the counter, shards of broken pottery sprinkled about. Then he saw Danny sitting beside the downed shelf, his expression urgent. The shelf heaved. Clint's heart stopped beating.

He threw the wood structure to the side. Beneath it lay Jenna. She struggled to kneel but then collapsed again. He caught her with an arm under her torso before she could hit the floor.

"Son of a bitch, are you all right?"

She nodded as he turned her over, sliding to his knees as he eased her onto her back.

"Like hell you are," he muttered, more to himself than to her. Her expression was contorted with pain, her body arched over his knees as she struggled to contain the agony. He couldn't stand seeing her like this. He caught her shoulders, holding her still.

"Hell, Sunshine, scream if you want to, but tell me where you're hurt."

She didn't scream. Her short nails bit through his denims into his thighs as she gasped, "My leg."

Danny growled deep in his throat a second before Rebecca asked, "Is she all right?"

Clint wanted to echo the growl as he looked over his shoulder and saw all the faces staring through the door. Jenna would be mortified. A quick glance down told him she already was. Her bright blue eyes were awash in tears.

"She's fine, but if you could tell everyone that the restaurant's closed for the rest of the day, I'd appreciate it." He ignored Jenna's violent shaking of her head. "Mrs. Hennesey needs a rest."

Damn, calling her by that name stuck in his craw. She should never have been married to that brutal bastard. Jenna struggled to get up. He overrode her with a simple placement of his hand on her stomach.

Behind him he heard Rebecca explaining to everyone, adding a reminder not to forget to pay their bills. She was an efficient, capable woman. She'd make someone else a fine wife.

Beneath his hand Jenna's seductively soft stomach heaved as she took a deep breath and gasped, "Jonas."

"What about him?"

"Supper."

"He'll no doubt drink it as usual."

A little shriek escaped the seal of her lips as she lurched against him. He caught her and held her against his chest, tucking her face into his throat, every pant of her breath ripping him up inside.

"I'm going to look at your leg."

She clamped her hand down on her skirt and shook her head.

"Jonas," she gasped again. He tugged at her wrist. She clamped down harder. She was going to fight him until this was settled, he could tell.

"Son of a bitch, you have got to be the most stubborn woman." He turned and hollered out the door. "Rebecca!"

She came through the door a second later, her hands filled with dirty plates. "Yes?"

"Is that drunk still here?"

She glanced over her shoulder. "He's just leaving, and I'm sure he has a name."

Just what he needed, two soft-hearted, soft-headed women.

"Jonas," Jenna gasped again the last syllable rising on high whimper.

"Ladle up a bowl of soup and a dessert for him, and send him on his way."

Rebecca didn't immediately move. Clint glanced over his shoulder. She was staring at Jenna, not so much with pity but with inquiry.

He swore under his breath, realizing nothing important was going to get done until the women had their way.

"What kind of dessert does Jonas like?" he asked Jenna.

He had to wait through four pants before she found enough breath to answer, "Chocolate."

Ah hell, first his pie to a dog and now his cake to a drunk. "Give him a piece of the chocolate torte and tell him if the plates don't come back in one piece I'm taking it out of his hide."

Jenna was shaking her head again as another spasm took her.

"What the hell is it now?"

"Eat here."

"No." There was no way he'd get her to rest if she had someone in the shop.

"Take it," she moaned.

"That's what I want him to do. Take his meal elsewhere."

"I think she means someone will take it from him," Rebecca offered, putting the plates on the floor by the door.

"Son of a fucking bitch!"

Rebecca gasped and Jenna groaned. With an unnecessary "Guard her" to Danny, Clint stormed into the other room. He took his Stetson, with its distinctive band, from his head and held it out to the downtrodden man. "Anyone messes with you—you point to my hat and tell them they're messing with me."

Instead of being grateful, the man looked in the direction from which Clint had just come. "Is Miss Jenna okay?"

"That's Mrs. Hennesey to you."

"Don't like that name."

Clint didn't know if Jonas meant Jenna didn't like the name or he didn't like the name, but since he didn't like it either, he didn't have much room to argue. He stood there holding the hat and waited. Jonas stood there with a set to his shoulders that said he wasn't taking anything until his question was answered. Was everyone trying to get on his bad side?

"She'll be fine. I just have to take care of her, and she won't let me do that until she's sure you're okay."

"She's a good woman." His eyes when they met Clint's were suddenly clear. "You need to take better care of her."

Clint thrust the hat into the man's hands. "Do you want my protection or not?"

Jonas nodded and reached for the hat.

As soon as Jonas touched the brim, Clint spun on his heel. He didn't trust Jenna to wait for him. The woman had a flare for getting into trouble. As if that thought gave birth to reality, Danny howled. Jenna screamed. And there was another god-awful crash.

"Goddamn, Jenna!" he swore, coming through the door. "I told you to stay put." She lay on the floor clutching her leg, her face a mask of agony, a new stack of pots around her.

"Rebecca," he called over his shoulder as he kicked debris out of his way so he could kneel beside her. "Can you get Doc for me? He should be over at Pearl's. Tell him I need laudanum."

"I'll go right away," she called from the other room. He heard the outside door jingle and then slam. Maybe he ought to reconsider Rebecca. He did like a woman who knew how to obey. Unlike Jenna who'd been shaking her head since he'd mentioned Doc and laudanum. He was through arguing with her.

"You're taking it." He couldn't stand to see her in pain any longer than she had to be.

"Can't," she whispered, her gaze skirting his.

He touched her cheek, knowing what she feared. The anger in him fled. "I won't let you have too much for too long, Sunshine."

He'd give her just enough to get them both through this.

He stood, grabbed a towel off the counter and tossed it into a bowl. He grabbed the hot tea water off the burner and poured it onto the towel, soaking it. Steam rose around his face. He grabbed a pitcher of water off the counter and poured just enough to take the edge off.

"This is going to hurt, Jenna, but it's the quickest way to making you feel better."

He covered the hand that clutched her skirt, squeezed her fingers, then slid his hand under hers, gathering the skirt into his palm, drawing the material up over her thighs, revealing the threadbare pantaloons beneath and the dimples in her plump, luscious knees.

Before she could stop him, he draped the hot cloth over the spasming muscles and raw nerves. At the same time, he pulled her up into his arms, taking her scream against his chest, rocking her as her nails dug into his collarbone under his shirt. With his free hand, he tucked the towel more securely, and then through its thick folds, started massaging the knotted muscles.

"It's okay, Sunshine." At first she arched higher, clawed deeper, but then as the heat and the massage got through, she began to ease. "It's going to be okay."

Her nails loosened their hold. Her breath soughed in and out of her lungs as she collapsed against him. "I'm sorry," she whispered.

"For what," he asked,

"I scratched you."

"No big deal." He leaned back against the counter and lifted her fully into his lap. She looked at him like he was loco, then down at his neck where the mark of her nails lingered.

"Is it better?" he asked, ignoring the look and focusing on her leg, feeling the lessening of tension in her muscles that said it was.

"Yes." She moved as if to get away.

"Whoa there." He pulled her back against him. "You know as soon as you use that leg it's going to get unbearable again." He suspected it was only a little less than that now.

Her soft little hands clenched at her side. "I can't stay like this."

"Why not?"

"It's unseemly."

"No one can see."

"That doesn't make it right."

"Amazingly enough, I'm not interested in 'right' at this moment." He forcibly pressed her head back against his chest. Danny whined. He shot him a glare. "I'm more interested in keeping your pain down until Doc gets here."

"What if Doc sees us like this?"

The door swung open and Doc strode in, crunching broken pottery under his boots, his hair, as always, on end, his light blue eyes sympathetic.

"He'd think his nephew was a damned smart man for keeping the damage down to a minimum."

Over Jenna's head, Doc's gaze met Clint's. The smile in his eyes said a damned lucky one, too. Doc had always liked Jenna.

"You said it wouldn't get any worse!" Jenna cried out. She pushed off Clint's chest to glance at Doc. Clint allowed it. When she tugged at his hand on her thigh, he simply ignored her efforts and continued his massage.

"Your leg won't," Doc retorted, glancing around the disaster area. "But I can't say the same for your shop."

Jenna's thighs tensed over his, and her breath sucked in. Another cramp was building. Clint tilted her face to his, not letting her duck his gaze. "Breathe with me on this one, Jenna. Don't fight it. That only makes it worse." He felt along her thigh, defining the extent of the muscle involved as he breathed with her, wishing he could take the pain for her. She didn't deserve this. As she caught his rhythm, he began to massage.

"That's it, Sunshine. Let it flow through you. Let it go, and let Doc do his stuff."

Doc's stuff was a reapplication of the hot cloth. When he would have taken over the massaging, Clint resisted. He tried to keep it nonchalant, but the laughter in Doc's eyes let him know that the older man knew it was because he couldn't bear another man's hands on her. Jenna rested against his chest, her ear pressed to his heart, breathing as he did, trying to do as he asked. He could tell the peak of this spasm was nowhere near the peak of the last. When she collapsed against him, he shifted slightly, just enough that her full breast squashed into his chest. Damn, she was something.

The soft pop of a cork out of a bottle brought her up straight. "No laudanum."

"You need to rest and those muscles need to relax," Doc pointed out.

"I'll apply the warm towels and massage," Jenna countered, pushing at Clint's chest in the mistaken belief that he would let her go before he had to.

"And how are you going to get to the towels?" he asked, continuing to work the damaged muscles.

Her chin ducked down. "I'll hop."

Clint could just see her hopping, losing her balance, and falling headfirst into the hot water. "No."

She clenched her hands in her lap. "I don't want this."

"I do."

That shut her up as he'd intended, but didn't diminish the stubbornness in her expression. He looked to Doc for help.

Doc cocked a grizzled eyebrow at him in reply. Clint sighed. Apparently, since he'd started this argument, he was going to have to be the one to settle it.

"You need this, Jenna." Her chin set and though she was too shy to look him in the eye, he'd be a fool to underestimate her devotion to stubbornness.

"I need to keep my shop open."

"If you get a good night's sleep you might be right as rain in the morning, but if you keep pushing like this, you're going to be down for a month."

It chafed that she looked to Doc for confirmation. He'd never lied to her.

"He's got a point," Doc agreed.

"All right, I'll rest."

Clint could tell from the assessment in her gaze as she looked around the little kitchen that their definitions of rest were worlds apart.

"All night," he clarified.

"I can't do that!" she gasped.

"Why the hell not? It's not like you have a family to take care of."

Her chin set stubbornly. "I can't."

"Why not?"

"I can't tell you."

"Then I guess you're going to have to go with my plan."

"You're not my husband."

"No, I'm not. But I'm as close to a protector as you've got, and that gives me some play."

"I don't need your help."

"I am of a different opinion."

"Why do you always have to win?" She surged against his hand, ran into the barrier of his strength, and lost.

"Just ornery that way, I guess."

Danny growled, Doc laughed, and Clint caught her back against his chest.

"That's so unfair."

"Life is unfair." He turned her carefully in his arms. "Where are the stairs to your room?"

There was a pause where she clearly considered not telling him, but he caught her eye, and the rebellion died a quick death. With a jerk of her chin, she indicated the curtain in the right corner. The smug smile hovering around the corner of her mouth brought up his sense of challenge. Clearly, she thought she had him over a barrel. Why he had no idea, but he was reasonably sure it would occur to him soon enough.

"Brace yourself." He carefully put his hands under her legs, keeping the good one close to him, he stood, and the smug smile on her face disappeared into shock. And then panic. Her arms flew around his neck.

"Don't drop me."

"Didn't have any intention of it." There was something very satisfying about unsettling Jenna. She went all fluttery, and her defenses dropped to the floor.

"I'm too heavy."

"No you're not." She wasn't a featherweight like Cougar's wife. She was definitely a lush tempting armful, but she felt good in his arms. "I'd say you're just about right."

She clearly didn't believe him. She held herself perfectly still in his arms and sucked her lip between her teeth. Her dimples were deep slashes in her cheeks and every sneak peek she took at his expression, looking for imminent signs of dropping, brought a spurt of genuine humor to his soul.

Until he got to the curtain. As Doc held it aside for them, the smug smile was back on Jenna's face, and it was easy to see why. The stairway was simply too narrow for him to carry her through.

"Guess we'll just have to do things my way," she said in a very respectful tone that didn't fool him for an instant.

"Like hell." He let her slide until her weight landed on her good leg. Before she could totally catch her balance, he put his shoulder into her stomach and hoisted her up and over.

He was halfway up the narrow flight before she started complaining. Even her protests were soft, the old wooden steps squeaked much louder than her voice. There were only two doors at the top of the stairs. The one on the right was open. He picked that on a hunch. It played out. Doc's heavier tread came up behind him, followed by the clacking of Danny's nails.

He looked around the little room. There was a plain quilt on the bed, a single window, four hooks on the wall—two of which had a dresses hanging on them—and a chest at the foot of the bed. It was spotless and tidy and spoke deeply of the lack of anything real in Jenna's life that resonated with the emptiness that he felt inside. In some ways they were two peas in a pod. Happy on the outside. Empty on the inside. But at least now that her no-account husband was dead, Jenna had a chance to move on.

He set her down in front of the bed. Holding her shoulders, he balanced her as she sat. Her hair was falling out of its bun and her face was red, whether from being upside down or embarrassment, he didn't know. Didn't figure it mattered. Her eyes flashed to his legs, and then skittered up to his arms before glancing off to study the floor.

"You're very strong."

He tugged his shirt back into place and shrugged. "Nah. You're just not that heavy."

She looked down at herself as if checking to see that they were talking about the same person, shook her hair off her face and then folded her hands in her lap. "I'll be okay now."

He wasn't leaving her alone. "I'll wait for Doc to make the decision."

He looked over his shoulder, fully expecting Doc to be there, but he wasn't. The door across the hall creaked.

"Oh no." Jenna was on her feet and moving. Clint caught her against him, taking her weight before she got to the second step.

A baby wailed.

She stiffened.

"You baby-sitting for someone?" he asked, enjoying the slide of her curves against him as he set her on the bed.

Jenna bit her lip and shook her head. Doc came through the door, the bottle of laudanum sticking out of his pants pocket and a tiny, blanketed bundle over his shoulder.

"Look who Danny found fussing in her…" he paused and looked to Jenna for confirmation. At her nod, he continued, "Her bed." Doc patted the baby's butt. "From the feel of things she needs changing."

"Oh no." Jenna slid to the edge of the mattress. Clint stepped forward, blocking her with his body.

"Whose baby is it, Jenna?"

Her chin set in a stubborn line, and she didn't meet his gaze. "Mine."

Doc didn't even break stride at the ridiculous proclamation. "Then I'd be guessing she wants her momma."

"You can't have children, Jenna." Clint pointed out, stepping back as Doc elbowed him in the gut. Jenna reached for the fussing bundle. From the noise level, the baby was working up to a wail.

Her voice as soft as down, Jenna curved her arms around the wiggling bundle. "Come here, sweetie."

Doc stepped back, his gaze locked on Jenna, who cradled the child like she was a miracle.

"She can't have children," Clint pointed out again. Forget the fact that he'd have noticed if she'd been pregnant.

Doc shrugged. "Sometimes God takes care of these things."

Jenna laid the now squalling infant on the bed. Amidst a bunch of cooing and softly worded nonsense, Jenna unwrapped the baby.

"Is this why you left word you needed to see me, Jenna?" Doc asked.

"Yes." Jenna whispered. "Hush little baby." She looked up at Doc, her big eyes dark with worry. "She has a horrible diaper rash and I don't know how to fix it."

She held a sopping wet diaper out to the side clearly expecting Clint to take it. He did, dropping it immediately, stepping back quickly as it hit the floor with a wet splat. She glanced at him. "Could you get some fresh diapers from her room?"

He wasn't exactly sure what a diaper looked like, but from the sodden mess on the floor he was looking for squares of pale yellow cloth. When he got to the other room they were easy to find. They were folded neatly on the top of the chest of drawers. From the looks of things, she'd cut up one of her three dresses. The only one that was not wool. Her most comfortable. The one that made him think of her as a walking ray of sunshine. He picked up the stack and paused. If he needed any more proof that Jenna was serious about the baby, he had it.

As he came back into the room, Doc was leaning over the little girl.

"I'd say she's about a week old. Still got her umbilical cord. Healthy from the sound of those lungs. Just needs a few things taken care of and she'll be right as rain. Where'd you find her?"

"She was left on my back step."

"No one around?" Doc asked, checking the baby's eyes.

"No."

Doc chucked the little one under her chin, "She's a beauty, but it's a cinch no one's going to want her."

Clint tossed the diapers on the bed. His "Why the hell not?" coincided with Jenna's "I want her".

Clint shot her a look. There was no way she could take care of a baby alone.

Jenna leaned over and kissed the child. "She's just the most beautiful little girl in the world."

Doc stepped back, and Clint got his first good look at the baby.

It was quite a sight. And not for the faint of heart. Great shocks of black hair stood straight out from her tiny skull. Her face was red and blotchy, screwed up in another scream. Small pimples covered her everywhere and her tiny fists waved in desperation. Her little body was painfully thin, her ribs poking out from beneath her pale, red-brown skin, and her hip bones were prominent. More distressing was the bloody rash covering her privates.

She was a tiny little mite, in a sad state of disrepair. Indian — which didn't bode well for her future. Her scream hiccupped to a stop. She opened her bright blue eyes and looked at him for help, her lower lip trembling, puffing in and out between her gums. He knew it was only a factor of poor eyesight, but her hazy gaze seemed desolate.

And well it should. A half-breed little girl of questionable background didn't have a prayer in hell of finding a future. Not without something upping the ante. As he watched, Jenna stroked the little head, smoothing down the flyaway shocks of hair, smiling as they sprang back up. The little legs kicked and stretched, and her little arms seemed to reach out for him in a silent plea. As if the last of her hope disappeared with his lack of response, that tiny little face crumpled.

"Ah hell." He scooped her up. She was no bigger than a minute in his hands. A tiny, helpless, shivering dot with the deck stacked against her and nothing to stand between her and the big bad world out there. He eased her against his shoulder, using his hand like a blanket to warm her painfully thin body. She latched onto the collar of his shirt with her rosebud mouth and commenced sucking. Her shudders lapsed to shivers as she rested against his chest.

From the bed, Jenna watched him warily. Behind him, Doc pointed out the obvious. "No one's going to want a half-breed little girl in their midst."

Jenna's hands clenched to fists. "They won't have a choice."

"I'm afraid they will," Doc countered in his gruff voice.

Jenna set her chin and Clint caught a glimpse of the strength he knew she harbored. "She's mine."

"Saying it doesn't make it so unless you have the muscle to back it." Doc shrugged and snapped a diaper out into a triangle on the bed. "And while the townfolk will go through the motions of finding her a home, when no one steps forward to claim her, the town fathers will ship her off to one of those orphanages east of here."

"No!" Jenna stroked the little girl's back, her fingers catching on the ridge of Clint's palm before dropping off. "I won't let that happen."

Clint cupped the small bottom a little firmer in his hand. Those orphanages were hellholes, places of no hope. If the kids survived, they became slaves to factories. No future, no past, just an unrelenting hell of the present. For however long it lasted.

Doc held his hands out for the little girl. Clint lifted her away, but as soon as her little body lost touch with his, she started to tense and puff. A quick glance down showed her lower lip flapping like a sheet in a wind. He resettled her and shrugged at Doc's puzzled look. "She still needs a minute."

Doc touched Jenna's shoulder kindly, every line on his face deep with regret. "They won't let you keep her Jenna, what with you being unmarried and all."

Jenna's big blue eyes locked on the baby. Tears washed their bright color and spilled onto her cheeks. Against his shoulder, the little one started fussing. He cradled her on her back in his two hands, and looked down into her face. On a little hiccoughing sob, she stared back at him, her midnight eyes brimming with desolation. He looked at

Jenna, her eyes brimming with the same panicked desperation, and lastly at Doc.

His uncle didn't look sad or upset, just expectant, the way he always did when he was waiting for him to do the right thing. Ah hell, they were ganging up on him. He handed the little girl to Jenna, who clutched her close, buried her face in the little one's neck and whispered, "I won't let them take you away."

"So the bottom line is, without a husband, there isn't a prayer in hell that Jenna can keep Button," he said, watching the two women — one full grown and the other new, both too good to be true.

Doc's "No" was matter of fact. Jenna's "Watch me" was a growl of determination.

This growl from his timid little Jenna who never said boo to a ghost. She must want the baby very much. He tipped her chin up. When her gaze didn't rise to his, he tapped her nose with his thumb until it did. "So I take it you're dead set on keeping her."

"Yes."

"Then you need a husband."

Panic flickered over her determined face. "I'll find one."

"Where?"

"There has to be someone."

Brave words, but she had to know, as he did, that a barren woman with a half-breed child and no land or prospects would find few takers, and few of those would be the type that the town fathers would approve.

Except for maybe a half-breed man with more money than sense who needed a reason to continue more than he needed his next breath. That was if he was in the market to drag someone as sweet and kind as Jenna into his private hell.

"Seems to me Clint's available and he's made quite a spectacle about being in the market," Doc pointed out helpfully.

Clint shot him a dirty look. Jenna intercepted the look, and the faint glimmer of hope on her face faded. He frowned. She couldn't read him worth a plugged nickel. She obviously thought he was angered with Doc's suggestion while in reality the unscrupulous, selfish part of him leapt for the opportunity to make her his, good intentions be damned. Having Jenna in his bleak world would brighten a few dark corners. Until she learned he didn't have anything to give, and all that optimism faded to disillusionment.

Jenna ducked her face into the baby's neck and whispered, "I'm not his type."

"I wasn't aware that I had a type." Her grip on the baby tightened.

"Seems to me that's why the boy's been doing so much courting." Doc offered. "Because he can't settle on one."

Jenna clutched the baby to her ample breasts. The little one grunted a protest, the sound almost but not quite covering her quiet reply. "He deserves better."

She stroked the baby's back with desperate intensity before vowing, "But I'll find someone."

Clint couldn't imagine what she'd dredge up if she thought he was too good for her. "That won't be necessary."

"You serious son?" Doc asked.

Jenna straightened on the bed, her gaze clinging to his, her lips set between her teeth, looking so uncertain, so torn, so damned innocently optimistic that it hurt him to look at her. He'd meant to keep her free of his taint. It didn't look like that was going to happen. In his experience, fate had made a habit of messing with his good intentions. Didn't seem like it intended to stop now. That being the case, there was no sense bucking tradition. He reached out and ran his index finger down the deep crease of Jenna's left dimple, rested his thumb against that tempting mouth, and sealed her fate to his.

"Yes. I am."

Chapter Three

Jenna clutched little Brianna to her and stared at Clint. He couldn't mean what she thought he meant. He couldn't mean that he was going to marry her. Clint McKinnely was a legend. People feared and admired him in equal parts. The same way they did his cousin. Half-breed or not, there wasn't a woman in the territory who wouldn't—hadn't—thrown herself or her virgin daughter at his feet. All sacrificial offerings to his wealth and his strength.

And there was a lot of strength. She looked up, way up, his body as he stood before her. He was big, the muscles in his thighs pressing against his denims, his chest rising powerfully from his lean hips. She didn't dare look into his face. Instead, she let her gaze slide across his massive shoulders before traveling down over the bulge of his biceps until it came to the strong bones of his wrists. The wrist attached to the hand on her cheek. He could snap her neck with a flick of that wrist, but his grasp, while firm, wasn't angry. Still, it worried her. Especially when he cupped her cheek and his fingers slid around to caress the base of her skull. It was all she could do to sit still. He made her so nervous.

She bit her lip and considered her options. The McKinnelys were strong, bold, and possessive. Everyone knew that once a McKinnely claimed something as his, there was no going back, and woe to whoever tried to take it. The McKinnely men were hard, scary people, but when they decided something was theirs, they'd move heaven and earth to protect it. Which proved even more that Clint couldn't mean what she thought he'd meant. He couldn't be claiming Brianna.

Brianna fussed again. Her little belly no doubt empty. Jenna jostled her lightly, biting back a moan when the movement sent her muscles to cramping.

"Well what about it, Jenna?" Doc asked. "You going to marry the boy?"

Boy. She looked up at the breadth of Clint's chest, her attention lingering on the point of his collar, still dark from Brianna's sucking. Only Doc would consider Clint a boy. She forced the answer past her lips, wishing she was bolder. "No."

She couldn't bear for him to know how much she wanted the McKinnely name for Brianna. How much she wanted for her new baby the protection she'd never had. It would be too humiliating when Clint let Doc know that he hadn't meant his words the way they had sounded.

To her surprise, it wasn't Doc who answered, but Clint himself. His finger slid under her chin, the calluses dragging on her flesh as he tilted her face up, forcing her to meet the intensity of his deep black gaze. "Yes."

"You don't mean it."

His gaze didn't waver, demanding her compliance. "It's not often I say things I don't mean."

"But what about Brianna?"

"Is that Button's name?"

"Yes."

"What about her?"

"You can't..." She tried to duck his gaze. He wouldn't allow it, holding her centered with the tip of his finger and the force of his personality.

"I can't what?"

"You can't want her."

His left eyebrow rose. "Why not?"

"Because!" Because she was a throwaway. Worthless in the eyes of society. Because she'd always look more Indian than white. Like he did, except the world was harder on women, and so intolerant of differences. Because raising a half-breed little girl was not going to be easy. She wasn't stupid enough to insult Clint openly by stating the obvious so she settled for, "Just because."

"Not good enough."

She patted Brianna's back as her fussing became more insistent, and shifted her weight off of her aching leg, pulling her chin free of Clint's touch.

"She's mine." She stared hard at the faded knees of his denims.

"No one's taking her away from you."

He had that right. She would fight with everything she had to keep Brianna, but the knowledge of how little that actually mattered almost overwhelmed her with hopelessness.

The floor creaked. Doc's boots came into view a second before his capable hands slid around Brianna's little chest. He pulled gently. Inexorably. Jenna held onto Brianna right up until the last second, reluctant to lose the buffer of her soft body, to trust her to someone other than herself. But Doc, for all his calm, gruff manner was a McKinnely, and once set on a course of action was not easily dissuaded. In two seconds, he had the little girl cuddled in his arms.

"Looks like you two have things to talk about, and this little one needs her diaper and her lunch." He brought the baby to eye level. She froze, staring at his face.

Clint chuckled. "Don't go scaring her, Doc."

Doc smiled into the baby's face. "She's not scared, just admiring the family resemblance."

As if to prove him right, Brianna gurgled and kicked her feet and waved her little hands. And her gaze did seem focused on Doc's gray-streaked locks that stuck up off his head in a manner that was very similar to Brianna's.

He settled her over his shoulder, grabbed up the nappy and asked, "Do you have milk for her?"

Jenna clenched her fists, not only against the pain eating at her ability to think, but also at the way events were whirling out of control. Maybe she should just take Brianna and leave. Start over somewhere else. But with what? She had no savings. She stared at that too thin, square little face and felt desperation squeeze at her heart. And where could she take Brianna that she'd be safe and accepted?

"Jenna?" Doc prompted, still waiting for a response.

"Milk is in the icebox downstairs. The bottles are in the bottom cabinet." Out of sight so as not to arouse suspicions. So she wouldn't be forced to make decisions she didn't want to. So she wouldn't be forced to fight a nearly hopeless battle.

"Then little Brianna and I will go get us a bit to eat."

"Stay out of my torte," Clint warned.

His tone, as quiet as always, had an undertone that sent a dart of fear down Jenna's spine, and had her inching away. Danny whined and nuzzled her hand with his nose. Clint shot her a considering look, and Doc...well Doc merely smiled at the growl.

"Then I suggest you turn real sweet and convince the young lady that you're worth taking on as a husband."

"He doesn't need to marry me." Her first marriage had been bad enough, but at least when sober, Jack had been manageable. She'd never be able to handle someone like Clint.

Clint cut her another one of those looks out of the corner of his eye that sent a strange shiver through her. She worked farther back on the bed. Her leg immediately spasmed. The cry was past her lips before she could stifle it.

Clint swore under his breath. Doc shifted Brianna up and pulled the laudanum bottle out of his hip pocket. "I left the tea in the other room."

Clint took the bottle. "I'll get it."

"Not too much," Doc warned.

"I know."

They were talking about her as though she wasn't there. If she hadn't been in such agony, she would have protested more strongly, but the most she could work up to was a gasped, "I'm not taking laudanum."

The men continued as if she hadn't spoken.

"A good dose of sugar will cover the taste."

Jenna grabbed her thigh and took deep breaths as the muscles beneath her fingers writhed and contracted. *Oh, heavens! This hurt.*

"I am not taking that medicine."

The only response she got was both men's appraising glances settling on the grimace she couldn't hide.

Doc frowned. "Take care of her right."

"Never had any intention of doing anything else." Clint stepped toward the bed and his big hand cupped Jenna's shoulder, steadying her against his hard hip as she gasped at another surge of agony. "You take care of my daughter."

Jenna knew from the pressure of his fingers that he hadn't missed her start at his proclamation. Clint's expression wavered through the tears she couldn't suppress. Doc stared at Clint a minute, then he smiled and kissed Brianna's spiky hair. "Never had any intention of doing anything else."

Brianna kicked out her tiny feet and sucked in a wavering breath before letting loose with a wail. Clint touched her cheek with his lean callused finger. Brianna immediately turned and latched onto the tip, sucking for all she was worth.

Doc pulled her away, making a face. "Here now, you don't want any of that. Not when we've got cake and milk downstairs."

Clint's finger dropped to Brianna's chest where it rested dark and huge. He ran it over her ribs. His full lips settled into a hard line. "Better get her fed before she brings the house down."

"She's just hungry," Jenna interjected quickly. "She's usually very good."

"I know."

Clint moved his free hand across Jenna's shoulder until his fingers stretched to stroke the nape of her neck. The gesture was strangely soothing. He was still touching Brianna, and for the one heartbeat before he dropped his finger from Brianna's chest, he connected them both.

Brianna wailed louder. Jenna apologized again. "She's very sweet normally, but she's hungry."

Clint met her gaze, his as usual, dark and unreadable, "I know."

"And we're going to do something about it right now." Doc rubbed Brianna's tiny head, causing the wild black tufts of hair to crackle and wave as he turned. Brianna worked up another decibel. Doc appeared totally unfazed, just stroking her head and murmuring, "I agree little one. We have been kept way too long from our dinner."

He was out the door, Danny beside him, before the last word was finished, Brianna's wail floating in his wake. Her little cry was full of nuance, the ones yanking at Jenna's heart were the tones of desolation and confusion. She knew just how her little girl felt and she never wanted to hear that in her voice again. Jenna attempted to stand. She made it an inch before Clint stopped her with his grip on her neck. She struggled against his hand, moaning with the pain but not letting it stop her.

"She needs me."

"Uh-huh."

"Let me go!" Not caring if he slapped her for it, only needing to get to Brianna she swung at his groin. He sidestepped the blow, catching her forearm on his thigh. She glanced up. He was frowning.

"You need to learn to fight."

She could still hear Brianna's cry. She yanked at her arm. It didn't seem that he even felt her struggles.

"Let me go to her."

"First, I take care of you."

She didn't need taking care of. She dug in her heels and pushed back. Pain seared her leg. She cried out. He let her go. She doubled her over, grabbing her thigh.

"She needs me," she sobbed against her calf.

Clint unclenched her hands and removed her nails from her thighs. His fingers under her chin brought her gaze to his.

"Yes, she does." His hand replaced hers on her thigh, covering much more area, its warmth seeping past her pain. "But not right now."

Jenna could barely hear Brianna anymore. She tried to jerk her chin free. "Yes, now."

Clint kept her chin right where he wanted it. She didn't have any choice but to meet his gaze. "You aren't any use to her like this."

She hated him for pointing that out. "I'll be fine."

"Tomorrow you will be."

"I'm not a cripple." All her vehemence got was a rise of his brow.

"No you're not, but you are in a lot of pain, and I'm not going to let that continue." His fingers began a gentle massage. "Breathe, Jenna."

She didn't realize she'd been holding her breath. She let it out on a shudder, and he worked the spasming muscles, seeming to read their intent with his hands and forestalling further rebellion. Controlling them the way he controlled everything around him.

"When I get you settled through this, I'm going to get you that tea, dose it with laudanum, and you are going to rest until your leg recovers."

"I am?"

"Yes."

"And who will take care of Brianna?"

"I will."

"You can't take care of a baby!"

His dark gaze dropped to her breasts with an intensity that shook her.

43

"If you were feeding her yourself, that would be true, but as you're not, I figure I've got it covered."

"You can't want to do this." What man wanted to take care of a fretful, crying newborn?

"It needs to be done." Which told her nothing about how he felt.

The cramping was easing. She stretched her leg just a little, experimenting.

"Better?" he asked, his eyes meeting hers, expressionless as usual, not revealing anything to her while she felt he knew everything about her.

"A little." It still ached, but the knifing pains had stopped.

"Good. I'll get the tea in a minute."

"I'm not taking that stuff."

"You are." He worked down by her knee at the base of the scar, and a driving pain ripped through her. She fell against him, needing his strength just for this moment, hoping that he would give it to her as he had once before. He did, turning so that she rested more comfortably against him.

"Breathe, Sunshine," he whispered in her ear. "Just breathe and let me make this better."

"You're making it worse," she gasped, her head resting weakly on his shoulder. She took a breath and inhaled the scents of pine and the outdoors. She recognized it immediately. It was etched into her brain from that awful night six months ago when he'd held her in his arms and driven her demons away. As he was doing now.

"Just for a minute." The sympathy in his voice undermined her control. Tears burned behind her eyelids. She was so weak and he made it so easy to lean on him. To let him take over. As if he knew, his voice grew softer, his drawl slower. "Just for a minute more it's going to hurt, Sunshine, and then you'll be a whole lot more comfortable."

He made it so hard to remember that she was learning to be strong for a reason. "Just because you say so?"

His cheek brushed hers as he nodded, his voice as compelling as always, coaxing her to relax. To give in. To him.

"Yes. Because I say so." His fingers pressed deeper, working the same magic on the muscle that his voice did on her nerves. Soothing and coaxing, yet somehow commanding. Her leg relaxed and the excruciating agony faded to a throbbing ache.

"Ah." The whisper of satisfaction drifted past her ear as the knot let loose. "There you go."

He stroked her thigh through her pantaloons, from the top of the scar to the bottom. "And after a night's rest, you'll be as good as new."

"Why does it matter so much to you?"

"I'm your husband, father to your daughter."

"Just saying it doesn't make it so."

Clint didn't let his gaze waver from hers, but a smile tugged the corner of his mouth.

"Unless I have the muscle to back it up," he finished with the part she'd left off. "And Sunshine, I have plenty of muscle."

Her big blue eyes widened at that, staring at him in a mixture of shock and disbelief. Clint didn't care. He'd been in lust with the voluptuous little optimist since the day he'd seen her standing in front of the mercantile, head bowed, earnestly listening to a set of instructions rapped out by her husband. She'd looked so soft, so inviting, so radiant with some sort of inner glow, that he'd fallen ass-over-band-box, and he was tired of fighting it. Tired of fighting the fate that kept throwing her in his path. Tired of resisting the shy, curious, unconsciously hungry yearning in her eyes when she looked at him. He'd been a selfish bastard since the day he was born. He was pretty much set in his ways at thirty. No sense trying to change things at this point in the game.

And he wanted Jenna like hell on fire. He knew her husband had been a bastard. Knew more than he would ever tell her on that subject. It was his experience that women tended to marry the same kind of man the second time around. Maybe settling for the devil they knew. He could see Jenna doing that. She didn't have her feet under her yet. She was scared, hungry, and vulnerable in ways that she didn't even recognize.

Jenna deserved better than a repeat of her first marriage. She deserved security. Dignity. Respect. He could give her those things.

He worked at the lingering tightness under the scar tissue, the softer than soft, unburned flesh on the outside skimming his fingertips, reminding him again of the lushness he coveted. Craved. He cut a glance out of the corner of his eye at her troubled face, keeping his expression blank as he let the reality of his claim sink in. He might be a selfish bastard, but there were three things he knew how to do well — kill, make love, and keep what was his. He'd just claimed this woman and that spiky-haired urchin as his own, before Doc. They belonged to him now. His family. He pictured coming home to Jenna. Waking with her in his bed. He inhaled the rose scent of her shampoo, and felt a small measure of peace settle amidst the turmoil inside. This was right.

"You don't have anything to worry about," he told her as she shifted back.

He saw her mouth open, and just as quickly saw the caution that had been beaten into her drive the protest away. Her gaze dropped and her husky voice emerged in a whisper. "You don't have to marry me."

"No, I don't." But the more he thought on it, the more he wanted it. He moved his fingers down to her knee, being especially gentle there. Stroking and soothing the tired muscles, trying to ease the tension in the rest of her body as she leaned back. He knew she was afraid of his size. So far he couldn't tell if it was just him or all big men, but one way or another, he'd be getting rid of that fear.

"I can take care of Brianna on my own." Her fingers were laced tighter than a cinch in her lap. Her spine was rod straight, but her chin tucked. Hiding her face.

"No. You can't." He cut off her protest with a shake of his head, "You might get by for a few years, but what about when she gets bigger and men start thinking she's fair game because of her skin color? How will you protect her then?"

She didn't have a ready answer. An occasional glimpse of blue told him she was peeking at him from beneath her lashes.

"What does it matter to you?" she finally asked.

"I suspect for the same reason it matters to you. She's little and helpless and needs someone to stand for her." He shrugged and gave her the truth. "And I've a hankering for a family of my own."

"I don't want her hurt," she said, revealing what he suspected was her greatest fear.

"Neither do I."

"She'll be hurt when you leave."

He circled that for a moment. "Why would I leave?"

"You'll get bored. Find something better."

He suspected the phrase she really wanted to use was "someone better". Her knuckles gleamed white under her skin. She really didn't think much of herself. He put both thumbs on either side of her knee and started sliding them up her thigh. "Then I guess it'll be up to you to make me want to stay."

As he expected, his hands moving up her thigh provided a bit of distraction.

"What are you doing?" It was practically a squeak.

"Relaxing your muscles."

"I don't have any muscles there."

Yes, she did. Wonderfully enticing ones, but he'd have to save those for another day. He reversed the direction of his hands, stopping when he cradled the rough scar tissue in his palms, just resting his hands on her soft flesh, letting the heat soothe, the contact fluster. He wanted her very aware of him.

"Jenna?"

She cut him a quick glance.

"Look at me." She did, but he could see what it cost her.

"I want a family. Someone to come home to. I'm not looking for a grand love. I just want someone I can respect. Someone I can talk to. Someone who thinks about things the way I do. Someone to build a home with."

"And you think that's me?" She couldn't sound more disbelieving if he'd told her the sky was pink with brown polka dots.

"Yes." He patted her thigh and stood. "I want to marry you, Jenna. I want Brianna as my daughter. You just have to make up your mind to say yes."

Her hands twisted in her lap. "I don't know."

The confusion on her face told him she wasn't leading him on. She'd honestly never thought he'd consider her.

"I haven't made it a secret I'm looking for a wife."

Her eyes narrowed in an involuntary flinch. He studied her more closely. "Surely you had to know I'd get around to asking you out?"

"Of course not!"

"You think I'd pick a wife without at least having dinner with the most beautiful woman in the territory?"

"You never asked me." Her teeth were worrying her lips, and her glance kept flickering over his face as if searching for clues to his thoughts.

"I'm asking you now." He refused to let her look away. "Are you going to marry me?"

She shoved her skirt down over her thighs. He was beginning to get the idea that it wasn't him but the act of making a decision that was bothering her. He waited a good two minutes while she fussed with her clothes and the bed linens before she blurted out, "I've been married before."

"I know."

"I'm not a…virgin."

"I don't remember that being a requirement."

"I'm not very good in social situations."

"I don't throw a lot of parties."

"I'm fat."

At that, he tipped her chin up. "Look at me."

She did, but with reluctance and a great deal of embarrassment.

"I'm going to speak plainly here because both of us have been around enough to know what matters. I'm a normal man with normal hungers. Probably not much different than your previous husband in that respect."

That information didn't appear to soothe her. He slid his fingers around to the side of her cheek. His skin was very dark against hers. "The truth is Jenna Hennesey, soon to be McKinnely, I've been hankering to have you in my bed since the first time I saw you."

The blush fled her cheeks only to return in a brilliant flare of scarlet. "You have?"

He wouldn't have heard that tiny squeak if he hadn't been listening so closely. "Yes."

"Oh." A long pause and then, "You like fat women?"

"I've always liked you, but you were married and off-limits. Now you're not."

It really was as simple as that, but apparently not to Jenna because her expression went from disbelief to alarm in two blinks of her long, dark lashes. He sighed and tested the softness of her skin with the pad of his thumb.

"Maybe you'd better tell me what's got you so worried."

"I wasn't planning on getting married again."

"I also imagine you weren't planning on being a mother, but things change."

"Yes. They do."

"And you need to make a decision."

"Now?"

"I can give you until I get back with your tea."

Indignation flashed across her expressive face to be quickly cloaked. "That's not much time."

"I'm not a patient man."

Nor a stupid one. He had the advantage and he had every intention of pressing it.

"Oh."

In the soft syllable, he heard the acceptance she had yet to reach. He touched the curl at her temple. The silken blonde strand caught on his calluses. He tipped his hand and let it slide off. She was his now. The knowledge slid into the emptiness within, stirring it, causing waves of…something to spread out. He fought back the feeling, burying everything except the satisfaction of possession.

That was one feeling he didn't mind experiencing. And while he might not have love to give Jenna, he'd treat her better than any man she'd ever met. Better, certainly, than that drunken ass she'd married. He'd respect her, please her, and do his best to make her happy. And no bastard would ever put a mark on her again.

"I'm going to get your tea."

He let his hand drift down her cheek. The warmth of her skin was astonishing. Her lashes fluttered against the back of his knuckles. He looked closer. She was holding herself unnaturally still. No doubt wondering what he was up to. No doubt expecting the worst. No doubt preparing to bolt.

"Don't even think about getting out of that bed before I get back." Her jump told him not only had she thought it, but in her mind was halfway down the stairs. "I mean it Jenna. I'll paddle your butt if I catch you out of bed."

One scared look and she settled down. She'd stay until he got back. He left to fetch her tea from the room across the hall. This room was as baren as the other, showing none of the feminine gewgaws he was accustomed to seeing in a woman's home. Bare of all the little knickknacks and feminine things that made a woman smile and marked a place as hers. A woman like Jenna should be surrounded by all the delicate pretty things that made her feel special and wanted. He'd have to see that she got them.

The cup was on the wood crate beside the bed. As he picked it up, he looked at the lined drawer Jenna used as a crib. He ran his hand over the blanket set into the drawer for cushioning. It was damp and smelled faintly of urine. He'd have to do something about that, too. Brianna was bound to have more needs than he could think of right now. From the look of that hair and the strength of her lungs, it sounded like Brianna was going to be a demanding little thing. He pictured the chaos Jenna and Brianna were going to wreak on his quiet, orderly house, and smiled. He was, amazingly, looking forward to it.

Chapter Four

Saying something apparently made it so. Jenna stood in the little alcove of the small church six days later and clutched her bouquet in her hands. In about three minutes, she would be wed to Clint McKinnely. She didn't know whether to breathe a sigh of relief or whether to collapse in terror. She was thinking about doing both. She could never, ever win a fight with Clint. Not verbally, and certainly not physically. The man was a walking giant, and he had more muscles than the town blacksmith.

Her first husband had been muscular too, but slow to react and slow to move, giving her time if he turned ugly. Clint, however, moved with the grace and confidence of a predator. If she ran, he'd catch her. Her chest tightened with panic at the thought. She closed her eyes and breathed through her nose.

She had to have faith. Believe in the rightness of this. Believe God hadn't deserted her or Bri. She'd told God she'd do anything at all if He'd just show her a way she could keep little Bri. And then Clint was there, offering marriage and security. If that wasn't an answer to a prayer she didn't know what was. As much as she didn't want to invoke Clint's wrath, she sincerely did not want to annoy the Almighty. So she'd just be a good wife, figure out what Clint needed, and give it to him. And all would be well.

There was a soft knock at the door.

Oh heavens! This was it. "Yes?"

Cougar's tiny wife peeked around the door, her brown eyes shimmering with excitement. It was easy to see why Cougar loved her. She just sparkled with life. "Are you all set?"

As much as she'd ever be. "Yes."

She wished her voice sounded stronger, but she didn't want to walk down the aisle in front of the whole town. She didn't want to feel their pitying stares as she limped along, hear the whispers and speculation as to why Clint would marry someone like her. She'd tried to talk Clint into a quick, private ceremony but he'd just looked at her with those deep, black eyes and said that he was proud of his family and wasn't getting married in any way that said differently.

How could she argue with that? He wouldn't understand how horrible this was. How she hated being on display. A man like him had probably never had an uncertain moment in his life.

Mara stepped around the door and shut it behind her. Her smile faded. "Are you okay?"

Jenna tucked the bouquet tighter against her body to hide her trembling hands. "Just a little nervous."

"Nervous good or bad?" Mara asked as she came over, stepping around the long train of the gown, straightening the right side.

Jenna opened her mouth to answer and then closed it. She really didn't know what to say. She settled for, "I don't know."

Mara stepped behind her and then came around front again. "Heavens that man has an eye."

"Who has an eye?"

Mara glanced up. "Clint." She twitched a fold of the train into place. "You are absolutely beautiful."

Jenna touched the white satin skirt of her dress. "Clint picked out my dress?"

No wonder he had refused to let her take it back when she'd said it was too fine.

"Not only did he pick it out, he had to ride eighteen hours straight to get the material here in time for Pearl and her girls to make it up since the freighters wouldn't be able to get it here until next week."

Jenna hid her hands in her bouquet. She hadn't known. "I told him white wasn't appropriate for a second marriage."

Mara laughed. "Bet he didn't care."

Jenna shook her head. "No."

"You'll find these McKinnely men don't pay much heed to convention."

Jenna gripped the bouquet harder, the stems biting into her palms. "He said he'd never seen a woman more deserving to wear white."

Mara smiled. "That's another McKinnely trait. They see what they want."

She felt like such a fraud. "I'm not innocent."

Mara stopped fussing with the dress. "Jenna, I imagine Clint knows exactly who you are, and from the way he's fidgeting at the altar, he's anxious to have you as his."

His. In a month of Sundays, she'd never get used to being Clint McKinnely's. She just couldn't wrap her mind around that anymore than she could conceive of Clint fidgeting.

"I wasn't planning on getting married again," Jenna confessed.

Mara bent to straighten the other side of the train, her cinnamon eyes flashing with wry amusement. "Well, you're one step ahead of me on my wedding day. I wasn't planning on getting married at all."

Jenna had heard rumors. "Is it true that Cougar compromised you?" Jenna wished the words back into her mouth as soon as they left. "I'm sorry. That was rude."

That was why she never spoke up. She always said the wrong thing.

Mara laughed and shook her head as she straightened. "Pretty much. These McKinnely men can be very devious in getting their way."

"They are persistent."

"That, too." Mara stepped back and put her hands on her slender hips. "I think you're ready."

Jenna's knees started to knock and she took another breath. She was never going to be ready.

A sharp rap on the door saved her from having to say anything, which was good, because panic had her too short of breath for words. Another knock at the door and Mara was in motion. Jenna couldn't see who was behind the door or hear the conversation, but she didn't need schooling to know people were beginning to wonder where the bride was. Her stomach knotted, knowing the delay would give the townsfolk even more reason to whisper.

Mara turned back to her. "Ready?"

Jenna fought back a wave of nausea, took a slow breath, and nodded. Mara opened the door. Doc strode in, his hair, for once, smoothed flat, a smile on his kind face.

"Well now, it's easy to see why Clint calls you Sunshine. You look like a bit of heavenly light in that dress."

She'd been unsure about the style, but Mara and Elizabeth had been adamant about the cut of the bodice, which showed the tops of her breasts. They had ignored her protests until she'd had no choice but to go along. Now that the dress was fitted, she had to admit that it did make the most of her few assets, but just thinking about all those male guests seeing her in it caused another surge of nausea.

Doc grabbed her elbow as she swayed. "Are you all right?"

She shook off her weakness and put some starch in her spine. "I'm fine."

"You look a far cry from fine."

"It's all this waiting," she explained, holding out her hand. "It makes me nervous."

The sooner this was over, the better she'd feel. She hoped.

Doc tucked her hand into the crook of his arm and patted it. "Then let's get the waiting over with, 'cause truth be told, if you don't come down that aisle soon, Clint will be coming up it to fetch you."

The door creaked as Mara slipped through.

"He's that mad?" Jenna asked.

Doc sent her a look that went from confused to understanding in one blink. "He's that anxious."

She doubted that.

Organ music swelled on a long building note. It was time. She took a breath and pasted a smile on her face. The shakes started as they always did when she was forced to be the center of attention. She knew Doc could feel her trembling by the sharp glance he cut her. She stared straight ahead as the organ started playing her wedding hymn. She would not shame Clint by acting the weakling on their wedding day.

Doc started forward. The three steps to the door passed much too quickly. She had a chance for another breath as Doc pulled the door open. She took it and held it. She could do this. Just one step at a time. That's all she needed to do. Put one foot in front of the other, follow Doc's lead, and in no time this would be over with. She made it as far as the top of the aisle before disaster struck. Someone had laid down a beautiful, white shimmery cloth on the aisle. Her slipper on her good leg slid. The unexpected weight on her bad leg sent a knifing pain through her thigh. She pulled up short, jerking Doc back, almost falling, holding back her groan through sheer force of will. There was a murmur in the crowd as she stood there unmoving. It took all her concentration to control the pain. When it faded, she was faced with a church full of curious attendees.

"Think she's planning on leaving McKinnely at the altar?" she heard a man mumble.

"Might just be worth getting all decked out to see that," another whispered back.

She glanced up. Ahead of her, there was nothing but a mass of people staring at her, judging her. Expecting the worst of her. At the end of the aisle stood Clint. His broad shoulders squared and straight. His expression impassive. She didn't know what he thought, but as she stood there, the whispers around her piling up into rampant speculation, she could imagine. Inside, the tiny kernel of courage she'd been drawing from withered.

Cougar stood beside Clint, his impatience clear on his face. As her gaze touched his golden one, he shook his head. His long black hair swung in punctuation to the jerk of his chin—a clear order to get moving. An order he expected to be obeyed.

But she couldn't. God help her, she couldn't. She couldn't even release the breath she'd been holding as everything in her rushed toward panic.

Doc patted her hand. "Jenna?"

She shook her head, feeling the tightness pulling at her arms, closing off her breath. Oh God, not now. Please not now. She couldn't do this to Clint. To herself. She couldn't mess up her one shot at keeping Brianna.

The murmuring became a soft roar. Halfway down the aisle, Asa's wife Elizabeth stood, her brand new baby girl a splash of pink ruffles on her shoulder, the pity and confusion on her face a mirror of everyone else's expression. Beside her, Doc was encouraging her to sit down, but she couldn't do that either. She couldn't sit and be married. She had to make it down the aisle. To Clint.

There was a louder murmur and then a sudden deafening, expectant silence. She looked up. Clint was coming toward her, his long hair flaring around his shoulders, his long legs eating up the distance between them. He didn't look angry. He didn't look anything. He just kept coming toward her. When he was close enough that she could see the slight lines fanning out from the corner of his eyes, she closed hers, accepting the reality—it was over.

His "Ah, Sunshine" reached her first and then his arms wrapped around her, pulling her into the solid strength of his chest, taking her weight off her legs and making it his responsibility.

"A little too much too soon?" he queried against her ear.

She nodded and gulped in a painful effort to respond. She hadn't wanted to fail him.

"Shh." His lips brushed her ear, laid bare by her upswept hair. "I want you just to relax, Jenna."

She tried to twist away. His lips brushed her temple. His left hand opened on the small of her back. "No one can see, Sunshine, so I want you to rest here against me and find your breath."

Easy for him to say. Her ribs heaved, but nothing happened.

"Jenna, baby." A down comforter wasn't as soft as his deep voice at that moment. "I should be shot."

For what? she wondered with the one calm section of her brain. His fingers brushed her jaw

"I should have known being on display would upset you."

He shifted, pulling her closer with his hand on her spine so that her skirts wrapped around his boots. His lips brushed her cheek. "Breathe, baby. For me. Just once."

She stiffened remembering the last time he'd said that. He pulled her a little closer, seeming to absorb her whole body into his as his laughter puffed against her ear.

"Ah, you remember that, do you?'

How could she forget?

"I promise you this time, baby, no pain. You just take this one tiny breath, and the rest will be a cakewalk."

Air wheezed in and choked out of her lungs while he just stood there as if the whole church full of witnesses didn't matter and crooned nonsense into her ear. She tried to look under his arm to see what kind of spectacle they were making, but he wouldn't allow it.

He tucked her head against his chest and said, "The only people who matter here are you and me, and I'm just fine with this."

"She okay?"

That deep, slow drawl drew her chin up. Asa MacIntyre's silver eyes met hers.

"She's fine, but she could use a minute, if you could arrange it," Clint answered, his voice too quiet for anyone else to hear.

Asa winked at Jenna and on a "You got it" stood and sighed loud enough for everyone to hear. "Wish I had me a girl who wanted a hug from me bad enough to hold up her wedding to get it."

A slow trickle of laughter followed the pronouncement. Doc picked up the theme and ran with it. "Heck. I tried to see Dorothy before the ceremony and she threw a shoe at me."

"That might have been because we were late and I was getting dressed at the time!" Dorothy called to him.

"You're a randy one, aren't you Doc?" a male voice Jenna didn't recognize teased good-naturedly.

"I'm not sure I want you treating my wife after hearing this!" another called.

"Ah heck, Jerome," the first voice countered, "No offense to Fran, but she's got more years on her than Old Ben's dog. If Doc was going to get up to something funny, he'd pick someone else."

"She's a damned handsome woman to this day," Jerome harrumphed.

Jenna, leaning against Clint, listened to the joking and smiled. Jerome was sixty if he was a day and dearly loved his plump wife. Everyone knew it. Growing up, Jenna had hoped to have a man look at her the way Jerome looked at Fran—as if the sun rose and the moon set in her eyes—but she'd long since outgrown that notion.

The jokes continued. A little of her tension eased.

"There's my girl," Clint whispered. His thick black hair brushed her cheeks and bare shoulders as his lips glided across her neck. She shivered at the strange sensation. Against her ear, she felt Clint's smile. "You let Asa do what he does best, and just concentrate on giving me that nice deep breath I asked for."

Surprisingly, breathing was easier now, even though she was still standing in the middle of the aisle and everyone still watched.

Clint cupped her throat in his hand. "That's it, Sunshine."

His fingers stroked from her ear to her shoulder, launching a quivery sensation inside her. "Look at me."

She did. She always did what he said when he used that tone. His eyes were deep, black, fathomless, and totally compelling. His fingers curled until he was rubbing her throat with the back of his hand. It was the lightest of caresses. She felt it to the tips of her toes.

"Breathe for me."

She hesitated.

"Now." She did, expecting nothing, but shockingly, getting a breath of cool, fresh air. Her reward was the relaxing of his expression and a return to his embrace. She put her palms against his chest.

"I'm okay now."

"Just to be on the safe side, we'll rest here a bit."

"We're in the middle of a wedding."

"Since we're the main attraction, I expect they'll wait."

His hands on her back didn't allow her to move away. She was eternally grateful she'd chosen a heavy-duty corset. She might feel like a sausage, but all Clint would feel was a smooth silhouette.

As if reading her mind, he tapped one of the ribs. "This can't be helping your breathing."

The blush started at her toes and burned over her face. "I just get nervous."

A quick glance up showed he was frowning at that piece of information. She dropped her gaze to his throat. He had the most beautiful skin. The hint of red under the brown always made her want to nibble, just a little to see if he tasted as hot and spicy as the cinnamon he reminded her of. She dropped her forehead against his chest. Oh heaven! She was in church and she was having carnal thoughts. She was as bad as her father always said.

"You can let me go now." As always, her voice lacked the force she wanted so she wasn't surprised when he merely held her.

"In a minute."

"I won't seize up again."

"I know."

She frowned, pressing lightly with her fingers. There was no give to the man. "How do you know?"

"Because you know you're safe with me."

"I do?" It came out louder than she anticipated, bringing everyone's attention back to her.

"You're supposed to save that for the reverend," someone hollered.

The panic began again, deep inside where it always started. A finger slid under her chin, the rough skin scarping her softer flesh.

"Look at me."

She did.

"You're not going to panic."

"I'm not?" It sure felt like it to her.

"No. You're going to stay calm, and walk with me up to the front of the church and say your vows. Then we're going to have some of that wedding cake Priscilla's daughter baked."

"I am?"

"Yes."

"And I'm not going to panic?" The last was said on a wheeze as she glanced around his arm to see everyone watching her again. Especially Cougar. His darkly handsome face hard with disapproval.

Clint turned her face back to his. "You aren't."

"How can you be so sure?"

"Because I have you."

And just like that, he turned, tucked her into his side as if she were tiny and delicate, and calmly started down the aisle. She had no choice but to go with him. Her skirt swishing around his legs, his arm taking most of her weight. When she stumbled, he turned her to face him, bringing her hand to his lips, kissing the palm, staring into her eyes as he backed her the rest of the way to her position.

The sigh that rose from the young women in the crowd let her know the gesture looked wildly romantic. In reality, it had kept her from falling on her face.

He'd done as he'd promised. He'd gotten her to the altar, safely, her pride intact. She shouldn't have been surprised. Clint was known to be a man of his word. His hand at her elbow steadied her as she faced the reverend. The eyes on her back were like the touch of a stranger. Uncomfortable.

"All set now?" Reverend Swanson asked. Clint cocked an eyebrow at her.

She whispered, "Yes."

A floorboard creaked as Cougar leaned around his cousin. His deep gold gaze flickered over her before he leaned back and asked out of the side of his mouth, "You're dead set on this?"

The words weren't meant for her to hear, but she did. She didn't look at Cougar or Clint as he debated his answer. She'd seen the signs.

God had sent her Clint as an answer to her prayers. If she just believed in that, everything would be all right.

Still, when Clint's "Yes" rumbled out in his deep voice, she breathed a sigh of relief. She was doing the right thing.

* * * * *

"It's time to go, Jenna," Clint said two hours later.

Jenna clutched Brianna a little closer. Fed and changed, the little girl was almost asleep, and her muffled grunt said she didn't appreciate the gesture.

"We'll take very good care of her," Mara promised. The hunger in her voice made Jenna uneasy. Everyone knew that Mara wanted a baby as much as they knew that Cougar feared losing her to childbirth. She didn't want to leave Brianna here. What if they didn't give her back?

Cougar took a step forward. His long hair slid over his massive shoulders as he reached out. Jenna barely kept from pulling back as he stroked Brianna's tiny back.

"I'll keep her safe for you," he promised, his golden eyes dark. Everyone knew a promise from a McKinnely could be taken to the bank. Still, Jenna couldn't let her go.

"It's okay, Jenna," Clint said.

But it wasn't. A dribble of drool dampened the shoulder of the blue traveling dress she'd changed into. "I think maybe we should reconsider—"

"If you're going to tell me again that we don't need time alone," Clint interrupted, a smile hovering around his mouth, "you're wasting your breath."

"Every couple needs some get-acquainted time," Dorothy, Doc's wife, spoke up as she came closer, the basket Jenna had packed in her hand.

"But we're not…"

Clint sighed and pried the baby out of her arms. "We're married, Jenna."

Reverend Swanson stepped forward, licking frosting from his fingers. "And in one of my nicer ceremonies, too, if I do say so myself."

He ran his tongue around his thumb. The gesture was so unconsciously sensual that Jenna did a double take. Sometimes it was hard to remember that this tall, lean, muscular man was a man of God.

"I wasn't going to say we weren't married." She watched in agony as Clint passed Brianna over to Mara.

"Doesn't matter what excuse you were working on," he said, "I want to be alone with you."

"But five days…"

"Will be just enough to whet my appetite."

The men laughed. Jenna blushed, and Dorothy swatted Clint with a towel. "If your mother was here she'd wash your mouth out with soap."

Clint ducked a second swat. "Lucky for me then that she's living the easy life back East with Dad."

Dorothy handed Jenna the basket. "You just ignore those buffoons, Jenna. Too many trips to the back door has addled their brains."

The basket weighed a ton. Jenna shifted her grip. Clint had been drinking? The feeling that her life was spinning out of control intensified.

"My shop…"

"Is in good hands with Lorie," Clint countered, taking the thick, expensive wool cloak he'd insisted she needed off the hook by the door.

"Lorie is very competent," Mara said, looking totally natural rocking the tiny baby in her arms. The image of the perfect little family was completed when Cougar stepped beside his wife, and she immediately relaxed into the shelter of his side.

"But will she remember to feed Harry? And that Jonas has to eat in the restaurant or someone will take his food away?"

"I'm sure she will," Clint countered, holding out her cloak. She ignored his hint.

"Sometimes the other customers complain."

"I can handle complaints," Lorie said, coming forward. Jenna looked at the tall competent woman. She just bet she could. Lorie looked the type who could handle anything. She'd probably handle her shop better than she did without one single blonde hair on her head falling out of place. Her customers probably wouldn't even miss her.

"You have to remember to feed Harry. I've just started putting weight on him."

"I'll remember. Every day at sundown a plate of food at the back door."

"With milk. Make sure you give him enough. I don't want—"

"Him to lose weight," Lorie, Clint, Mara, Asa, Cougar, and Doc finished for her.

Their amusement hit her like a blow. She ducked her head, her voice dropped to a whisper but she couldn't let it go. "He's just come so far…"

They probably thought she was ridiculous for worrying about another discard, but Harry mattered to her and so did Jonas even if they weren't particularly pretty right now.

The heavy weight of the cloak settled on her shoulders, the fur trim on the hood brushing her cheeks. "Harry, Jonas, your shop, and little Brianna are in good hands, Jenna."

Clint's hands lingered after the cloak was settled, but the stroking of his fingers didn't alleviate the finality of his words. The life she'd so carefully built for herself the last six months was now firmly in the care of others, and she was once more a wife with nothing to call her own.

She stepped out of Clint's hold and said the only thing she could. "Thank you."

She put the basket on the floor, shrugged out of the heavy cloak, and put it back on the hook. She reached for her old one.

"What are you doing?"

She turned to Clint. "Getting ready to go."

"It's cold outside."

"I know."

"You need a cloak."

"I'm getting one."

"What's wrong with the one you just had on?"

A bark of laughter came from the other side of the room, quickly followed by, "This ought to be good."

Jenna wished she had the courage to shoot Asa a glare for his interruption, but she just didn't dare rile the ex-gunslinger. She pulled her perfectly serviceable cloak off the hook.

"It's new," she told Clint.

"I know. I bought it for you."

"It's snowing outside."

"I know."

She buttoned the top two buttons of her cloak, the others having long since disappeared. "It'll get wet."

"It's supposed to get wet."

She reached in her pocket to pull out her knitted gloves. "I'm not having my brand-new cloak get wet and muddy."

Clint took the gloves out of her hand and tossed them on the table. "I'm not having my brand-new wife get cold."

"This cloak is fine."

"That cloak is only fit for fire starter."

"I made this cloak myself." Maybe it wasn't fancy but she'd scrimped and saved and taken beatings to get the money for the material. It had seen her through four winters just fine.

"Now you've done it."

"Shut up Asa," Clint growled.

Jenna added her own glare from under her lashes as the big gunslinger leaned with indolent grace against the doorjamb.

"Just trying to point out that you can't win arguing with a woman about her clothes," Asa mentioned, faking injury when his wife slapped his midsection. As if Elizabeth's fist could make a dent in his big frame.

Clint held out his hand. "I'm not insulting your clothes, Jenna. I just want you warm."

She ignored the order in his outstretched hand and tucked the thin material closer around her. "I'm warm."

She thought she detected a softening in his dark eyes, but then the wind howled and shook the building's windows. Clint's jaw set. "Not as warm as you're going to be if you don't hand me that cloak."

"Oh that will make for a right companionable wedding night," Asa laughed.

Elizabeth's "You're not helping" carried clearly. Just as clearly as Asa's "Wasn't aware I was trying to help".

A muffled snort came from Cougar. Jenna had a strong suspicion that he was laughing but then he slapped his chest and coughed. He could have just swallowed wrong.

She knew she was going to have to back down. She'd been foolish enough to make the confrontation public and no man gave ground when faced with an audience. She used to be smarter than this, but six months of peace and that moment in the church had apparently dulled her wits.

She unbuttoned the cloak. Clint's approving nod grated on her nerves as she handed it to him. She expected him to throw it on the floor. Instead, he folded it and set it on top of the basket.

"Thank you." He held the luxurious cloak out again.

"For what?"

"Sparing me worry."

She stared at him. He would worry? "You're welcome."

Jenna tried not to step back as he snuggled the hood under her chin. The whole cloak was lined with soft fur. It was the most luxurious thing she'd ever seen, and it felt as good as she'd always imagined decadence would.

He tugged at the cloak around her hips. She stumbled forward. He placed a pair of shearling mittens in her hands. "These should keep your hands warm."

She didn't know what to say. She wanted to resent him for forcing his way, but at the same time, she couldn't ever remember a time when someone had worried about her, let alone made sure she was comfortable. It made her feel strange. Beholden. She didn't like it.

She yanked the mittens on. She was warm, draped in luxury, and surrounded by kind people who wished her well. It was nothing like her first wedding. Nothing like what she was used to. She just wanted to find a corner and hide. Instead, she pasted a smile on her lips.

"I want to thank you all for coming and wishing us well."

"It was our pleasure," Cougar said, as if he hadn't been cautioning Clint against her just hours before.

Clint shrugged into his coat, looking bigger than ever beneath the bulky shearling. He reached for his hat while his free hand settled on her back. She was taking a step toward the door before she realized he hadn't intended to push her along. He was just doing as every other male in the place. Touching his woman.

Oh heavens. She looked up, way up to his deep black eyes as he followed her toward the door. She was his woman now. If there was anything guaranteed to make a woman feel inadequate, it was knowing that.

"Hold on now." Reverend Swanson put his empty plate on the small end table. "You weren't planning on leaving without giving us a chance to kiss the bride, were you?"

"Of course, she wasn't," Asa said, pushing off the door frame. It took only three strides of his long legs to cross the room. There was some good-natured teasing and jostling and then there was a line of men between her and the door.

Oh heavens, she hated this part of weddings.

She looked up. Clint was scowling at the men. It did nothing to ease her nerves. He was frowning so hard that she halfway expected him to tell the men to back off, but then his hand in the small of her back urged her forward as he said in a tight voice, "Let's get this over with so we can get to our own celebrating."

The men hooted, the ladies laughed, and she blushed and lost her voice. Clint urged her forward another step, right into the reverend's grasp. Before she could react he had her hands, sweeping her away from Clint's comforting presence and into his arms. Her small shriek floated on the air as his chaste kiss landed on her forehead along with his congratulations.

"Watch her leg!" Clint warned as the reverend gave her a little toss to the next man.

"I've got her." There was no mistaking that deep drawl so similar to her husband's, or the strength in the arms that caught her and lightly set her on her feet, holding her for that fraction of a second it took her to get her balance. Then the light was blocked as Cougar bent and his long hair fell around her. There was a soft scent of sage and then his lips touched her left cheek. She held herself perfectly still, afraid to move.

He leaned further in. Her breath caught in her throat. His lips hovered near her ear. "You hold your head up, Jenna McKinnely."

There was a break of light and then darkness again as he kissed her other cheek. He stepped back. "Welcome to our family."

She had a brief glimpse of his handsome, serious face before she was whisked into another man's arms as if she weighed nothing more than a feather. She only had time to absorb steel gray eyes lit with humor before firm lips glanced off hers. She flinched back and then screamed as a hard arm locked around her waist and yanked her against a harder torso, and a growl rumbled through the room.

"Go kiss your own wife, MacIntyre!"

Asa looked totally unperturbed. Actually, he looked ready to burst into laughter. Jenna didn't understand it, but a quick glance around the room showed everyone in the same state. Probably because Clint had her dangling with her feet six inches off the ground.

"Please put me down," she whispered.

He hesitated but eventually did as she bid. He didn't release her though, just kept his hand scandalously splayed across her midsection, keeping her back pressed against his front.

His erection was solid against her spine, definable even through their clothing and it all made sense. She held back her shudder. She was well-acquainted with the uncertainty of male jealousy. Her effort to see his expression was thwarted by the cloak's hood. With no indicator to work from, not knowing if he was angry with the men, but blamed her for tempting them, she settled for folding her hands in front of her and waiting.

"Are you ready to go, Jenna?"

She took a steadying breath. "Yes."

Mara stood a little to her left. It was all Jenna could do not to rip Brianna out of her arms and run. As if he felt her inner battle, Clint's hand pressed a little harder before he tucked her into his side.

"Then let's go."

He angled his hat down on his head and ushered Jenna through the door. "You all know where to reach us if you need us." He turned and reached for the basket, "And if you value your life, I wouldn't suggest needing us."

A bark of male laughter punctuated his closing of the door.

Chapter Five

Clint closed the door on the remnants of Asa's laughter. He straightened his hat on his head and looked at his wife. Jenna stood waiting on him in the twilight, rubbing her arms, her breath rising in the wind in nervous frosty puffs. She was his now. His wife. And he could take care of her the way he'd always wanted to.

"Cold?" he asked, stepping toward her.

She stopped rubbing her arms immediately. "I'm fine."

He adjusted the hood around her face and tipped her chin up. His finger slid between the soft fur and her softer cheek. He wished she'd smile. She hadn't smiled since he'd proposed.

"You let me know if you're cold."

"I'm sure I'll be fine."

She should be. He'd bought the most expensive cloak he could find, choosing the one that would complement her lush beauty, but instead of being pleased, she'd seemed upset. Still seemed upset.

He slid his hand behind her head. The thick fur lining the hood wasn't nearly as fine as the curve of her cheek, the silk of her hair. He pulled her into his body, putting his back to the wind, taking the brunt with his bigger body, sighing when she eyed him warily. Did she think he was going to turn into a monster now that the ceremony was over?

"It's not going to be so bad being married to me, Jenna."

He wasn't upset by her start of surprise. Instead, he used that moment of confusion, propping his thumb under her chin, holding her ready for the descent of his mouth. He was very careful with her, fitting his lips gently to hers, trying not to scare her, but he needed to taste her, to remove the image of Asa's mouth on hers. It didn't matter that Asa had kissed her just to rile him. The fact that Asa's lips had touched hers was driving him crazy.

Her breath puffed into his mouth in a soft expulsion of shock. He took it as his own, savoring the intimacy after such a long time of anticipation, moving closer, following her as she stepped back, almost groaning in frustration as the layers of their clothing kept him from the lushness of her body.

Her lips parted under his. He accepted the invitation, slipping his tongue past the soft seam of moist flesh into the heat beyond. She tasted so good. So damned good. Like tea and chocolate nestled on a warm, moist bed of pure womanly essence. She went limp beneath him, relaxing against the wall, letting him do as he pleased, her acquiescence adding a sharper spike to his already soaring passion. She was his. She was willing.

A rap on the window pulled him out of her spell. Dorothy was frowning at him through the window, the tolerant smile on her face the kind he was used to seeing growing up whenever he'd let his impatience get ahead of his good sense. Like now. He was kissing his wife on the front step of Doc's house with an audience not more than ten inches away. He eased his body from hers, stroking the moisture from the corner of her pink lips with his thumb.

"Guess I'd better be saving that for more privacy."

Jenna swallowed hard twice then nodded.

He grabbed her hand, feeling almost happy as he pulled her out of the shelter of the overhang to the edge of the steps and into the swirling flakes of snow. He caught her around the waist and swung her off the stairs. Her little gasp tickled his humor as much as her frantic grasp at his shoulders. It'd be a cold day in hell before he'd drop her.

Snowflakes clung to her hood, and settled on her nose before melting into her skin. He wanted to lick them off her lashes, her cheeks. He wanted to lick her from head to toe. He kissed her hard, and let her hand slide from his as he headed to the barn, eager to get home.

"Clint." Jenna calling his name in that breathless little voice pulled him up short halfway to the barn. He turned. Jenna was about twenty feet behind him. Even from here he could see the flush on her cheeks and the rapid puffs of air as she panted.

"I can't keep up," she called as she limped heavily in his wake, the slippery snow making it more difficult for her to walk.

Damn. He'd forgotten. "Sorry."

He turned and met her halfway, scooping her up in his arms, getting another of those amusing shrieks. "Hold on, Sunshine."

He tossed her just a little, just enough to have her arms clinging to his neck and her face buried in his throat. He kept moving to the barn, savoring the warmth of her breath sliding over his skin. After waiting a year for Jenna, he was suddenly fresh out of his legendary patience.

He had to put her down at the barn. As soon as her feet hit the ground, she stepped away, fussing with her cloak and her hair. He smiled as he pulled the door open. She was cute when she was flustered.

He sighed when he saw the buggy just inside the barn door. It was adorned in more tin cans, paper and hope than any wedding send-off he'd ever seen. A quick glance at Jenna showed that she was a bit stunned.

"Seems like everyone had a part in wishing us well."

"Apparently." She touched an empty whiskey bottle dangling off the wheel. "Looks like they put in a lot of work." Her lip was between her teeth.

"Can you drive a buggy?"

She cast him one of those uncertain glances as if he was asking more than a simple question before she squared her shoulders. "I can learn."

"Not necessary." He just needed to come up with another plan. He would never get his high-strung buckskin to stay close to this monstrosity, but it would take too long to clean it off. They were losing daylight fast. "Can you ride?"

She looked at him and then at his horse still waiting in the barn.

"No." There was wistfulness in her gaze.

"Ever want to learn?"

"It doesn't matter anymore." She looked down at the ground.

There was no inflection in her husky voice and without being able to see her expression he had no way to judge whether she was happy with that or not. The bottle rocked against the wheel as she took her hand away.

"Why doesn't it matter anymore?" He stepped forward and steadied the bottle.

"What?"

"Why doesn't it matter anymore whether you want to learn to ride?"

"Oh." Her hand smoothed her thigh through the cloak. "My leg is too weak."

Clint shoved a can out of the way and leaned against the buckboard. "Did I ever tell you about the time I rode Ornery with a broken leg?"

There was a slight shifting of the hood. With a flick of his fingers, he pushed it back. Jenna flashed him a startled glance as the hood slid down her back, her eyes a deep blue in the gloom.

"I can't tell if you're 'yesing' me or 'noing' me."

"Oh." There was a pause and then, "I said no."

"Well, I did, and seeing as I could manage that, I expect you could manage to ride, if you wanted to."

Another of those wistful glances toward Ornery. "It would probably take me a long time to learn."

"I haven't noticed we're running short on it."

She hunched her shoulders and looked down. "I don't learn things quickly."

"I'm known for my patience." Except tonight. Tonight he wanted to be home as fast as possible.

"I'm not very graceful." If her head dropped any lower her chin would be resting on the ground.

"Jenna, look at me."

She did, and even in the descending twilight, he could see the hunger in her mixing with the uncertainty. She wanted to ride so badly that she could taste it, so why was she throwing up so many barriers?

"I'm teaching you to ride."

Delight flashed across her face before she smothered it with caution. He uncrossed his arms. He pushed off the carriage. "Starting tonight."

Alarm replaced caution, and her eyes flew wide.

"Tonight?" she echoed as he took the reins of the horse.

"Yup." He led the docile horse standing prepared in its harness beside the buggy into an empty stall, tossing it some oats and patting its neck before shutting the stall door and motioning Jenna over. "Come with me."

He could feel her gaze boring a hole in his back, and hear her slightly uneven gait as she felt her way across the barn. There was a thump and a muffled curse. He turned to find her rubbing her forehead, glaring at the pole clearly before her. "You okay?"

"Yes." She reached forward with her hand as if confirming where the pole was.

"Sunshine, are you having trouble seeing?"

"It's just so dark in here."

Not to him. "Just stay where you are." He settled the roan in front of a bale of hay, traded his head harness for a halter, and swung back toward her. "Here. Take my hand."

Jenna's fingers clenched over his, with just a hint of desperation. He made a mental note of her lack of night vision.

"This way." She followed the tug of his hand. "There's a bucket to your right."

"You can see in here?" she asked as she gave the bucket a wide berth.

He pulled her in before she collided with a stack of hay. "Yup."

"I guess it's just me then."

"Just you what?"

"Just me who can't see at night. I always thought Jack was just gifted that way, but I guess I'm the one who's different."

"It's not a big thing."

"It can make things difficult in the winter. I get lost sometimes." Her fingers tightened on his as they stepped into a shadow.

He stopped dead. He caught her before she could crash into him. He tipped her chin up, wanting to see her face. "Lost?"

"Sometimes things get confusing, especially when it snows."

"And you got lost?" He could feel her skin heating beneath his fingers. She was blushing.

"Just a couple times."

His stomach clenched at the thought. Wyoming winters were nothing to sneeze at. "Were you hurt?"

"Just a little frostbite."

"Where was your husband?"

She didn't answer. Probably because it was a damned fool question. Anyone who knew Jack Hennesey knew he could be found at the bottom of any bottle, shouting about the evil of lust and the strength of temptation while he wallowed in both.

"Never mind. I've a good idea."

"He was a good man when he wasn't drinking," she said defensively.

"I'll take your word for it." He'd never seen the man sober. He brushed a curl off her temple. "You won't get lost again."

"I won't?"

"No." He wouldn't allow it.

"Oh."

He patted the buckskin's rump as he stepped behind Jenna and caught her waist in his hands. "Spread your legs."

He had her airborne before her gasped "What?" had drifted away. Though she'd said that she didn't catch on quickly, she was savvy enough to throw her leg over the saddle and take the horn in a death grip. Ornery shifted his feet and she shrieked. Clint vaulted up behind her.

"Don't go scaring him now or this lesson will be over before it starts," he murmured as he hitched her higher up against him.

She slapped one hand over her mouth, cutting off the outcry, and from the way her ribs swelled under his hand, her air.

"Breathe, Sunshine," he ordered as he flattened his hand over her midriff and pulled her back against him.

She did. Just until he nudged Ornery toward the door. Then she was back to clutching the horn and freezing.

"First lesson in riding a horse is to relax and go with the motion."

Her "Okay" was a nearly inaudible high-pitched squeak. He didn't notice any relaxing.

"Jenna, I won't let you fall. Now, relax your back and let your weight come against me."

She did, a fraction of an inch at a time, clearly ready at the slightest inattention to spring back to her petrified state. Finally, her head came to rest under his chin. The fur trimming the hood tickled his nose.

"That's my girl." He pulled her a little closer. The cloak blocked any sensation, but just the weight of her in his arms was enough to have his cock straining. "I'm going to slide my hand under your cloak now, to get a better grip," he warned her as he unfastened the wooden frogs.

"For what?" Her hands were back to death gripping the pommel.

"So you won't be so nervous." And so he could enjoy the weight of her magnificent breasts on his forearm, but he didn't think she'd appreciate hearing that. He slid his hand inside the cloak just under her breasts. But he did. Son of a bitch, he did. Even though she had herself bound up tight, he could still feel the soft swells shudder with each step Ornery took as he urged the horse out of the barn. Damn, he couldn't wait to get her under him. Those plump, fleshy mounds in his mouth. Were her nipples as plump and luscious as the rest of her? If he sucked on them long enough and carefully enough, would she come for him? Would she shriek his name when he brought her to climax? Or sigh it softly as her body shuddered under his? Whatever way she came, it'd be his name on her lips. He'd make sure of that.

"Clint?"

She was looking up at him, snowflakes sparkling in her blonde hair, apprehension on her face. He was gripping her too tightly. He dropped a kiss on her brow, smiled at her airy intake of breath, and relaxed his grip.

"Right here, Sunshine."

"I can ride in the buggy."

"I like you where you are."

"Oh."

"Nothing more to say?" There was a pause in which he actually felt her gathering her courage. Damn, Hennessy had left her shortchanged on confidence.

"Yes."

"What?"

"I need my basket."

Clint looked toward the porch where they'd left it. It would be a challenge to lug it along. "We'll get it later."

She bit her lip, but didn't disagree. He nudged Ornery on. She looked back four times as they passed the house, but didn't say a word which he should have taken as acceptance. On the fifth turn of her head, he pulled Ornery up short.

"What's in the basket, Jenna?"

"Nothing important." Her voice was a whisper of sound, bare of inflection as if she were staying as neutral as possible.

"How not important?"

"It's just your wedding present."

Just? "You got me a wedding present?"

Her voice dropped to almost nonexistent as she answered, "Yes."

Now that was a surprise. Brides didn't normally give their husbands a present. Let alone brides who were marrying out of necessity.

"Will it keep?"

She ducked her head. "It's not important."

The way she tried to sink inside herself told him this was very important to her. Important enough that she worried about his reaction. That meant it was personal. He wheeled Ornery around.

"What are you doing?"

"I'm getting my present."

"There's no need. It's nothing special."

"I think I'll see that for myself."

He reached the porch. With a cluck of his tongue, he urged Ornery on. Jenna squealed and pressed back against his chest as the horse lurched up the steps. He hugged her tighter with one arm as he leaned over and grabbed up the basket. It was heavy, and not because of the threadbare cloak that sat on top.

"What's in it, Jenna?"

"I know how much you like chocolate."

"Chocolate?" Clint asked, nudging the lid. "Jenna, you baked me something chocolate?"

Her "Yes" was shy, sweet, and uncertain.

"Ah baby, I'm going to love being married to you."

She clearly didn't know what to do with that. She shifted in the saddle, bringing the fullness of her buttocks against the top of his aching shaft.

"It's just a little something."

"Sunshine, the littlest something from you can have a man in ecstasy."

Including the littlest movement of her ass on his cock. As she straightened, the soft fullness caressed his length. He pushed up with his right leg, prolonging the pressure. She gasped, but couldn't do anything but let him enjoy her. He liked her sweet and submissive against him. He kissed the top of her head, and turned toward home.

As soon as Ornery slowed to a walk, he touched his lips to Jenna's ear. "Did I get a chance to tell you how beautiful you look today?"

She stiffened slightly and then relaxed. "No."

"Now that's a shame, because you are beautiful."

"Thank you."

"And I'm very hungry for you."

"Oh."

"Which brings me to a question." He brought his hand to her back under her cloak, trailing his fingers up the multitude of buttons covering her spine.

"What?"

"How averse are you to my unbuttoning this dress and pleasuring those beautiful breasts of yours while we ride?"

She was completely averse to that idea, but before she could even voice her opinion, Jenna felt the give that said Clint had her dress unbuttoned to her chest. She clutched the basket to her and whispered her thanks for the concealment of her cloak.

"Nothing to say?"

She shook her head. What could she say? He was her husband.

"Ah, I like that."

That was her dress sagging off her shoulders. She took comfort in the fact that not a lot of her flesh was exposed, thanks to her heavy corset and chemise. Then his hand slid across her corset. The calluses caught on the smooth material as it traversed her side to the fullness of her breast. Inwardly, she cringed as his big hand opened and stretched over her curves.

She was so big. Had always been too big. Like a big fat cow that no amount of squishing and compressing could ever hide. Especially when a man held her in his hand. Like Jack had done. Like Clint was doing.

She braced herself for the scathing comment that was sure to come. She'd heard them all since her breasts had surged to prominence during her twelfth year. Someday, she'd be immune.

"Sunshine?" Clint's lips brushed the side of her neck.

"What?"

"Slide your arms out of your dress."

"Here? Are you serious?"

There was a flick of something hot and moist on her neck—his tongue? It sent shivers of goose bumps down her arms.

"Dead serious."

"But we're out in the open."

"The cloak covers you."

"Ornery might bolt." Jack had been demanding in his needs, but never like this.

"Nah." Clint's fingers slid back and forth on the side of her camisole—whisper-light, inching the fabric of her dress forward, freeing the path for his fingers.

"He hates snow. He'll just plod all the way to the barn door."

She was out of excuses. She unbuttoned her cuffs. Heat burned up her chest and over her cheeks in a wave of embarrassment as she slid her hands out slowly. Behind her, Clint chuckled.

She didn't want to know why, but some suicidal part of her just had to ask, "What?"

The answer was a low, deep murmur of sound against her ear. "I've never felt a woman blush before."

"I can't help it."

He nuzzled his face into the curve of her neck. "I don't want you to help it. Just commenting on the facts." He pressed the reins into her hands as soon as her arms were clear. "Hold these."

"What are you doing?"

"I'm freeing up my hands."

Was he out of his mind? "I can't drive a horse."

"No driving to be done. Just hold them steady."

She curled her fingers into the basket and repeated the obvious, "I can't drive this horse."

"Sure you can." Against her hand, she felt his fingers relax. Good heavens! He was going to get them both killed!

"Grab hold now."

She did, clutching the basket with her forearms and grabbing the falling reins with her gloved fingers. Someone had to exercise some common sense. "You're crazy!"

She felt his smile slide against her hair. "Nah. Just hungry for my wife."

His mouth settled on her shoulder while his hand worked under her cloak, and then before she could draw a breath to protest, he had both of her breasts in his hands. The thin cotton of her camisole did nothing to diminish the impact of his touch. His hands were hard, sure, and firm. Not hurting. Not fumbling. Just holding her, as if weighing her assets. In an agony of suspense she awaited his verdict.

"Sunshine, you are one pleasant handful for a man."

"You don't think I'm too big?" If he was just being nice, she'd rather know up-front. His laugh puffed over her neck, raising more goose bumps.

"You feel just right in my hands."

"Oh."

"Nothing more to say?" he asked, his tongue sliding over the path of bumps on her skin. Wet and hot. She should be repulsed. She wasn't. Maybe it was because he wasn't overwhelming her. With the exception of Ornery's potential flight, she didn't have a sense of impending doom that overtook her every time things spun out of control.

"No."

The cool air blew over the flesh he'd moistened. New bumps arose, and she shivered. He sucked at the curve of her shoulder. "Hmm, you smell good. Like fresh air and roses."

"It's the powder."

"The powder?" She felt the edge of his teeth on the cord of her neck. She held herself very still. He was very big behind her. Very intimidating.

"Mara loaned it to me," she whispered.

"I like it."

"Thank you."

"You should get some."

"Oh, I couldn't."

His mouth separated from her skin. His lips nibbled at her earlobe as his hands began a subtle massage on her breasts. She bit her lip, all her attention shifting to his hands.

"Why not?"

"It's expensive."

"If you like it, get it."

He said that now, when he had his hands on her body and bedding on his mind, but she knew how attitudes changed when the urge passed. "I'll think on it."

The wind blew, and soft fat flakes swirled in her face. She blinked and pulled back. Straight into the unyielding support of his chest. He seemed to tuck her in, absorb her weight. Shelter her. She wasn't a small woman, but Clint made her feel that way for the simple reason that he was so big. And he handled her so carefully. Not like something he owned, but like something he valued. She couldn't figure him out.

"That's right, Sunshine, cuddle back here and let me make us both feel good."

Clint felt Jenna's small surrender in the way she rested against him, but there was a fine tension humming under her skin. She was doing what he asked, but she was wary. Clint slid his palms up Jenna's magnificent breasts, tightening his grip as he tugged ever so slightly at their weight, enjoying their soft resiliency as he worked his way up to their equally soft peaks. With a curl of his pinkies, he pulled her camisole down.

He wished the cloak wasn't in his way so he could see their color. He imagined they were a soft pink, maybe with a hint of red on the tips. He explored their textures with his index fingers, taking advantage of Jenna's uneasy shifting to rub the tender tips. They were flat. Unresponsive.

He wasn't deterred. He never figured she'd light up like a torch right away. For all the talk, he'd never imagined Jenna as loose. He'd call her a lot of things—shy, stubborn, opinionated, and oddly courageous—but round in the heels was not a term he'd lay on her. This ride was more of a "get acquainted" session for them, but she was such a sweet handful, it was a challenge to remember her bedroom experiences to date might not have left her enthusiastic.

Ornery stumbled on a rock. Jenna yanked back on the reins. Ornery hopped a protest. Jenna dropped the reins and almost threw herself to the ground. For a few seconds, Clint had all he could do to hold Jenna, rescue his present, and keep Ornery from crow-hopping the joy out of this wedding night.

"Son of a bitch." He pulled Ornery to a halt, resettled Jenna in front of him, and handed her the basket. "I'll give you one thing, Sunshine. You sure can ruin a moment."

"I told you I couldn't drive a horse," she whispered.

He eyed her flushed cheeks, wide eyes and death grip on the basket.

"So you did." He squeezed his knees, putting Ornery back into motion. Jenna sat so stiffly in front of him that it was almost a dare. He never could resist a dare. He pressed the reins back against her hands. She shook her head vigorously, her hair glowing in the last bits of daylight.

"Either you hold them, or we just let them go." She turned in his arms, her expression one of horror and incredulity.

"You can't want to go through that again?"

"You've got to learn sometime. Now is as good as any." And he really wanted to see if he could make her nipples perk just a little in the time he had left.

"I can't."

"Why not?" he asked as he reached under her cloak and hooked his fingers in her camisole.

"Because I'm just not good at things. I'll get us killed."

"Sunshine, I'd never give you something you couldn't handle."

"But I *almost* got us killed."

"The worst that would have happened is I would have lost my present."

"We could have fallen off!"

"I haven't fallen off a horse since I was four, and I would never let you fall."

She gasped as his cool fingers cradled her nipples. He couldn't tell whether from pleasure, shock, or cold.

"You wouldn't have a say." A breathless, airy quality entered her voice.

"Sunshine, I have a say in everything when it comes to you." Her nipples contracted under his touch, and he had the answer to one of his questions. She had dainty, delicate nipples that peaked into his touch with deceptive eagerness. He withdrew his hands, but left her breasts bare. He knew the minute the fur lining of the cloak registered on her skin. Her lids flicked up, and her restless shifting stilled.

He stroked her cloak over her breasts, dragging the material over the tips.

"I bought this cloak thinking about how good it would look against your skin," he whispered in her ear, stoking the soft fur over her breasts. "How good it would feel against your skin.

He repeated the caress. "Does it feel good to you, Jenna? Do you like how all that silky fur feels against your bare breasts?"

She sat very still in front of him and didn't answer. He cupped her breasts through the cloak. As always, she didn't struggle, but she didn't encourage him either. She had to be uncomfortable with his touch, maybe even afraid. He was a big man with a bad reputation, a virtual stranger, but she held her ground. Held to her bargain. She had such courage, his Jenna. Not the flashy kind, but the "stick it out" kind. The kind that helped her endure. He gentled his touch, and pulled her back against him. He wouldn't betray her trust, but he also wouldn't let her hide.

"Answer me, Jenna. Does it fell good when I rub this soft fur over your breasts?"

She swallowed hard. Her shoulder blades flexed against his chest. Then, almost imperceptibly, she nodded.

He kissed the top of her head and just held her against him, satisfied with that concession, enjoying the scent of woman and roses that drifted up from the warmth of her cloak, blending with the crisp evening air. She was his. In time she'd come to accept him. Trust him. Until then, he'd just work at convincing her he was worth the effort.

Chapter Six

It was almost dark by the time they arrived at the barn. Clint slid off Ornery, and Jenna immediately panicked at being left alone up on the big buckskin. He put one hand on her thigh and one on the horse's shoulder, soothing both with his touch. When they were calmer, he held his hands up to her.

"Slide on down here, Jenna."

Jenna shoved the basket at him instead of dropping into his arms. He took it and put it on the ground. The whole move took about two seconds, but by the time he was upright, Jenna had managed to get herself tangled, hanging halfway off the horse. It was easy to see why she didn't complete the move. Her skirt was caught on the saddle horn, and she couldn't swing her leg over to fall the rest of the way off.

"Need a little help?" he asked, admiring the turn of her calf as it was exposed by her hiked up skirt.

She didn't answer and didn't move. He was getting used to her silences. He figured they either meant she was nervous or embarrassed. Tonight, it was probably a little of both.

Ornery sidestepped, uncomfortable with the placement of weight. Jenna abandoned her paralysis. Ornery abandoned complacency. With a snort, he bucked. Just enough to let Clint know that he wasn't happy, but it was enough to send Jenna into a full panic. She let go of the horn to grab her skirt. A mistake, but one Clint had anticipated. He waited, a knife in his hands. On the next hop, she flopped back into his arms. With one hand he held her against his chest, and with the other, he cut her skirt loose. As she lay gasping against him, he sheathed his knife.

"It would have been better if you'd let me help you."

"I just wanted to do it myself."

He set her feet on the ground.

"Independence is a good thing," he turned her and pushed her hair off her face, noting the faint sheen of tears in her eyes, "but it needs to be tempered by intelligence."

Her flinch was mostly internal, but it lingered in the flicker of her lashes and the slight tightening of her lips. He tucked another strand of hair behind her ear. "And patience. Jenna, you've got to learn patience."

"I'm patient."

"Sometimes."

She didn't say more, but he knew she wanted to. He wondered if there had been a time when she would have said more, before the fire inside her had been smothered by criticism and beatings.

She stepped back. He allowed her a foot before he hooked a hand behind her neck and stopped her. There was a sizable pile of manure one step back.

"I don't think you're stupid, Jenna, but I do think you're impulsive, and I'd appreciate it if you could curb that tendency."

She ducked her chin, "Or what?"

He tipped her chin up. She seemed to be staring at a point just south of meeting his gaze. With her lack of night vision, it was hard to tell if she was avoiding his gaze or just didn't know where it was.

"Are you asking me what will happen if you don't?"

"Yes."

"I'll be unhappy."

"Oh."

He caught her hand in his and guided her toward where Ornery stood by the barn door patiently waiting to be let in.

"You don't have to hold my hand."

"You can see where we're going?"

"No."

"Then I'm holding your hand. And watch out for the rock there."

"Where?" Her toe hit it, and she stumbled. He steadied her.

"Right there."

"Oh." A pause and then, "Thank you." There was a certain note in that "thank you" that hit him wrong.

Her hand, so much smaller and softer rocked in his. It took him a second to figure out why, and then he realized she was furtively feeling around with her toe, looking for more rocks. He slipped the rope latch off the iron hook that kept the barn door closed.

"Jenna?"

"What?"

"I won't let you fall." All movement stopped.

"Thank you." That off note in her voice was stronger now.

"You're welcome. Now let's get Ornery settled." He grabbed Ornery's reins just below the bridle. He slid his hand up her arm to her shoulder before sliding it down to her waist. He wouldn't say she tucked willingly into his side, but she went. He made his first step small, accommodating her stride, but it wasn't small enough to accommodate a dead stop.

"What are you doing?" she asked.

"Guiding you into the barn."

"I'm not helpless."

"Never said you were."

"I can walk by myself."

"Fine." He let go of her and guided Ornery along the familiar path to his stall. Behind him, he heard Jenna shuffling her feet. The stall door creaked as he opened it. Jenna gasped and stopped.

Ornery pushed past him, eager to have his oats. Clint supposed he could light the lantern by the stall but he could still see, barely, and some perverse part of him didn't want to make things easy for Jenna. Not when she was so determined to make them hard for herself.

There was more shuffling as he undid the girth and pulled off the saddle and blanket. He swung the saddle onto the sawhorse with ease of long practice. He could make out her outline in the doorway. She'd made it just inside the barn, no doubt clinging to the faint light coming from outside. From the way she was bent, he figured she was checking out the damage his knife had done to her dress. He removed his rifle from the leather scabbard and propped it against the outside of the stall. She was a stubborn little thing.

The lid to the oat box slammed open. Jenna jumped. He scooped out a measure, pushed Ornery's eager nose out of the way as he reentered the stall, and dumped it into the horse's bin. Grabbing the water bucket, he went to the pump just inside the door and started pumping up the water. Everything was quiet with that peculiar hush that comes with the first snow of winter, amplifying the other sounds — the grinding metal efforts of the pump, Ornery's munching, and Jenna's sudden shriek. A shriek that quickly turned into a panicked scream.

"Jenna?"

She didn't answer, just shrieked again and started spinning in circles, beating at her clothes. He dropped the bucket. It took him four strides to get to her side. He caught her by the shoulders, stopping her hysterical spinning. It took him a second to decipher what she was saying.

"Oh, not rats. Not rats, not rats, not rats."

"Not rats, Sunshine. Kittens." He plucked a kitten off the back of her skirt and pulled her into his arms.

Wrestling against him, she didn't seem to hear. He put the kitten on his shoulder, and grabbed at the bulge moving beneath her cloak in the vicinity of her stomach. She grabbed, too, her short nails gouging into his hands. The bulge howled and hissed. Jenna screamed and fought. He anchored her with a hand at the back of her neck, left her to contain the bulge, and made short work of the buttons on the cloak. It fell to the floor, revealing the whiteness of her skin and the problem. The kitten was stuck in the fold of her loosened top as it fell over her waist, trapped by her hands and the material.

"Let go, Jenna."

Her chant shortened to staccato "nos" as she wrestled to contain the little kitten, which was just as determined to get free.

He grabbed her hands and pulled them from her body. She lashed out with her feet. Her eyes flashed white in the darkness.

"Nononononononononononono."

Holding both her hands in one of his, he pulled the equally hysterical kitten from under the bodice, tugging hard when the sharp little claws clung to the material. As soon as the kitten was free, it spun in his grip. He winced as it clawed its way up his arm to the security of his shoulder.

"It was just kittens, Jenna." She shuddered under his hand. He pulled her into his chest and wrapped his arms around her. "Just two little pesky, more-trouble-than-they are-worth, kittens."

She burrowed against him as if wanting to get beneath his skin. He wrapped his arms tighter, holding her harder.

"Just kittens, Sunshine," he repeated.

She gave one last violent shake, and then released her pent-up breath. "Kittens?"

"Just kittens."

She went limp. He backed them up until he got to the side of the stall. He sat her on a bale of hay. She resisted, her soft hands sliding over his stomach, wrapping around his thighs as he pulled out his sulfurs and lit one. Her eyes were huge in her pale face as the match flared. He lit the lamp, sitting beside her as the glow intensified, unbuttoning his coat and pulling her into the warmth of his body. What in hell had made her so fearful of rats?

She was still trembling, tiny little shakes that he knew she was trying to contain from the way she tensed though each occurrence.

"I've got you, Sunshine. You're safe." He cupped her head in his hand and cradled her close.

She lay against him, her breath coming hot and moist against his chest through his shirt, the mounds of her full breasts pushing against his stomach, and her left hand resting against his erection, which stretched down his thigh, uncaring about the fear draining from her body. Only aware of her womanly smell and the lush temptation just the thickness of the fabric away.

The kittens mewled in his ears. One draped itself into the curve of his neck, and started grooming his ear. He'd kick them off if he didn't know they'd just cause a ruckus crawling back up.

"Are they yours?" The soft whisper drifted up from the level of his chest.

He shrugged the kitten away from his earlobe. "They certainly think so."

"Why?"

"I made the mistake of feeding them when their mother abandoned them." The kitten came back with a vengeance, determined to have its comfort. There was another silence.

"Jack used to bang their heads on rocks."

That did not surprise him. "A lot of folk feel that way."

He shrugged the kitten away again. The kitten dug its claws in and pushed back.

Jenna didn't say anything, just lay against him. The kitten took advantage of his distraction to latch onto his earlobe. In two seconds it was happily slurping away, sucking on his ear, like a baby with a sugar tit. He knew from experience if he yanked it off he'd have to listen to ten minutes of yowling protest. It was easier to just wait until it went to sleep.

Jenna shifted against him. He looked down to find her looking up with something like amazement in her eyes. "You have a kitten sucking on your ear."

He winced. "She'll go to sleep soon."

"It looks uncomfortable."

"It isn't my favorite experience."

"Do you want me to pull it off?"

"You want to hear her yowl for the next ten minutes?"

"No."

"Me neither."

She stared at him for so long that he didn't know what to make of it. Then she blinked and the smallest of smiles touched her lips. "You are a nice man, Clint McKinnely."

"I'm a selfish bastard, and you'd do well to remember it."

She slid off the bale of hay, settling between his thighs. The light from the lamp cast her bare breasts in golden shadow. His cock jerked in his pants. She had to have felt the leap of hard flesh beneath her open palm. He expected her to flinch away. He never expected her to smile. Or the delicate touch of her hands on the buttons of his pants.

"Jenna…"

"What?" She didn't halt in her unbuttoning.

"There's a house just a few yards away."

"Good." She unfastened the last button.

"There's a big ol' bed upstairs with a brand-new mattress sitting on it."

"Good." She tugged at the waistband of his denims. He lifted his hips so she could work them down.

"So why are you undressing me?"

She pulled those softly aggressive hands from his eager flesh and folded them in her lap.

"I'm sorry. I didn't realize…"

He liked her better with the light of confidence in her eyes. He caught her hands and put them back on his pants.

"There's nothing to realize." He removed the now-sleeping kitten from his shoulder and put it on the bale of hay. "I was just a little surprised."

She'd been too forward, Jenna realized. How many times had Jack slapped her for taking charge? She'd just been so touched that he'd fed and sheltered the two little kittens that she'd wanted to do something equally nice for him.

He released her hands. For a moment she didn't know what to do. Would he be offended if she resumed touching him? Would he be mad if she stopped now that she'd begun?

His hands slid up over his thighs, over his lean hips, and under the worn blue fabric of his pants. He shifted. The material bulged as his hands worked beneath. Little by little he revealed the solid length of his cock. Every time she thought there must be an end, another dark, throbbing inch appeared until at last the broad head lay heavily against his hair-dusted thigh.

She stared. She couldn't help it. She'd never, ever seen a man's organ that was so large. Never, ever dreamed a man could be built so. Jack's cock had barely cleared his fly. Clint's would not only clear his fly, but reach the elk horn button just above his navel. It was dark, wide, and tinted with the same red as the rest of his skin. Part of her was appalled, but another part of her, the shameful part that had led her astray in her youth, wanted to touch him to see how he'd feel under her fingers. To stroke the power that simmered under his skin.

As if knowing what she was thinking, and the demons she wrestled with, Clint held his impressive length in his hand—stroking it, making it grow even more.

"Is that what you wanted, Sunshine?" Deep mystery blended with the night, edging his drawl with temptation. "Were you curious as to what I looked like? How I was built?"

How could he know so much about her in so short a time? She ducked her head, bracing herself for the condemnation that always came with honesty. "Yes."

"Then come satisfy your curiosity."

It was a long way up to his face, but she needed to see his expression. To understand the motive behind the invitation. His eyes met hers. His gaze was intent, serious, and unflinchingly dark with desire. He wanted her to touch him. She relaxed inside.

"Come take what you want, Sunshine. Let me feel those soft lips on my cock." He angled his cock toward her with three long strokes of his big hand.

His thighs flexed under her hands as she leaned forward. He was such a big man, so strong. And he was hers. She'd do well to please him.

The rough fabric of his denims scraped the sides of her breasts as she touched her tongue to the smooth, hot tip.

"Yes, baby. That's it," he groaned, as he pressed his cock up into her touch.

She let her tongue flatten against him, measuring the pulse of his hunger with her mouth. His hand cupped the back of her head, the weight alone pulling her forward, onto his cock.

"Kiss it, Jenna," he groaned in that low drawl that made everything in her want to obey. "Give me a taste of how sweet loving you is going to be."

She did, relaxing. He was no different than Jack in this. He wanted to be admired. Praised.

"You're so big…" She didn't have to fake the wonder in her voice as she rained light kisses over the mushroom head.

"Not too big." His thumb stroked the corner of her mouth. "Open for me, Jenna."

She parted her lips just a little, teasing him with the promise of the heat within, knowing it would increase his pleasure. He growled and leaned back, pushing his hips forward. He rubbed his cock over her lips, from corner to corner, touching her teeth, seeming to enjoy their smooth glide over the sensitive tip.

"Open, baby."

She did, but he was too big to just slide in. She stretched her jaws as far as she could, working him past her teeth, flinching when she accidentally scraped him, relaxing when he moaned instead of lashing out.

When he was settled against her tongue, she peeked up from under her lashes. His big shoulders looked massive in the shearling coat, braced against the stall, his black hair swinging forward, framing his dark face, the shadows casting the sharp planes in stark relief. Beneath his lowered lids, his eyes glittered. He was watching her take him into her mouth. He touched her lips with his finger.

"Now that's a pretty sight. Those beautiful lips tight around my cock."

He was going to be easy to please. She smiled up at him and suckled lightly. One hand slid over her hair and then down to her shoulders.

"Scoot up a bit." She did, taking more of his cock in the process, the broad head filling her mouth too full. For an awful moment, she thought she'd gag. His fingers on her cheek stilled her panic.

"Easy, Sunshine. Breathe through your nose and relax."

She knew that. Knew how to do this. Jack had spent most of their marriage teaching her to do this right. She took a slow breath and forced her throat to relax. It would be so helpful if she could remember it all now. If she pleased Clint tonight, maybe her second marriage didn't have to go the way of the first.

She worked him deeper in short little jabs. He was so much bigger than Jack that she couldn't be sure she was pleasing him. Giving him enough stimulation. His finger under her chin made her jump.

"Look at me."

She did, dreading what she'd see in his face. Surprisingly, he didn't look upset, just very…intent.

"Keep your eyes on me as you suck me. I want to see everything you feel, everything you think as I come."

She had to rely on her raised eyebrows to communicate her "Why?"

"Because I want it."

And his tone said that was that. She shivered, but held his gaze. Clint's eyes narrowed, and he swore.

"Damn, I'm sorry." He leaned forward. "You make me forget my head."

She had no idea what he was talking about.

"Just hold me, darling, while I get you settled." She needed to be settled?

His cock surged and jerked in her mouth as he shrugged out of his coat and then the heavy weight and warmth of it settled over her bare shoulders. She was immediately enveloped in the moist aroma of pine, smoke, and man. He seemed to surround her, his cock in her mouth. His scent in her nostrils. His hand in her hair.

"It's a shame though, to cover those magnificent breasts."

He thought her beasts were magnificent? She glanced down, but all she could see was the thick stalk of his penis and the curly edge of the coat he'd draped over her shoulders. His finger touched her cheek and she immediately brought her gaze back to his.

She touched the edge of the coat and then stroked his penis gently. He was such a kind man. She wrapped her hand around his staff, marveling that her fingers didn't meet, marveling at how he throbbed with life. Touching had involved as much fear as purpose with Jack. He could be volatile when aroused, though Clint was prodigiously aroused, she didn't sense any violence in him. He was in control. Enjoying her mouth, but not on edge. It gave her the courage to experiment.

She hugged the coat to her with her one hand while with the other she pumped in counterpoint to the motion of her lips. Twisting lightly as she pulled away, swirling her tongue over the tip before sucking strongly. Keeping her eyes on his as he'd ordered.

"That's it Sunshine." His lids slipped lower. "Do that again."

She did and was rewarded by the salty taste of his pleasure. But she didn't need to taste to know she was pleasing him. She could see it in his face, the way his eyes narrowed, and his lips pulled back from his teeth. His big hands drifted up from her shoulders until both were in her hair. Three short tugs and the thick mass fell around her shoulders. He ran his hands through the heavy tresses as they spilled over her back and face.

"Son of a bitch, you're something," he groaned as his cock pulsed again.

She wasn't, but for this moment in time if he thought so, she was content. His finger touched her cheek and pressed, feeling himself through her flesh.

"Faster now, Jenna."

She obliged, taking him deeper, sucking harder, pacing herself to the harsh tension of his breathing, the pulse she could feel throbbing just beneath the satin-smooth skin of his cock. He was huge, hard, so swollen with the need to come that she thought he must split, and still he didn't give her his seed.

She redoubled her efforts. His breath hissed through his teeth and his head fell forward, his hair framing his dark face as the angles sharpened with his torment. Then his eyes opened and locked with hers, searing her with the intensity of his passion. His hand slid over hers, working her fingers free, replacing them with his own. Holding his cock steady for the descent of her mouth.

"Open the coat. Just for a minute, Sunshine. Let me see those beautiful breasts of yours."

She did, but she couldn't help blushing. This was so much more intimate than anything she'd ever done with Jack. The air chilled her nipples pulling them tight. Clint's hard mouth tilted in a smile.

"Put your hands under them and lift them up, like you're offering them to me."

She had to shift forward to do so. She worked back off his cock as she cupped the underside of her breasts, not sure what he wanted. He arched his hips, reclaiming lost ground.

"Such a shy little wife." He touched her cheek. "Do you want me to tell you what to do?"

She lashed his cock with her tongue as she nodded.

"I want you to pretend those are my hands on your breasts. I want you to stroke them and fondle them and give yourself pleasure."

Oh heavens. She had absolutely no idea how to do that. His big hand cupped her chin, his thumb pressing against the bulge of his cock.

"Shh, don't panic. We can work up to that." His voice was a harsh growl. "I'm not going to last much longer anyway. Your mouth is sweeter than honey."

Hay rustled as his hips arched, reflecting his need. "Take me as deep as you can, Sunshine. Slow and deep, and I'll take care of the other."

She blinked as his hands closed over her breasts. They were huge and cold. Very cold. She shivered and he laughed, a deep husky sound of pleasure and pain. Despite the fact that she was the one wearing a coat, he was the one sweating. His hips arched up, feeding her more of his cock.

"That's the way. Just stay relaxed and take it, Jenna. All that you can. Slow and deep."

His hands on her breasts were gentle without that mean edge she was accustomed to, and his voice was so soft as he asked rather than slamming into her throat. She did her best, swallowing as he nudged the back of her throat, feeling the painful pressure as he pushed in, blinking back the tears and pushing forward, wanting to please him, hoping this time her marriage could be more friendship than anger. She groaned in relief when he pulled back. Her relief was short-lived. His fingers slid up to her nipples. She blinked, bracing herself for the wrenching pain that always came when a man put his hands there.

"Ah, baby, you have the prettiest nipples." His fingers stroked lightly, rhythmically, the calluses dragging on her flesh. "They're like delicate, silky pebbles of flesh under my hands. And your mouth. Damn, Jenna, you have an incredible mouth."

He pinched her nipples lightly. A warning? She wasn't taking any chances. She took him all the way to the back of her throat, suppressing the urge to gag, struggling to relax enough to let him in.

"Son of a bitch, you're going to make me come too soon," he said as he pressed against her, his cock pulsing with the caress of her spasming throat.

Too soon? Her jaws already ached. She checked his expression to see if he was serious. He laughed deep in his throat. A lazy sound.

"I want a chance to play with these sweet nipples before I come," he explained. She started. He circled the pebbled flesh with his thumb. "Nothing too hard. You're not ready for that. Maybe just a little stroking at first. Just enough to make them sit up and take notice." He pulled out, not as slowly as before, and his movement wasn't as smooth. Was his calm a lie?

"Would you like that, Sunshine?" he asked on a tight note. "Would you like me to pleasure your breasts?"

She'd like anything that didn't bring that awful pain. She nodded as she suckled the tip of his cock. A spurt of warm seed flooded her mouth. His hands left her breasts to cup her head.

"Later then." His voice was a hoarse expression of sound. "Later, I'll pleasure them until you scream, but right now I need your mouth."

She gave it to him, taking him as deeply as she could, wetting his shaft with saliva as she withdrew, using the slick surface to facilitate the strong strokes of her fist. Sucking hard, working him hard, taking him so deep it ached, and still it wasn't enough. His hands on her head urged her closer, urged her to go just that little bit further.

"Just a little more, baby." His cock pressed the back of her throat. "A little more and you'll have it all. C'mon Jenna. Take me. Take me."

She took a deep breath and did, moaning as he popped through her resistance at last and as her muscles spasmed a protest around him he came, flooding her throat with his hot seed, holding her to him as he cried out and bucked. He held her to him so long that she began to panic, needing air, and still he came.

She caught his wrists in her hands. On a rough "Jesus" he let her go. She wanted to throw herself to the ground and gasp for air, but she knew better. Instead she drew on every bit of control she had, hauled air in through her nose, and carefully caught every silken wash of his seed, not spilling a drop, swallowing it while nurturing the last remnants of his pleasure, cementing his good will the only way she knew that worked. Taking a small measure of pride in her ability to do so.

Finally, he pulled her up into his chest and wrapped his big arms around her. The buttons on his shirt dug into her breasts as he kissed the curve of her shoulder before he slanted his mouth over hers and kissed her hard, his tongue stroking her lips as his hand massaged her sore throat.

"Damn, baby. No one's ever taken me like that. Given me that."

He was shaking against her. Against her stomach, his cock rose hard, undiminished. She touched his heaving chest. She'd done this to him. With nothing more than her mouth she'd taken his strength and given him pleasure. She curled her fingers around his cock.

"Would you like me to do it again?" Her voice was hoarse from the strain and the words were awkward as her tired jaw muscles tried to shape syllables. To her surprise, he shook his head.

"Sounds like that mouth of yours could use a little rest." He touched the corner of her lips with his thumb. He held it up for her inspection. It glistened with moisture. Very slowly, she stuck out her tongue and licked his finger clean. His nostrils flared and his eyelids twitched. "You are a hot little thing, aren't you?"

He sounded very happy with that conclusion. He pressed his thumb against her lips, rubbing it over the moist lining, his dark gaze holding hers while a strange shiver of sensation shot through her body. His eyes narrowed as he registered the tremble. His thumb pressed a little harder. She closed her lips around it and sucked, holding his gaze as she did so, watching the heat flare anew.

"Shit."

His cock came fully erect. In a flash, he had their positions reversed—the prickly hay bale was beneath her, the wall behind her, and before her stood Clint, looking totally pagan with his big cock jutting out from the open fly of his pants and his long hair loose about his exotic face. She jerked as he seemed to fall forward, expecting to be crushed under his weight, but there were only a couple of thunks in rapid succession above her head, and then the steady push of his cock against her mouth.

She looked up. His wide lips parted on a wickedly primitive smile.

"One more time to take the edge off, and then it will be my turn to make you scream."

Chapter Seven

Clint opened the basket containing his wedding present. The cake was a little worse for wear, but a few dents weren't going to put him off. Not with the way Jenna could take simple ingredients and make a man's taste buds scream for mercy. Above his head, he listened to the small creaks that indicated Jenna's progress around the bedroom. He'd left her to get changed and ready for bed while he brought up their snack. His cock throbbed in his denims, as eager as if he hadn't come twice so hard down Jenna's tight throat that he'd thought his head would explode.

He grabbed the knife off the table. Damn, she had a mouth that could make a man cry uncle. And that body. That "drop a man to his knees" body… He placed the knife in the middle of the cake and cut a large slice. He was so hungry for her that he felt like a green boy going after his first woman. He just wanted to bury himself in all that lush heat over and over until she was so full of his seed it would pour out of her when she stood. He wanted to permanently mark her as his so no other man could trespass. That she was his wife didn't seem to be enough. In a demand he'd never known before, his body wanted to mark her physically, making it obvious beyond a shadow of a doubt to whom she belonged. So much so that he'd lost his head and started his honeymoon in the barn.

He put a second piece of cake on another plate, hooked a couple of wine glasses on his finger and grabbed the bottle of wine. Hopefully, chocolate and wine would keep Jenna from dwelling on that less-than-romantic start to their life together. For a man with a reputation for having a way with the ladies, he wasn't putting his best foot forward with his wife.

Danny whined from where he lay in the center of the big kitchen floor. Clint didn't even need to look down to know what he wanted.

"Forget it, fella. This is my present." Danny cocked his head at him and let the muscles in his face sag. Clint snorted. "I stopped falling for that hang-dog look about a year ago."

He stepped over the big dog and Danny rolled, presenting his stomach. Clint petted him with the toe of his boot before heading out. This time his snort was one of disgust as the big dog's jowls fell back and he wiggled like a puppy.

"You know, there used to be a time when you inspired fear in people." Danny gave a blissful moan and wagged his tail. Clint shook his head and popped the door open with his elbow. "Damned shame you went and got yourself domesticated."

He was still shaking his head as he climbed the stairs to the bedroom. Sure enough, he was going to have to get another dog to guard the place. The good life had flat-out taken the mean out of a perfectly good dog. The scramble of feet behind him let him know that Danny wasn't letting that chocolate cake out of his sight. Clint tapped lightly at the bedroom door with the toe of his boot. He heard a sharp, "Oh" followed by a thump as something hit the floor. He was about to kick the door open, thinking Jenna had fallen, when he heard a string of curses. One corner of his mouth kicked up. Who would have known sweet little "wouldn't say boo to a ghost" Jenna could curse like a wrangler?

"Jenna?"

"What?" The disgruntled tone kicked the other side of his mouth up.

"Open the door."

"Just a minute."

Something nudged his elbow. Danny had meandered his way over and was looking expectantly at the door. "No way, bub."

Danny moaned and slumped to the floor. The doorknob rattled. Danny perked up. Clint pushed him back down with his foot. He did not need Jenna falling for that hang-dog look and bringing an audience to their wedding night. The door cracked and he had a perfect view of the left side of her face.

"You going to let me in?"

"I'm not quite ready."

As nervous as she looked, he figured he could be staring down his ninetieth birthday and still be standing outside the door. "Sunshine, if you're trying to make yourself beautiful, I've never seen you less than gorgeous."

"Even that night?"

He knew what night she was talking about in that whisper. He'd never forget it or the panic he'd felt running into that inferno and knowing he was probably too late.

"Yes. Even that night." The one eye he could see blinked once, twice, but the door didn't open. He shifted the wine bottle into his hand with his knee. "Can you tell me what the problem is?"

Her mouth worked. He had a glimpse of white before her teeth sank into her lower lip. "I want to turn out the lamp."

It took him a second to remember he'd sent her upstairs with a comment about leaving the light on so he could see her lying on that big bed with that wonderful mane of hair spread about her.

"Why?"

"Mara and Elizabeth bought me a nightgown as a wedding present."

That sounded promising. "I'm not following."

"It's too short."

Now there was a fact to perk up a man's cock.

"How short?" His drawl was a little more intense than normal. More of her lower lip slipped out of sight.

"Short enough to be showing things better left covered."

"Somehow, I'm not seeing that as a problem."

"You will."

That agonized whisper pulled his sense of humor up short. He kept his tone as gentle as possible, considering he was more used to using his voice to intimidate than cajole.

"Jenna, open the door."

"Can I turn out the light first?"

"No." He wasn't starting this marriage off creating barriers between them.

With a deep breath, she stepped back, staying behind the wood panel as the gap widened. Clint stepped through the opening. The wine glasses clinked together as his elbow bumped the door.

Danny whined and scrambled to his feet. Clint put his shoulder to the door and pressed it closed, locking Danny out. He turned, to see Jenna in all her glorious splendor. And she *was* glorious. That thick, wavy mane of long hair tumbled past her shoulders, framing her softly rounded face and providing the perfect backdrop for the rosy pink glow of flesh left so enticingly exposed by the bodice that barely clung to her shoulders. He couldn't take his eyes off those shoulders and that filmy white fabric gracing them. Just one push with his finger and it would slide down those soft arms and waft away from those incredible breasts. He might have to nudge it again if it got hung up on the plump tips, but then it would float down to the wide flare of her hips, catching again before it slid down her thighs.

His gaze dropped to her thighs, which she was doing her best to keep tucked behind the flounced hem of the gown. Her scarred thighs.

"They must have taken my robe out of my valise."

If she could have disappeared through the floor, he had no doubt that she would have. The flush on her cheeks begged the brush of his fingers. The agony of insecurity in her blue eyes offended him. She had nothing to be ashamed of. Because his hands were full, he bent. She ducked her head. His kiss landed on the part in her hair. The faint scent of roses teased his nostrils.

"Ah Sunshine, did you think you had me beat in the scar department?" She wouldn't meet his gaze, just clung to that doorknob like it was her lifeline.

"It's different for a man."

"Guarantee you, collecting them hurts the same." She glanced up as if surprised that he could know pain. Damned if he could figure her out. "You're beautiful, Jenna."

He put the wine and cake on the dresser. Behind the door Danny moaned. Jenna reached for the knob.

"Don't you dare." She jumped. He softened his tone. "We'll never get him out of here if he gets in."

"What harm—"

He tucked the long fall of her hair behind her shoulder. "I'm not looking for an audience tonight." The flush rose from her chest and flooded her cheeks as she caught his meaning.

"But surely after the barn?" She looked so damned adorable, so innocent, though he knew she wasn't.

"Got to admit that warmed me right up." Impossibly, the blush deepened.

"But Jack…"

He didn't want to hear about her first husband. Especially not on his wedding night. He slid his hand around the nape of her neck.

"Do me a favor and don't mention him." She flinched from the anger in his tone. He bit back an "ever" and added a softer, "Not tonight at least."

"I'm sorry."

The little bit of confidence she'd displayed since the barn disappeared as if it had never existed. She seemed to shrink in on herself, hunching her shoulders, and as much as the move provided him with a clear view of her breasts and accented the rich valley between, he hated the meekness she drew around herself like a shield.

"Don't be sorry, just don't mention him."

"I won't."

He sighed. So much for his legendary finesse. He pulled her away from the door. She lurched against him. She caught his forearm in her hands. Her palms were damp. She was nervous. He wrapped his arm around her waist and took her weight against his chest. "You feel good in my arms."

"I do?"

"Yes."

"Oh."

"And I'm an ass."

"You are?"

"Yes."

"Why?"

"Because you were married and I have no right to begrudge you that."

She took a little shuddering breath. "I'm just trying to do what you want."

He took a handful of her hair and tipped her head back. "How about you just relax and let me fill you in on my preferences?" She blinked, but didn't argue. He couldn't read what was going on behind her eyes. Damn, her father and first husband had about crushed the life out of her. "That was an apology, Sunshine."

"Oh."

Her breasts pressed into his stomach. Her breath seared him through his shirt. How could she ever doubt that she pleased him? He stepped back from her, immediately missing her soft breasts and hot breath. "Come here."

He didn't give her much choice but to follow. With his hand on the nape of her neck she was forced to tag along, a wary shadow. When he got to the bed, her eyes widened. The pulse in her throat picked up speed. He laid money it was nerves and not desire that set her heart to pounding.

He turned her and gave her a little push. She sat on the bed. He noticed she didn't bend her right knee.

"Is your leg bothering you?" He ran his hand over her thigh. There wasn't any tension in the muscle.

"No."

Desire replaced worry. He had her in his home, in his bed, and her thigh under his hand. There was only one thing that could make tonight better. "Would you like some cake?"

"Cake?"

"Yes." That decadently rich chocolate cake his wife had baked him. As a present. For her husband. It put the earrings he had purchased for her to shame.

"Uhm…no."

"Mind if I have some?" He wanted it all, his wife and her gift.

"Now?"

"Yes."

"Go right ahead."

If he wasn't mistaken, that was relief in her voice. Why she would be shy now when she wasn't in the barn eluded him, but she clearly was. He brushed his fingers over the remnants of heat in her cheek. "Smile for me, Sunshine."

She did, a tentative twitch of the lips, but it was enough to spark those dimples. He moved his finger over one. All the while she stared at him.

She had the biggest eyes, the softest skin, and the most vulnerable personality. He'd have to be very careful to gentle his ways around her. She was wounded and needed protection. He could give her that.

He just wouldn't be able to leave her alone. She was a walking fantasy with all those full womanly curves and he wasn't the type to rise above his baser moments. But he could give her a minute to collect herself and something to ease her through whatever was giving her a case of the jitters.

It only took a minute to pour the wine into the glasses and grab his plate. She was still sitting where he'd left her, a temptress in a froth of white, staring at him with wide apprehensive eyes. She had, however, pulled the quilt up as high as she could to cover as much as possible without actually lying down.

"Is that spirits?"

"Nope. Just some wine." He hoped she wasn't going to be one of those teetotalers.

"Ugh!" Her nose wrinkled.

"You don't like wine?"

"My father made it every year from leftover apples." She eyed the expensive bottle on the dresser as if it were poison.

"I think you might find this more to your liking." Clint had had a bit of that type of wine himself. He held out the glass.

She took the glass. He sat beside her, his hip catching hers as she slid toward him with the dip of the mattress. This close, his view down her bodice was unimpeded. He took a bite of his cake, and she took a sip of her wine.

"This is good." She couldn't have sounded more surprised.

"Did you think I'd skimp on my wedding night?"

She ducked his gaze. "I didn't think…"

He tipped the glass back up to her mouth with his finger before licking a smear of frosting off his thumb. "I wasn't criticizing."

"Oh."

She took another sip, striving to look calm, but he could tell from the betraying flush on her cheeks, and the nervous looks she flashed him that she was flustered.

He took another bite of cake, savoring the flavor as he savored the reality of his wife. She was such an outwardly unassuming little thing. So sweetly shy. So completely passive, and yet surprisingly bold when she needed to be.

She shifted under his gaze and took a bigger sip. He kept staring at her, knowing it made her nervous, deliberately keeping her off balance so she'd fall back on sipping the wine to cover her nerves. He watched her drink, calmly eating his cake, savoring the buttery chocolate flavor as he watched the alcohol take effect. He'd figured it wouldn't take much to relax her, and he was right. By the time the glass was empty she was leaning unselfconsciously against him, staring at the wall.

"Jenna?"

"What?"

He ran his finger around the last of the icing on his plate. "You ready for your piece of cake yet?"

"No." She held her glass in both hands and bit her lip.

"Then I think I'll have it."

She handed him her empty glass as he stood. He glanced down, waiting for her to ask him for what she wanted. She didn't, though she glanced at the bottle.

"Would you like another glass of wine?" he asked.

Her nod was shy. "Please."

He took the glass. His fingers grazed hers. "You know you can have whatever you want, Jenna. You don't have to ask me."

"Thank you."

Her acquiescence didn't fool him. She was a long way from asking him for anything.

He filled it half full and brought it back with his cake. She scooted over as he sat. He handed her the glass. She was careful her fingers didn't touch his even as she fell against him with the dip of the mattress.

She took a sip, smiled shyly. "This is decadent."

"Wine?"

"Eating in bed."

She'd swallowed his cock down her throat in the barn, but she thought eating in bed was decadent? He added that to her list of contradictions. "I guess it is."

She smiled, revealing those dimples that intrigued him. "But it's our wedding night."

"The perfect time to be decadent," Clint agreed.

He put his unfinished cake on the floor and settled his arm behind her on the bed. She tumbled into him without a murmur of protest. He tipped her glass to her lips. She obligingly took a sip. He gently removed it from her hands. Her "I wasn't done" followed him down as he placed it on the floor. He straightened and then kept leaning back, taking her with him until they landed on the soft mattress, her head cushioned on his shoulder.

"I want you relaxed, Sunshine, not unconscious."

"You tried to get me drunk?"

"Relaxed," he reiterated, turning to his side. The quilt slipped from Jenna as he tucked in his elbow. When he looked down, Jenna was staring at him, two faint lines between her brows.

"Why do you call me little?"

He smoothed a curl off her cheek and turned her a little more into his arms. "Because you are. You're soft, small, and very appealing."

"I'm fat." She said that as if confessing a sin.

He slid his thigh over hers, making sure his knee took most of the weight on her other side. The sheets rustled as he propped himself over her.

"Compared to me, Sunshine, you're just a little bit. As for being fat…" He slid his fingers from her cheek, down over the gentle sweep of her throat, until he got to the sumptuous swell of her shoulder. The curve filled his palm perfectly. "Baby, you're so deliciously rounded you make my back teeth ache with the need to start nibbling on you. I want to start at the tips of your toes and gradually, thoroughly, taste my way back up."

She looked down at herself than back at him, frowning. "Are you sure you don't need spectacles?"

The burst of laughter caught him by surprise.

"I'm very sure." With a nudge of his thumb, he turned her face to his. "Just looking at you makes me horny," he whispered, leaning down.

"Really?"

"Really." The last syllable bled into her mouth, drifting on his breath. She lay passive under him. "Kiss me back, Jenna."

She obediently pursed her lips under his. If he didn't know she'd been married, he would have sworn she didn't know how to kiss.

He tickled her lips with his tongue, working past her inhibitions, stroking their plump fullness with the tip, tickling the corners until she gasped and then repeating the procedure on the other one for the simple reason that he liked the way she lifted against him. He gently eased his tongue into the enfolding heat of her mouth. At first she froze, staring at him with those big blue eyes, not understanding, but even as he moved his tongue on hers, he could see her brain working, assimilating. Then her tongue was stroking his, her hands coming tentatively up to grip his shoulders.

He did enjoy an intelligent woman.

He adjusted the angle of the kiss, giving them both better access. He pulled her hips a little tighter to his, groaning into her mouth as her thigh cushioned the aching length of his cock. Damn, he wanted to wallow in her, her softness, her gentleness, her sweet giving nature—wanted to pull it into himself and use it to fill the blank void where his emotions used to be. He kissed her lips, rubbing his nose against hers.

"Ah Sunshine, you make me hunger."

"*I* do?"

"Can't you feel how much?" He was really going to have to work on her confidence.

Her "Yes" was whispered. No doubt she was shy, because he kept his eyes open and his lips on hers, too close for a lie to slip past.

"That didn't sound too convincing." The mattress creaked as he straddled her. Bracing his weight on his forearms, he notched his cock into the V of her thighs, still keeping his lips to hers, catching her gasp as she absorbed his intent. "There, now can you tell how hungry you make me?"

She nodded.

"How hungry?"

"Very?" He smiled at the lingering question mark.

"I can see you're a tough woman to convince." He kissed her deeply as he reached between them and unfastened his denims. "Push my pants down a bit."

She frowned at him and then obeyed. He needed a few inches before he could work the hard length of his cock free. He caught her hand before she could retreat and brought it to him. His breath hissed through his teeth as her fingers encircled his shaft, not meeting but squeezing him erotically as she tried to encompass all of it.

"God! I could come from this alone!"

Her "Do you want to?" stroked along his cock with the tempting possibility. Lord knows he'd be good to go again afterward, but he'd already had his pleasure twice while making her wait for hers. He was a selfish bastard, but not that selfish. He shook his head, curled his fingers over hers and pumped himself through her fist — once, twice — just enough to draw his seed to the tip of his cock and confusion to her gaze.

He kissed her again and said, "Sorry, Sunshine, you make me lose my head."

"I don't mind."

"I do." He pulled her hand from between them, and pressed a kiss to the center of her palm before putting it back on his shoulder. His cock nudged at her thigh, bobbing and straining to get closer, the way he wanted to get closer. He held off, not only because he wouldn't be able to reach her breasts, but because he was so close to the edge of his control that he didn't trust himself. She was just the hottest woman he'd ever met. And so innocently unaware of her appeal. She drove him crazy with the conflicting desires to fuck her raw, or to sweep her away to seclusion and protect that aura of innocence. Even from himself.

Her breasts quivered as her next breath caught in her throat. He watched the jiggle fade to a shimmer of motion that blended with her breathing. His blood thrummed through his veins. He touched the gossamer sheer bodice where it lay just above her nipple. That soft, pink nipple just begging to be awakened. Maybe he'd just settle for a compromise between his conflicting desires — putting her on a pedestal during the day and wallowing in her innate sensuality at night.

"Jenna?"

"What?"

"You are going to have to trust me. You are one damned beautiful woman."

He pulled the bodice down. Her lip slipped between her teeth. Her fingers tightened on his shoulder, her short nails pricking him. He forced his breath to come evenly, not wanting to make her more nervous. He was one inch from having that tempting breast in his mouth when she whispered his name.

It was his turn to ask, "What?"

"I'm not ready." Did she think he was going to jump on her?

"I know, Sunshine, but we'll get there."

He brushed his lips across her nipple. Her gasp wafted over his head. Her palms pressed on his shoulder. He shifted up. His hair fell forward, sliding over her cheeks, casting her face in shadow, obscuring her expression. He lowered his mouth to hers. Her lips parted immediately beneath his. Her tongue met his. She was soft and eager and still she pushed at his shoulders.

"What is it?"

"I need to get ready." Obviously, she wasn't talking more kissing.

"What more do you need?"

"My cream. Please let me get my cream." She pushed harder. He leaned back. Her "I'm sorry" was breathless as she scrambled out from under him. "I dropped it when you knocked on the door. I think it rolled under the bed."

As she talked she was moving, the sheer gown billowing around her as she dropped to her knees. He sat up. Her head disappeared under the bed.

"Jenna?"

"I'm sorry. It's just so dark I can't find it."

He leaned back on his elbow and admired her ass as it wiggled back and forth. If he was reading the signs right, they'd be getting much better acquainted in just a few minutes.

"Take your time." The light rumble of glass across uneven wood alerted him to the fact that she'd found the jar.

She backed out from under the bed. He stroked her ass, squeezing the left globe, taking her into his palm, smacking that full nether cheek lightly as she popped up, clutching the jar to her chest. Her gaze dropped to his straining cock and then back to his face. Her free hand rubbed the sting from his swat as she stood, poised as though to flee.

It wasn't hard to read her mind. She was worried she couldn't take him. He held out his hand. Not only would she take him, he'd make damned sure she enjoyed it.

"Give me the jar, Jenna."

She bit her lip and actually took a step back. He caught her before she could take another, pulling her into his lap, shifting her weight so her ass cushioned his cock. She wiggled. Sensation shot outward reverberating against his control. He cupped her thigh in his hand, spreading his fingers out for maximum contact. He took the jar from her hands. She was an adventurous little thing for sure.

He tipped her face up with his finger. "Kiss me, Sunshine."

She did, using her lips and tongue without hesitation, making him wonder how he could have ever thought her inexperienced. He turned her so that she fell back on the bed. Her hair surrounded her in a golden cloud, setting off her bright blue eyes above her fiery cheeks. He caught her head in his palm, easing her down, smiling at the surprise on her face. He held up the jar.

"You sure this is what you want our first time?"

She nodded. "I prefer it."

No doubt there. The lust he'd been holding under a tight lid burst free. He had all night to get to the rest of her, but now he had an open invite to his favorite playground.

"Roll on your stomach." His voice was hoarse with the desire ripping at him. She frowned at him but turned over, slowly, so slowly that she had to know what it was doing to him. Had to be doing it deliberately. He slapped her rear again for her impudence, a light smack that had her falling into position. Her ass was gorgeous, full and wide, beautifully white. The faint pink of his handprint lingered on the left cheek. He placed his hand over the mark, a brand of dark flesh against her pale skin. He curled his fingers into her fullness, making four indents in that soft flesh. He released the pressure. The flesh sprang back, resilient. Like her.

He stood. The bed was high, built to his specifications. Built so he could enjoy a woman in comfort while standing. He slid his hand under Jenna's waist. With a tug he drew her to the edge of the bed so that her legs dangled off. She was just tall enough that her toes skimmed the floor. She would be helpless when he took her. Unable to do anything but accept the pleasure he coaxed from her body. Son of a bitch, he liked the thought of that.

She propped her torso up on her elbows, and shot him one of those glances over her shoulder. "I don't think this is the best way."

"I do."

He popped the metal bar holding the lid in place and opened the jar. It had a light honey scent. He scooped a bit out and rubbed it between his fingers. It seemed to be merely a scented lubricant and nothing more. He had some creams in his supply that she might like better. Creams that would add to her enjoyment.

He rubbed the base of her spine with his fingertips. "Baby, would you like to try one of my creams this time?"

"No." She jumped against his hand. "Mine works just fine."

The tension in her muscles spread outward.

"Shh, it was just a thought." He kissed her right buttock, then her left, and then the tiny rosette between.

Her shriek was an inward draw of breath. There was no mistaking her shock. Damn! He would have liked to linger there, but she was too nervous. Her husband must have been an ignorant SOB.

He straightened and stepped up to the bed. His cock touched her right cheek, pressing into the lush swell, sliding outward, his seed leaving a shiny mark. With his hand in the middle of her back, he held her still while he bathed the other side.

"You have a beautiful ass, Jenna."

"Thank you."

"Wiggle it for me."

"What?"

"Make it dance for me."

"I don't understand."

"Yes, you do. Use that ass to make me burn. Tempt me, Jenna."

She managed a few tentative wiggles. He rested his cock high in her crack, letting the vibrations drag his come past his control, bathing her in his enthusiasm. He couldn't help the groan that dragged from his throat as she clenched her cheeks, catching his cock in an intimate kiss.

"Do that again, baby. Kiss my cock with your ass again."

She did. He thrust against her, his cock sliding up between her buttocks, skating just above the pink little rosette. He tossed the lid to the jar on the bed and coated his fingers.

"Hold still now, Jenna. Just for a little bit, and then I'll pleasure you like you asked for as long as you want. As hard as you want."

She held still, compliant, but a little tense under his hand. He could understand that. When a woman gave herself to a man this way, she put a lot on the line. He rubbed the base of her spine soothingly with his free hand. He started at the top of her crease, just the lightest of touches. More a grazing than a stroke. He hadn't gone more than an inch toward his destination when goose bumps sprang up. His cock throbbed against his thigh. Ah, they were going to have so much fun.

"Here it comes, baby. Just hold still. All you have to do is hold still while I work this cream nice and deep. We'll get you all ready, then we'll play, and then I'll make you mine."

He reached her anus. She shuddered from the inside out. Damn, she was sensitive. She froze, except for her ass, which clenched in an intimate little kiss against his fingertips. He kissed it back, pressing his finger in. Her muscles tightened, resisted.

"Relax, Jenna. Just relax and push back for me, baby." She wiggled beneath his hands. He pressed harder. He gained the barest of entrance. Her shriek nearly took out his eardrums.

"What are you doing?"

Chapter Eight

He let her pull away. His finger left its incredible haven with a mournful pop. He caught her before she could leave the bed, dragging himself up beside her. Flopping onto his back, he tugged her against him, curving his arm so that she tumbled onto his chest, her cheek naturally falling into the curve of his shoulder. He locked her there with his arm around her waist.

Against his ribs, he could feel her heart thumping. Its heavy beat echoed his own, but he was beginning to understand, not for the same reason. He slipped his hand between her thighs, through the springy curls, then up between her legs. She quivered but didn't resist. As he suspected, she was dry, her soft folds tucked tightly against her body. He doubted she'd been aroused at any time that evening, which brought up some pretty serious questions.

He sucked in a steadying breath, ordered his cock down, and said in as normal a tone as he could, "Sunshine, we need to talk."

She pulled tighter into him, her knee digging into his thigh. "I won't do that. I won't!"

The words hissed against his shoulder. He propped himself up on his forearm to better see her face. She threw her arm up, obviously expecting to be hit. A cold, sick feeling settled in his stomach. Hell, if he took a notion to pound on her, there wouldn't even be a grease spot left. He pulled her arm down. She glared at him, her expression tight with fear and defiance, every muscle braced.

"Ah damn, Jenna. What in hell did they do to you?"

Panic flared in her eyes. "Nothing. Nobody's done anything."

He severely doubted that, but he wasn't going to spend his wedding night arguing the point. "What do you use the cream for, Jenna?"

Her gaze skirted his. "Not for that!"

"So I gathered. So what do you use it for?"

There was a long pause, and then she said in a very shaky whisper, "So it won't hurt so much."

"You think I'd force myself on you?"

"You can't force me."

He looked at the size of his arm as it stretched across her torso. He could make her do any goddamn thing he wanted and not even work up a sweat. "Why?"

"I'm your wife. It's my duty to satisfy your needs."

"Ah."

"Except that. I'm not doing that."

"So you said."

"I mean it."

"I know you do, but that still doesn't explain why you think I'd hurt you."

Some of the tension left her body as she frowned at him. "It always hurts."

He touched the crease between her brows. "Did it hurt in the barn?"

She nodded, studying his expression intently, no doubt waiting for the moment when he lost patience and turned on her.

"Then why'd you do it?"

"You were in need, and so nice to the kittens, and I thought it might make you happy."

"But it hurt you."

"You liked it!" Resentment began to replace her wariness.

There was a challenge in the statement. As if she expected him to deny it. He ran his finger down the short bridge of her nose, and then slid it off the side so he could touch her cheek.

"Yes, I did." He tipped her chin up and waited until she met his gaze. "It's not supposed to hurt, Sunshine."

She didn't answer, just stared to the left of his ear and ignored him. There was a stubborn set to her jaw that communicated more clearly than words that she knew what she knew and wasn't falling for any of his statements to the contrary.

He let her certainty sink through his pride, let it dip and weave through his confidence until the unpleasant truth was reached.

Whatever her motivations in the barn to do what she'd done, they weren't born of desire. Son of a bitch! He'd been so certain he could manage Jenna that he hadn't managed a thing. He'd mistaken complacency for eagerness and desperation for pleasure.

He had a lot to make up for.

With the tips of two fingers, he turned her face to his. "Look at me, Jenna."

She did, the mutiny erased from her face. In its place, blank expectancy. As if she only waited on his bidding, as if her happiness was wrapped up in pleasing him. It was one hell of a survival technique. One he wouldn't be falling for again, either.

"If anything I do to you ever hurts, you need to stop me immediately. No lying, no enduring. You stop me."

The flicker in her gaze was disbelief, but she nodded.

"I'm serious, Jenna."

"How?"

"How will you stop me?"

"Yes."

"All you have to do is tell me, Sunshine. Just let me know, and I'll stop." That she didn't believe a word he said was clear in the subtle tensing of her expression. However, her agreement was immediate.

"Fine."

"That's an order, Jenna." He had a long way to go with her.

"I know." She didn't bat an eyelash as she agreed in that husky, quiet voice.

"Good."

He spread his hand across her throat, marveling that she'd taken him there, wondering what that miserable bastard she'd been married to had done to her to make her so good at faking it. The silence stretched.

"Are we going to sleep now?" she asked, breaking it. There was nothing in her tone to indicate a preference.

"Are you tired?"

"Are you?"

Hell no, it was his wedding night and he was as randy as a billy goat. "A little."

"I'll stoke the fire."

The room was chilling fast. She'd freeze in that scrap of nothing she was wearing. He caught her before her bare feet touched the floor. "I'll get the fire."

He slid out of bed, and shoved his still hard cock back into his pants, watching as she perched nervously on the edge. When he came back from stoking the small stove, she was still perched on the edge, her lower lip between her teeth.

"What's wrong?"

"Nothing."

The sigh escaped before he could suppress it. "Jenna…"

She immediately started chewing on her lip. "I'm a restless sleeper."

"I'll get used to it," he shrugged.

"Apparently I can be very loud…" Her hands twisted in her lap. The glance she flashed him was too quick for him to decipher.

"Are you trying to tell me you have nightmares?"

"I don't know. I never remember, but Jack preferred I sleep elsewhere." Just the sound of the man's name put him in a murderous rage.

"I prefer you sleep next to me."

"I won't go far. I know a wife should be available for her husband's convenience." Well, that certainly cleared up how she saw her place.

"Glad to hear it."

"I could make up a bed on the floor."

He kicked off his boots. His toes were already curling away from the cold floor and she wanted to sleep on it? "Not necessary."

"I can be pretty bad."

"We'll work it out." He shucked his pants and dropped his shirt on the chair by the bed. Her eyes rounded as she took in his naked body.

"You'll be tired."

Ah, now they were at the crux of the matter. No doubt she saw a tired, cranky man as something to be avoided at all costs. He took the covers out of her hands, slid into bed beside her and nudged her over with his hip. As soon as he had enough room, he lay down. The mattress sagged, and she rolled against him. She shivered at the bite of the cold sheets. He pulled her into his arms, dragging her on top of him despite her resistance.

"Looks like it'll be a cold winter."

Her "Yes" was a squeak of agreement. He tucked her head under his chin as he said, "Tonight and every night from here on out, Jenna, you'll sleep in my arms."

"But—"

"No buts."

"My dreams…"

"Will be my problem." The softness of her stomach cradled his cock, caressing it with every breath. From the way she held herself unnaturally still he knew she debated what to do about it. "Jenna?"

"What?"

Her hair slid over his ribs in a silken brush. He sucked in a steadying breath.

"Go to sleep."

* * * * *

The scream in his ear jolted him awake. He was reaching for his gun before he realized there wasn't a threat. Beside him Jenna screamed again, bolted up straight, and flailed at invisible demons. Before he could do anything more than push up onto his elbows, she was swinging at him, the bed, the wall, all the while begging—begging—for someone to help her to get them off of her.

He sat up and grabbed her hands. She threw herself backwards.

"Jenna!"

"Oh God, help me!"

"Jenna. Wake up, baby."

She twisted in his grip. "Get them off me!" The last syllable broke on a scream.

He caught her head just before it slammed into the wall as she threw herself away from whatever haunted her dreams. He yanked her against his chest, anchoring her legs with his thigh, holding her arms at her side with one of his.

"I'll do whatever you want, I promise," she moaned.

He snagged her chin in his hand. "Jenna?"

Her head fell back, her throat arched and she screamed a horrible, grating sound that had the hair on the back of his neck standing on end. Her body jerked against his. Her knee knifed up into his stomach.

"Nononooooo..."

"Jesus Christ!" She hadn't been kidding about the dreams. He shook her, trying to wake her up. She fought harder.

The screaming stopped as suddenly as it began. She went limp in his arms. Her eyes flew open and locked unseeingly on the ceiling. In a despairing little whisper that tore at his heart with its total lack of hope, she begged, "Please, someone help me."

He pushed her hair off her face. She flinched and stiffened. "It's me, Sunshine."

"Clint?"

"Right here."

Her nails gouged desperate furrows into his forearms, but her gaze didn't leave the ceiling. She was still dreaming. "Don't let them eat me, Clint."

"Never, baby."

"Please?"

"I've got you."

"I can't keep them off me." Her voice rose with every syllable.

"I'll take care of it." He started brushing at her body with hard short strokes, hoping he was doing it right so she'd believe he got whatever it was.

"All gone now," he told her, putting as much authority into his voice as he could.

"They'll come back." She glanced past his shoulder. "They always come back."

"I won't let them."

Her gaze drifted in his direction. "Promise?"

"I promise."

"You won't forget?"

"No."

She held herself absolutely still, as if weighing the value of his promise, then she shuddered and collapsed against his chest. He moved her hair out of the way. Her eyes were closed. She was asleep again, clutching his arm as if afraid he would leave. He pulled the comforter up over her sweaty body, protecting her from the chill, holding her as tightly as she needed, holding her as the night stretched on, soothing her when she got restless, comforting her when she cried out, holding her while the rage that boiled inside of him coiled to a hard knot of determination. Come morning, they were going to talk.

Jenna murmured in her sleep. He kissed her gently on top of her head.

And come morning, he'd have the name of the son of a bitch he was going to kill.

* * * * *

"I told you, I don't remember."

"And I told you I don't believe you."

Jenna placed the platter of steak, eggs, and home fries in front of Clint. "There isn't anything I can do about that."

Clint picked up his knife and fork. The implements looked deadly in his large hands. "You can start by telling me his name."

She stepped back from the table. "I don't know what you're talking about."

"That was more than a nightmare last night, Jenna."

"I don't remember any of it."

"You expect me to believe you don't remember a time in your life when you were trapped somewhere with something crawling on you."

She shuddered at the thought. "No."

Clint took a bite of the steak, chewed, and swallowed. "It won't do you any good to hide from me. I will find out."

"When you do, you can tell me."

He took another bite, staring at her over his fork. He chewed, and raised an eyebrow. "You really don't remember anything?"

"No."

"Of the dream? Or what causes it?"

"Neither."

"Then it's going to take me a little longer."

She wiped her hands on the towel. "For what?"

"Someone hurt you, Jenna. I want to know who and why."

"It was just a dream."

"It's more than that, whether you remember or not." His fork clinked on his plate as he cut off some egg.

"Can't you forget about it?"

His eyes narrowed and his lean jaw set as he placed his knife and fork on his plate with deliberate care. "No."

She wrapped her hand in the faded blue towel and gathered her courage. "Maybe I don't want to know. If it's as bad as you say, maybe it's better if it stays forgotten."

Clint leaned back in his chair. "No."

"Why not?"

"Because whoever it is could still be a threat."

"That's preposterous."

"Why?"

"Because." She refused to believe that what had happened before could happen again.

"That's not much of an answer."

"No one wants to hurt me." *Not anymore.*

"You just got through saying that you don't remember."

She didn't, but when she tried to remember, her head hurt and she couldn't breathe. And that scared her almost as much as Clint did when he got the expression in his dark eyes that he had now. He was so cold and remote. Unreachable.

She motioned to his breakfast, hoping to change the subject. "Is everything all right with your food?"

"It's fine." His expression didn't lighten. If anything, it got harder. "Where's yours?"

"I'll eat when you're done."

"Why?"

Because Jack had always insisted that she do so. But Clint had forbidden her to mention Jack to him. "I thought you'd prefer it."

"You thought wrong."

"Oh."

"Jenna?"

The deep note in his voice stroked along her nerves. She liked his voice. It contained such strength, such calm. Just hearing it soothed the panic she so often felt inside. "What?"

"Sit down and eat."

"I didn't cook anything for myself yet."

"Bring me a plate."

His gaze burned into her back as she crossed to the oak hutch. She tried to minimize her limp, but she knew there was no way he wouldn't notice. She wished, just for once, that she could be graceful. She took one of the fine china plates off the shelf. Because she was focusing so hard, she overcompensated. Her toe caught on the rug. She stumbled, caught herself on the table edge, but the plate—that beautiful blue flowered plate—went flying. For a second, she couldn't move. She just stood there, watching the plate sail through air. With a sense of finality, she watched it hit the floor, closing her eyes as it shattered, knowing there was no excuse for its breaking. Nothing except her own clumsiness.

"Oh God!"

Clint stood and cut her a glance, his expression unreadable. She hadn't meant to call attention to herself. The exclamation had just slipped out.

She licked her dry lips. "That was horribly expensive wasn't it?"

"I have no idea." He squatted and picked up the large chunks. The powerful muscles in his thighs stretched his pants. "But it doesn't matter."

"Of course, it matters." The next time he got mad at her, it would matter. He looked up, as he reached for a piece under the table.

"It's just a plate, Jenna." He placed the pieces on the table.

"I'll try not to be so clumsy again."

He studied her. "You can drop as many plates as you like."

"I…" She didn't know what to say to that. To him.

He straightened and shrugged. "Hell, if you don't like what's here you can pitch the whole lot and start over."

He turned. She turned with him, keeping him in her line of sight as he stepped past her, clutching the table behind her for strength. His clean scent drifted back to her.

It only took him one step to reach the hutch. It was a fluid movement containing none of her imperfections. The man was all masculine grace and strength. He turned back to her. With his hair tied back in a leather thong, his cheekbones were in sharp relief, lending a powerful, feral look to his appearance.

He was so much bigger than her first husband. So much less predictable. She had no idea what to do with him. No idea what to expect. As he came back to her with the delicate china in his lean hand, she caught her breath and held it. She didn't release it until he passed. When he didn't make a biting comment, or backhand her, she began to relax. Maybe he really wasn't mad.

"Sit down, Jenna." The chair he pulled back was kitty-corner to his. She didn't want to sit that close to him.

"I should just finish sweeping up these pieces."

"Breakfast will be cold by then."

She shrugged. "It won't hurt me to miss a meal."

"I wouldn't like it."

"Like what?"

"You missing meals."

"Oh."

Wishing he weren't watching her so intently, she took the necessary steps to get to the chair. She was rather proud of how she managed to minimize her limp by taking small steps. He was still watching her. His dark eyes as inscrutable as ever. She had to turn her back to him to sit. She caught her breath, every sense, every nerve ending excruciatingly aware of him as he stood behind her. She sat. For a second nothing happened. She didn't breathe. He didn't move. Then his fingertips brushed her shoulders and his lips brushed her hair.

"It's going to be all right, Jenna."

So he kept telling her. "Thank you."

He moved around her and divided the food on his plate in half. "Is this enough?"

"I couldn't possibly eat that much!"

"Are you sure?"

"Half of that will be fine." Putting away that much food would mean even her corsets wouldn't be able to squeeze her into her dresses.

"You're going to need to keep your strength up."

"For what?" She wished the words back as soon as they left her mouth. Clint's expression mellowed into a hint of amusement.

"We're on our honeymoon, Sunshine. I have a lot of plans." He took his seat and motioned with his fork. "Eat."

It was an order. She ate, keeping her head down, methodically bringing food to her mouth, her cheeks burning with embarrassment. Out of the corner of her eye, she could see the amusement on Clint's face. His laughter was evident in the slight lift of his lips and the barest of narrowing of his eyes. Why did she always act the fool in front of him?

Like last night. She'd started off hiding behind the door like a naive virgin, then she'd lost the cream, which had led to the other misunderstanding. She didn't want Clint to see her as someone who needed to be pitied. She wanted him to see her as a woman he could respect. Like Asa looked at Elizabeth. Like Cougar looked at Mara.

She pushed a piece of potato across the plate. But she wasn't anything like Mara or Elizabeth. Her only skills were cooking and, apparently, disappointing husbands. She bet Cougar and Asa didn't go to sleep unsatisfied rather than bedding their wives. She gave the potato another shove. It popped off the plate, landing on the tablecloth. When she picked it up, there would be a greasy stain left on the blue checked cloth. If she couldn't get it out, it would be just one more example of how she messed up everything she touched.

"Jenna."

She didn't look up. Clint repeated her name in that low, deep drawl that slid right under her defenses and seduced her away from good sense. He tapped her plate with his fork. She looked up to find him staring at her, his black eyes so deep and dark she was in danger of falling in. Into what, she didn't know, but if she fell, there'd be no going back and she wasn't ready to travel down a path of no return. It was bad enough she'd agreed to marry the man. She stabbed the spilled potato with her fork.

Clint plucked the piece of potato off the tines and dropped it back onto her plate. "Are you finished eating?"

"Yes."

He frowned and touched her cheek. "You sure?"

"Yes." Maybe if she were thinner Clint would be more inclined to exercise his rights. Not that she particularly wanted him to, but if she couldn't keep him in her bed she wouldn't have a prayer of a peaceful marriage. Her stomach chose that minute to rumble.

He shook his head, took the fork from her hand, scooped a piece of egg and held it to her lips. "Eat."

She did immediately, hearing the order in his voice, wanting to refuse but not daring. She expected him to hand her the fork, but he didn't. He just kept presenting forkful after forkful for her to chew and swallow. Which she did, long after the point where she was full. And still he didn't stop. He had to be testing her. Seeing if she knew how a proper wife behaved. Seeing how well she obeyed. She breathed through her nose to control the nausea as she chewed a piece of the nearly raw meat. Her stomach lurched as he cut off another piece. Blood-red juice dripped off the tines as he held the meat up to her lips.

"Open up, Sunshine."

She did, her jaws slowly separating as her gorge rose. She pushed it back through sheer force of will. She got the bloody mess in her mouth. She even managed two whole chews before her stomach rebelled.

She jumped up. Her chair clattered to the floor. She didn't glance at Clint though she heard him following her. She couldn't deal with him now. Couldn't worry about his retaliation for failing to obey. She barely made it to through the door in time. She hit the porch rail and the contents of her stomach vaulted over the side. Her stays cut into her middle with every violent heave, compressing her ribs, gouging into her hips, robbing her of the breath she needed between bouts.

"Jesus God, Jenna." One of Clint's hands pulled her back against him. The other caught her forehead. She clawed at him while she struggled to find a position that didn't hurt. She twisted to get free, tangled her feet in her skirt and ended up vomiting on them both. He swore and let her go. She threw her hands up, protecting her face as she stumbled in the direction of the steps.

Her only hope was to run.

He had her in two steps. The scream tore from her throat. He would hurt her so bad she'd never survive his revenge. Never. He was too big. Too cold. Too relentless. She spun around, ignoring the stays bruising her torso, and sank her teeth into his arm. He swore and angled her down. She went to her knees under the pressure, knowing what was coming. Better he kill her quickly than she live long enough for him to punish her at his leisure. He swore again. The coppery taste of blood filled her mouth. Out of the corner of her eye she saw sunlight flash off metal. She braced herself for the pain, a part of her glad that at last it would be over, while another desperately wished for a chance at the life she'd always wanted. For the chance to raise her daughter. She ignored the inner struggle. It never mattered what she wanted. She closed her eyes and waited.

There was a thunk as the knife sank deep. She waited for the explosion of pain to sear through her. For the light to come for her. For the angels. For the devil. For something to make this end. To just end.

Hard fingers pried her jaw open. Hot liquid dripped down her chin as she opened her eyes. Out of the corner of her eye, she could see his knife quivering in the porch rail as Clint went to his knees in front of her. She didn't know what to make of his expression as he stared at her. The hand on her right wrist kept her anchored on her knees. With her bad leg she didn't have the leverage to get up. His right hand he brought to her face. Blood welled from his wrist and spilled on her chest as he cupped her cheek in his hand, his fingers on the back of her neck preventing her from pulling away.

"What in hell did they do to you, Sunshine?" Sorrow, strength, pity, and calm colored the depths of his low drawl.

She didn't have an answer for him. Didn't know what he wanted to hear, so she knelt there mute, her leg aching almost as much as her spirit, and waited.

Chapter Nine

She didn't answer his question, and Clint wasn't surprised. Whatever had been done to her had been done over time. Had to have been to have created such knee-jerk reactions, and no doubt, it wasn't something she was proud of.

Under his fingers he could feel the tremors running through her. She'd been coldly accepting when she thought he was going to kill her, but now that she was faced with living, she was terrified. He took the sleeve of his uninjured arm and wiped as much as he could of his blood off of her mouth. She knelt there and let him. Not fighting. Not begging. Just accepting. Son of a bitch, it made him want to go out and kill someone.

"Come here, baby. Let me warm you." He pulled her into his chest, needing to offer her comfort even if she wouldn't take it. He needed to hold her. "I'm sorry, Jenna."

He should have known she couldn't eat that much, but every time he lifted the fork to her mouth, she'd taken the food. Chewed it. Eaten like he'd ordered. Like she'd been trained to do. Continued eating, he was beginning to suspect, because he hadn't told her to stop. He smoothed her hair away from her pale face.

"Looks like I'm going to have to be changing my ways around you, Sunshine. Otherwise we're never going to get this marriage off the ground."

"I didn't ask you to change." The voice came, small and cautious, from against his chest.

No, she hadn't. But having his wife vomit on him, bite him to the bone, and then wait for him to kill her just wasn't how he planned on spending his days. He left her statement unchallenged.

"Does a bath sound as good to you as it does to me?" He took her hitch in breathing as a "Yes". "Then let's go get one."

He stood up, taking her with him, not missing her wince as her right foot took her weight. Without missing a beat, he swung her up in his arms. She squealed and threw her arms around his neck. She smelled of fear, sweat, and vomit, but her arms were soft around his neck and her breath moist in the hollow of his throat. He hefted her a little higher. She was such an intriguing mixture of strength and terror, sprinkled with the oddest moments of trust. Like now. She needed a protector more than anyone he'd ever seen. More so than even little Brianna.

She needed someone to make her feel safe, cherished. Someone to bring the light back into her life. He yanked his knife out of the rail where he'd driven it to keep it out of her hands. Unfortunately for her, she was stuck with him.

"If you put me down, I'll get the water started," she whispered.

"How about I hold you and we see if the plumbing works?"

"Plumbing?"

"Yup. Doc and Cougar convinced me I needed one of those new bathing rooms if I was intending to take a wife." He headed toward the back door. "I've had the reservoir heating since I got up."

"Reservoir?"

"A big tank of hot water."

She seemed to stop breathing. "Are you talking about one of those fancy bathtubs where you just turn a knob and all the hot water you want comes pouring out? The kind they have in the catalogue at the mercantile?"

He smiled at the disbelief in her voice. "Yes."

"And I can use it?" This time the disbelief didn't make him smile.

"I bought it for my wife." His tone was harder than it should be, but damn, it pissed him off when she acted like she was nothing.

"But I'm…"

He glanced down at her and finished her sentence with the only truth that mattered. "The only wife I'll ever have."

He kicked the door fully open with his foot and stepped into the warmth of the kitchen. The house smelled of food, wood smoke, and hope. Hard to believe it had been the scene of such chaos moments before. He debated sitting in the kitchen, but the chair was too small for what he had in mind.

The parlor, though. The parlor had a nice big settee that would do just fine. And it was next to the bath addition. He ignored Jenna's stiffening as he stepped over Danny's sprawled form in the doorway to the hall. He hadn't managed to keep the dog out of the house, but he was slowly training him to stay in the hallways. As he went down the hall, he heard the click of Danny's nails on the wood floor behind him.

When he got to the parlor, he used his pinkie to slide the pocket door closed. Danny flopped to the floor with a disgruntled sigh. The door rattled as his massive body settled against it. Jenna stiffened in his arms with a wary breath. He very carefully set her on the settee, rubbing his forearm where the steel of the stays had bitten into it. She stayed where he placed her, watching him from wide blue eyes, every muscle tensed in case he turned ornery. He touched the lace collar of the simple brown dress. He was going to turn something, but ornery didn't quite fit it.

"Unbutton your dress." Her fingers went immediately to the long line of cloth-covered buttons. There was no hesitation to show resentment, though he knew she had to be feeling something. He ran his fingers down the side of her face, and up along the line of her jaw until her chin balanced on his fingertips. "I need to see you, Sunshine."

Her gaze flicked up, as usual too fast to read, but there was a tremble in her fingers as she worked the third button loose. She was afraid. At the very least, nervous.

He went over to the little parlor stove and added some more wood. The room was warm, but not warm enough to lounge naked. And he wanted her naked, before and after their bath. Especially after.

By the time he turned back to her, she had all of the buttons undone down to her stomach, revealing the cotton-covered stays beneath, and the full swell of her breasts. She was watching him from under her lashes, her fingers pausing as he knelt beside her. Her breath caught in her throat as his hands replaced hers.

"It's all right, Jenna."

"I know," she whispered.

"Then how come you're not breathing?" He smiled as the last two buttons gave up the fight.

"I am. It's just a little difficult, sitting like this with the stays."

"Then let's get them off."

"I could just change positions." The suggestion was offered cautiously. No doubt she wanted out of her dirty clothes, quickly and efficiently, with him out of the room, but it wasn't going to happen that way. She was his wife. She needed to understand that even though he

125

was calling the shots, he was here to care for her. The only way he knew to do that was to show her.

"I like off better. Lift up." He spread the dress off her shoulders, and tapped the inside of her rounded white arm. Her breasts shimmied with the motion, their full white curves suffused with rose, bulging over the top of her cotton camisole.

He supported her head with his hand, sliding a tasseled pillow underneath. Her big blue eyes were fastened on him with a mixture of confusion and trepidation, but she didn't argue and didn't resist. There was something very seductive about knowing that she would let him do whatever he wanted without protest. He could see where it could tempt a lover to go too far, to push her too hard. She gave a man free license to unleash all his baser instincts with that air of acceptance, and tempted him to do so with every breath she took. He untied her camisole and spread the material wide. Her breasts rose white and full, shivering slightly with her breath.

"You're perfect, Sunshine."

"I'm not perfect."

He shook his head at that flat little statement. "On that, we are never going to agree." He tucked the camisole beneath her large breasts. Her nipples were small, pert little nubs on top of dainty areolas, petal pink and infinitely tempting. She *was* perfect, everything about her lushly inviting, and he wanted nothing more than to just sink into her.

"I don't want you to panic, Sunshine, but later on I'm going to want to kiss your breasts."

"Why would I panic?"

"Because you always seem to expect the worst. But right now I'm going to get you ready for your bath."

"I can do it myself."

She could, but letting her hide from him was something that he was unwilling to do. "It's our honeymoon and this is a husband's privilege that I'm not willing to give up."

"Undressing me?"

"Undressing you. Bathing you. Drying you off." He shrugged. "Pampering you." She stared at him with her lips parted, apparently speechless. "What part has you flummoxed?"

She didn't answer. He unfastened the hooks to her stays. It wasn't easy. Damn she had herself trussed up tighter than a Christmas goose.

He cocked an eyebrow at her. "I'm guessing it's not the undressing part as you didn't seem overly concerned last night."

Her hands clenched into fists beside her. "I'm not loose!"

"Never thought you were."

He slid the stays apart. Even through her camisole he could see how the boning had bitten into her tender skin, the cotton damp and sticking to the deep grooves.

She shivered.

"Are you cold?"

She shook her head.

"Nervous?"

Her lip slid between her teeth. Her nod was the faintest move of her head.

"No need to be. I may be new to being a husband, but I've been studying up for a long time on what to do with a wife."

"You have?"

"Yes." He reached for the pins in her hair. She eyed him warily as pin after pin came free, and the heavy, wavy mass slid down to surround her face. "My own personal angel."

She touched the messy wound on his wrist. "Not much of an angel."

"An angel with a bite." He smiled.

"It will scar."

He looked at the bite, caked with dry blood and already bruising. "Sure enough, you put your brand on me."

Her gaze slid from his. "I'm sorry."

He tipped her face back to his. "I kind of like the idea of carrying your mark."

Confusion replaced worry. He let her chew on that while he unbuttoned her camisole and pulled it over her head. Her hair got tangled in the buttons before he could pull it free, leaving her with her arms pulled over her head and her torso stretched high. Those full breasts, with their dainty enticing tips, were face-level. With the faintest of movements, he could have one against his tongue, know her taste. Saliva flooded his mouth and his cock jerked in his pants. All he had to do was be bastard enough to lean forward, and he could have what he wanted. She'd let him. She wouldn't fight him. She'd hold still and let him do whatever he wanted.

And probably die a little bit in the process.

He took a steadying breath, reined in his lust, and untangled her hair from the buttons. He needed to back off with her. Forget all his big talk and base plans and start over.

When she lowered her arms, her face and chest were beet red. The only indication of what she wanted to do was the twitch of her hands toward her breasts, but then she placed her hands at her sides, palms up, and lowered her gaze.

He took her hands and crossed them over her breasts, pressing them into her upper arms as her gaze flew to his. "If you don't want to show me your body, you don't have to."

"But…"

"No buts. Except in a situation where you're hurt and there's a need, I won't touch you again without permission."

"You're my husband!"

"Yes I am, but I don't rape women."

"I'm your wife."

"And a damned tempting one, but that doesn't change anything."

"I can't tell you no."

He touched the full curve of her lower lip. "Yes, you can. It's a one syllable word and real easy for most people to get out."

Her fingers dug into her arms, her lip slipped between her teeth, betraying her confusion and revealing her dimples. "You don't understand."

"No, I don't. But I've never forced myself on a woman, and I'm not about to start now."

He pushed to his feet. Son of a bitch, doing the right thing was painful. "Which means, as much as I'd like otherwise, I'll be letting you handle your own bath."

It almost killed him to say that, too. She was so tempting, with her plump arms squeezing her breasts together and up, creating a valley he'd love to explore, her dimples teasing him from the redness of her cheeks, and those big blue eyes shining bright in her face. As he watched, a tear slid out of the corner of the left one and trickled down her temple to blend into the bright gold of her hair, darkening a strand.

"I'm going to fill the tub." He dropped the blanket over her. "You just lie here and relax while I get it ready."

"I don't understand you."

"I know, and that's a damned shame."

She clutched the blanket to her chest, bounced a glance off of his erection as it strained down his thigh, and another off of the wet stain on the leg of his denims near where his cock head rested.

"I repulse you."

"You know that's a lie."

"You're ashamed of me."

He admired the gumption that kept her head up while she put forward her convictions. "Not hardly."

"You will be." He didn't like the way her eyes skirted his. He tilted her head up.

"I won't."

"You don't know—"

"I don't need to," he cut her off, holding her gaze through sheer force of will.

"But—"

He cut her off with a shake of his head. "Here's where my being half-Indian plays in your favor. I was raised white, but a lot of my mother's beliefs stuck with me. One being, if you say it, it's true."

"Like when you said I was your wife and Brianna was your daughter?"

"Yes." He tugged her lower lip free of her teeth, letting his thumb slide along the moist inner lining. "The other is, all you need to do to start over is to put one foot in front of the other and do it."

"That's crazy."

He shrugged, stroking the smooth skin of her cheek where her dimple would be if she were happy. "Maybe, but it sure can be a useful philosophy if you want to grab hold."

He dropped his hand back to his side. She didn't say a word or look at him again. She just kept twisting her hands under the blanket and chewing on her lip. He turned on his heel and entered the bath.

* * * * *

She was going to have to leave the bathing room sometime. Jenna knew that. The last fill on the tub had exhausted the hot water and while the air surrounding her was warm and scented with the rose bath oil Clint had dumped in, the water itself was getting chilled. The problem being she didn't know what she wanted to do when she got out.

She'd never heard of a man giving a woman a choice when it came to anything. Her father had ruled her house with a heavy hand and her husband had made her father look positively benevolent. Having the protection of a man's name without having to suffer the attentions of a husband was every woman's dream. It was her dream. She just couldn't shake the feeling that it was too good to be true.

Which meant she had to think. She had to make this work for her. Not just for today, but down the road, because as of yesterday she was Mrs. Clint McKinnely, married to one of the most powerful, respected men in the territory. She'd asked God for a miracle and He'd seen fit to send one to her in the form of Clint, and she wouldn't be offending the Almighty by snubbing his offering. Or treating it shabbily. Which she would be doing if she took on all the trappings of being Mrs. McKinnely without keeping up her end.

She stood. Water poured off her body in a cascade of sound. She glanced at the door while grabbing a towel off the rack, half-expecting Clint to come through it like Jack always had. Jack had liked catching her vulnerable and naked. Liked turning her pleasure to humiliation. Seemed to relish the power he felt when he did. But there were no sounds of footsteps and the knob didn't rattle.

And now that she thought on it, there wouldn't be. By all accounts, Clint wasn't like that. He was a hard man. A dangerous man, but he wasn't a bully. Tales about his ruthlessness when it came to criminals were widespread and the whispers that followed him when he came to town were many. Enough so that she knew he was hard on women, but no one ever complained that he had a heavy hand, which was more than she could say for Jack. And he was fair. Clint McKinnely was scrupulously fair.

She squeezed out the thick rope of her hair and then wrapped it up in a towel. She took the second towel and dried off her shoulders. Stepping out of the tub, she wrapped the towel around her and probed her knowledge of Clint. He was a sucker for little things. He'd held Brianna for all of two minutes before he was under her spell. He liked kittens and fed them rather than killing them. And more importantly, he tolerated their affection. He'd been demanding in the barn, but not cruel. And to be fair, she'd started it. And last night, he'd been kind, not beating her when she'd unthinkingly refused him. She could do a lot worse. It was scary that he was so different in that she couldn't predict what he'd do, and it was possible that she could inadvertently trigger his temper. But, if she were careful, and did as he asked, there would be no reason to anticipate him losing his temper.

She pulled the towel from her hair. And tonight he'd asked for the right to pamper her. And she'd turned him down. She closed her eyes. Her husband had wanted to be nice to her, and she'd rejected him. Oh God, how stupid could she be? She hung the towel on the hook. She'd prayed for the Almighty to send her a husband, one who would be kind to her, and when he had tried, she'd told him no.

She had to fix that. She eyed the doorknob. It looked so innocuous. A simple black metal latch, but if she did what she was thinking, there'd be no going back. No changing her mind. She bit her lip so hard it brought tears to her eyes. The knob blurred out of focus.

If she did this, and Clint took it wrong, there would be no forgiveness. She reached for the handle, doubt eating at her gut. She'd never been bold and this went against everything she'd been taught, but she honestly didn't know what else to do to fix the mess she'd made. She turned the handle, lifted the latch quietly, let the towel drop, and stepped through the door.

Clint was sitting in the big leather armchair to the right of the settee. His forearms were resting on his knees. He cradled a cup in his hands. The scent of coffee filled the room along with a hint of wood smoke from the stove. On the table before him was a tray with a porcelain pot and another cup. Bright light spilled through the windows, the sun amplified by the freshly fallen snow. The harsh light accented his hawk-like profile, the firm set of his lips, the harsh set of his jaw. He did not look like a happy man.

Oh God, this was such a bad idea. Such a stupid plan. She was always coming up with stupid plans. She grabbed for the towel. Clint looked up. The cup dropped from his hands, and his eyes — those black eyes — lit from within with a searing heat.

"Jenna?"

She swallowed hard, all her courage gone right along with her voice. She straightened, the towel dangling from her hands. She stood there while he looked her over, vividly aware of every bulge, every scar. Such a stupid plan. He called to her again, his drawl deeper, hoarser.

"Come here, Sunshine."

She wanted to. Knew she had to, but her feet wouldn't move. She was frozen in the door, the soft scent of the rose bath salts she'd used wafting around her, incapable of doing anything except drawing short hard breaths and panicking.

Unbelievably, Clint smiled. A genuine smile that softened his hard face and took it from handsome to mesmerizing. He rolled to his full height with a lazy flex of muscle.

"Cat got your tongue?" he asked as he came toward her.

It took him only ten steps to get to her side. She knew because she counted them, trying to focus on anything except her pounding heart and her inability to breathe. She expected him to stop, but he didn't. He just kept on coming until she was in his arms, her cheek pressed against the hard muscles of his chest and her body flush against his. All she could think of to say was, "You changed your clothes."

"And you lost yours."

"I'm sorry."

"Care to tell me why?"

"Please don't make me." His big hand cupped her head, dwarfing her, overwhelming her with the gentleness of his touch when she was expecting roughness.

"Can I guess?"

She nodded, the button on his shirt scraping her cheek. Anything was better than trying to make her voice work again.

"Would you be trying to tell me you want me?"

"I want our marriage to work."

Which wasn't exactly the same thing, Clint knew. Jenna's muscles were like rock under his hands and she was shaking. She was scared to death. He just wasn't sure of what.

"So you decided to step out here and catch my eye?"

"You said you wouldn't touch me." He couldn't tell if she was complaining or reminding.

"Unless you asked," he qualified.

There was a long pause and then a harshly croaked truth, "I don't know how to ask."

He suspected she didn't know what to ask for either, but this was a start and he could teach her what she needed to know. He let his hand slide down to the base of her spine, urging her closer. Her flesh was soft under his hands. A silky, delicate, womanly expanse he'd love to run his mouth over.

"Lean into me, baby." She did immediately. He took advantage of her distraction to swing her up in his arms. Her squeal and grab made him smile. "I won't drop you, Sunshine."

"But…"

"No buts." He shook his head at her. His words didn't result in an appreciable lessening of her grip, but since holding him so tightly kept her breasts squashed against him, he wasn't going to complain. The damp towel was wadded between them. The first thing he did after settling them on the settee was to discard it. "I don't think we need this."

For all that she agreed, her fingers were reluctant to let it go. He grabbed the knitted comforter off the back of the settee and draped it over her. She seemed flustered by the small consideration but let the towel go. He tossed it in the direction of the stove. It landed on the hardwood floor.

"Oh no!" Jenna sat up straight in his lap. He had to duck her elbows as she tucked the throw around her. He recognized that tone. He'd heard it from Mara often enough.

"What?"

She froze, looked at him, the towel, and then back at him before dropping her gaze. "Nothing."

It was obviously something. She was practically twitching. "Out with it, Jenna."

"The towel will stain the wood."

"Ah hell." If Jenna felt halfway about household things the way Mara did, he wasn't going to get anywhere until the towel was moved. He slid her onto the settee and grabbed the towel off the floor. With a flick of the wrist he tossed it over the arm of the parlor chair. A quick glance at Jenna had him checking it again. Her lip was between her teeth and a frown pleated her brow. Son of a bitch. He took it off the chair and draped it over the handle of the stove. If she didn't like that it was just too damned bad.

He headed back to the settee, unbuttoning his shirt as he went. From the way Jenna shrank back into the seat, he might be letting his impatience show through. He worked on gentling his expression. He needn't have bothered. She took one look at his chest, and all the fear left her face.

"Oh my God!" Her eyes rounded in horror.

Damn! He'd forgotten about the scars. "Sorry." He started buttoning back up.

She was off the settee and at his side, her hands undoing buttons faster than he could do them.

"No one told me," she whispered as she parted the halves of his shirt. Her soft hands were infinitely careful on his chest. She looked up at him, her eyes brimming with tears and pity. "Why didn't anyone tell me?"

"Because it didn't matter." And he didn't want it mattering now. He caught her hands and pulled them away from his body.

She yanked her hands free and swatted his arm. "Of course it matters."

He looked down to where she'd hit him. Hit him. This from the woman who ate until she vomited because he'd ordered her to.

She traced the broad puckered scar that cut diagonally across his chest and abdomen. "You got these that night, didn't you?" she whispered.

"Yes."

"My God." Jenna stared at those scars that covered his hard muscled chest and abdomen. They were broad, newly healed, and had to have hurt like hell. She couldn't imagine voluntarily enduring them for any reason. Least of all saving her. She rode the ridges of the biggest as it followed the hills and valleys of the slabs of muscle cutting across his abdomen until it disappeared beneath the waistband of his denims. She'd never thought, not once, that he'd been hurt saving her. Never thought it because she couldn't conceive of a man doing something so unselfish. She placed her palm over the scar, feeling the smoothness of the new skin, the ridges of the perimeter and the heat and strength of the man beneath. "My God."

He'd endured hell for her and had never said a word, asked for a thing. Except last night when he'd asked for her trust. She leaned forward and kissed the smaller round burn just to the left of his breastbone. He could have anything he wanted of her. Anything at all.

"Son of a bitch!" Clint's hands on her arms were rough. Not hurting, but not gentle either, as he set her away from him. "I don't want a goddamned gratitude fuck."

The words hit her like blows until she looked into his face. His face was like stone, not an emotion showing. In her experience the only time a man hid his emotions was when he felt vulnerable. Of course, her experience was limited, and if she called this wrong, she would be paying for it for the rest of her life, but she touched his chest. She didn't think she was calling this wrong.

"Clint." He didn't let her go, but he did frown.

"What?"

"I want to be your wife."

"You already are."

"Your real wife."

"Because you think handing over your body is going to make up for a few scars?"

The derision in his tone flicked her like a whip.

"No." She was no reward for anything. She took a step back. He didn't let her go. Just held her with an ease that sent flickers of panic racing up her spine. He wanted his pound of flesh. She could understand that.

"I don't have anything else to give you." She took a steadying breath. "I can never thank you enough for what you did." She tightened her grip on the throw and squared her shoulders. It took everything she had to meet his gaze. "You can have anything you want of me."

"Anything?"

His face, his voice, his grip—all three were as implacable as the man himself. Her stomach sank. There was no end to the demands he could make, but she'd given her word. "Yes."

"Then I want your trust."

She couldn't have heard him right. "What?"

"I want your trust."

"But I've done everything…"

But she hadn't. She'd refused him last night.

His finger under her chin brought her gaze to his.

"I don't want your obedience, Jenna."

She didn't believe that for a minute. "I don't understand."

His thumb stroked cross her lower lip. It was a strangely possessive, yet soothing caress.

"I want you to trust me to take care of you." He tugged the throw from around her. "Starting now."

Chapter Ten

"I don't have anything else to give."

He'd been pissed right up until she'd whispered that truth. She'd held his gaze and offered him everything she had, leaving herself vulnerable in a way that he couldn't conceive of ever making himself vulnerable to anyone. And he'd been bastard enough to throw her offer back in her face, attacking her where he knew it would hurt the most.

She believed herself worthless. It was like an open wound on her soul, and he'd gone for it right off, getting his own back with his usual efficiency. And she'd stood there, taking it like she deserved it. Like any of that nonsense was the truth. He'd never hated himself more than when he'd seen that flicker of acceptance in her blue eyes. If he lived to be a hundred, he'd never forgive himself. If he lived to be two hundred, no one would ever put that look in her eyes again.

"Sunshine?"

"Yes?"

"Do you want to catch that throw?"

"What?"

"Either you catch it or it's going to hit the floor."

She didn't move. "I don't know what you want."

"Do you want to be naked in front of me?"

She shifted and avoided his gaze before finally admitting, "I want to please you."

"And do you think your body pleases me?" He caught the throw from behind. As long as she stayed pressed against him, she was covered.

"No."

He hadn't been expecting that. "I wouldn't have guessed from the way you're always taking your clothes off."

The glance she cut him was purely defensive. "Men like that."

"That's the truth."

"It makes them feel powerful."

If he wasn't mistaken, that was a shot, though it was delivered in the softest, gentlest, most inoffensive tone possible.

"Now that's where you're wrong." He snuggled his fingers into her hair, shaping his palm to her skull, supporting her head when she tilted it back to look at him. "The sight of you naked would drop any man to his knees."

"Not you."

"Especially me." She made him weak in all kinds of ways.

"Not last night."

That was an accusation. "Last night was different."

"How?"

"You weren't ready."

She closed her eyes and rested her forehead against his chest. "Please tell me what you want."

"I want you."

"Now?"

"Yes."

She took a step back and released the throw. He caught it and tossed it across the settee. She stood before him, hands folded in front of her, a blush rising from her chest. She hadn't blushed last night, which meant she was feeling vulnerable now. Which meant she wasn't hiding behind a shield of docility. He was seeing the real Jenna. He dropped his shirt to the floor. She stared, her eyes going to his scars, following them down, dipping below the waistband of his pants, widening before flashing back up to measure the width of his shoulders. He imagined he must look pretty intimidating to someone like her.

He held out his hand. "Trust me, Jenna."

She placed her small hand in his larger one, her skin fair and delicate against his, her magnificent breasts jiggling with each step she took as he backed to the settee.

He sat while she stood, her weight balanced carefully on her feet, poised for flight. With a tug he pulled her into his lap. Her hip cuddled his cock. Her shoulder nestled under his and the soft scent of roses teased his nostrils. She turned her torso into his, put her arms around his neck and raised her mouth. He shook his head. "No."

"What?"

"I don't want you giving me what you think I need."

She frowned. "You want me to just sit here?"

"I only want you to give me what you feel."

"But I don't feel anything."

"Ever?"

"No."

"Now that's a damned shame."

"Am I supposed to?"

He brushed the damp fall of hair from her forehead. "If I do my job right, you should feel a whole hell of a lot."

She shifted, weighing his words. "But you'll let me use my cream."

He couldn't blame her for not taking chances. "If you want the cream when the time comes, I'll use it."

"Promise?"

"I promise."

She relaxed against him. "What do I do now?"

He let her slide back on his arm, his hand on her head controlling her descent until the deep green fabric of the settee cushioned her back. "You just lie there and let me play."

"And that will make you happy?"

He propped himself over her, closing his eyes briefly as the tips of her breasts pressed against his scarred chest. "Very happy."

The bright sun reflecting off the new snow outside lit her skin with a pure white light, highlighting that inner glow that always enthralled him. Her breath was coming in little pants that caused her breasts to shiver as she watched him warily. He shifted his hips, sliding his knee between her legs. She tensed immediately.

"Easy, Sunshine."

She took a breath and stilled.

"That's it," he whispered against her cheek. "There's nothing to be afraid of. You just trust me to make you feel good."

It didn't escape his notice that she ducked his gaze on that statement. He kissed her cheek. Her hands gripped his forearm. She had a lot to learn about him. He wasn't a man who rushed his fences. He could take as long as she needed. He kissed the tip of her nose, smiling when her eyes crossed as she watched, kissed her forehead, and then closed those big blue eyes with a brush of his lips across her dark tipped lashes. They tickled his lips as they fluttered a response, but they closed. He kissed the blue veined lids softly.

"There you go. Just focus on how I make you feel."

He made her feel small, feminine, vulnerable. Jenna gasped as his lips brushed her ears. Very vulnerable. He was so big, so strong, The muscles of his chest bulged as he supported himself above her, and though he obviously intended to do his best to make this not hurt, she didn't see how he could avoid it. Jack wasn't anywhere near as big as Clint and he could make her scream. Another of those butterfly kisses on her neck and she shivered.

"Did you like that, Sunshine?"

It was a rhetorical question because Clint didn't wait for an answer, just did it again, lingering a little longer on the spot just beneath her ear. Another dart of sensation raced down her spine. He laved the area with his tongue and then sucked the flesh between his teeth. The tingle of sensation exploded into something more, something hot and demanding. Something that made her breasts swell and peak. Something that scared her. She pushed against his forearms.

He didn't pull back, but rather tucked her closer into his chest, his mouth. Tucked her into that out-of-control feeling, and nurtured it with hot whispers of approval as she shivered and arched.

"That's my girl. Go with it."

Go where? She had no idea what he was doing, where he was taking her, what he expected her to do along the way. She'd hoped for a lack of pain, but this lack of control was something altogether different. Before she had a chance to study it, contain it, he was moving again, his lips brushing her cheek in a light series of caresses on the way to her mouth.

It was with a feeling of relief that she felt him kiss the corner of her mouth. She knew what to do here. He'd taught her last night. As soon as he kissed the other corner, she opened her mouth, sliding her hands up the hard bulge of his biceps to the unrelenting firmness of his shoulders. His nose brushed hers as he shook his head. A strand of his hair slipped its tie and slid along her cheek.

"Don't rush it, baby."

Rush what? As a married woman, an intelligent woman, she'd thought she knew everything about relations between a man and a woman, and how to survive them. She didn't know a thing about this. About the way that the he could make her lip tingle with the brush of his tongue, the way he could make her breath catch and her body twist just by sucking her lower lip into his mouth.

His laugh mingled with her gasp. A low masculine sound of pleasure as his hand eased under her torso and held her chest to his. She braced herself for the bruising to come, but instead he just held her, letting her get used to the feel of him as he got used to the taste of her.

Gradually, her muscles relaxed, letting him bear her weight, letting him take responsibility for their position. Her reward was another of those approving murmurs before he slanted his mouth across hers, and his tongue pushed past her parted lips in a slow, easy thrust that rode her breath and her anticipation before culminating in a lazy curl around her own.

He didn't appear to be in any rush, or working toward any particular goal. His mouth on hers was gentle, his hand on her back supportive, the fingers on her cheek coaxing. She was surrounded by his smoky scent, his strength, and his gentleness. Her fingers caught in his hair tie and when she tugged, his hair sprang free, sliding around her face, blocking out the sun, locking her into the sensual world of his creation where nothing else existed except the fragile new feelings he was coaxing from her body and the diminishing of her resistance. She dropped the leather hair tie on his back as, through the shock hazing her brain, the reality pushed forth.

"You're seducing me!"

It was a breathless accusation that lacked any real strength. Clint met it with the truth. His "Yes" was strong in contrast, his amusement somehow kind instead of mocking. "Is that a problem?"

She shook her head, feeling foolish.

He brushed her nose with his. "Must be I'm doing it right then."

He smiled. Another real smile that took his face from handsome to devastating, and more of the shield she'd put up around her heart dissolved. She'd always wanted to see him smile, never dreaming she'd actually get to be the one to make it happen. And here she'd done it twice in one morning. She touched the corner of his lips.

"You're actually smiling." He raised an eyebrow at her. "You never smile."

"I've never had you in my arms before."

She blushed. She could feel it starting in her toes and burning its way up over her chest. She couldn't help it. The way he looked at her made everything seem more intimate. More personal. He looked at her as if she were something special, which only made her more aware of all the ways she wasn't.

"You must say that to all the ladies."

"No. I don't." He wouldn't let her look away. His smile was gone and in its place was the man she was used to seeing. The one who asked no quarter and gave none. The one who gave the truth with no apologies or acknowledgment to decorum. Another spurt of hope shot past her defenses. Maybe she really was pretty to him. She quashed it immediately as foolishness.

"Thank you." His focus intensified. She shifted uneasily. Sometimes she swore he could see so deep inside of her that she had no secrets left. His nose brushed hers again.

"Sunshine, someone sure put some strange notions in your head."

"I'm sorry." She so wanted to give him what he wanted, to react the way he was used to. His hand worked up her back until he was cupping her head, her shoulders supported by his forearm.

"Nothing to be sorry for. Just means we have a few things to get straight."

"Just a few?" He smiled at her stab at humor. Just a quirk of his lips, but it made her so hungry for more. He nodded.

"The main one being that I think you're so beautiful I'm about to come in my pants just from looking at you."

"Really?" The starkness of his words shocked her. The possibility of them intrigued her. He dropped his forehead against hers. This close she only had a vague sense of his expression, but there was no denying the harshness of his breathing or the pounding of his heart.

"Really."

"But we've only kissed." She felt his shrug all along her torso, especially on her breasts where his chest hair dragged on her nipples.

"You're one hell of a kisser."

The compliment warmed another spot deep inside that she'd thought forever frozen. She stroked his shoulder and back, enjoying the ladder of muscle flexing beneath her touch.

"I can go get my cream."

His "No" was so abrupt it made her jump.

"There's no need to wait."

He kissed her hard. "It'll be sweeter for the waiting."

She didn't know how that would be possible, but he was the man, and he certainly knew what he liked.

"Fine." Then because she was curious and because his lips on her neck had her heart fluttering and racing she asked, "Is it allowed, I mean would you like…" He rose up and eased his body down hers as she searched for the correct way to ask. The settee creaked as he pulled his arm from under her and propped himself over her with his arm beside her chest.

"Spit it out, Sunshine."

Because she hadn't come up with any better approach she did. "Can I touch you?"

It seemed as if the question hung between them unanswered for an eternity as he studied her expression, and then he relaxed and the smile began. It started in his eyes, warming their flat dark depths with light as it spread outwards over his full lips with pure carnal anticipation.

"Yes."

"Thank you." Another blush surged up from her toes but she held her ground.

"My pleasure." His hands brushed up over her ribs to the side of her breasts.

She couldn't help her involuntary stiffening. His gaze sharpened and his eyes left hers and dropped to her chest, searching for the cause of her unease. In the bright light he couldn't help but notice and she didn't want him to see her that way. Didn't want him to know. She tugged at his hair.

"I thought I was going to get to touch you." She was rather proud of the seductive quality of her complaint.

"In a minute."

He had incredible hands. With a touch he could both soothe and coax. It was no wonder he was the best horse trainer around. But she didn't need soothing, she needed a distraction. His breath hissed in and she knew it was too late. She closed her eyes against the pity she'd see in his. The curiosity. The disgust.

"Tell me who, Sunshine." The rough tip of his finger lightly touched her breast just to the left of her nipple.

"It doesn't matter anymore." She looked down. All she could see was the dark width of his shoulder spreading across her line of vision, and the black spill of his hair over the stark whiteness of her skin.

"It matters." He cradled the fullness of her breast protectively in the width of his palm. The coldness of his gaze when he looked up made her shiver.

"You're scaring me." She could feel him withdrawing from her, back into that place she couldn't go, where no one could reach.

"You're not the one who needs to be scared." In contrast to the lethal growl in his voice, his lips on her breast were infinitely gentle— hot soothing kisses of…apology? "Tell me, Jenna."

"It's not important."

"Was it that son of a bitch your father forced you to marry?"

"It doesn't matter. I'm with you now. No one can hurt me." She couldn't bring herself to lie. She petted his shoulders. The muscles tensed to rock-hard under her hands. The fingers of his left hand bit painfully into her soft flesh.

"I'll kill the son of a bitch who so much as thinks about trying." The calmness with which he stated that fact had her shivering again.

Clint felt the shiver all along his body. He turned on his side, squeezing them both onto the settee, taking her unease into himself while he tried to quell the murderous rage swelling under his skin, breaking out of his control, threatening to explode him from within.

His Jenna, his sweet, gentle Jenna had been whipped. On her breasts. Hard enough to leave scars. Son of a bitch, no wonder she'd been so obedient, blindly doing what he'd asked without a murmur. She had to be in terror of that happening again. And she didn't think it mattered?

He dropped his forehead to hers and eased his grip on her breast. Damn! He'd been squeezing hard enough to leave a mark. Which had to make him little better than the bastard who had released such savagery on her. "I'm sorry, baby."

"It's all right." She was always telling him that but he didn't believe it.

"Do you want to call a halt?"

His cock jerked in protest, but he fought back the selfish urge to push on, to force her to acknowledge him as different. He felt the heat of her blush before he saw it.

"I..."

"It's okay." He tucked her into his torso, needing to shelter her as much as he needed to claim her. She tore him up with her vulnerability combined with that inner strength that she relied on to keep going. "This doesn't have to happen all at once."

She swallowed so hard her head butted his chin. "I don't want to stop."

"What?" He couldn't have heard her right.

"It's never felt good before. I know it's a sin, but I just want..." The rest of the sentence faded off into nothingness.

"You just want what?" Her hands clenched on one of his.

"I just want to know what it would be like with you."

"Shit!" He was in no condition to take her gently. He was too raw, his anger simmering too close to the surface, blending with his lust in a volatile, unpredictable mix.

"I'm sorry." She cringed away.

"Damn it, come here." She did immediately, lying stiffly against him. It didn't take a genius to figure out why. "Jesus, you should never have married me."

"I told you I wasn't perfect."

He grabbed her chin and jerked it up. "There isn't a goddamned thing about you that isn't perfect, but there's a hell of a lot about me that should send you screaming for cover. Number one being that right now I'm in no condition to take you gently. Like you should be. Like you need to be."

Instead of flinching away, her chin came up. "Who says?"

"Who says what?"

"Who says I need to be taken gently?"

"I do. You should have soft words, gentle touches, and all the patience a man can muster."

"And you can't give me that?" She propped herself over him.

"Not this time. Not now."

"Why not?"

145

"Because you're mine, and you've been hurt, and it drives me crazy thinking I wasn't there to prevent it."

"And that makes you want to hurt me, too." She said that as if it made sense.

"Ah shit, baby, I don't want to hurt you ever." Her breasts dangled an inch from his mouth while her hand grazed its way down his stomach.

"But you want me."

"Yes."

"Just me?"

"Only you."

Her fingertips inched under the waistband of his denims. His stomach sucked in at the pleasure. Her breasts swung as she hitched up higher. Her nipple brushed his mouth. He caught it between his lips before it could swing back. Her breath left her in a rush. He didn't let go, just held her in his mouth, meeting her gaze with his, warning her to back off. Her eyebrows arched up. He pulled his lips back, letting her feel and see his teeth. Letting her know he was serious. Needing her to back off, so he could hold onto the little bit of self-liking he had left.

Fear flared in her eyes. Her gaze locked on his teeth. She stopped breathing. If he had any sense of self-preservation whatsoever, he would nip her, give her that bite that would send her flying, but he couldn't because in the time it took him to make the decision, the fear in her eyes was replaced with understanding.

"It's okay, Clint," she whispered, leaning forward, giving him access to her breasts. "It's okay if you need to hurt me this time."

His cock leapt and strained in his pants at her submission. Desire thickened his blood until it chugged painfully through his veins. Goddamn her! How could she do this to him? Give herself to him like this? With no holding back, knowing how close to the edge he was?

He kept her nipple locked between his teeth while he sank his fingers into her hair at the base of her skull and dragged her over him. When she was straddling his stomach, he arched her head back, forcing more of her breast into his mouth. He suckled her hard, probably too hard, but he needed her, needed her acceptance. Needed to test whether she meant it. Needed this culmination of years of hunger. Of waiting.

He lashed her nipple with his tongue as it rose to attention. Nibbled it with his lips, his free hand molding her breast to his liking, drawing it away from her body, toward his mouth, milking a response. Demanding it.

And she gave it to him, in soft pants and tiny surprised squeaks of pleasure. She didn't like it when he used his teeth. Just the hint of them would have her braced, but she loved it when he used his lips to nip and grind gently on the little nubs. She would moan when he suckled her, drawing hard on the sensitive tip. And she liked it when he worked her breast with his hands in time with his tugging on her nipples. Then she would rock on his torso, unconsciously rubbing her pussy over the ridges of muscle. He cupped the plump cheeks of her ass in his palms and forgot all about driving her away.

"Come up here, baby." He pushed with his hands and scooted down on the settee until the bottom arm stopped his progress. She only got as far as his chest before she stopped, just close enough to tease him with the first scent of her passion, but too far away for him to taste. And he needed to taste her. To know every little intimate thing about her.

He grabbed her waist and lifted her to the side. She was still wobbling on her feet, trying to get her bearings when he sat on the floor before her and took her hands in his, leaning back until he was supine and she was bent over him. It wasn't the smooth move he'd planned because she didn't have any clue as to his intent. He shook his head at her lack of education, and with a quick tug, overbalanced her so that she fell. Her squeal ended buried in his chest as he cushioned her fall.

"Straddle me, Sunshine." She did as ordered, pushing her wild tangle of hair off her face as she knelt above him. He brushed the plump swell of her stomach on his way up to the bright red tips of her nipples, taking the tiny bit of additional pressure against his thumb as she sucked in a breath.

"That's it," he whispered as her pussy dampened the flesh of his stomach. "Feel the pleasure. This isn't a sin, Jenna. It's the way it's supposed to be between us. Let me show you how good it should feel."

Her head dropped back and the long length of her hair lashed his thighs as she shook her head. "How can you do this to me?"

"Do what?"

"Make me forget."

"Practice." He'd had a lot of practice forgetting. "Now, come here."

He tugged her nipples. She leaned forward, catching her weight on her hands on the floor beside his head. He stroked his hands down her back, marveling at how soft she was to his touch. So different from him. Inside and out. He traced the line of her spine with the index fingers of both hands until they ended in the soft flesh of her buttocks.

He palmed her ass, massaging the giving flesh, sinking his fingers deep, pulling her up as he scooted down until with a last tug, he lifted her thighs over his shoulders one at a time so that she was kneeling over his face.

"Clint?"

He knew she was embarrassed. Unsure. Knew and didn't care. She had the prettiest pussy. Plump and lush like the rest of her, the delicate inner lips just beginning to unfurl with her desire. Just a few drops of moisture clinging to the springy blonde curls.

He scooped one pearly drop on his finger. It shimmered against his dark flesh, enticing him to look for more, bring forth more. He glanced up. She was looking down at him. He held her gaze while he brought his finger to his mouth, curling his tongue around that savory drop, groaning in his throat as her flavor spread through his mouth. Son of a bitch, he'd known she'd be sweet on his tongue.

The flush on her cheeks turned scarlet as she gasped. He slid his hands over her hip bones until he had a good grip and pulled her down. He did most of the tugging on the left side, supporting the right so she didn't have to, welcoming her weight on his chest as her pussy brushed his lips. Fear flared in her blues eyes. Her entire being seemed to cringe away. He stroked her hip with one hand while holding her still with the other.

"What is it, baby?"

Her lip slipped between her teeth, but she didn't say a word, just fisted her hands beside his head and braced herself. He kissed the inside of her thigh, dragging his lips across the warm, silken expanse, absorbing her start, stopping when the color drained from her face.

"What is it, Jenna?"

"Please don't."

"Don't what?"

"I know I said it was okay, but please don't bite me there. Please."

He took a deep breath and held it, the rage swelling higher than before. Damn, he'd put her husband in the ground again if he could.

"I won't bite you, baby. I just want to kiss you a little. Taste you. Make you feel good." He kissed her folds, once, twice, three times, easing her into the thought of his mouth there, gentling her with his lips and hands until she relaxed above him.

"Is...is this necessary?" she asked in that squeaky voice that made him smile.

"Very."

He teased her with his tongue, probing the crease with light flicks, working a little deeper each time until he reached the moist inner core of her desire. Her gasps were constant now, but no longer from fear. Her delicate flesh was swelling and her sweet channel lubricating, teasing him with her unique flavor. He wanted more.

He pulled her closer, delved deeper, lashed her faster. His cock jerked and throbbed in rhythm with his mouth.

He nuzzled his face deeper between her legs, searching for and finding her clit were it nestled. He lapped at it gently, gradually increasing the pressure as she arched against him. He was rewarded as the sensitive nubbin swelled against his tongue and a fresh burst of cream coated her thighs.

He wanted to eat her up. He wanted everything she had to give. He wanted her to give it to him, and he wanted to take it. He slipped a finger into her channel. She was very tight, her muscles clamping down on him immediately. He took her clit between his lips and sucked it gently while easing his finger in and out.

Her breath came faster, broken by incoherent whimpers. He upped the pace, the pressure, driving her desire higher, adding another finger to the first. He could feel her passion building, feel her response beginning to take over. Feel her fear growing right along with it in the tension of her muscles.

She gasped and pulled away. He growled and pulled her back, holding her still for the lash of his tongue, the suction of his mouth. He held her to him and drank of her essence as she spasmed above him, her nails digging into his shoulders as she cried out his name. He growled deep in his throat when she would have pulled away.

He wasn't done yet. Hadn't had nearly enough of her sweetness yet. She screamed his name again, another stronger climax coming on the first, the last consonant shattering on a note of panic as her pussy milked his finger and her juices flooded his tongue. The edge of pain in her next scream was the only thing that could have pulled him away from her at that moment.

He turned them on their sides, tucking her head onto his shoulder as she cried, stroking her spine while kissing her cheek, her neck, her jaw.

"It's all right, baby," he whispered in her ear as huge sobs shook her body. "It's all right."

And it was. Despite the fact that Jenna was crying rather than smiling, despite the fact that his cock ached for relief, for the first time in years, everything was right in his world.

Chapter Eleven

She couldn't stop crying. It was embarrassing, ridiculous, and stupid, but the more Clint stroked her back and kissed her hair, the more tears gathered and fell.

"Ah Sunshine, you've got to stop."

She would if she could. "I'm trying."

Her voice was a pathetic hiccup of sound, squeaked out between sobs.

"You're going to make me look bad. Folks will take one look at your face and know for sure I'm a real son of a bitch."

He wasn't a son of a bitch. She stroked the scars on his chest, her fingers sliding across the sweat-slicked muscle. He was a hard man and sometimes a cold man, but he was a man like no other. And he was hers. Another round of tears swelled. She sniffed and wiped at her nose. It figured that the first time she'd cried in years, she wouldn't have a hanky handy.

Behind the pocket doors, Danny whined. Beneath her, Clint moaned. She apologized again, sniffed and burrowed deeper into his arms. There was something so solid about the man that had nothing to do with all that heavy muscle and bone. She couldn't get close enough. He made her feel feminine, dainty, and...desired. He grunted as her elbow dug into his ribs.

"Are you going to cry like this every time you come?"

She had no idea. "Does it matter?"

His chuckle bounced her around. "Not really." He shifted beneath her, catching her with his arm when she almost tumbled off. "I might just pick a more comfortable place for the next round, though."

They were on the floor. Or more correctly, Clint was on the floor and she was sprawled on top of him.

"You must be freezing!" She scrambled up. He let her, catching her hand when she would have pulled away, rolling to his feet and pulling her back into his arms as he straightened.

The cotton of his denims rasped against her stomach as he tucked her into his embrace. Against her hip and thigh, his erection throbbed. She remembered how he'd held her this morning. His tenderness. His consideration. She quelled her reflex to shift away. Instead, she rubbed against him, lifting her face for the descent of his mouth when he touched her chin with his finger. His lips were firm and demanding, his tongue seeking hers with the urgency she could feel thrumming under his skin. He wanted her.

It still shocked her that someone like him could want someone like her, but he did, and she wanted to give him everything he needed. Whatever it was. However it was.

His hand dropped to her breast. She shivered first from the cold contact and then from the heat as he lifted her breast to the stroke of his thumb. Fire streaked out from her nipple, lingering sparks dancing erratically over her torso, flashing and tingling all the way down to her pussy, where they coalesced into a hot ball of greedy incentive.

She wanted more. Of the feeling. Of him. She rubbed her tongue against his, standing on tiptoe to get closer. His forearm at the base of her spine anchored her against him as his kiss got bolder, hotter. More demanding. She went with him, twining her arms around his neck when he lifted her feet off the floor, amazed that he could do so with one arm, secretly thrilled that he could.

He pulled his lips from hers.

She grabbed his hair and pulled him back. "No."

He ignored her protest. "Wrap your legs around my waist."

It should have terrified her to draw such a tone from a man, but it didn't. God help her it didn't. Instead, every guttural note hissed like hot sap along her nerve endings, heating her up like the main event at a bonfire. She wrapped her legs around his lean hips, leaning back so he could see her breasts, smiling when he licked his lips. His expression hardened to granite. His black eyes seared hers as he turned, carrying her out the door as if she weighed nothing.

They were at the foot of the stairs before she found her voice. "Where are we going?"

"Upstairs where I can love you right."

"I can't imagine you doing it wrong." The bold statement just popped out.

Clint s eyes flared and his breath sucked in. And then he was in motion again, spinning them around, backing her up. His arm hit the wall first, taking most of the impact snapping her into the equally hard wall of his chest. His mouth came down on hers, wild and hungry as if he wanted to devour her. His teeth grazed her neck as he arched and fumbled beneath her. He sucked at the cord of her neck and shoulder as he kicked free of his boots and pants, jostling a laugh from deep within. She didn't recognize him like this. Didn't recognize herself like this. But she liked it.

The broad head of his cock slid along her buttocks as he groaned in relief. His mouth came back to hers, and he was kissing her again, his mouth as possessive as his hands on her hips, his cock branding her with the heat of his passion, demanding that she give in and accept him.

And she did. He lifted her, a wicked smile on his exotic face, and slid his cock between them, tilting her so that he rode her crease, the broad head flicking her swollen clit as he speared up through her folds, sending shards of lighting flickering outward. She hunched her back and buried her face in his neck as he climbed the stairs, every step nudging the hot length of his shaft along her ultra-sensitive clit. It was sinful, decadent and she never wanted it to end. By the time they reached the top of the stairs she was whimpering and gasping, her mouth kissing and sucking at his shoulder in response to the blistering demands of her body.

He entered the bedroom without missing a beat, and kicked the door closed. His cock dipped and caught the top fold of her pussy where it pressed and strained.

"Son of a bitch!" The heated curse swept past her ear as Clint caught a fistful of her hair in his hand and pulled her head back. The salty taste of his flesh lingered on her lips as she stared up at him. She held his gaze as she licked it off.

He tossed her, his masculine laughter following her as she squealed and flailed for support. The softness of the mattress wrapped around her before it dipped to one side and then the other as Clint placed his hands beside her knees, his hair swinging forward between them. He started crawling up her body, his hands set with predatory precision alongside her as he covered her. Everything feminine in her went on alert. Even though she knew he was playing, he was too big, too masculine to just lie still. She propped herself on her elbows and wiggled backward.

"Clint?"

He just smiled wider and kept on coming, his biceps flexing with every move, his cock dragging up the inside of her thigh in a hot, silken caress. The sheer weight of the broad head of his cock pulled it down.

She looked over her shoulder. She was running out of bed. His arms drew even with her hips. He paused, grinned at her, and slowly, slowly lowered his head, holding her gaze the whole time. His hair pooled on either side of her thighs, while his tongue—his wickedly talented tongue—extended toward her pussy. He wiggled it once, making her shiver and arch up almost imperceptibly. His smile broadened and then he was licking her, swirling his tongue through her thick juices, tapping her clit with every other pass, while his eyes measured every response she made. It was too much. Too intimate. She let her lids flutter down on the next wave of passion.

A nip on her thigh had them flying open.

"Watch." She didn't know whether to be scared or soothed.

"You bit me." He cocked an eyebrow at her and sucked the injured area before laving it with his tongue.

"No, Sunshine. I just got your attention."

She rubbed the inside of her thigh. He kissed her hand, working his tongue between her fingers, tickling her with the promise of sensation.

"But…"

"Trust me, baby."

He held her with the power of his personality, the depth of the emotion in his eyes, the promise of passion in his touch. It might make her a weak woman, a loose woman, but she wanted that pleasure with him again. Wanted to give it back to him. No matter what.

She removed her hand and placed it on his head. His hair was silky and cool to the touch, soothing against the heat of her skin. He turned and kissed her palm. Feeling bold and daring, she curved her fingers over his jaw. The start of his beard rasped her skin. He paused and looked up at her over her hand. The heat under the question in his gaze seared her.

"I want to make you feel good, too."

"I'm feeling very good right now." His deep voice rolled over her the way it always did, soothing and stimulating at the same time.

She shook her head. "I don't want to just take. I want to give."

"Sweet thing, you're giving me heaven right now."

"I'm not giving you anything. I'm just lying here."

He kissed his way up her stomach, each brush of his lips on her flesh infinitely gentle. "You're giving me your trust."

It wasn't enough. "Please?"

He kissed the tip of each breast, sucking each in turn before nuzzling into the side of her neck. "How about we make a deal?" The question wafted against the sensitive cord of her neck. She curved her fingers over his shoulders.

"What?"

The bed dipped, shifting her to the right as he continued his climb. "You forgive me this time, and I'll let you run amok later."

His cock nestled into the damp well of her vagina as his hair fell over her face, obscuring her view. She shifted back to level as her left arm joined his right—even with her shoulders.

"Forgive you for what?"

"My impatience." The explanation ended on a hiss as he pressed against her.

"Oh." He was big. His fingers on her cheek soothed her nerves. He was still in control. But dear God, he was so big.

"Easy, Sunshine."

The mattress creaked as he shifted his weight onto his forearm. He was breathing hard, his breath hitting her cheeks in rapid puffs. He cupped the back of her head in his hand. He smelled of coffee, her and them.

"I'll be as easy as possible," he whispered against her mouth. "But I can't wait any longer to be inside you."

She could feel his urgency in the quiver of his muscles, the restrained power surging through him. She tilted her head back into his grip, knowing it was the right thing to do as he groaned and kissed her throat. She pushed his hair back to better see his expression. It was hard, almost savage with the desire tearing at him. For her.

"You need me."

The kiss he pressed into the hollow of her throat was violent with restrained hunger. And still he held back. "I'm aching for you."

She'd never known anyone like him. "Let me get my cream."

"You don't need cream." His laugh was more of a moan. He caught her hand in his, dragging it down between their bodies until her fingers dipped between her legs. Her flesh there was abnormally soft and wet. Slippery. "Feel how ready you are for me. How your sweet pussy is crying for me."

Her fingers bumped the head of his cock. She turned her hand in his, grasping the thick stalk. She couldn't wrap her fingers around the smooth, hard shaft, but she tried, squeezing what she could. Clint stopped breathing, his whole body caught in a desperate, expectant stillness. His huge cock leapt in her hand as his body jerked down. The resulting charge of sensation up into her womb had her gasping and instinctively arching up. He pushed harder against her. Her flesh tingled and ached as her muscles fought to accommodate his entry. A whimper tore from her throat.

"Son of a bitch." Clint's torso slammed her down into the mattress, keeping her from moving. "Don't do that, baby." He dragged her hand off him. "You've got to leave a man some control," he drawled as he brought her hand up between them.

His dark eyes held hers, his nostrils flaring as he caught her scent. He brought her fingers to his mouth with deliberate intent, and closed his lips over the first two. He shuddered, his eyelids lowered, and his cock rocked against her opening as his tongue lapped the underside of her fingers. With his gaze locked on hers, there was no way she could mistake his response for anything else than pleasure. He sucked and then paused, as if savoring her flavor, letting it roll across his tongue before he swallowed. His lids lifted and his pupils flared as he went after the third finger.

"You taste so good, Sunshine. You make me want to eat you from sunup to sundown."

Those words, spoken in that rough drawl, rode her nerves harder than a caress. He really did like her. As she was. There was no way anyone could fake that much passion.

Clint's lips and tongue worked her fingers, tugged at hidden nerve endings until it felt like he was so deep inside her, he was tonguing her womb. The tingling spread outward, making her ache and throb, tense with the need for more.

"That's it," Clint whispered in that deep, dark tone. "Just relax and let me in."

She was, she realized. Though it felt like some invisible spring was coiling tighter and tighter deep inside, her woman's flesh was actually relaxing against him. Welcoming him. With every pulse of his hips, he was gaining a fraction more entry. And her body was clamoring for more. Beyond sense and beyond reason, she wanted him in her. Wanted him to fill her.

She tried to push up. To help. A simple flex of his hips kept her in place.

"No." He kissed her palm before placing it on his shoulder. "You just relax and let me do this."

It was easier said than done, especially when he brought his big hand between them and paced the rough surface of his thumb high up on her pussy, just over her clit. He did nothing more than rest it there while he maintained the pressure of his cock against the tight ring of muscle guarding her passage. The inner urging to move, to mate, grew stronger.

"Clint, please." She was so empty, and she *needed* him to move. His fingers. His hips. She needed him to fill all the places in her that had been empty for so long.

"Please what?" His voice was hoarse and raspy. He needed her as much as she needed him.

She bit her lips, and tried to decipher all the needs clamoring for notice. Her nipples ached against his chest. Her clit ached against his thumb. Her pussy ached against his cock. Any place her body touched his, nerve endings screamed for attention. Stimulation. She couldn't isolate it to one need so she generalized it into one command.

"Move!"

Even as the words left her lips, she couldn't believe her daring, giving a man an order. But she needn't have worried. Rather than tensing up, Clint laughed that way he had that sent shivers down her spine, and she had a bit of what she wanted as his chest vibrated against her nipples, giving them a small taste of what they cried out for. His black eyes didn't miss a thing, least of all her surprised expression.

"Like this?" he asked with pseudo innocence as he dragged his chest across hers, the ripples of muscle and scar tissue abrading her nipples deliciously. Pleasure bound with desire, twisting around her chest, constricting the muscles, leaving her helpless to do anything, even breathe, as the sensations whipped through her, soothing and intensifying the painful need.

"Or like this?" he asked as he worked his thumb gently against the hood of her clit until she gasped and then, smiling a smile so wicked that Satan would be jealous, his teeth flashing white in his dark face, he rubbed that spot with deliberate slowness. He chuckled when she began to pant, laughed when she cried out, and encouraged her as a scream built in her throat.

"Oh you like that don't you, Sunshine? You like my thumb on your clit, rubbing it over and over, making it nice and hungry."

Oh she did. She did. He grazed that eager nubbin harder this time. A sensation just short of pain shot through her. Her head snapped into his shoulder as her body jerked helplessly.

Wetness gushed over her thighs.

"Give that to me again, baby."

As if she had any choice. The stroke that accompanied the deep whisper drove the scream from her throat. It was too much. He was too much.

Yet it wasn't enough. None of this was enough. She wanted to pull away. Push closer. Beg him and beat him at the same time. She wanted him to make it stop, and at the same time she never wanted it to end. She needed so badly that she didn't think she'd survive the want and he just kept making it worse, keeping up that relentless stroking as he pressed harder against her, his huge cock making demands at her body's entrance that she couldn't resist. With a hard stroke of his thumb he sent her over the edge. Amidst the echoes of her scream, he surged into her.

Reality splintered away as pain and pleasure combined in a tidal wave of sensation that tossed her up into his shoulder. She grabbed at him tooth and nail, struggling for purchase in a world that consisted of nothing but splintering emotion. He grunted, swore and pressed against her, his shout echoing in her ear as she bit down. His big body shuddered over hers as he pulled her into him—into the fire. His cock wedging deeper, taking her higher, driving her further away from what she knew about herself.

And then it was over. The maelstrom fading to swirls of foggy memory. Her body throbbed with the aftershocks as she slowly, slowly sank back into reality and the sobs that shook her. When she opened her eyes, Clint was staring down at her with that peculiar intensity that had her hunching uncomfortably.

And she immediately winced. He was still in her. As hard and as big as ever. Bigger than she remembered. She gave a tentative squeeze with her inner muscles. She had to abort the attempt. She was stretched so tightly around him that there wasn't any room to move.

Clint shifted in her, around her, as he leaned down and kissed her lips. "Wildcat."

There was a wealth of satisfaction in his whisper.

She closed her eyes and groaned as she remembered just how wild she had been. Had she really bitten him? She peeked through her lashes. There, on his left shoulder were two half crescent marks.

She touched them very gently as tears continued to well. "I'm so ashamed."

His teeth flashed white as her caught a tear on his finger. "It'll only be a shame if you never do it again."

She sniffed back another tear. "You liked it?"

"Having you go wild in my arms? Scream my name as you practically squeezed my cock off with your pleasure?" He wiped at a second tear. "Yes. I liked it."

"But I didn't satisfy you." Oh God, now she was thoroughly pathetic.

He stopped wiping at her tears. For a second he stared at her uncomprehendingly. Then he smiled a totally real, totally natural smile, one that took years off his face and made her forget how dangerous he could be.

"Sunshine, I came so hard my heart almost stopped." He nestled his cock a little deeper. "I'm just warming up for round two."

Round two? She was still discovering aches from round one. Maybe she wasn't woman enough for him. The thought sent another of those senseless tears spilling.

"Ah, you've just got to cry, don't you?" Clint asked, licking the tears from her cheeks, kissing her eyelids between drops.

She shook her head, changed her mind, nodded, and finally admitted, "I don't know why!"

He did. Jenna came like a woman who'd never known a moment's peace. She came like a woman who'd been looking her whole life for a chance to let go. "I'll get used to it."

Or go nuts from the need to stop them.

Clint worked his cock deeper into her snug pussy. "Son of a bitch, you're tight, Sunshine."

"I'm sorry."

He rubbed her nose with his. Marveling at her foolishness. "Jenna love, there's nothing to be sorry for. As long as it doesn't hurt you, tight is good. As for the tears, you can cry all over me all you want as long as they're happy tears." He wiped at a tear track with his thumb as he pulled out until her cunt clutched at just the tip of his cock. "And these are happy tears, right?"

Her cheeks turned a deeper red, but she gave him the truth. "Yes."

"Good."

He kissed her soft lips, taking her gasp into his mouth as he surged into her, letting it mingle with his breath before he exhaled, holding her to him as he wedged deeper, accepting the truth. She was hot, tight and completely his.

She winced again. He was definitely more than she was used to.

He brushed a kiss over her eyelids. "I know you're sore baby, so we'll just take this nice and easy."

Her nails bit into his forearm as he pulled back. Her brow pleated as he eased back into her beckoning heat, her eyes darkening with an emotion he couldn't define.

"Too much?"

She bit her lip and shook her head.

He didn't trust her. It would be just like her to take pain to make him happy. "You're sure?"

She nodded. He reached between them and sifted through the wet tangle of her curls until he touched the stretched point of their joining. Damn! He had to be hurting her.

He swore and pulled out.

Her knees came up around his hips. Her "Oh no" was a moan of pure feminine distress. He paused and reassessed. Her agony was of a woman denied, not of one used too hard. Her fingers clutched at his arms and her hips lifted desperately toward his cock. Half-smothered whimpers broke from her throat. She wanted him. Needed him. His heart swelled with the knowledge.

"Shh, baby. I'll give it back." He did, moaning himself as her silken walls clasped and dragged at his cock as he slid in.

"Better?" He could barely get the word out.

Her nod was enthusiastic but that full lower lip, the one he wanted to sink his teeth into, was still tucked into her teeth.

He found the strength to stop. "Does it hurt, Jenna?"

"Oh God," she moaned. "Don't stop."

"Am I hurting you, baby?"

"A little, but I don't care. You feel so good." Her back arched and her ankles hooked around his hips in the mistaken belief that her feminine muscles were going to win a war against his masculine ones.

He curved his spine so he could nibble on her shoulder, while he withheld what they both wanted. "How good?"

"So good…"

"So good what?"

She opened her eyes and glared at him while her heels drummed at his back. "So good I'll scream if you don't give me what I want."

He pretended to consider it. "Not much of an incentive as you'll do that anyway. What else you got?"

She was so naive that she didn't catch the growl in his throat that indicated how close he was to losing control. And so new to teasing, taking the game that far threw her into a quandary of uncertainty. For the longest moment, she lay under him, clearly debating what she had, and damned her hide, she must have come up empty, because she went soft and complacent, and son of a bitch, that might just be an unhappy tear forming in her eye. Her mouth opened. He forestalled the "nothing" he knew was coming out by simply filling in the blanks for her.

"I suppose you could offer up those gorgeous breasts of yours. That for sure would inspire me."

She stared at him, uncertain. He touched the end of her nose, tenderness mixing with passion in a potent combination. "Or you could smile. Those dimples of yours get me hotter than a stallion in mating season."

He counted three breaths before she dropped her hands from his shoulders and slowly, so slowly that sweat broke out on his brow, cupped her palms under her breasts. Her hands were way too small to do an adequate job with such largess, but when she stroked them to the tips and pushed those full mounds together, holding them up and out for him, he damned near came on the spot like a green boy. As he watched, her tongue smoothed over her lips, until they shone wet and pink as she smiled, bringing her dimples into play.

Lust hit him like a stampede, trampling all his good intentions, all his play.

"Now you did it, Sunshine. One I could have managed, but hitting me with both…" He shook his head and propped himself on his hands so that they were only joined at the hips. Cock to pussy. Male to female. Husband to wife. He shook his hair back out of his eyes. "Now I'm afraid you're in for it."

She didn't look scared, just the opposite. She looked femininely eager, hungry. The way he'd dreamed she'd look at him. The rightness of her in his arms, his bed, hit him like a sledgehammer.

"Son of a bitch, you're something, Jenna."

"I could say the same."

Her hands stroked his chest, lingering on the scar while her ankles hooked behind his back. The breathy catch to her speech hooked in his desire, dragged his lust past his control, sent his hips down into hers, his cock spearing deep. Her head fell back. Any doubts he had about her enjoyment were dispelled by her long, moaning "Yesssss!"

It was all over for him then. The bits of civilized restraint that he clung to blew away before the force of his passion. He drove into her over and over again, lunging deeper with every thrust, making a place for himself inside her body, her life. A place where he didn't have to think, where he could just be.

She groaned with every thrust and threw her hips up to meet him, taking what he had to give. Taking the pleasure, the desire, and in return, she gave him calm, her soft arms circling his neck when the climax hit him, anchoring him through the violence of his body's eruption, stroking him in the aftermath, her tears bathing his cheek as he found peace.

Chapter Twelve

"Button's not going anywhere, Jenna," Clint said, clucking his tongue as he backed the gelding into the traces of the small buggy.

Jenna stilled her fidgeting and folded her hands in the drape of her cloak.

"I know." It was her deepest fear. That Cougar and Mara would keep Brianna. Or worse, that Brianna would be so settled it would be impossible to take her away. "I'm just anxious."

Clint tossed a handful of hay onto the ground in front of the horse and then turned to face her. The brim of his hat shadowed his eyes, keeping her from determining his mood. "Anxious about what?"

"Just in general." He tilted his head to the side, studying her. Without the benefit of a hat like his, and with her hood down she had no defense against his perusal. She waved to the horse. "Shouldn't you be getting him harnessed before he eats all that hay?"

Clint pulled another handful of hay out of the bale and tossed it on the ground with the rest and grabbed the dangling strap under the black's belly. As he started pulling it tight, he glanced over his shoulder.

"You know, Sunshine, a lesser man might be discouraged to see his wife was in such a hurry to bring the honeymoon to an end."

"I'm glad you're not a lesser man."

Because a lesser man would be right. She did want the honeymoon over and considered it a blessing that her woman's time had made its infrequent appearance this morning. Clint was not a cruel man, but he was a very demanding man. He took everything she offered, accepting whatever she gave, never saying when it was enough. He made her so nervous that way. She didn't know what he wanted of her and maybe if Brianna was here, he'd be too distracted to notice she didn't have a clue.

"Nothing to be sorry for." He fastened the last strap, then grabbed the reins and threaded them through the guides before tossing the ends over the front edge of the buggy.

"It's not like we don't have fifty years or so to make up the difference." He slapped the black on the rump and headed for her, his long legs eating up the distance with disconcerting speed. "That being the case, what has you coming out of your skin?"

The wind gusted around the barn, blowing his hair into his face. He flicked it back with a toss of his head. The morning sun glanced off the sharp edge of his cheekbones and the uncompromising line of his jaw. There wasn't an ounce of insecurity in the man.

Jenna clenched the folds of the cloak in her hands. "What if she doesn't remember me?"

He pulled his leather gloves off and tucked the cuffs into the front pocket of his denims.

"She'll remember you." It might have been her imagination, but his drawl seemed deeper, softer. She focused her gaze on the tan gloves dangling from his pocket. There was a small tear on the back of one.

"She might not. We didn't have much time together."

"Brianna's not stupid." That flex of his thigh muscles could have meant anything—he could be uncomfortable or he could be getting impatient. The effort to keep her voice level had her hands aching.

"I did so many things wrong."

"You did a whole lot right." The side of his finger under her chin brought her head up. She couldn't yank her gaze from his.

"How can you know?" It was barely a whisper of sound, but he heard.

"There's not another woman in the territory with a bigger heart than you, Jenna McKinnely. Brianna isn't going to forget something like that."

She caught his wrist in her hand. His flesh was cool from the air. The sprinkle of hairs tickled her palm. "Are you sure?"

He slipped his hand around her neck. "I'm sure."

She let go of his wrist, letting her fingers slide up the rough fabric of his sheepskin jacket, until they rested atop the hard bulge of his biceps, clinging to the assurance in his gaze like it was a lifeline. The descent of his head blocked out the sun and then his lips were on hers, not with the passion she was used to but with a more soothing touch. He was comforting her, she realized as he brushed his mouth over hers again. The wind whipped the long stands of his hair against her cheeks, and she leaned into his chest, trusting him to support her as she sampled the astounding realization until the last possible moment, feeling a heartbeat of loss as he broke off the kiss.

Clint tucked her into his side with the same casual ease with which he tucked a tendril of hair behind her ear and said, "Let's go get our daughter, Jenna."

* * * * *

The thirty minutes it took to get to Cougar and Mara's house was the worst of Jenna's life. With each turn of the wheel along the frozen, rutted road she grew more and more convinced that she was doing the wrong thing. Mara and Cougar were married, in love, and desperate for a child. They could offer Brianna things she never could. Confidence. Security. Two loving parents who loved each other.

She absolutely knew she was doing the wrong thing when they pulled up in front of Mara's house. It was a mansion. A huge, sprawling log structure that intimidated with its grandeur. She could see Cougar living here. But more importantly, she could see Brianna growing up here. Safe. Respected. Loved.

She caught Clint's arm as he set the brake. "If Brianna doesn't remember me, I'm leaving her here."

It would about kill her, but she wasn't going to ruin Brianna's life with her selfish desires. Clint stared at her a long time, his black eyes unreadable, and then he calmly got down from the buggy. A thin layer of ice cracked under his weight. He still didn't say a word as he came around to her side. He just held his hand out for hers.

She stood. The buggy lurched. Clint caught her around the waist and steadied her. Her hands automatically settled on his shoulders. Through his heavy coat she could feel the shift of muscle. She gathered her courage as he lowered her. As soon as her feet hit the ground she said, "I mean it, Clint."

"I hear you." He steadied her as she found her balance. It was such a little thing, but he was always seeing to the little things, and it always made her feel more important than she probably was.

"Why don't you sound concerned?"

He cocked his eyebrow at her. "Probably because I came here to take my daughter home, and I'm not leaving without her."

She glanced at the house, and flinched away from the reality as wind whipped her cloak around her legs. "She may be settled."

"I'm sure Cougar and Mara have taken wonderful care of her, but she's our daughter."

"You keep saying that."

"Probably because it's true."

"But Cougar and Mara—"

His finger over her lips silenced the painful suspicion eating at her.

"Will have kids of their own some day," he finished for her. "Kids who will grow up as close as brother and sister with Brianna, but Brianna is ours."

The wind blew again. Clint watched his words sink past Jenna's confusion. She blinked as a stray hair blew across her eyes. He reached up and brushed it away, letting his fingers linger at her temple as she visibly wrestled with herself. And sighed.

She had no confidence, no belief that anyone would want her for anything, but that wasn't why she was willing to leave Brianna here. He knew that. He was beginning to see how her mind worked. She wanted the best for Brianna and she knew Cougar and Mara were guaranteed. In contrast, she saw herself as the wild card in the mix. The potential ruination of that little girl's life. As if anyone who could love so deeply, so unselfishly, could ever be anything but the best.

"I want our daughter, Jenna."

"Really?" She about tore his heart out with the desperate hope in her face.

"Really." She stood looking at him, saying nothing more, her expression a mixture of hope and fear, her doubts so loud he could hear them. He pulled her against his chest with the next gust of wind, turning them slightly so he took the brunt. "I want you both."

"I don't want to ruin her life." That plump lower lip of hers that drove him crazy with his need to nibble on it, slipped between her teeth.

"Then act like her mother."

He felt ten times a heel the minute the words left his mouth, but damn it, it pissed him off when she put herself down like that. His hand on her back kept her from flinching away.

"Brianna needs someone who will stick by her, Jenna, not run the minute the doubts start."

"I want to be her mother." No one hearing the hope in her voice could disbelieve it.

"Then do it."

"Just like that?"

He nodded. "Just like that."

Her hands came up against his chest, their pressure slight. She leaned back. He didn't give her room, so all she ended up doing was arching over his arm, exposing the vulnerable hollow of her throat. He leaned down, taking full advantage, pressing his lips against the rapidly beating pulse there.

"You're going to be a wonderful mother, Jenna."

Her "I am?" drifted over his head. He kissed the soft spot under her ear.

"Yes."

He pulled back as her breath hitched, just far enough that he could see her eyes. Flecks of deep blue broke up the clear sky blue of her eyes. Their shade darkened as determination shoved out doubt.

"I'll love her so much she'll never feel lonely."

"You do that." He couldn't imagine anyone loved by Jenna feeling lonely.

"I'll try to love you, too." Her fingertips curved into his chest hard enough that he could feel the pressure through his coat. He could tell that she meant it, and the part of him that he'd thought long dead stirred with hope. He squashed it.

"I left lovable behind me a long time ago, Sunshine."

"You don't want me to love you?"

"I don't think that's something that can be forced."

She didn't argue with him. She never argued with him, but her chin set in a stubborn tilt. She clearly had her own idea on the subject, and as much as he knew he should say something to knock down her plans, he didn't. If she was determined enough to find something lovable about him, he was selfish enough to take advantage of her soft side. He finally settled on, "I'll be content with your cooperation."

"With what?"

He slid his hand bend her neck tipping her chin back with his thumb. "This."

He brought his mouth to hers. Her lips parted immediately at the brush of his tongue, tempting him with the moist heat beyond. He pulled her closer, pressed deeper. She relaxed against him, accepting his lead, sparking his lust higher with the knowledge that she'd let him do whatever he wanted even as it prodded the remnants of his conscience with her vulnerability.

"Should I put Tidbit down for her nap so you all can go back and finish up your honeymoon?"

The amused question sliced through Jenna's complacency with the efficiency of a knife. She went from relaxed to board stiff in the space of a heartbeat. Clint pulled back a breath, pressing Jenna's face into his chest.

"Go devil your own wife, Cougar."

"Got her right here." A muted squeal punctuated the statement.

Clint shook his head. For a man who spent every waking moment making sure nothing ever disturbed a hair on his tiny wife's head, Cougar spent an inordinate amount of time deviling her. Looking down at Jenna's red face, her lips swollen from his kiss, he began to understand why. There was something very tempting about a woman caught between propriety and passion.

"We'll be right in," Clint called, running the backs of his fingers over Jenna's hot cheek, an inner smile springing to life as she closed her eyes and leaned into his hand.

"You might want to hurry it up before your wife freezes solid," Cougar admonished.

"Are you cold?" Clint arched a brow at Jenna. She shook her head, blushed anew, and took a deep breath. The wind gusted and his hair whipped across her face. The dark strands stood out starkly against her pale skin. He pulled them off her face, leaving it clear again. "Good."

"I'll put the coffee on," Mara called.

"Thanks." As soon as the door thunked shut, Jenna said, "I don't like that man."

"He grows on you." Clint kissed the top of her head. She remained silent on the subject, but tucking her into his side wasn't as easy as before due to the stiffness in her spine. He sighed, steering her in the direction of the house. "Cougar's a good man, Jenna. A good friend to have."

"He doesn't like me."

"He likes you as much as I want him to."

She stopped dead. "What does that mean?"

"Exactly what I said. " She didn't move, just stared at him. He sighed and gave her the truth. "I'm a possessive man, Jenna. I don't like the idea of any man taking a shine to you, married or not."

"I think you're pretty safe." Her cheeks pinkened up again, and she ducked her chin.

"If you promise not to get a swelled head, I'll fill you in on a little fact." He was safer letting her think no man found her desirable, but every woman deserved to know she was special, and his Jenna more so than most.

Her only response was a barely discernible, "What?" and a flash of blue in the corner of her eye. He put them back into motion.

"You are the talk of all the men at the saloon."

"They think I'm loose?" She stiffened and came to a halt. He shook his head at her, titled her chin up, and kissed her cold lips.

"They thought you were too beautiful to resist." Her mouth formed a startled "Oh". He traced it with his tongue before he whispered, "And I had to bloody more than one nose when talk wandered into disrespectful."

"Other men think I'm pretty?"

She acted as if she couldn't get her mind around the fact. He was surely shooting himself in the foot, but it galled him that she didn't see herself the way he saw her.

"Men get hard just at the mention of your name." That had her turning a brilliant red.

She caught his hand in hers. "No one ever approached me."

"You were in mourning, and didn't need a bunch of hungry men pestering you."

"You kept them away?" Her soft blue eyes searched his.

"Yes." Damn, she was quick. He braced himself for her anger. Her fingers squeezed his.

"Thank you."

"For what?"

"I wouldn't have liked men courting me then." Meaning she would now?

"You married me."

"Yes." She smiled just enough to have her dimples flirting in and out of view and resumed walking.

Which told him nothing.

"This house is very impressive." She paused at the foot of the steps to the porch, looking up at the ornate network of beams supporting the roof.

He'd rather talk about that "Yes" and how she felt about marrying him.

"Cougar was in a mood when he built it."

"What kind of mood?"

"A 'kick 'em in the teeth' kind of mood."

She stared at him, then at the building, and then back at him. "Who'd he want to kick?"

"Everyone who ever spit on him or looked down on him because of his blood."

She frowned. "Did you ever have a mood?"

"Nah." She was obviously not going back to the men subject. He took her elbow and helped her up the first step. "But it was different for me. Cougar's pa dragged him from pillar to post, whereas I grew up here, back when things were so small that everyone within spitting distance was kin."

"So you grew up happy?"

"Yes."

"And Cougar?"

"He grew up mean." The tension in her arm told him he'd chosen the wrong term. "Cougar hasn't had it easy, Jenna, but for all he can gut a man without blinking an eye, he's a man you can count on, and the man I turn to when I need someone to watch my back."

"I won't offend him."

"Good." The tension didn't leave her muscles. He squeezed her elbow. She took a step. He tugged her around. She fell against his chest with a startled cry. "If you ever need help, Jenna, and you can't find me, you go to Cougar."

She blinked. "I'm sure it won't be necessary."

"Promise me, Jenna." He didn't have the patience for evasion. Not on this. She glanced over her shoulder at the door and then back at him. He had to wait for her to make up her mind.

"I promise." She said it in that sexy, husky voice of hers that had him hard in an instant. He set her carefully away. If he walked through the door with a hard-on, Cougar wouldn't let him hear the end of it for a month of Sundays.

"Good."

She turned, back straight, and marched up the step. He admired the sway of her skirts as she reached the top, adjusting his denims as his cock thickened and stretched down his thigh. Four more days until her woman's time was over and he could have her again. She brushed her hands over her hips, smoothing her skirt, making his palms itch to smooth over the softer fullness of her buttocks.

Son of a bitch, he was never going to make it. He came up beside her and pinched her butt through her cloak. As she jumped, he opened the door, ushering her into the warmth of the house, feeling an equal warmth spreading out from inside as he entered his cousin's house for the first time as a married man.

* * * * *

"You still planning on keeping her?" Cougar asked as he passed Clint a cup of coffee an hour later.

Clint took the cup and glanced across the big room to where Jenna sat with Mara, exclaiming over Brianna's latest trick, which appeared to be waving her arm aimlessly over her head.

"Seeing as we're married, I don't see where that's relevant."

"You can always have the marriage annulled."

"The marriage has been consummated." Clint took a cautious sip of the hot coffee.

"Throw enough money at a problem, and anything can be fixed." Reading between the lines, Clint knew that meant Cougar would bankrupt himself if necessary to free Clint. Cougar smiled and shrugged as he settled back in the red leather chair.

"I'm happy with my marriage."

"Then why the long face?"

"Wasn't aware that it was."

"Uh-huh."

He leaned forward, rested his elbows on his knees and let the coffee dangle between them. "I think that husband of hers was a bigger son of a bitch than either of us guessed."

"Why?" The laziness left Cougar's posture as he sat up.

"She's been whipped."

"Jesus!"

"Yeah, that was about my thought."

"That bastard husband of hers died too quickly."

"At the time I was more interested in expediency than revenge." Clint tightened his grip on his cup and beat back the residual anger.

The corners of Cougar's lips curved in a lethal mockery of a smile. "A damned pity you can't call a do over and put him in the grave twice. This time not so fast, and not so clean."

"I'm not sure that would solve anything." Except maybe give him an outlet for the rage that kept creeping up on his blind side."

"You don't think he did it?"

"I'm not sure."

"Why not?"

He looked up, meeting Cougar's amber gaze with his own. "Because Jenna won't say so."

Cougar grunted and then asked, "Any chance her father did it? I heard he was a real Bible-thumper with some strange notions and a penchant for drink."

"Maybe." Clint shrugged.

"But you don't believe it?"

"No." Feeling like he was betraying a confidence he gave Cougar the unvarnished truth. "The scars are on her breasts."

"Damn." After a pause Cougar said, "A lover would be the type to take revenge that way."

"That occurred to me." More than once.

"Rumor was Jenna wasn't the most faithful of wives."

"Don't go there, Cougar."

Cougar lifted his brow at the warning, shrugged his broad shoulders, and added, "It's not as if a man could blame her if she did stray."

"If you don't want us coming to blows, you're going to have to trust me on this. Jenna isn't the type to step out on a man, no matter how bad the marriage." Clint tightened his grip on the cup, keeping his head down until the need to mess up Cougar's face was under control.

"My apologies."

"Apology accepted."

"So you think whoever did it is still out there?"

"Yes." Clint took a long pull of coffee, welcoming its scalding heat.

"Damn." Cougar took a pull on his own coffee and glanced over at the women. "It would drive me crazy to know Mara was in danger and not knowing from what, or who."

"I'm not the most serene right now." Clint watched as Jenna talked with Mara, clearly enjoying the start of a friendship, but still on edge. The set of her shoulders was stiff, as if expecting the moment to come crashing down on her. Damn, he wished she could just relax and let herself go.

"It'd be easiest if you could get her to tell you."

"That's not going to happen anytime soon."

Jenna smiled shyly at something Mara said, her dimples appearing and disappearing in her cheeks. His cock surged to attention, eagerly awaiting another glimpse.

Cougar chuckled and shook his head. "I know what that's like. Took me a good month to coax Mara around to my way of thinking."

Clint shot Cougar a disbelieving glance. "The way I remember it, Mara was the one who did the coaxing."

"Which reminds me. I've been waiting for the opportunity to pay you back." Cougar set his cup on the low oak table between them. His long hair swung over his shoulder as he again arched his brow at him.

"For what?" Clint sat back in his chair and feigned innocence.

Cougar paused before he let go of the cup. "For teaching the woman how to tie knots."

"What in hell did you expect me to do? She came to me for help."

"You could have sent her home."

"From what I understood, you weren't letting her come home, and that's what she intended to set to rights."

"It wasn't any of your business."

"You were being an ass."

"Almost as much of an ass as I'm sure you're being now." Cougar sat back in his chair and motioned in the direction of the women.

"All I've done is marry the woman."

"Uh-huh. On the outside that would appear to be so, but Clint, I've known you since you were twelve, and nothing is ever that simple with you."

It was Clint's turn to say, "Uh-huh."

"As a matter of fact," Cougar continued, "it wouldn't surprise me at all to find out that you've been hankering for Jenna all along and just looking for an excuse to hitch your wagon to hers."

Damn, Cougar knew him too well. "She's a good woman, and she needs help."

"There are a lot of good women who need help. I didn't see you marrying up with any of them."

"Which just goes to prove your theory is empty." Probably because just looking at the other women didn't make him ache so hard his back teeth wobbled. He shrugged. "One man can't save them all."

Cougar cut his glance to Clint's groin where his erection throbbed. The other man's smile was slow, and promised future ribbing.

"You just keep shoveling that bull. Truth is you married up with Jenna Hennesey—"

"McKinnely," Clint corrected.

Cougar nodded and continued, "Truth is you married up with Jenna for the same reason I married up with Mara."

"And what would that be?"

Cougar laughed. It was a low, deeply satisfied sound that had both women glancing their way, Mara with love and Jenna with wary curiosity. Clint sighed. He really was going to have to do something about Jenna's unreasonable fear of Cougar.

Clint smiled at Jenna, which immediately had her ducking her head and fussing with Brianna's blanket. He had to wait two seconds before she lifted her red face and smiled back.

"It was the only way to get any peace of mind," Cougar admitted, continuing their conversation. "The woman had the damnedest knack for getting into trouble."

"Not to mention she had you walking bent double with hunger."

"Not to mention that." This time Cougar's smile was wryly mocking.

"I'm not likely to get any peace of mind until I find out who Jenna's afraid of."

"That's the truth." Cougar shook his hair back and all laughter faded. He suddenly looked as intense and as dangerous as his namesake. Clint sighed. Figures Jenna would choose that moment to look over. Her grip on Brianna tightened and her glance as it bounced off Clint's was worried.

"You put someone on watch?" Cougar asked.

"Not yet. I was wondering if you had any idea who was free." Cougar's taunting smile let him know exactly who Cougar had in mind before he said a word.

"Jackson's free, and I'm sure he wouldn't mind keeping an eye on someone as pretty as Jenna."

"I thought Jackson was tied up with those rustlers over at the Rocking C?" Clint didn't want the handsome, sweet-talking wrangler and bounty hunter anywhere near his wife.

"Nope. He cleaned them out last week."

Damn. "You sure he's not looking for a break?"

"I'm sure."

"Damn."

Cougar shrugged. "If Jenna is as loyal as you say you don't have anything to worry about, and short of Asa, myself, or you, Jackson is the best there is now that the reverend is out of commission."

"I know."

"We're talking about my niece and sister-in-law, Clint. I'm not taking chances because of your jealousy."

"Neither am I." Clint forced the words between his teeth. His mind knew what was right while every possessive instinct forbade another male from being anywhere near Jenna.

"Jesus, can't you just take her to bed, work that magic you do that has all the women falling at your feet, and wrap her around your finger?"

He wished. "It's not that easy."

"Why the hell not? She's your wife."

"And that just has her waiting for me to turn into a monster. The woman doesn't have an ounce of trust left in her body."

"So what are you going to do about it?"

Clint drained the last of his coffee and listened to the quiet murmur of the women's voices, watching Jenna's expression as she nodded to whatever Mara was telling her, wanting to reach over and smooth the tension from her shoulders with his fingers, wanting to tell her it was going to be all right.

"I figured I'd spoil her rotten and see how she takes to it."

Chapter Thirteen

Spoiling Jenna was easier said than done. The woman had a bone-deep distrust of anyone doing anything nice for her. Taking Bri so she could enjoy a bath had her looking nervous. Cooking supper so she could bathe Brianna made her drop things. Walking Bri through a crying jag had her alternating between biting her lip and making excuses. As if there was something shocking about a baby crying.

Clint leaned his shoulder against the doorjamb and watched Jenna as she sat on the bed with Bri, rocking her in her arms, alternating between soothing noises and outlandish promises. Sure enough the two of them had worked themselves into quite a lather. Bri was clearly taking her cues from her mother, screaming in time with Jenna's frantic promises, sobbing through her tense croons.

He pushed away from the door. "Here's the bottle."

Jenna turned those frantic blue eyes on him and he felt his heart trip over itself, redoubling its beat when he spotted Bri. Damn, he didn't like to see his girls upset.

"What's the matter, Button?" Brianna kicked her feet and screamed again, the hoarse wail ending on a pathetic warble. Jenna nudged the corner of her wide-open mouth with the bottle. "Here, Bri. Here's your bottle." A bit of milk dribbled in. "Take it, sweetie, and you'll feel all better."

Bri obviously disagreed. She turned her head, letting the milk dribble down her trembling chin. Jenna tried again. Bri screamed louder, her body as stiff as a board in Jenna's arms.

"She doesn't want it."

Clint touched the little one's flushed cheek. "She's just got her tail in a knot, Sunshine."

"She's suffering!" And Jenna clearly saw that as her fault. Clint could practically see the knots forming in her spine. He cupped Jenna's shoulder in his hand.

"She's showing off that fine temper she has."

"She's too little to have a temper!"

"Uh-huh." From where he sat, Bri had one hell of a temper, but he could see that wasn't a point Jenna was willing to concede.

Jenna shifted so her back was slightly to him, and resumed her rocking and promising. Bri resumed her screaming. In the doorway, Danny whined. Son of a bitch, if he wanted any peace, he was going to have to step in. He motioned the dog to stay while he kicked off his right boot. Before it hit the floor, Jenna's promises to the little girl had reached the ridiculous. When she got to the point where she promised to return her to Mara if she'd only eat, Clint had had enough.

His left boot hit the floor with a clunk. The mattress sagged as he swung up behind Jenna. The sudden movement got him one moment of peace as surprise silenced both Jenna and Brianna. He wrapped his arm around Jenna's soft waist, gathering the volume of white material comprising her nightdress in his hand as he did. One tug and Jenna's back was resting against his chest, her soft buttocks cradling his groin. He looped his ankles over her shins, keeping her in place.

"What are you doing?" Jenna asked in a muted squeak.

Clint bent his head to nuzzle her neck. The scent of roses immediately enveloped him in its familiar embrace. "Helping you calm down."

Jenna wiggled against him. "I'm not the one who needs calming."

He held her in place. "I disagree."

Jenna's snort was as close to an argument as he'd ever heard her give.

She nudged Bri's mouth again with the bottle. Bri arched her back and let loose a scream that must have originated in her toes.

Jenna renewed her wiggling. Clint let her try to get free while he reached around her with his longer arms and tugged the blanket out from around Brianna.

"A lot of times, new moms have trouble nursing their babies," he began conversationally. "They're nervous, and their milk doesn't flow."

"I don't have any milk."

He kissed her cheek at the regret in her husky voice. "But you're still nervous and it's up to your husband to ease things along."

"What do you know about new mothers?" Her tone bordered on insolent. He kissed her again for that bit of courage.

"For awhile I had thoughts of being a doctor and tagged along behind Doc whenever I had the chance."

"And instead you became a marshal?" She touched the bottle to Bri's quivering lips. The little one arched her spine and wailed. Against him, Jenna lurched as if suppressing a sob.

"Pretty much." The blanket came free and he snapped it open. Brianna silenced mid-wail, her puffy eyes following the flash of white. He folded the blanket into a triangle and put it on the bed. "Lay Bri down on the blanket, Sunshine."

"She'll cry."

"No you won't, will you, Button?" He rested his chin on Jenna's shoulder. Brianna sucked in her lip and wrinkled her nose, clearly ready to make a liar out of him.

"What are you going to do?" Jenna asked as she carefully laid Bri down.

"Something Dorothy taught me."

"I don't know anything." The sad whisper was more sorrowful than a wail.

"Watch and you will." He eased a fold over Brianna's tiny arm. Her forearm was hardly the width of his finger. Her deep blues eyes stared at him with such high hope. A surge of protectiveness welled from inside as he wrapped the edge against her fragile body. He'd tear apart any man who hurt her. "That's it, Button. You just let me get you snuggled in here, and you'll feel a lot better."

Jenna's body was unnaturally still against him, watching every move he made.

"The secret, Sunshine, is to get Bri to a place where she feels safe." He folded Bri's other arm into the blanket, gentling his touch to feather light for fear of breaking her delicate bones. "Secure," he added as he tucked the long end of the blanket under her opposite hip. "Then she won't worry so much about things that can't touch her."

He pulled the bottom flap up and tucked it around, cocooning the baby in a snug bundle. Bri hiccupped and let out a shuddering sigh. He slid his hands under her body, amazed as always at how tiny she was. She almost fit in his palm. He made a mental note to check with Doc to see if she was all right. He didn't remember other babies being this small. He eased her back into Jenna's arms.

"I think she might take that bottle now." There was a moment of hesitation before Jenna pulled her spine taut and took Brianna from him. He brushed his lips over her ear. "That's my girl."

This time when Jenna put the nipple to her mouth, Bri closed her lips around it. One tentative suck and then she went at the bottle the way she'd been screaming earlier. Like there was no tomorrow.

"She's drinking!"

"That she is." Jenna's cheek brushed his as she tried to turn to see him.

"Thank you."

"Nothing to thank me for. We're in this together."

Another silence as she absorbed his words, and then she relaxed against him, one muscle at a time, cautiously entrusting herself to his care. He eased her a little higher into his lap. The lamp threw the room into a yellow glow, doing little to push away the shadows, creating the illusion of a warmly lit haven comprised of that moment, in that room, in that bed. Clint pulled Jenna a little closer, for the first time holding his wife and his daughter in his arms.

The fire crackled in the small potbellied stove as he stroked his daughter's flushed cheek while she drank her bottle and recognized a miracle when he saw it. Last week, he'd been trying to think of a reason to keep getting up in the morning. One that didn't have anything to do with anger or violence. Now, he had two of the sweetest reasons a man could ever hope to have. And they'd fallen into his lap like two ripe plums. If that was the last bit of luck the good Lord threw his way, he'd die a contented man.

He leaned forward to get a better view. The blanket was brushing Brianna's cheek. He could see from her frown it was annoying her. He inched it away with his fingertip. Over the bottle her eyes meet his, and though Doc swore babies couldn't see at this age, he knew she saw him. Lord save her, he had the distinct impression she approved. And he got a taste of the uncertainty Jenna lived with daily at the trust and faith imparted with that one glance.

"Does she scare you the way she does me?" he asked against Jenna's ear.

Her response was a hushed whisper of truth. "She makes me feel like I can conquer the world and at the same time, be terrified of not doing it right."

That was pretty much the way they both made him feel. "Guess we'll have to get used to it."

Jenna's fingers dipped down from Brianna's hip to touch the inside of his knee. It was a fleeting touch, but one of the first she'd ever offered him. The comfort of her touch was almost as undoing as her words.

"You'll be a wonderful father."

"You basing that conviction on hope?" His drawl wasn't as smooth as he'd planned.

She shook her head. "You're strong and confident and have a very good heart."

"You haven't been watching close enough if that's the picture you have of me." And when she did see the big picture, he had a feeling she wasn't going to be as content with this arrangement.

The bunching of her jaw muscles alerted him to the fact that, while she didn't dispute his claim, she wasn't agreeing with it. There was something very appealing about a woman with a stubborn streak. Made a man just want to devil her into revealing more of it, and then continue the deviling until he coaxed her around it. Except he didn't want to devil her into changing her mind. He wanted to devil her into revealing how deep her conviction was, which was a fool's journey, because her belief couldn't be that deep.

He settled for the alternative, which was enjoying the view down the loose neck of her nightgown. He hitched his arm up, pressing her breasts higher, deepening that enticing valley. His cock, already hard, surged painfully. Jenna didn't have any idea what he was doing. How a twice-married woman could be so naive baffled him.

"Would you like to know how I'd be with you, Jenna, if Brianna was ours and this was our first time together with our daughter?" He kissed her ear, feeling her shiver caress his chest. He kissed it again as he brought his hands up to the tiny buttons at the neckline of her gown. She held still, not looking right or left—not moving. Then, ever so subtly, she nodded her head.

"I'd be so tender, Sunshine. So careful." He slid his hands inside the neckline of her nightdress. Her skin was smooth and warm against his fingertips. Very white against the darkness of his hands. He cupped her breasts in his palms. She tensed even as she filled his hands to overflowing. "Ah Sunshine, you have beautiful breasts."

"You don't think I'm a cow?" The question came out haltingly, revealing a vulnerability he needed to soothe.

"In case you haven't noticed, I'm a big man. A little woman would be lost beneath me."

"Cougar likes Mara, and he's as big as you."

"And I like you." He skimmed his hands toward the tips, keeping his touch light.

"Oh." She clearly didn't have a rebuttal for that.

He ended the caress with the barest brush of her nipples. He retreated before she could finish her breath. He did it again, sliding his hands outward, pressing a little harder, smiling as she pretended not to notice what he was doing, but was clearly intent on every nuance as witnessed by how still she held herself. And the way she held her breath every time he got near her nipples.

Like now. They were hard and swollen—eager for his touch. He gave it to her, a little harder, rolling the sensitive peaks between his fingers before working his way back to the plump base.

"Sometimes," he explained, squeezing gently as he had as much of her breast in his hands as he could gather, "when a woman is nervous and her milk won't come down, her husband can help her by stimulating her." Her breath shuddered out of her lungs as he massaged the resilient flesh in his hands. "Finding the right stroke and pressure to make her relax." He tweaked her nipples smiling at her halting intake of breath. "A woman's milk flows better when she's relaxed."

"But I don't have any milk."

"But you're my wife, and this is the first time we're feeding our daughter together, and I want you to have the full experience."

He centered her nipples in his palms and pressed. The succulent flesh bloomed in his hands. She sighed and her head dropped back against his shoulder. She was giving him more than her permission. She was giving him her trust. He let his fingers cup the sides of her breasts, controlling the expansion as he controlled the moment.

"That's it, Sunshine. Lean back and let me take care of you."

"I'm feeding the baby."

"And I'm taking care of you."

He rolled her nipples in his palms, tilting his hand so that her breasts sprang back into his palms. They were heavy and full and if the baby wasn't in her lap, he would have turned her and tasted them. He resumed the milking motion, increasing the strength of each stroke, taking his cue from her increased respiration until, with the fourth pass, he captured her nipples between his thumbs and forefingers and squeezed, increasing the pressure until she moaned and pressed back against him.

"Ah, that's it then," he murmured, tucking her shoulders under his arms, keeping her still for the pleasure he wanted to give her. "Right there?"

It was a rhetorical question. He didn't need verbal proof of her pleasure. The involuntary shifting of her body against his, and her breathless moan told him all he needed to know.

He did it again, hungry for her response, her whimpers of pleasure, holding the pressure for a heartbeat more, reveling in her openness to him. Needing it.

Out of the corner of his eye he saw Brianna turn away from the bottle.

"I think Brianna needs to be burped." He let the words drift down her neck, the goose bumps that sprang up equally pleasing.

Her head snapped up. "Oh."

He relaxed his grip, sliding his hands back until they were once again just supporting her heavy breasts. He felt her blush in his hands before he saw it on her cheeks. She carefully sat Brianna up, supporting her with a hand on her chest. Brianna sat there, her big blue eyes full of surprise as if she wasn't sure how she got there, and then they filled with intelligent curiosity as she viewed her world from this new position. Clint couldn't suppress a smile. She was such a little dickens.

Three taps on her little back had the child burping loud enough to have Danny lifting his head off the floor. As soon as the noise abated, Brianna's head jerked and one corner of her mouth kicked up in an unmistakable expression.

"She smiled!" Jenna exclaimed turning to him. "Did you see that? She smiled."

"She sure did," Clint kissed the corner of Jenna's mouth, watching Brianna bob in her blanket, her movements jerky, her pleasure at being able to do them contagious. "And over a belch no less. That child's going to be a hellion for sure."

"She is not!" Jenna kissed Brianna on her beaming face as she bucked in her blanket and smiled again, this time getting both corners of her mouth into the action. "She's perfect."

Clint looked at the square little face topped by all that spiky hair and shook his head. The girl had hellion written all over her.

"Now that would be a darned shame." He tickled Brianna's cheek. She turned instinctively toward his finger her mouth open, looking like a little bird. "I always thought a little bit of hellion was an attractive quality in a woman."

Jenna stilled again in that way he was beginning to understand meant that she was thinking.

"It's a woman's duty to submit to a man." She threw that piece of wisdom out like a shield.

His "hmmm" was noncommittal as he kissed the side of her neck.

"In all things to follow his direction." She was obviously quoting an oft-heard dictate.

He pulled the pins from her hair, and the heavy mass fell in a silken waterfall between them, pooling where his chest met her back before sliding off to the side. Damn, he'd love to wrap himself in her hair.

"What if the man's wrong?"

"What?" She sounded shocked.

"What if the man's wrong?"

There was another of those long pauses. "A woman must trust and pray God will provide direction."

If that wasn't the biggest load of bull he'd every heard. "Sunshine, I've met a lot men in my time, and some of them wouldn't hear God's guidance if he boomed it in their ears. What does a woman do then?"

There was defeated pain in her voice as she said, "She prays and does the best she can."

"Is that what you did with your first husband, baby? Pray and endure?"

She shook her head. "I'm not a very good wife."

He hugged her simply because he'd never held anyone who sounded like she needed it more. "The son of a bitch didn't deserve you."

"I was willful and disobedient."

He'd had a gut full of her defending that worthless piece of shit. "He was a drunk and a bully and a few straws short of a bale."

"He was my husband."

"And I for one am glad he's dead."

She didn't have an answer for that. Brianna screwed up her face, clearly ready to lay into her mother again. Clint gently flicked her cheek with his finger. He couldn't allow that.

"Brianna wants the rest of her bottle, Jenna."

She jumped and hurriedly propped Brianna up on her knee. As soon as the nipple touched her cheek the little girl turned and latched onto it, sucking strongly but without that desperate edge, as before.

"She's a strong eater," Jenna said, pleasure in her voice.

"Yes, she is." It was probably the wrong time, but Clint couldn't stomach the thought of Brianna growing up to be a shadow of the woman she was supposed to be. "She's going to be a strong woman, Jenna. I don't want her growing up thinking she has to kiss the ass of every man she meets."

"She'll never find a husband if she's willful."

"Then she won't, but no one's going to tell my daughter she's worthless."

"You're a man. You don't understand what it's like." He tipped her head back with a finger under her chin until her head rested on his shoulder.

"I'm getting a glimmer of what things have been like for you, but they're not going to be like that for Brianna because we're not going to let them be that way."

"We're not?" Her eyes were huge as they met his.

"No." He cupped her jaw and turned her head so that her cheek pressed against his collarbone. "We're going to raise her to be strong—to think—and we'll protect her from any son of a bitch who tries to put her down."

"We may not always be available."

"If we aren't, then Cougar or Asa will be stepping up to kick ass. And trust me, you haven't seen an ass-whupping until you've seen those two take someone to task."

"I'd forgotten..." Her voice drifted off on what might have been a note of wonder. And hope.

"Well. I haven't. Brianna's a McKinnely now and we take care of our own. If I'm not available when there's a need, she's got a family to watch out for her." He kissed her lips, stroking her cheek, willing her to trust him. "And so do you."

"Thank you." She ducked her head away from his gaze. There was no increase of confidence in her words. Clearly she didn't think anyone would hit the ground running for her. He tipped her gaze back to his.

"Sunshine, I'm very good at taking care of what's mine, and you're mine now."

"I know." She didn't blink or flinch.

"I want you happy, baby." He stroked her cheek beside her mouth. "I want to see these dimples at least twenty times a day."

Her eyes widened briefly. "You do?"

"Yes, and not just because they get me hard." While her mind wrapped around the knowledge that he found her dimples lust-provoking, he pressed on. "You can be as willful and as disobedient as you like as long as, at the end of the day, you're smiling."

"Why?" She blinked twice.

He rubbed his nose on hers. "Because I've waited a long time to have a wife to pamper and spoil, and as determined as you are to take the fun out of it, I'm just as determined to enjoy myself."

"You are?"

"Yup." He rested his forehead on her temple. "I'm not planning on settling for less than happy."

She didn't answer right away. Her gaze left his and she stilled against him. When she looked back into his eyes, her answer almost ripped the heart from his chest. "I don't know if I know how to be that."

He kissed her very, very gently on her lips. "Then maybe we'll get to have some fun figuring that out together."

"Do you know how to be happy?"

The question hung between them in the quiet room, and as much as he wanted to be glib and smooth, he found he couldn't be. Not with her, so he gave her the truth. "Not anymore."

This time when he touched his lips to hers, she was ready for him, kissing him back, tenderly, leading with that generous heart of hers, whispering into his mouth, "I want to make you happy."

The words went through his system like a flame. He shifted her higher, held her closer, welcoming her softness even while he felt driven to protect her from herself. "I'll be happy as long as you are."

She shook her head, her mouth set in a mutinous line, checked Brianna, and then tentatively laid her head on his chest again. "I want more."

"You're just going to have to accept that I'm past redemption in some ways."

"No. I'm not accepting that."

"You might not have a choice." He slid his hands up over her arms. Her muscles were tight under his fingers. She was scared of bucking him, even on something as sweet as her determination to make him happy. She was so soft inside and out, and yet so damned incredibly strong in ways he couldn't be. He massaged the tense muscles, keeping his touch light.

"There's always a choice." How she could believe that after all that had happened to her was one of the mysteries of what made her who she was.

"Not in this."

"I won't be happy unless you are." Stubborn laced her husky voice and fought the purpose of his massage. He sighed and set his thumbs on either side of her spine, just inside her shoulder blades and worked at the tension there.

"Okay, baby. How about we agree that we'll both try to get acquainted with happy, but neither will expect too much."

"Okay."

She really thought he meant that. He kissed the top of her head, breathing the scents of roses and woman. There was no way he was going to be content until she smiled from dawn to dusk. He looked down at little Bri. Her eyes were closed and her lips slack around the nipple. A trickle of milk dribbled down her chin.

"She's asleep," he whispered.

"Oh. Good." Jenna made as if to get up. He kept her still with a hand on her shoulder.

"I'll put her to bed."

He slid around her, bracing himself above her as he eased his feet to the floor. His hair swung down around her face. To his surprise she smiled, tentatively touching the dark strands. Her "I like your hair" was as shy as her touch on his chest. Lust ricocheted through his body like a bullet shot off in a barrel. He couldn't move. His cock ached and throbbed. She leaned forward and pressed a kiss to the hollow of his throat. It seared him to his toes. He took a breath. It didn't help. His drawl was a hoarse parody of its normal tones.

"What brought that on?"

Her gaze fell from his as she whispered, "You're a nice man, Clint McKinnely."

"I'd probably believe that if you looked me in the eye when you said it."

"You're a nice man." She met and held his gaze, but with effort.

She had a lot to learn about him. He slid his hands under Brianna, lifted her up, and smiled at Jenna.

"Tell me that again after I get Button here settled and see what it gets you."

Chapter Fourteen

Tell me again and see what it gets you.

Jenna bit her lip and followed Clint's progress across the room. He paused when the floorboard squeaked under his weight, jostling Brianna slightly to keep her asleep. She'd never seen a man holding a baby before. Never dreamed a man would want to, but Clint seemed to actually enjoy it. Brianna was so tiny in his massive arms, a speck against his chest. He held her close, not too tight, but with an instinctive protectiveness that screamed "Mine."

She had no doubt he'd die for Brianna.

As much as every instinct told her not to take Clint up on his dare—and that's what it was, a dare—she was going to. Dry-mouthed and shaking in her nightgown, she was going to repeat her statement. Just as soon as he got back to her. Which hopefully wouldn't be before she got some spit in her mouth, because right now she wouldn't be able to yell "fire" if the room were ablaze.

He scared her so much. Not because he was big and could hurt her. She'd been hurt so many times another scar wasn't even going to make a dent, but Clint could hurt her way down deep where the last of her dreams hid out. Part of her wanted to give him those dreams, but she couldn't because there were things that he couldn't know about her if she wanted him to respect her.

Clint turned from depositing Bri in the drawer that was functioning as a makeshift bed until her brand-new crib came in. He grabbed a clean towel off the stack on the dresser and tossed it onto the bed beside Jenna. His black eyes smoldered, and the way the corner of his mouth kicked up set her heart to racing. Clint's lean, dark fingers went to the buttons on his white shirt.

"Tell me again, Jenna."

The first button slipped its hole. His gaze dropped to her chest. The set of his mouth went from serious to sensuous in the blink of an eye. She looked down. Dear God, her breasts were exposed to the nipples! The heat started in her chest and rose to her cheeks. Clint's chuckle drifted through the quiet room.

When she looked back up, he was standing only two feet away, his legs slightly spread, wide shoulders set in a clear challenge. The last button on his shirt slipped free of its mooring. He hooked the shirttails behind his wrists and put his hands on his lean hips, exposing the hard, muscled expanse of his torso, and the thick bulge of his cock as it stretched down his thigh beneath the worn material of his denims.

"Tell me again, Sunshine." His drawl was deep, hoarse, persuasive.

Jenna licked her dry lips and sought the courage to take him up on his dare. She dawdled, looking up, her gaze slowly climbing the rock-hard muscles slabbing his stomach, riding the hills and valleys of his abdomen until she reached the solid wall of his chest. The deep scars from where he was burned only accentuated the power inherent in all of that dense muscle. She forced her gaze higher, lingering at the hollow of his throat where the force of his pulse belied his easygoing drawl. And ran out of courage.

"If I do, will you think me forward?"

"Tell me and find out." He shrugged out of his shirt. It fell to the floor with a soft click of buttons striking wood.

"You're not Jack." She clenched her fingers in her gown, wrestling with the need to do as he wished, and the rules she'd been raised with.

"No."

"You won't trick me."

He cocked his head as if considering that before admitting, "Only on April Fool's day, and only if you let me catch you napping."

His hands went to the fastening of the denims riding low on his hips. He undid the top two buttons, revealing the dark line of hair arrowing down from his navel. Her mouth went dry even as the outrageous urge to run her tongue down the groove of muscle slanting inward from his hipbone swept over her. To sink her teeth into that red-brown flesh, to see if he tasted as good as she remembered. The bite of pain in her palms alerted her to the fact that she was pulling her gown so hard it was in danger of ripping. She gentled her hold and groped for reality.

"It's my woman's time."

"I know."

"We can't."

"So you said." He shrugged, and the slightest hint of a smile touched his mouth. The last button on his pants gave way. The thin line of hair broadened to a thick patch as he spread the heavy material.

"I'm dirty." Embarrassment choked her voice to a whisper. His finger under her chin lifted her face. She wouldn't—couldn't—meet his eyes. His thumb brushed her lips.

"All your woman's time means is that you'll be hotter, wetter, and be able to take me easier." His thumb brushed her lips. "And Sunshine…" The tap on her lips was an order. She met his gaze, mortification burning her from the inside out. "You couldn't be dirty if you spent three days in a wallow."

Whore. Filthy bitch. The words swarmed out of the past, striking her like blows. She pulled her chin free and ducked her head. Strong hands on her arms lifted her and tossed her up and back as a low masculine laugh surrounded her like a hug. It happened so fast she didn't have time to scream. The mattress cushioned her landing. She clutched the front of her gown closed as she glared at Clint.

He stood at the foot of the bed, two hands on the edge of the mattress, one knee firmly planted to the right of her foot. He leaned toward her. His long black hair swung forward, giving his already handsome face a primitive cast as he looked up at her from under his brows. Laughter and lust shimmered about him in a seductive combination. His shoulder muscles flexed in an intimidating display of power as he rested his hands on the mattress on either side of her knees.

"Tell me again, Sunshine."

She propped herself up on her elbows and crept back. He placed his knee on the hem of her nightgown, holding her there as he put his other knee on the bed, looming over her—dark and threatening.

"Tell me," he ordered, his drawl as intent as his expression. Holding her gaze, he lowered his head, smiling slightly as he nipped her thigh just at her knee. It didn't hurt, but caused all sorts of alarming sensations to streak through her. She swallowed hard and tugged at the edge of her gown while keeping one hand firmly clamped on the bodice. He smiled a purely predatory smile and continued to advance.

Fear fought with a foreign skitter of excitement as the mattress dipped by her hip and his head lowered again, this time letting her feel his teeth high on the inside of her thigh.

"Let go of the gown, Sunshine." She stopped tugging at the hem. She felt his smile against her thigh, a brief relief from the pressure and then his teeth touched just to the inside of her hipbone. "Let go with the other hand."

She did, reluctantly. As if he sensed that she didn't know what to do with her hands when they weren't protecting her modesty, he drawled, "Put them over your head."

She did, instinctively putting one inside the other. He moved again, enfolding her wrists in his hand, pinning her arms to the mattress.

He held her captive, his big body trapping hers, his dark gaze holding hers. He was above her. Around her. Every breath she took drew his familiar smoky scent into her lungs, binding them further together until there wasn't any distance between them. Emotional or physical. She was his. In the eyes of God. In the eyes of the law. In the depths of her soul.

"Clint?" She wasn't surprised when he ignored the quavery question, but when he dipped his head and nuzzled aside the lapels of her nightgown, she found her voice. "What are you doing?"

"Clearing the way." The sin they preached against in church wasn't as wicked as his expression.

"We agreed—"

"I agreed that I wouldn't make love to you if you didn't want it during your woman's time," he finished for her.

"Than what are you doing?"

He kissed the valley between her breasts. His lips were firm and dry, his breath moist, his evening whiskers a delicious rasp on the inside of her breasts. Her nipples drew taut as he used his chin to fully expose her left breast.

"Making you want it."

She should have seen that coming, but the man addled her brain to the point of no return. She closed her eyes against the rampage of sensation swarming over her. She was the slut her father accused her of being. And she was beginning not to care.

Moist heat engulfed her nipple, followed by a gentle suction. Tiny trickles of pleasure wove out through her torso pulling invisible wires of need taut. She squirmed and pushed up. Clint's deep chuckle buffeted her sensitive nipple with deep throbs of pleasure. He rubbed the rough base of his chin over her nipple, using his beard to lightly abrade her sensitive tip. Each short pass made her gasp at the fire that streaked straight to her womb.

"Tell me again, Sunshine."

"Tell you what?" She arched into his mouth needing more. She couldn't remember anything beyond the ache in her nipple and the anticipation of his mouth.

"Tell me again what a *nice* man I am." He nipped her with his lips. Sparks flashed behind her eyelids as he did it again, not giving her time to react, demanding a response from her, laughing when she cried out, sucking harder when she pushed up. He released her breast with a soft pop. Cool air washed over her damp skin, making her shiver.

"You're going to have to be quiet, Sunshine."

"What?" The next brush if his chin had her crying out again. She couldn't catch a full breath. Her nipple ached. Her pussy throbbed. His lips came down on hers just in time to catch her moan.

"We don't want to wake Button," he whispered against her lips.

No. She didn't want to do that. She didn't want anything to interfere with this. Clint made her feel so wild, and yet somehow, so incredibly safe. As though there was nothing she could do or say that he would hold against her. As though she could trust him.

His lips parted hers. His breath mingled with hers a heartbeat before he slid his tongue into her mouth, his taste flooding her senses. He tasted clean, this man who'd pulled her from the flames, away from the death that had looked so enticing, and made her live. This man who could make her feel when she was numb, live when she wanted to die, and hope when common sense said to give up. He tasted of power and fantasy and she couldn't resist.

She touched his tongue with hers. He moaned and levered himself over her. The scars on his chest teased her swollen nipples. His hand tightened on her wrists and he deepened the kiss, his tongue delving deep. Demanding. Receiving. She gave him everything that he asked for, matching him thrust for thrust, stroke for stroke.

He broke the kiss. Her gasping breath was loud in the room. She closed her eyes. The kiss he pressed to the corner of her mouth was incredibly gentle, in sharp contrast to the violent passion she could feel humming beneath his skin.

"Tell me, Jenna." The nip he placed under her chin was not as tender as the others. Some of that tension in him was anger, she realized. She tugged on her hands. He let her go. She gave him what he wanted.

"You're a nice man, Clint McKinnely." The tension surged in his body again and that cold look broke over his face. She cupped his cheeks in her hands, smoothing the tension in his jaw with her thumbs. "I know you've told me not to see you as nice, but I can't help it. You're nice to me, to Brianna, and you make me feel like I've never felt before."

"How's that?" He turned his mouth into her palm and tickled the center with his tongue.

"Special." She skirted his gaze.

"You are special, Sunshine." Speaking softly so that each word breathed new life into her soul, he found her mouth with his, mating their lips in the way with which she was becoming familiar,

"Only to you." Tears welled.

"To anyone with half a brain," he growled deep in his throat.

"Why can't I feel the same way about you?"

"Because it's not the same."

"You keep saying I'm yours."

"You are."

"Then that makes you mine, too." It was the boldest statement she'd ever made. Women just didn't contradict men, let alone lay claim to them. She closed her eyes against her own temerity. Clint's teeth tested the pad of her thumb in a sharp nip. She kept her eyes closed.

"Look at me, baby."

"Are you mad again?" She wasn't going to open her eyes if he was mad.

"No." His hair slid over her cheeks on a smooth caress as he pressed his forehead to hers.

She cracked her eyes and checked. He didn't look mad, just fierce and…amused.

"Maybe if you were mean to me I could see you differently," she suggested, wrapping her arms around his neck. He touched her cheek with his finger. He was so gentle with her.

"I'll work on it."

"And I'll work on thinking less of you." She pulled him down to her. He buried his face in the curve of her neck. His shoulders shook under her hands.

"Sunshine, you are something." The amusement in his voice soothed her worry.

"I'm glad you think so." And she was. More than glad. She opened her palms on his back, enjoying the flex of muscle beneath her hands as he kissed his way down her chest until he got to her breasts. There he lingered, running his lips over every inch, lifting her breasts so he could kiss the underside. Shards of fire shot out from everywhere his mouth touched. Her nails dug into his back. Her gasp as he curled his tongue around her nipple drew another laugh from his lips.

"Want that again?"

She nodded. He gave it to her and then some, pushing her breasts together, drawing her nipples into his mouth, sucking them gently and then harder and harder with drawing motions of his mouth, keeping pace with the clenching of her fingers. When she whimpered, he lashed them with his tongue until she writhed on the bed.

She felt bereft when he drew back, withdrawing his heat but not his passion. That simmered between them, arcing across the distance. She clung to his shoulders as he stood. He stared at her, a smile ghosting his lips as he towered above her. She moved to draw the comforter over her. He shook his head.

"Let me look at you."

She did, feeling foolish lying there with her hands reaching for him and her body clamoring for his attention. He stared for so long that she couldn't bear it. She needed to move, to do something. She remembered what he'd asked her before. As his hands went to his waistband, hers went to her breasts.

At first she just held them, but when he swore and his hands froze on his fly, power rushed through her. She might be a mere woman, no match for Clint in muscle, but she had some control here. She ran her fingertips up and down her breasts, tracing patterns on the smooth surface. The darts of pleasure caught her by surprise. She hadn't expected that, biting her lip as tingles shot out from her hands, experimenting with what felt good.

"Son of a bitch, Jenna. You're going to make me come."

"What's wrong with that?" she asked, some demon possessing her voice and drawing the words past her caution.

"Not a goddamned thing." His mouth thinned to a straight line. Desire chiseled his features. He shoved his pants down. They caught on the swell of his cock and he swore again, drawing his cock out before kicking them aside. "Hold those pretty breasts up for me, Sunshine."

She did.

"Higher," he ordered in a deep voice as he pumped his cock through his fist. She couldn't take her eyes off of the head of his cock as it appeared and disappeared in his fist. The head was broad and fat, dark with desire and dripping with moisture. For her. She lifted her breasts as high as she could so that they pulled at her ribs. Clint nodded.

"Now push them together." She did, following his gaze, seeing what he saw. The large mounds of her breasts rose high, almost to her chin, the cleavage between them looking deep and somehow erotically inviting. "Offer them to me, Sunshine."

She opened her fingers, resting her breasts on her palms, holding them out in an open invitation. A muscle in his cheek jerked. A quick glance down revealed another bead of seed glistening on the head of his cock. She licked her lips, remembering his flavor, the way he'd shaken against her as he'd come.

"Do you want it?" Clint asked, his dark fingers framing the pearly drop. A glance at his face and she knew what her answer would be.

"Yes."

"How much?"

She answered with the truth. "I want to pleasure you."

"You do that just by breathing." He smiled.

"The way you want," she elaborated. He paused, and uncertainty flooded her confidence. "Please."

"Shhh!" His hand cupped her cheek, instantly soothing her. "Keep your hands on your breasts and don't panic."

She bit her lip before blurting out, "I'm never sure what to do."

"You're seducing me beautifully."

"I am?" She couldn't call his smile gentle, but his, "Yes" was infinitely so.

"Without taking your hands off your breasts, scoot over here to the side of the bed." It was awkward and she felt foolish, but by the time her hip hit the edge of the mattress, his smile was gone and the hard planes of his face settled into harsh lines of passion. A quick glance showed his cock was steadily leaking pre-come. He leaned forward, bringing his cock closer and closer until the head of it touched the tip of her breast, bathing the turgid nipple in silky wet heat.

"Lick it off." Keeping her gaze locked with his passionate one, she tilted her breast and lowered her mouth. As her lips parted he whispered, "Slowly, baby. Nice and slow."

She followed his orders to the letter, holding his gaze as she swirled her tongue around the pebbled nipple, lapping delicately at the pink flesh, shivering as his eyes flared and his grip spasmed on his cock. When she couldn't find another drop of salty fluid, she leaned back. He leaned in, treating her other nipple to the same bath. He didn't have to tell her what to do. She knew what he wanted and loved giving it to him. Every catch in his breath, every flicker of his eyes spiked her own passion until the glide of her own tongue over her flesh began to feel like his.

The bed dipped as he knelt on it. She rolled into his thigh, reaching for that beautiful cock. He caught her hand and brought it to his mouth. "Not yet."

"Why not?"

"I don't want to come yet."

"You're that close?" She couldn't believe the conversations she got into with him.

"You have that effect on me." His smiled — a tight, strained twist of his lips. In contrast, her smile came easily. She turned and kissed the inside of his thigh while holding his gaze.

"I like that."

The mattress dipped as his hands came down by her shoulders.

"Are you gloating woman?" he asked as he straddled her torso. She bit her lip as his heavy cock dragged across her stomach, setting her belly to quivering.

"Yes."

He laughed as he sat back on his heels, the thick length of his cock lying like a vertical brand across her ribs, the head resting in the valley between her breasts. His hands brushed hers from her breasts.

"I'll take over here." She closed her eyes as the rough warmth of his strong hands enveloped her breasts. She just loved the way he touched her. All that strength blanketed with gentleness. He squeezed and her breath caught. Fear mixed with passion as the pressure increased.

"Open your eyes, baby." She did, automatically falling into the order, only to fall into his passion as he shook his head at her. "Who's touching you?"

"You are," she whispered as he continued to squeeze and release, each time just a little harder than the previous.

"And who am I?"

"Clint."

"Then why are you afraid?"

"I'm not—"

"I can see and feel your tension." He shook his head again, drawing her breasts up as he squeezed. She didn't have an answer that he wanted to hear. "Did Jack hurt you this way?"

She nodded. She bit her lip as his fingers slid up to her nipples. How could one man's hands feel so good when another's had felt like a violation?

Clint had figured as much from the way she lay so tense under his hands. Breathlessly excited while nervously expectant. Clint pinched Jenna's nipples lightly. They immediately drew tight. Her stomach muscles jerked under his cock, massaging his balls as she quivered beneath him. Her breasts were incredibly sensitive. The lightest of tugs had her body jerking.

"I'm not Jack."

"I know."

"I'm not going to hurt you."

She nodded.

"But I am going to make you come."

Her eyes flew wide, and she blinked.

"Is that okay with you?"

"Yes."

"Good. Then go over behind the screen and prepare yourself for me."

She blushed fiery red as soon as she understood his meaning, but she did as told, returning to the bed with her head down and her hair shielding her face. As soon as she got close enough, he hooked his hand behind her neck, pulled her to him, and kissed her hard before helping her back up on the bed.

"Lie down now."

Impossibly, her face got redder. He laughed, knelt on the bed, and rearranged them until her buttocks rested on his thighs and the length of his cock snuggled into the hot, wet folds of her pussy. She blinked again, that plump lower lip sliding between her teeth, her expression one of doubtful expectation.

"We'll make a mess," she whispered.

"That's what the towel is for," he whispered back, leaning forward until the hard points of her nipples snuggled into his chest the way his cock nestled deeper into the embrace of her pussy. As she gasped and arched under him, he pulled her lip free of her teeth and into his mouth.

He sucked it lightly, wanting to smile when her eyes flew wide and she jerked back the way she always did. He held on, not letting her pull back from him or the pleasure she felt, working his palm behind her head, tilting it back, releasing her lip long enough to murmur, "Don't fight it, Jenna. Let me make you feel good."

Her eyes closed. She was running from him again.

"Open your eyes."

She did, reluctantly, all the conflict she felt inside revealed as her lids lifted.

She was so open and so vulnerable. She filled him with the need to give her the world, while at the same time wanting to shelter her from it. He probed the corner of her mouth with his tongue. Against the base of his cock, her pussy clenched.

"You liked that." She nodded, a sheen of tears in her eyes.

"Why the tears?" He caught one at the corner with his thumb before it could spill over.

"You make me feel so much."

"I just want you to be happy."

"It scares me."

"Why?" He cupped her breast in his hand, giving her the pressure he knew she enjoyed.

"You want everything."

"Yes." He did. He stroked his thumb over her pert nipple. She lurched against him, her pussy riding his cock hard. She jerked again.

Her nails dug into his thighs as he speared his cock up through its warm nest. He wanted her defenseless before him. He wanted her trust, her innocence, her hope, her passion. He wanted everything. Every nuance of who she was.

"You make me feel too much," she gasped.

He shook his head, tenderness welling to mix again with lust. "I won't take you past your limits, Jenna."

"You already have."

"No. I've just taken you past your fear." He wiped another tear from her eyes. He bent to her breast. Her "What's the difference?" whispered over his head. He kissed her nipple gently and smiled. "Pleasure."

He opened his mouth just enough for her nipple to slide inside. Her whole body tightened as she waited. He stretched the moment out, keeping her on edge until her breath caught in her throat and her pussy pulsed against his cock, spilling her hot juices over his aching balls. He circled her nipple with his tongue, riding the intriguing bumps and ridges, probing the dip in the center. She shuddered and tried to arch again. He held her in place with his weight and his fingers in her hair. By the time he was done with loving her, the only reaction she'd have to his mouth on her breast would be sighs of pleasure. He kissed his way down the side of her breast.

"You're going to come for me Jenna," he murmured into the deep valley. She bit her lip and skirted his gaze. He caught the drop of perspiration on his tongue as it trickled down the slope of her breast. "And then you're going to come again, simply because it'll please me."

"What about you?" Her voice was a tense grope for sound.

"I'll come when you're satisfied."

"But you're ready now."

He was more than ready. Being wrapped in her heat was pure torture. His cock ached and a steady stream of pre-come dribbled past his control, but the drive to bury himself in her was nothing compared to his need to watch her flower for him. To see her lose her sense of self, to know that she'd put her trust in him, and to know that he'd delivered. He wanted that more than he wanted his next breath.

"It'll be better for the wait." Her pussy clenched against him and he pressed his open mouth to her flesh. His good intentions took a dive.

Son of a bitch, she was going to be the death of him. For sure he wasn't going to last as long as he'd hoped.

As if she felt that momentary lapse, she touched his hair and whispered, "You don't have to wait."

She was too generous, too willing to put him first. Her giving nature and her soft heart ganged up with his selfish side to deny her the pleasure she deserved. For a moment, he was tempted. But only for a moment. This was his Jenna. His one good thing. He was her husband. The one person in the world she should be able to count on to put her first. And tonight she was definitely coming first. Hot, hard, and long. And as many times as he could manage.

"No trying to talk me out of it. I've made up my mind."

"You have?"

"Yes. You come first." He tested the firmness of her breast with his teeth. The heat that surged against his lips let him know that she'd gotten his meaning.

"I like the way you pinken up for me." He arched her head back, kissing the hollow of her throat before returning to her breast. "And I like the way your breath catches when you feel my teeth.

"The way you shiver when I kiss your breasts." He kissed his way down over her collarbone before pressing a kiss into the upper curve of her chest. He moved down, smiling when she sucked in a breath and held it as he trailed his hand from the back of her neck, down the side of her throat, and along the ridge of her collarbone until he got to the crease of her arm. He lingered there a bit, teasing those betraying goose bumps to the fore before skimming his thumb across her other nipple.

"But I especially like the way you arch and moan when I take these sensitive little nipples into my mouth." She did more than arch and moan—she grabbed his hair and pulled him closer. He was happy to oblige, taking as much as he could, suckling her lightly at first, ignoring her demands for more, keeping it easy until a fine sweat broke out over her body, and she was yanking on his hair while the sweetest pleas for more broke from her lips. Against the length of his cock, her pussy spasmed with equal desperation.

"That's it, baby," he murmured, flexing his hips so that his shaft stroked in a smooth glide along her clit in time with his fingers. "Burn for me."

"I need you now." She tossed her head as she bit her lip.

"I want to see you going up in flames first."

"Please."

He looked up. Her lips were full and red from her biting, her cheeks flushed, and her eyes glowed dark with a need that had his balls pulling up tight. He gave her what they both wanted. Changing his pace, increasing the pressure of his hand and mouth, judging from her high-pitched whimpers when he had it right, knowing from her staggered breath and inner tension when he could give her more. He lashed her nipple with his tongue before sucking it hard, drawing her deep into his mouth, then pinching her other nipple between his fingers and holding tight while jiggling her breast.

Her climax caught them both by surprise. Her legs snapped tight, her back arched, and her breath exploded from her lungs before she jackknifed up into him. He caught her against his chest, holding her to him as her tears flooded his chest and her juices drenched his groin.

"Son of a bitch, Sunshine," he muttered, lifting her limp body, holding her with one arm under her hips while he positioned his cock at the still-twitching entrance to her pussy, lowering her gently onto his shaft, moaning as her heat seared him, pulling his balls up tight. "It's damn fun playing with you."

She took all of him in one smooth stroke, her quivering muscles offering no resistance to the firm push of his cock, shuddering against him as he seated himself to the hilt, her head falling back as the broad base spread her to her limit.

He kissed the exposed hollow of her throat, tasting the salt of her passion and her tears, wallowing in her warmth and acceptance. No matter how he came at her, she welcomed him with open arms. Like now. He raised her again and she whimpered a protest, but wrapped her arms around neck.

"And to think," he whispered against her ear as he lowered her onto the thick wedge of his cock again. "I've just gotten started."

Chapter Fifteen

"Wake up, Sunshine, it's time to have fun."

Jenna stirred, her eyes closed. She stretched languidly in the warm bed, luxuriating in the softness, and a solid night's sleep. The fact that Brianna hadn't woken her penetrated her complacency.

She was moving before her eyes opened. "Bri!"

"Is fine." Clint caught her and held her against his chest as he fussed with the pillows. With her cheek pressed against his shoulder, she inhaled his scent. She just loved the way he always smelled of smoke and the outdoors. The smoky smell was a little stronger today, meaning he'd been up for a while. Long enough to have a cigarette.

"How long have you been up?"

"Button wanted to see the sunrise."

"I would have taken care of her."

"You needed some sleep. And she's decided to take a nap now so drink up and enjoy the peace." He eased her back onto the pillows he'd stacked, and pushed a cup of coffee into her hand.

A strand of hair fell over her brow. She reached to move it out of the way, but Clint's hand intercepted hers, taking care of the matter for her. As he was always doing. She took a sip of her coffee. It was hot and rich with just the right amount of cream, though short a couple of sugar chips. She hid her grimace in another sip.

The mattress dipped as Clint sat on the edge.

"Coffee all right?" he asked slipping his arm around her back, pulling her into his side.

"Perfect." She leaned against the shoulder he provided. "Thank you for taking care of Bri, and for the coffee."

He took a drink of coffee, his black eyes alight with humor over the cup brim, alerting her to the fact that there was something she should be remembering.

"I had an ulterior motive."

She shook her head. No doubt he wanted a chocolate cake for dessert tonight.

The cup lowered, revealing the predatory edge of his smile. She reevaluated. Maybe something more than a chocolate cake.

"Is your woman's time over?" He slipped the question into the conversation as though he was asking about the weather.

She gasped. Coffee went down the wrong way. As she choked and coughed, Clint took her cup with one hand, slapped her on the back with the other, and swore when he knocked her forward. His second slap landed much more gently, merely jostling her. She kept her head down for a minute after the urge to cough had faded. She knew she was blushing beet red. Her cup waved under her nose, the steam from the hot liquid mixing with the moisture in her eyes. The scent soothed her nerves.

"Sorry," Clint apologized. "Should have eased into that one."

"It's all right. She didn't think they needed to discuss it at all. She took the cup.

"So is it?"

"Yes." She'd seen stray dogs with a bone display less tenacity.

"Good."

His smile broadened before he raised his mug to his lips. She watched the muscles in his throat work as he drained it, letting her gaze drift over his face while he was distracted. He was such a handsome man with those even features and chiseled lips. Just looking at his lips had her nipples tingling. It had been a rare moment during the time they'd been together the last few days that those lips hadn't been on her breasts, nibbling and kissing. Ever since he'd found out that he could make her orgasm that way, he'd been relentless in his attentions. To the point that she was getting sore.

He put the mug on the table with a decisive click and cocked an eyebrow at her when he caught her staring. The right corner of his lip kicked up knowingly. Every nerve ending in her body leapt in response. Nothing—nothing on this earth—was as mesmerizing as Clint McKinnely when he smiled.

"Penny for your thoughts?" She buried her face in her cup and shook her head. He sighed and gave her one of those quick hugs that warmed her way down deep. "You're a selfish woman, Jenna McKinnely."

He didn't sound upset.

Clint leaned to the left, pulling her with him as he went. She held her coffee up and trusted him to control her descent to the mattress. The sound of wood sliding on wood caught her attention, but when Clint pulled his hand back, she couldn't see what he'd pulled from the bed stand drawer.

He loomed over her as she lay there, his hair falling around his naked shoulders and a wicked grin hovering on his lips.

"Stay put." As if she had any choice with his big hand on her belly keeping her there. The sheets rustled as he turned and slid to the floor. The high bed put her hips level with his shoulders. His hand disappeared under the comforter while the smile on his lips spread to his eyes.

"Now we get to really play."

His fingers closed on her calf, squeezing lightly before sliding up and between them. The muscles in her throat appeared to be connected to the muscles in her leg, because every time he stroked her thigh, her throat tightened until it was almost impossible to swallow. She cleared her throat and found a parody of her voice.

"Play what?"

"With toys."

Toys? She blinked and tried to concentrate but his hand moved, the rough surface of his palm rasped across sensitive nerves until his knuckles brushed the curls shielding her pussy. Pleasure—sharp, sweet, and unexpected—shot through her body. Clint held her still for another touch, equally feather-light, equally devastating. It was as if all the play of the last few days had been designed to culminate in this one moment.

Moisture flooded her thighs, and for one horrible moment she thought her woman's time had returned. But even as she stiffened, Clint was pushing her gown out of the way, the roughness of his morning beard scraping along already attentive nerves. She couldn't help the cry that escaped her lips or the moisture that leaked from her pussy as he parted her with his fingertips.

"Ah, Sunshine, you're getting wet for me." His tongue swept the tender inner flesh. "I like that."

That was good because she didn't have any choice.

A dull thud penetrated her senses. The coffee cup hitting the floor. There was going to be a mess. She didn't care. Couldn't care, because Clint was working her clit like he did her nipples. Soft tender kisses followed by gentle laps and then a series of nips and nibbles that had her fingers digging into the coverlet and her teeth biting her lip.

"Dear God."

"Just you and me here, baby."

Desire drove through her like a steam engine, gathering speed with every pass of his hot tongue. He pulled her hips down into his face. His beard pricked. His tongue lapped, and she cried out, shifting her grip to his hair. The smooth strands tangled with her fingers as she pulled him closer.

"What do you want, Jenna?"

She wanted him. Harder. Higher. But all that came out of her mouth was a ruptured, "Please."

"Please what?" His chin brushed the top of her pussy, dusting her clit with a sprinkle of sensation. So close to giving her what she needed. So close. He paused. "Too much?"

She shook her head. The pleasure ebbed back from the high of the moment before. She didn't know whether to cry or laugh.

"Not enough?"

She nodded.

"Tell me."

"I can't."

"Sure you can. Just picture it in your mind and then give me the words."

"I can't say that!"

He cocked his eyebrow at her. "That good, huh?"

She groaned and closed her eyes.

"How about I just take a guess?" His guess had to be better than her saying anything. She nodded.

There was a soft thunk as whatever he took from the drawer landed on the floor. His hands slid up her calves, and over her knees, slowly parting her legs while holding her gaze. He hooked first one and then the other ankle on his shoulders. His flesh was hot against hers. He turned his head, brushing her ankle with his mouth. Fire streaked up her leg. She jerked and he laughed, trailing the backs of his fingers up the inside of her knees, then turning his wrist so that his palms hugged her thighs until his thumbs reached her labia.

"I like you wet like this."

His thumbs traced the crease of her outer lips, tugging at the hairs, tempting her. On her next breath, his thumbs slipped between the slick folds, the calluses rasping the sensitive tissues. Her womb contracted. Her fingers dug into the quilt as she struggled to contain the sinful sensation streaking outward, knowing it was hopeless even as she made the attempt.

Clint wouldn't allow it. Never allowed it. Sure enough, his fingers dipped within, gliding on her cream to the center of her heat before working with deliberate torment back to the top of her cleft. He rubbed the inside of each engorged lip in a gentle circular motion, grazing her swollen, aching clit in random patterns, nudging her desire higher with erratic strokes she couldn't foresee, couldn't control. Until she couldn't hold still. She needed him. His touch, his mouth.

"Please."

"Please what?"

"Please don't make me beg." She wrapped his hair around her fingers and pulled.

His fingers circled her clit, spreading them out and then narrowing in until he had the eager nubbin trapped in his grasp. It wasn't enough. She lifted her hips up toward his hands and mouth, offering herself to him in helpless need. He laughed and squeezed gently. She dug her heels into the hard muscles of his back, and yanked hard. His laugh deepened, but didn't give her what she wanted.

"Please," she whispered again, her voice breaking on a humiliated sob, feeling as if her whole being centered for this moment in this one little spot, hating herself for the weakness he drew from her so easily.

"Shh, baby," His deep drawl worked under her insecurity, soothing her fear with the stroke of softness, building her confidence with the promise of strength. "I'm just making it good."

If he made it any better she'd die. Even as she had the thought, he took her higher, closing those teasing fingers on her clit in a steady pinch. Not hard enough to hurt but hard enough to have every fiber of her being straining to get closer. And then he started milking her clit the way he milked her breast—light, short, deliberate strokes that pulled every one of those fibers to a grinding pitch of desire until the tormenting need exploded in a burning conflagration of lust so strong that she screamed. Her hips lurched as he lunged upward. His broad palm slapped over her mouth.

The suddenness of the move scared her into silence. When she dared to look over his hand, he was staring down at her, shaking his head, an impossibly wicked smile playing on his lips.

"Quiet, or you'll wake Brianna."

Oh heavens, she didn't want to wake Brianna, but she didn't know how she was going to survive this. Not as she was now, her legs over his shoulders, her hips raised off the bed, her body open and vulnerable to anything he wanted.

"Take a breath now, baby."

She did, resting her fingers on the solid muscle of his shoulders.

"Hold it." He eased his palm from her mouth. "Don't scream, no matter what."

She dug her fingers in and nodded.

"Good girl." He kissed his way down her torso, stopping at the undercurve of her breast to draw an intricate pattern over that spot that was connected directly to her pussy. Her breath caught in her throat, and her juices pulsed from her womanhood to flow over her buttocks, dampening the comforter. He abandoned her breast and slid down, his chest hair tickling her abdomen. He spread her thighs wider and then pressed that prickly soft mat of hair against her distended clitoris. His tongue dipped into her navel as he rubbed against her like a big, contented cat—his smile pressing into her belly as she whimpered. "Now that's a sweet little noise. Give it to me again."

She did, helpless to do anything else as he lifted her up, spreading her thighs wide with his shoulders, leaving her open to his mercy.

He had none.

He held her there for a heartbeat, his breath blowing on her flesh, wafting over her dripping folds before crashing into the barrier of her clit, seeming to wrap around the hypersensitive spot in an undulating promise.

"Oh heavens." She couldn't breathe, couldn't move. All she could do was wait and hope.

He leaned forward, riding the depth of her need, rasping her clit with his chin, sending the wild sensation shrieking outward. Every muscle snapped taut. He soothed the slight pain with his tongue before lashing the arousal back into full force, holding his tongue against her when she needed more, driving her upward when she wanted to rest, never letting her calm, keeping her on the edge until she shoved her hand in her mouth and bit back the welling scream. Only then did he take pity on her, curling his tongue gently around her clit, easing it into his mouth with a gentle suction that increased little by little until breathing became impossible. All she could do was strain toward the fulfillment that he held out before her like a glittering promise. Then with a nip and a scrape of his teeth he sent her hurtling toward it, giving her an extra boost with his clever tongue as she reached the pinnacle, catching her as she came back down to earth. Stroking her thighs and stomach soothingly as she did, he nursed her back to reality with light, easy suctions as his tongue restored her sanity. She relaxed into his caress, needing it, needing the break from the wildness to gather her control. His mouth pressed hard against her as he tugged his hand free. The mattress dipped and then something solid and round pressed against the dripping well of her vagina.

"Clint?"

"Just hold still and relax, baby."

"What is that?"

"A very fun toy we're going to play with today."

The pressure against her increased. He was putting it in her. She tried to back up but the headboard prevented her flight. His arms over her thighs kept her from going anywhere. She took a breath as the round object spread her.

"Easy, Sunshine, just a little more."

"Clint, this isn't right!"

"I want it."

"But…"

"Are you denying me?" He looked up at her, his expression calm, his eyes burning hot.

Dare she? She bit her lip and shook her head. It wasn't her place to deny him anything. And then it was too late. With a pinch, the object slipped inside her. She didn't know what to do. What to say. She'd never dreamed a man would want to put something other than himself inside of her. Had no idea why he'd want to do that.

"That's my girl." His tongue smoothed over her clit in a lash of rasping heat. That low drawl combined with that soft, rough tongue on her ultra-sensitive flesh sent fire racing to her core. The shiver started at her toes, worked up her torso, and ended with a sporadic twist of her head. Her hair tumbled over her face as his appreciative laugh buffeted her sensitive nub. The shiver started all over again. Before it reached her shoulders, another one of those smooth balls was pressing against her, spreading her. She grabbed Clint's shoulders. "Just a little bit more, Sunshine, and we'll be all set."

She bit her lip against the instinctive denial. Her nails dug into his shoulders through his shirt. Her breath came in tense pants.

"How do you do this to me?" she blurted as the second ball seated.

"Do what?" As if he didn't know. She glared at him. He patted her throbbing pussy with the flat of his fingers, letting them rest against her wet flesh after the third pat.

"Make me feel like this."

"Just lucky I guess." He kissed her stomach hard and pulled her nightgown down over her thighs.

She didn't believe that for a moment, but she also didn't want to hear about all the women he'd practiced on before her. She shifted and pulled back, the balls an alien weight inside her.

"Take them out."

"No." He took her right breast into his mouth through her nightgown, giving it a nip on the tip before letting it go. Her breast felt heavy and swollen in the aftermath. Her hands slid down his shoulders as he rose above her.

"Please?"

The smile slipped from his eyes. Years of teachings told her to drop her eyes. The flicker of a frown on Clint's face changed her mind. Clint didn't want her that way. He saw her as something different than what she was. Something stronger. She fought the urge and held his gaze. Her reward was a kiss on her nose and a cryptic denial of her request.

"They're all part of today's fun."

He came up the side of the bed near her head. She unfastened the buttons of his denims and then licked her lips as he lifted the hard length of his cock free. He was dark, swollen, and throbbing for her. And for this moment in time he was hers. Only hers. She opened her mouth, moistening her lower lip as she pushed forward, kissing the spongy head softly the way he liked, daintily licking his pre-come off as he groaned. His hands sank into her hair before she opened her mouth and took him deep. Completely without reservation. The way that pleased him best.

* * * * *

She was not having fun. Those balls that had seemed so innocuous at first were, in reality, instruments of torture. With every step she took, they shifted and struck against inner nerves that flowered open, eager for the contact. Her pussy ached and her nerves were stretched taut. She needed relief, but Clint was nowhere in sight.

Jenna wiped the last cake tin and put it on the stack. Her arm brushed her nipple. She clenched the counter with her fingers, bracing herself against the surge of sinful desire. As she turned she bumped the tins. She caught them and quickly silenced the clatter. She did not need Bri up yet. She still needed to frost the cakes so they'd be set to go when Jackson had time to take them into town for sale. A quick glance revealed the baby was still sleeping in her makeshift bed on the kitchen table.

Jenna rubbed the condensation on the window over the basin. The sun was bright, sparking here and there off patches of ice. In the corral, two horses stood hip-shot, soaking up what warmth there was from the late morning sunshine. Chickens pecked around the henhouse.

She leaned forward to look toward the front of the house. All she could see was the support holding up the roof and the edge of the porch. No Clint. A flicker of black caught her eye. It repeated and she sighed. It was nothing more than Danny's tail ruffling in the breeze. The knob of the cabinet door brushed her privates as she settled back to her feet. She jumped back, horrified by her body's reaction.

She'd never suspected a human being could hunger so. Never known another human being could be so cruel as to leave a woman in this much need. She gripped the towel tightly, took a breath, and counted to ten. She curled her fingers into fists. Clint had forbidden her to touch herself. She'd readily agreed, such actions being against God's teaching and never having suffered the inclination. But now…now she understood why preachers ranted against the temptations of the flesh, because her flesh was tormenting her so badly that she wanted to scream.

The horses in the corral whinnied a greeting. Danny barked. Someone was here. Her pussy throbbed and her nipples perked as every nerve leapt to attention in an all-out hope that it was Clint.

She rubbed at the window again. Two riders cantered into the yard. One of the hands immediately came out of the barn, rifle cradled in his arm. She couldn't see his face for the angle of the sun, but she knew who he was from the way he held himself. Jackson. Lorie's brother. They had similar, even features, though Jackson's hair was darker, but whereas Lorie impressed first with her kind heart and then her abilities, Jackson impressed with an aura of lethal competence. It was only when she saw how he treated his sister and the way he smiled at Mara and Elizabeth that she realized he was a very nice man. Still, he nodded and smiled at the two riders, she was glad he was keeping an eye on things. She'd be scared witless to have to face down two men on her own.

The two strangers swung down off of their horses. They didn't get any smaller for dismounting. The one on the left turned. She sucked in a breath as long hair flew about his silhouette. Oh Lord, Cougar. Which had to mean that the other man was Asa, based on his size and the fact that where there was one, there was usually the other. They turned and headed for the house. Jackson didn't come with them. And no matter where she looked, there was no Clint. Panic snapped at arousal, beating it back. It was going to be just them and her!

She ran to the small chest in the hall, ignoring the near crippling sensation skidding out of her pussy with the rapid motion. Pressing her hand against her spasming womb, she pulled open the drawer. The heavy tread of boots on the porch steps made her fumble. She grabbed the gun hidden inside and shoved the muzzle into the back of her skirt. It was a heavy, comforting weight as it dug into her spine and buttocks. Two short raps on the wooden door made her jump. She took a calming breath. No need to panic. She wasn't married to Jack and these weren't his drunken friends. Cougar and Asa were probably just here to see Clint. She'd tell them he wasn't here and send them on their way. The gun was just to make her feel better. She wasn't going to need it.

She straightened her apron and tucked all the wayward strands of hair behind her ears. The rap came again, harder as she made sure her dress was buttoned up under her chin. She was reaching for the knob when the door swung open.

"Anybody home?"

She quickly stepped back as Asa's broad shoulders blocked the light. Cool air swirled around her as he removed his hat, his dark gray eyes inspecting her from head to toe. "Ma'am."

"Move it on in Ace. It's dammed cold out here."

The door hit Asa in the shoulder as Cougar pushed forward. Asa caught it in his hand and stepped aside. He shot a glare at the door. "I apologize for the language."

Cougar froze. His strange golden eyes lighted on her for an instant and then swept the foyer and the adjoining rooms before coming back to her again, and sticking. "Sorry about that."

He didn't remove his hat. Jenna bit her lip, and clasped her hands in front of her to hide her nerves while she wrestled to find her voice.

Cougar cocked his eyebrow at her and exchanged a look with Asa before stepping into the foyer. He narrowed her escape route with a push of his hand to a small glimmer of sunlight, and then to nothing. The foyer filled with the scent of leather and horse.

She took another step back, and fire shot up through her womb, throwing off her balance. She bumped the table. She steadied it, feeling the flush start.

"No harm done." The door clicked shut and then it was just her and the two giants standing in the foyer.

"Clint's not here."

Cougar shrugged out of his coat. "I expect he'll be around shortly."

"You do?" She didn't like the gleam in his dark gold eyes. She couldn't hold his gaze. He wasn't like Clint. There wasn't any kindness visible beneath the intensity, just a wildness that terrified her.

"Seeing as how he invited us over to play," Asa cut in, "I think it's a safe bet." He tossed his coat to Cougar who caught it deftly and hung it on the hat tree with his own.

Time stood still for a horrifying second as the words sank past Jenna's naive hopes and foolish trust—sank until it hit square on the reality that she kept trying to forget. Her vision darkened at the edges, and the room swayed as the past pushed forward into the present.

It's damn fun playing with you. Oh God, Not again. She couldn't survive it again. The table teetered under her weight.

"Jesus Christ." The curse came from her right while Cougar's growled, "Catch her," came from her left.

Danny whined from behind the door as the edges of her vision went black and her lungs refused to work.

Oh God! She couldn't let them catch her. She felt more than heard the men move toward her. She lurched back, reaching for the gun with her free hand. The table tipped. She tripped on the clawed foot and came down on her bad leg. It buckled. A grip of iron closed over her upper arm, pulling her up short.

"Gotcha."

"Let me go!" The butt of the revolver settled into her palm. She swung it around, tightening her grip as the heavy muzzle threatened to tip it out of her grasp.

Asa did immediately, holding one hand up as he stepped back. The look he exchanged with Cougar put the hairs on the back of her neck on alert.

"Easy, Jenna." Cougar's easy drawl did little to settle them down.

She wasn't stupid. The only thing between her and them was the gun, and her willingness to use it.

"Get away from me." Instead of a shout, it came out in a whisper as shaky as her arms. Both men just stood there, not more than three feet way from her. Not by a twitch of a muscle did they indicate an awareness of how close she was to pulling the trigger.

Asa motioned with his hand. "Jenna, darling, is that one of Clint's guns?"

"I'm not your darling." Her voice was still pathetically weak.

"Sure enough you're not, but that doesn't answer my question."

"You need to leave." She didn't want to answer questions. She wanted them to go.

The muscles in her arms were beginning to ache and her courage was fast dwindling to zero. All she had left was desperation.

"Answer his question, Jenna." Cougar's deep voice rapped out the order so hard and fast that she obeyed instinctively.

"Yes."

"Damn." Asa took a step forward.

She raised the muzzle higher. "Get back!"

He didn't move, just held out his hand. "Very carefully, Jenna, give me the gun."

His voice was smooth as silk, his drawl an invitation to trust.

She tightened her grip on the gun. Both men tensed. She didn't lower the muzzle and didn't hand over the gun.

"The gun has a hair trigger, Jenna," Asa offered as if that meant something to her.

"And a kick like a mule," Cougar added. It sounded distinctly like a warning.

"If you leave, none of that will matter."

Asa shrugged and said almost apologetically. "Clint won't be happy if you get hurt."

"If you leave now, he'll never know."

Her shoulders ached and her forearms burned like fire. She needed to put the gun down, but if she did, she'd be defenseless, and she was never going through that again. Never.

Tears blurred her vision and the shaking in her arms spread out through her body. Dear God, she couldn't survive another rape, but she didn't think she could kill a man either.

Courage. She needed courage.

"Clint's going to blister your butt for sure, Jenna McKinnely," Cougar said, his eyes narrowing as he took in her expression and the tension there.

Asa shot him a sharp glance. "Shut up, Cougar."

In contrast to Cougar's growl, Asa's drawl was easy and gentle. Deceptively so, but she'd seen his eyes, and no one looking into his cold gray eyes could ever imagine him as anything but deadly.

"No one's going to hurt anyone, Jenna, but you're going to have to make a decision soon. Either shoot or drop the gun." He shrugged. "A little bit of a thing like you can't hold out much longer."

He was right. That just made it more imperative that they go.

"Please leave," she ordered. There wasn't a prayer that either man would see her as brave. All she had to threaten them with was her desperation. And that she had plenty of. Fractured memories of male voices, lust, pain, gauged her grasp on reality. Past mixed with present, old faces blurred over new. Her screams, her constant pointless screams echoed in her ears until she wasn't sure what was real and what was memory. The only thing she knew for sure was that Clint had betrayed her. The pain of that overrode everything else, feeding her panic, draining her hope and reason.

"Mind if I get my coat?" Cougar shifted his weight. His moccasins made no sound on the plank floor as he took a step to the right.

She just wanted him gone. The muscles in his forearms flexed as he reached for his coat. She took a step back. She couldn't let him touch her. He was too strong. Too unpredictable.

"Just take it and leave."

His hair fell over his broad shoulders as he reached for his coat. The gun weighed heavily in her hand. A bead of sweat trickled down her spine as he slowly, slowly took the coat off the hook.

To his right, Asa stood, no less lethal for all that he smiled easily. She'd heard stories. She knew what he was capable of. But Cougar was closer and the bigger threat. She kept the gun trained on him, forcing herself to meet his gaze in case he gave a split second of warning.

He didn't hide from her, but he did frown, his eyes searching hers before saying, "Your demons can't win here, Jenna."

She was clinging to sanity by a thread, but even this close to the edge she wasn't fooled by the gentleness in Cougar's voice. She'd fallen for that kindness trick one too many times to tumble again.

"I don't have demons." Just men who hurt.

"I'm not leaving until I get the gun," Asa interrupted in his easygoing tone. The floorboards creaked and for a second time Jenna didn't know who to train the gun on. She bit her lip and re-centered it on Cougar's chest.

"You trying to get me shot?" Cougar asked with an arch of his dark brow.

"You know how touchy Clint's guns are. Just setting them down wrong can set them off. It's a wonder she hasn't shot herself already."

"Right now I'm the one in danger of getting shot," Cougar pointed out dryly.

"Won't be the first time." Asa shrugged and settled his hat forward on his head, hiding his expression in the shadow of the brim. The floorboard creaked under his foot as he took another step forward.

Jenna's muscles burned with agony. She couldn't hold the gun much longer. She turned the gun on Asa. "Don't make me do this."

He kept coming.

"Mrs. McKinnely, I've survived this long by knowing someone's going to pull the trigger." He reached forward. "And when they're not."

He was right. She couldn't kill him. She couldn't avoid this that way. It didn't make her any less determined to avoid it. She turned the muzzle toward her chest and closed her eyes.

Asa's "Son of a bitch!" coincided with Cougar's succinct "Fuck!"

She pulled the trigger. In the instant her finger met resistance, her arm was slammed up and back into the wall and a force hit her in the stomach just as a loud explosion detonated by her left ear. The gun tore out of her hand, and there was another earsplitting explosion before she was tossed up and around.

There was a terrible growling, some more swearing. She opened her eyes, receiving a brief impression of the door and then the ceiling before she landed with a bone-jarring thud on top of someone.

She tried to turn, but couldn't.

"You got her?" Cougar asked.

From beneath her, Asa grunted, "Yeah."

"She hurt?" Metal clanking against metal punctuated the words.

"Don't think so." His arms tightened around her.

Oh God, she'd failed. Failed. She slammed her head back into Asa's rock-solid chest and screamed a protest against the unfairness of it all. Of the cruelty of knowing what was to come and the agony of having to endure it again. Screaming again as the terror rolled over her, keeping it up because at least it was something, no matter how ineffective — something she could do. As she screamed she dug her nails into the hands wrapped around her torso and upper arms and raked hard, slamming her head back, trying to hit Asa in the face, kicking with her feet, desperately searching for a soft spot to hurt him. It wasn't happening again. Not again. Not again.

* * * * *

Clint rode into the yard, his cock and his thoughts full of the next few hours with Jenna. She'd come so far in the last few days, losing some of that ingrained submissiveness and gaining a little confidence. Even had almost challenged him when he slid those little balls into that sweet pussy. He licked his lips. His muscles tightened with the memory of her delicate, musky flavor. His cock throbbed and jerked. Damn, he could come just from the taste of her.

He pulled Ornery to the hitching post in front of the barn. He noted Cougar's big black and Asa's buckskin in the corral. And sighed. He'd forgotten about inviting them over.

He'd just have to wait a little longer to play. Jackson nodded from where he was dumping fresh water into the trough for the two horses.

"Everything all right?"

Jackson nodded. "Cougar and Asa went up to the house about five minutes ago."

"Anything else?"

"With the exception that I'd like to take that roan off your hands, no."

Clint returned the other man's smile. "Not a chance."

"Figured you'd say that."

"So why do I get the impression you'll be back?"

Jackson's teeth flashed white in the shadow from the brim of his hat. "Probably because I haven't got what I want yet."

Clint chuckled. "Heard you could be difficult that way."

He lifted the reins over Ornery's head, "Could you cool him down for me?"

"Sure." Again that smile. "I'll just add it to your bill."

Clint shook his head. "You can't run a bill up high enough to get that roan."

Jackson took the reins from his hands. "Can't blame a man for trying."

Clint pushed his hat back. "Don't suppose I can."

A shot shattered the morning quiet. Clint was running for the house before the second one rang out, hot on the heels of the first, a woman's terrified scream echoing in the reverberations. Danny's wild barking punctuated the shrill cry.

Clint bit back his instinct to yell for Jenna. Instead, he ran harder, pulling his gun as he went, the two hundred feet between him and the house seeming like miles.

He pulled up short on the porch, staying to the left of the door. Two cautious steps and he flattened himself against the wall. He reached around Danny's big body, using the dog's noise to cover the sound of the door opening. As soon as the door cracked, Danny burst forward with a feral snarl. The door slammed against the wall. A man cursed a blue streak and Danny's snarls turned to battle cries. Clint sprang into the doorway ready to fire, but jerked his arm up at the sight that greeted him.

Cougar was dragging Danny away from Asa who lay on the floor, his long legs and arms wrapped around Jenna who struggled atop him. She yanked her head back, and screamed again—the kind he'd heard before during her nightmares. The kind that made the hair on the back of his neck stand on end.

He holstered his gun. "What the hell is going on?"

"Son of a bitch!" Asa swore as Jenna's head hit his chin.

"Get your wife and your dog under control," Cougar snapped.

Clint motioned Danny off. The dog dropped to an uneasy sit. Clint knelt and grabbed Jenna's arms, pulling her into his chest, falling back against the opposite wall as Asa pushed her toward him.

He expected her to stop fighting. She didn't. Her fingers curved into claws and headed for his face while mutters of "No, no, no" fell incessantly from her lips.

"It's Clint, baby. Calm down."

He blocked her hands with his forearm, pressing them against her chest. She twisted her head and sank her teeth into his biceps.

He cast a quick glance at Cougar while yanking his arm free of her teeth. "What in hell did you two do to her?"

"Not a goddamned thing," Cougar stated flatly.

Danny's snarls dropped to whines. Cougar let him go. He immediately laid his big head on top of Jenna's thrashing one, drool sliding into her hair. She didn't even seem to notice. Clint pulled her closer, pressing her head to his chest, and wincing when she immediately bit.

Asa got up from the floor, his gray eyes staring at Jenna with a mixture of pity and concern. "We came in. She seemed a bit nervous but civil. I made some comment about you inviting us to play," he waved his hand toward the barn, visible through the window, "with that mustang you've been trying to break and she went loco."

"She lost it over breaking a mustang?" Clint controlled Jenna's thrashing by pinning her arms to her sides with his. Her tears soaked his shoulder as she struggled against his hold, her teeth biting deeper.

Cougar stepped closer, his moccasins making no sound, his golden gaze considering, a grim set to his mouth.

"Actually, I think all he said was that you had invited us over to play," Cougar clarified.

It's damn fun playing with you. The words he'd said to Jenna last night rang in his mind. He thought of her past, and realized how Cougar's greeting might have struck her.

Ah, shit! Shit! Shit!

"I heard shots," he finally said, guilt tearing a hole in his chest bigger than Jenna's teeth could ever hope to.

Asa rubbed his bruised chin, his eyes meeting his with the forthrightness Clint appreciated in the man. "She turned the gun on herself, Clint."

"Son of a bitch."

The heavy weight of Cougar's hand on his shoulder was welcome. Clint met his cousin's gaze. They'd seen this reaction before. In other women. Women who'd been raped. Women they'd tried to bring home to their families. That it was his Jenna going through it made him want to rage. Instead, he fought for calm. Jenna needed that more than she needed his anger.

Jenna's breath was coming in harsh, erratic gasps. Her ribs heaved under his hands as she struggled for air. In the other room, he noted Bri's cries. He bent his head to murmur in Jenna's ear, keeping his voice mellow and soothing. "Jenna, baby, you've got to calm down. You're scaring Button."

He might as well have been talking to the wall. The fury he normally kept contained threatened to break free.

Asa knelt beside him. There was a tug on his gun belt. Asa reached around Jenna and handed Clint's revolver to Cougar. "No need for repeats."

He didn't immediately stand like Clint expected him to. Instead he caught Jenna's chin in his hand, freeing her teeth from Clint's flesh, and turning her face to his. His expression was devoid of its normal humor as he said to her, with deadly quiet, "When you get to feeling better, you tell me their names, and I'll take care of it."

Apparently Asa had seen his share of broken women, too. Clint didn't know if Jenna heard over her breathing and the lingering panic, but when Asa let go of her chin she didn't look away. Then she slowly shook her head.

"No."

"It will be settled," Cougar said, stepping into Jenna's line of vision. The same lethal purpose surrounded him that surrounded Asa. Hell…was probably surrounding himself, as well.

From the door, Jackson spoke up. "I'd be happy to tag along."

In his arms, Jenna became even stiffer. Christ, did she think they wouldn't put it together?

"When the time comes," Clint said, putting all doubts to rest, "I'll be settling the accounts." Jenna buried her face in his throat, her breath heating his skin but not touching the coldness in his soul. In the other room, Bri's screams rose in volume.

"Not alone, you won't," Cougar stated implacably.

"It's not your problem," Clint pointed out.

Asa put his hands on his knees and stood, his eyes never leaving Jenna. "I don't know about the rest of you, but I'm making it mine."

"Yup," Jackson agreed.

"That pretty much makes it a done deal." Cougar jerked his chin in the direction of the kitchen. His long hair flowed over his shoulder and chest as he turned. "I'm going to see to Tidbit while you two get things settled."

"Bring her out to watch us play with that mustang," Asa suggested, motioning Jackson ahead of him out the door.

"Will do." Cougar paused at the kitchen door, turned and came back, his eyes a dark gold and his expression serious. He stopped and motioned to Jenna. Clint gave his permission with a nod.

Cougar squatted down. Jenna tensed. Cougar placed his large hand on the back of her head, his skin looking very dark against the bright blonde of her hair. "You tell Clint what happened, Jenna. You tell him everything, and then you let it go."

The shake of Jenna's head was almost imperceptible. Clint barely felt it against his neck.

"Whatever it is, Jenna," Clint said, stroking his hand up her back, "it's not going to matter to me." He touched his finger to her cheek. "I just want you, Sunshine. Anyway I can get you."

Cougar pulled back, his eyes reflecting the sadness that didn't reach his voice. "You need to trust that Clint will handle the men who hurt you. You need to trust that he won't allow you to be taken from him."

"Never, baby. I won't let you go for anything or anyone — living or dead."

Clint felt the shaking start in Jenna. It started way down deep inside her with barely perceptible trembles, but then it moved outward to her limbs, jostling him as she vibrated against him. Her arms crept around his neck, her nails dug into his nape. Her tears soaked his collar as she gasped, "Oh God! Oh God!"

He felt the bite of her nails as she pulled herself closer, as if she needed to sink inside him.

"Oh God, Clint. Am I crazy?"

"No, Sunshine," he whispered, holding her as tightly as she could stand. "You've just been scared one time too many."

"But you don't need to fear anymore," Cougar said, standing.

"No." Clint cupped her head in his hand. "You don't have to be afraid anymore."

She felt small and soft in his arms. A gentle woman who wouldn't hurt a fly. Someone, some man had abused that softness. Tried to crush her. Terrified her to the point that she thought she was insane.

"I almost killed myself for nothing."

"But you didn't."

"What if I do it again?"

"You won't." He wiped the tears from her cheeks. "As soon as you get your feet back under you, you'll be right as rain."

He stroked her hair, tugging the few straggling pieces free. She'd been through hell, but she'd survived. He kissed her hair. She was his wife now. He knew her value. He'd cherish that softness. Protect it. And anyone who messed with her again would die. "I'm your husband now, Jenna. Not some weak-ass bully. I know how to protect my family."

"We will all protect you," Cougar added, his drawl resonating with the assurance of a man who knew how to back his promise. "You're one of us now."

Clint flashed him a grateful look as Jenna relaxed the tiniest bit.

"You have nothing to fear anymore," Clint told her, adding his assurances to Cougar's, telling himself it wasn't too much of a lie. She'd be fine until the day she discovered the truth about him and tried to leave. Then she'd see what a bastard he was, but between now and then he'd keep her safe.

Chapter Sixteen

Oh God. She'd almost killed herself. Over a misunderstanding. Left Bri without a mother. Left her husband without a wife. All because she hadn't fought the memories. Maybe she was as crazy as Jack had always claimed. Except she didn't feel crazy when Clint held her. She felt safe. Whole. Until something like today happened and she knew how fragile her reality really was. She couldn't go on like this.

The back door slammed. Cougar taking Bri outside.

"I'm sorry."

Clint's hold gentled. "For what?"

"For threatening to shoot your friends."

"It's not the first time someone's taken a potshot at them."

"I don't know what happened."

"You got scared."

"That's no excuse."

"For a while, we'll let it slide as one."

"I'm still sorry." He was so kind. So patient. She turned her cheek against his chest.

"For pointing a gun at Cougar and Asa? Or for trying to kill yourself?"

She didn't know how to answer that. A tug at her nape had her head tilting back. The sun from the parlor window slanted off his right cheekbone, illuminating his dark eyes with streaks of light.

"The latter you need to spend a lifetime apologizing for." His lips touched hers. "You're mine, Sunshine. Forever. No matter what."

She'd never been kissed with so much emotion. Never been held with so much tenderness. And never, ever wanted to believe something so badly. He held her until her heartbeat slowed. Until her panic ebbed, and until her embarrassment faded beneath the steadiness of his touch. As it did, she noted that while she was relaxed, he was not. The arms that held her were tense, the heart beating beneath her cheek did so faster than normal, and when she glanced at his face there were white lines carved beside his mouth.

"Clint?"

He looked down. "What do you need Jenna?"

Not an abrupt, "What?" No lecture—just an instant offer of comfort.

"You're upset," she began, not sure how to broach the subject.

"You scared the shit out of me."

She stroked his chest. "I scared myself."

"We'll get past it." He had such faith in her. For absolutely no reason.

"We have to."

"I know."

She touched the corner of his mouth where the skin showed white. He deserved a reason. He deserved a wife he could count on. "I can't be her anymore, Clint."

He frowned. "Who?"

She moved her touch to the lines between his dark brows. "That woman who gets so mindless with fear that she does stupid things."

"Glad to hear it." The lines around his eyes might have softened imperceptibly.

"I don't know how, but I'm going to change." She meant every word. "I'm not leaving you or Brianna because of the past."

"There's no rush. I'll be more careful."

How much more careful could he be?

"I think some of this has to come from me." She ran her finger down the straight bridge of his nose, taking strength from his confidence. She could be the woman he saw when he looked at her.

"When you're ready." His hand smoothed over her hair, his pinkie catching in a snarl.

"I'm ready now."

"Now?" He raised an eyebrow at her and eased his finger free.

She nodded. "I want to make you feel better."

"I'm fine." He hugged her as carefully as if she were fine china and in danger of shattering.

He wasn't. She could feel the tension humming beneath his skin. "Please?"

He tipped her chin up. "What I need, you're not in any condition to give me."

The rejection hit her hard. She dropped her gaze and folded her hands in her lap. It took about two seconds for her to realize what she'd done. And after she'd vowed to change. She tipped her face up and looked Clint dead in the eye.

"No."

"No?" Both his eyebrows went winging up.

She couldn't blame him for his surprise. She'd never said that to him without being out of her head, but she was saying it to him now. She clenched her fingers tighter. "You can't keep treating me like I'll break, and then expect me to be strong."

"I don't expect you to be strong."

That hurt more than the rejection. "I want to be, and you have to help me."

"I do?" He leaned back as if to see her better.

"Yes, starting now." She took a breath and let it out. "You have to tell me what you need and let me decide if I can give it to you."

"That sounded like an order."

She took another breath, held it in an agony of daring and answered, "It was."

He didn't move or seem to breathe for three heartbeats, and then, unbelievably, he laughed. "You are an amazing woman, Jenna McKinnely."

The back of his fingers brushed her cheek, his dark eyes thoughtful. She leaned into them and waited. He sighed, and she knew she'd won.

"I came too damned close to losing you." He paused, and a muscle in his jaw leapt. "I need you."

"You want to make love to me?"

"More than just make love." He shook his head as if disgusted with himself. "I want to bury myself in you until you can't separate where I end and you begin."

"And you think I wouldn't want to give you that?" She turned in his arms, her breast pressing into his stomach, one hand going to where she knew his scars were, imagining she could feel them through all the barriers. She'd give him anything he wanted.

"You're very vulnerable right now."

She shook her head, avoiding his gaze. The thought of making love right now with the memories so strong made her cringe, but the thought of disappointing Clint when he needed her was worse.

"Maybe I need you like that, too. Maybe I need to know you still want me."

"I'll always want you." His hand curved around the back of her skull, cradling her head. She slid her hands over his shoulders, skimming her fingers up the side of his neck, stroking his jaw with her thumbs before cupping his cheeks and pulling his mouth to hers. She focused on Clint. He was the only one who mattered right now.

"Then kiss me." She needed him to make the demons go away. To remind her of how things were now.

He did, his mouth gentle as it touched hers, a mere brushing of lips when she expected possession. The easy ebb and flow of his mouth on hers gave her time to adjust fully to the moment. To push away the last remnants of the past. She gave herself to his kiss, the strength in it, the comfort. Beneath her hands she felt the finest of tremors hit him before his kiss changed, became harder, deeper, more passionate, as if he needed to stake his claim.

She opened her mouth to the thrust of his tongue, taking him into her, holding him, understanding his need as she shared it. She needed to know he was real, too. That he would be there for her when she reached out. That he was hers. No matter what.

His hand slipped down to the back of her neck, tilting her head for a better angle. Deepening the thrust, taking control away from her, leaving her helpless to do anything but receive his desire.

His hand dipped to the hollow of her back as he mated his mouth to hers, arching her over his arm. Pain stabbed up from her leg as the pressure increased. She moaned and pushed at his broad shoulders. There was only the minimal give of his shearling coat before she hit rock-hard muscle. His mouth parted a breath from hers.

"It's okay, baby. Just give me a little more."

She pressed harder. "My leg."

The words were lost in his mouth as her breath swirled with his. For the space of a heartbeat, she didn't think he'd heard, but then he was in motion, lifting her off his lap as if she weighed nothing. Holding her so that none of her weight was on her legs as he pushed off the wall. She grabbed for his neck as he stood.

He swung her up in his arms, his chest shuddering against her as he drew in a deep breath. She tightened her grip around his neck as he cradled her close.

"I'm sorry, Sunshine."

She didn't want him sorry. She tilted her head back to see his face. "It was just the position."

He was shaking his head before she finished the sentence, his long hair brushing her cheek in a soft caress. "I should be horsewhipped for going at you like that after what you've been through." He headed into the parlor.

"It was a long time ago."

He paused in the parlor door. His eyes were knowing, his expression hard. "Close enough in your mind that I almost lost you because of it."

She couldn't argue that. She rested her cheek on his shoulder as he carried her into the comfortable room. He laid her on the soft cushions of the settee, the worry in his eyes telling her that he wasn't going to pick up where they had left off.

"I won't slip like that again."

"I know."

He didn't sound like he believed her. "I won't, Clint."

In the aftermath of that hysterical moment, she felt free. For the first time in her life—free. As if everything that had been too confusing for understanding was now suddenly clear and firmly in place, where it belonged. As if it really was possible to start over. One step at a time. Away from the past, into her future.

"Good." He cupped her face in his hands as he knelt beside her. "I want you to rest now."

"I don't need to rest."

He traced the line of her cheekbones with his thumbs. "I want you to try." He reached for the throw and covered her up.

"What about you?" She caught his hand as he would have pulled back.

"I'm going to work the edge off on that damned horse."

She almost felt sorry for the horse. Clint practically vibrated with tension.

She sighed. "I wish you'd work it off on me."

His eyes flared with heat before it was quickly banked. She knew what the answer was before he shook his head. "I'm too raw for careful, and you're too raw for wild."

He was right. Darn it. She moved his hair behind his shoulder, guilt gnawing at her. He needed her, and once again she was falling short of giving him what he wanted. "But later?"

"You can count on later." He kissed the inside of her arm. The abrupt move was a poor imitation of his normal smoothness, telling her more than words about how on edge he really was beneath his control. His hair fell forward again, as stubborn as he about doing what it wanted.

"What about Bri?"

He smiled and tucked the comforter around her shoulders. "I think the three of us can handle one sweet little girl for a couple of hours."

"You said she was a hellion," she reminded him with a faint smile.

"I like that in her."

Yes, he did. He seemed to enjoy everything about the little girl, from her good moods to her bad. Delighting in her temper and her smiles with equal fervor. He was unlike anyone she'd ever met before.

The cushion dipped as he pushed to his feet. "I'll stoke the stove before I go. You relax and take a nap."

"I'm not sick."

"No, but you've been up with Bri the last few nights and you're still tired." He crossed to the small stove. The door creaked as he opened it. "And that leg could use a rest," he added as he stuffed a few logs onto the glowing embers.

Would he always see her as a cripple? "You promise you'll come back?"

His right eyebrow arched as he reminded her, "You're my wife. This is my home."

And he was a good man who'd made a promise to honor both. Her fingers twisted in the throw. She wanted to be more to him than a duty.

His boots made soft thumps as he crossed the wide planked floor. His hand was heavy on hers as he unknotted her fingers.

"I'm not going anywhere, Jenna." He brought her hand to his mouth, kissing her knuckles. His brow creased with worry and strain as his eyes met hers. "I'll be outside. If you need me, just ring the bell."

She pushed up on her elbows, determined that he know this one thing. "And I'll be in here if you need me."

He nodded, but his expression didn't relax. "I'll keep that in mind."

He didn't believe she meant it.

Inside of her, something shifted, and guilt and fear died beneath a surge of determination as she watched him leave the room. She was going to have to do something about that.

* * * * *

"Wake up, Jenna."

The low drawl wove into her dreams. She turned toward the voice and opened her eyes. Clint knelt before her, his expression unreadable.

"I fell asleep?" She pushed her hair off her face. Clint's eyes followed the movement and a smile softened the hard line of his mouth.

"Looks like it."

"Where's Bri?"

"She just went down for her nap."

Which meant that they had a couple of hours free. She waited for the nervousness to come, but instead, all she felt was the same determination that she'd experienced earlier. And anticipation. She touched the edge of his smile.

"Does this mean it's later?"

"Do you want it to be?" She loved the way his eyebrow rose when he was amused. She slid her finger into his mouth, jumping at the bolt of sensation that shot down her arm when he sucked it. The hitch in her "Yes" would have been embarrassing if it hadn't had such a profound effect on Clint.

His expression went hard in an instant while his eyes burned with an intensity she'd grown to appreciate. His voice, however, was calm. Too calm. The way it was when he was hiding how he really felt. Did he still feel that she wouldn't be able to handle his desire for her? He had a lot to learn about her.

She slid her arms over his shoulders. "Help me up, please."

The ease with which he lifted her sent a quiver of excitement down her spine.

"Can you stand?" he asked, supporting her as she reached her feet.

She tested her leg. "I'm fine."

He steadied her with one hand. The little balls made their presence known with a vengeance. Her knees buckled on the sharp surge of pleasure. Clint caught her and swore.

"Your leg?"

The blush burned up from her toes, leaving her slightly lightheaded as she confessed, "It's not my leg."

Clint frowned. "You said you weren't hurt." As he talked, his big hands were running over her body, searching for wounds.

Oh heavens. This couldn't get more embarrassing. "I'm not hurt."

One beat. Two beats. She could see his mind working. When understanding hit, his smile was pure male satisfaction, and his eyes flared with sensual heat. He closed the distance between them with one step.

"Those toys giving you a bit of trouble?"

"Yes." Not only were they giving her trouble, but it felt like every nerve ending in her body had joined the fray.

He pulled her against his body. The hard length of his cock leapt against her, as if straining to reach her through her skirts. She had an incredible urge to yank the cumbersome material out of the way. Her pussy wept with an equal need. He pushed a strand of hair off of her cheek, that ghost of a smile touching his mouth.

"Can you feel the balls now?"

She shook her head. "Only when I move."

"And you're sure your leg's not hurting?" His hand slipped behind her neck.

"Yes." She knew better than to ask, but she did anyway. "Why?"

A genuine smile formed as he pulled her forward and lowered his head. "'Cause I think it's time you moved."

She closed her eyes as his firm lips eased hers open. She curved her arms around to grip his forearms with her hands. She loved the way he kissed, all heat and patience and yet so completely carnal that she felt it all the way to her womb, which clenched in delight, triggering a shift of those torturous balls.

"Can't we just take them out?" she gasped as the spike of desire eased.

"Yes."

She sighed in relief. He turned her around. With his hands on her shoulders he urged her toward the door.

"As soon as we get upstairs."

She looked over her shoulder at him. "You can't mean to…"

"I can't?" He raised his dark brow and laughter blended with the lust in his gaze.

"Brianna?"

"Will be asleep for at least two hours."

His hand in the middle of her back propelled her forward, the balls shifted, bumped together, sending shards of sensation splintering outward. She bit her lip and took a deep breath.

"Oh, this is going to be fun," Clint murmured.

For him maybe, but it was going to be pure torture for her. She took a step. The balls shifted, and she bit her lip on the moan that snuck past. Clint's laughter followed her as she took another. There was the sound of something hitting the chair. A quick glance revealed his coat. The next step got her as far as the bottom of the stairs. She grabbed the rail for support. A board creaked, and then she felt him against her back. His heat and scent seeped into her senses like an insidious drug, making her weaker, more susceptible to the sensations racing out from her core. This time there was no suppressing the moan as she swayed.

"Problems, Sunshine?" His arm came around her waist.

"I can't do this."

"But I want it." His fingers rested on her stomach, just above her pubic bone. "I want you hot and aching, that sweet pussy open for my cock."

She was already there. "It's not fair."

"What's not?"

"I want you aching, too."

His lips brushed the side of her neck. "Do you think I can hear your moans, know you're hurting for my touch, and remain unmoved?" His teeth nipped her ear. "That's some damned image you have of me." He pressed with his fingers, massaging the ache deep inside to a more urgent pulse, at the same time letting her feel the rock-hard length of his cock through her skirts.

"I want you baby. I'm just enjoying the anticipation."

She couldn't come up with anything more eloquent to say than "Oh."

"So why don't you get this luscious ass moving up those stairs so I can get onto playing?"

Luscious? He thought her ass was luscious? The compliment almost made the thought of moving bearable. She put one foot on the stairs. The balls pressed against her inner walls. Hot licks of fire radiated out. She glanced up. There were fourteen stairs to go. She licked her lip and took another step. Clint was right behind her, his hand on her stomach measuring every hitch in her breath. Her pussy swelled and ached. Her skin beneath his fingers became ultra-sensitive, straining for his touch through her clothing. She paused, gripping the post for strength. Clint eased her back against him.

"Don't fight it," he murmured in her ear. "Just let it flow over you. Let yourself feel good. It's not a sin baby, but a gift."

A gift? It was torture, pure and simple. Her head found the hollow of his shoulder. His lips brushed her ear.

"Climb the stairs, Jenna."

Why did he have to say it just that way, in that voice? She took one step, and then another. The fire rose up from her groin, raging over her senses, burning out her ability to do anything but feel. She fell back against him. "I can't."

"What if I say I want you to?" Still that seductive voice that coated her need with honeyed promise. Her pussy clenched and wept as the inherent promise slid down her spine.

"Please don't."

She shivered as his lips found the side of her neck. "Do you ache for me, Sunshine?"

"Yes."

He laughed and pushed her forward. She caught herself with her hands on the stair, her back curved, taking most of her weight on her good leg. He came down over her, surrounding her with his body, his hips aligned against her buttocks with blatant intent.

"I like you like this, all bent over." His hands drooped down to her knees. He started gathering her skirt.

"Accessible." He piled layer after layer of material into the small of her back. His big hand slipped between her thighs, catching on her moist pantaloons. "Ah Jenna, you get so wet for me."

"I can't help it." She shifted her legs apart to accommodate the width of his hand as he cupped her pussy.

"That wasn't a complaint." His fingers dipped inside the slit of her pantaloons, the callused tips scraping the hungry flesh. She pushed back against him. He leaned in, his cock grinding into her ass. "That's it. Show me what you want."

"You." The embarrassing confession whispered into the quiet of the house. "I want you."

"You've always had me, Sunshine." His teeth scraped the back of her neck.

Not like she wanted. She'd never have him that way. The stray thought whisked away as his tongue lapped at the spot. Her knees buckled. How could her neck be connected to her pussy?

He laughed and did it again. The sharp spark joined the others, building the internal fire. She twisted against him. His fingers brushed her swollen clit in a searing caress.

"Oh God!" Her knees buckled.

"Hold yourself up." He gave her pussy a soft pat.

She couldn't if he kept doing things like that.

"Do it, Jenna." The order rode the heels of the last shuddering sensation. She braced her knees and tried. She swayed as he removed his heat and support, but she didn't fall. She considered that a huge success. His hands slid over her hips. "Good."

There was a tug and a ripping sound and then a wash of cool air on her buttocks as the remnants of her pantaloons slid down her thighs.

"Clint…"

"Who else?"

No one else. No one else could make her feel like this. No one else could make her burn with fire as she bent over, exposed and vulnerable. Only Clint. She only trusted Clint this much.

"Damn, you have a fantastic ass." His palms curved around each cheek, his fingers braced on her hip bones, the thumbs dipping into the shallow creases at the top.

Her skin throbbed beneath his touch with the same pulse as her pussy.

"You don't think…" She bit back the rest of what she was going to say. Only a weak woman would ask if he though her ass was too big when the truth was in his caress, the way his fingers kneaded in sensual bliss. The way his thumbs glided down the sensitive crease between. The soft hum of appreciation he made in his throat as she involuntarily pushed back into his caress, her body knowing what her mind fought to accept. Clint McKinnely loved the way she looked. She—fat, worthless, almost invisible Jenna Hennesey—could make big strong Clint McKinnely moan from just the sight of her butt.

As an experiment, feeling awkward and terribly exposed, she wiggled her hips.

"Oh yeah." His hands left her. "Do that again."

It was harder without his touch, but she focused on him and measured her success in the harshness of his quickly drawn breath as she did as he ordered.

The sound of leather sliding through metal pulled her up short. She knew that sound intimately. He was taking off his belt.

The little voice inside that had kept her alive for years told her to freeze. To be passive so as not to risk provoking him. She was so tired of listening to that voice.

Another, newer voice rose out of the confusion, insidious in its message. It whispered for her to move, to tempt him, to test her power, to see how far she could drive this powerful man.

She wiggled her rear again, slowing the move, listening to the inner rhythm, withdrawing when she heard his breath catch, pushing back when he released it in a tormented curse.

"You're making me burn, Sunshine."

Power and pride washed through her in equal parts. She waved her ass again.

He laughed. "What happened to my timid little wife?"

She gave him the truth. "She's tired of being afraid all the time."

"I like how she's chasing away her fear." A ghost of a caress on her right buttock and then he said, "Spread your legs a little more so I can see that sweet pussy."

A wave of awkwardness washed over her, blending with the heat simmering through her, but she didn't give into it. Refused to give into it. This was her husband and he wanted to see her. What was wrong with that? She spread her legs.

"Now, that's a pretty sight."

She wondered how she looked to him, if the swollen, achy feeling in her pussy was visible. She arched her back and presented him a better view. When he moaned, she curved her spine, taking his view away, smiling when he hissed, "Witch," knowing from the stroke of his hand on her flank that he liked it. Rewarding him by arching her back again. Moaning when the smooth move sent those devilish balls shifting inside of her again.

"Damn, Sunshine, you're going to make me come."

"From just this?" she gasped.

"Yes."

"You don't mind?"

"That my wife is such a hot little temptress that just the sight of her makes me want to come?"

"Yes."

"Not a bit. Tempt away." His finger dragged along the sensitive crease where her buttock met her thigh before sliding inward, the move enhanced by the juices coating her thighs.

His finger circled her clit with the barest of touches. She took it as an incentive, riding the wave of pleasure that he drew from her with each delicious circle of his finger. Wanting to give him the same pleasure that he gave her, she waved her ass at him like a cat in heat, letting him see what he did to her, hoping he liked it, wanting to be the kind of lover he deserved.

"Son of a bitch." The curse came out a hoarse parody of Clint's normally soothing drawl. The smile that rose from deep within shocked her as much as it delighted her. She was a temptress, because only a temptress could bring a sound that tortured, that delighted from a man's lips. From Clint McKinnely's lips. She pushed back with her arms, reaching for him with her ass. His fingers slid off her clit, but that didn't matter, because she found something better. The broad head of his cock nudged her thigh. "Is that what you want, Jenna?"

The head moved up until it settled against the pad of her pussy. He had to be holding it with his hand. His cock was too long, the head too heavy to stand on its own. He shifted. The rim behind the head caught on her clit, plucking it gently.

"Yes." She closed her eyes and threw her head back as the sensation charged through her. Oh yes. That was definitely what she wanted.

"Good, because it's what I want, too." He pressed the head of his thick cock against her clit, pushing it up into her vulva, holding it against her so tightly that she felt the heavy throb of his pulse vibrating down her engorged clit. She bit her lip and bent her knees. Wanting more.

She almost cried when he pulled away. She tried to close her thighs, but he slipped along the well-juiced flesh with no resistance.

"Shhh, baby." His hand patted her ass. "We'll get back to that, but there's something I've been dreaming about all morning that I want to get to."

What could be better than what they were doing now? She didn't have to wait long to find out. There was a soft thud and then the moist heat of his breath on her starving pussy.

"A little wider, Sunshine." The order was emphasized by his palms on the insides of her thighs. She shifted her grip and her feet until she was braced to the side of the stairs.

"I can't go any further."

"That'll do." His tongue lapped the juices on the inside of her thighs. "Damn, you're sweet."

She looked between her legs to see him running his tongue over his lips, savoring her taste. His gaze, blacker than night with the emotions riding him, met hers. She closed her eyes as mortification and lust rolled over her, but nothing could block the memory of his expression, the desire stamped on the lean, chiseled features, the lust burning inside him, the openness with which he showed her his desire. Not as though it was something dirty, but something to cherish. As if it was a…gift, she realized. She opened her eyes.

"Clint?"

"What?"

He nipped the inside of her thigh. She jerked. He steadied her with his hands as she gasped, "I need to say this."

"No one's stopping you." He breathed the words against her. The reverberations shivered up her spine. His tongue tapped at the seam of her labia, wiggling between the soft nether lips.

He was. How could she talk with that insidious tongue vibrating against her? He turned beneath her.

"Bend your knees." As soon as she did Clint slid his massive shoulders through as he leaned back on the stair under her. His mouth was even with her groin. He looked up at her as he cupped her buttocks in his big hands. "Sit back on my hands."

"I'm okay."

"Your leg's hurting."

"I'm all right." It was, but how could he know?

"Sit back, Jenna."

"I'm too heavy."

"Sit back." She did, eyes closed, keeping most of her weight on her hands, gingerly giving him just a tiny fraction of it. Enough to satisfy him. She was wrong. "All of it, Sunshine."

"You can't—"

"I can." There was no hesitation in his voice or his expression. He expected complete obedience.

She gave it, expecting his arms to buckle. Instead, he didn't even seem to notice, merely humming in satisfaction as he tilted his head in and pressed a kiss at the top of her pussy.

"Now, what did you want to tell me?"

She was used to feeling big. Awkward. Bulky. Clint made her feel dainty, feminine, and beautiful. Irresistibly beautiful.

"I just wanted to say thank you."

He drew back, the tip of his tongue lingering against her moist flesh as he cocked an eyebrow at her. "For what?"

Heat washed over her cheeks. Darn it, she was blushing again. But how could she not when the handsomest man alive knelt between her thighs, his mouth an inch from her throbbing pussy, anticipation lightening his expression and tilting the corners of his beautiful mouth?

"For…" Oh God, what had she been going to say? For liking her? That was too pathetic and not at all who she wanted to be. And it wasn't even what she wanted to say. She gathered her courage and the truth he deserved. "For making this beautiful."

Approval joined the other emotions on his face. "Sunshine, if anyone is going to be thanking anyone, it's me."

"Why?"

He shrugged. "You make me feel."

"I'm glad." She noted that he didn't add anything to the end of that. Not good, not hot. Just feel. She touched his hair where it pooled on the step between her hands. It was cool and silky. Soothing.

"Good," he murmured as he leaned in.

She felt as though he touched her with more than his tongue. That in this moment, she had more of him than she'd ever had before. She didn't know what it was, but she wanted it. She wanted this openness with her husband, even if she didn't know what to do with it.

And then she stopped thinking as he took her into his mouth, holding her in the position he wanted with his hands, nibbling and sucking at her clit before lapping at the juices that welled, humming against her sensitive bud as he took his pleasure, causing more cream to flow, driving her higher—away from conscious thought, straight into pure sensation.

She rocked on his mouth, the little balls going with her, adding their own brand of torment to the moment. With every stroke of his tongue, she climbed higher. With every nibble of his lips, the invisible wires inside coiled tighter and tighter, until she couldn't hold back her scream.

"Shh, baby," he murmured. "I'll make it better in a minute."

She didn't want to wait a minute. She wanted it now. As he attempted to slide out from between her thighs, she clamped down. Her strength was no match for his. He laughed, nipped her inner thigh and slid free, shifting her weight back to her responsibility as he rose behind her.

His fingers slipped into her wet slit, moving gently against her flesh, and then he pulled out. The balls shifted, moved, stretched her outward before popping free. He dropped them, catching her as her knees buckled. The balls rolled down the stairs with loud thumps as she futilely tried to suppress a scream. Her body ached for him.

"I'm right here, Jenna."

His chest came down over her back, his hands settled beside hers. Between her thighs she could see his cock, hard and engorged, stretching almost to the stair with the weight of the wide plum-shaped head. As she watched, a pearl of fluid beaded the tip, dangled precariously a second before falling to the stair tread.

"Oh God."

His chin came to rest on her shoulder. His hair swung into view, bringing with it the scent of pine and smoke and outdoors. "Bring me home, Jenna."

She reached between them. His cock was hot to the touch. Rock-hard. She just needed to angle him up and they'd both have what they wanted. She hesitated.

"What if someone comes in?"

"Then you'll stand up."

He was right, all she had to do was stand up and her skirts would fall into place and no one except she would know about the fire raging inside. She looked between their legs. Unless they recognized those little balls down there at the foot of the stairs.

Another bead of moisture formed on the tip of his cock, growing bigger, stretching into a teardrop. She caught it with her thumb, smoothing it over the slit, tracing it back and forth, back and forth. She didn't want to waste any of this.

"Jenna, if you don't want me to come in your hand, you'll stop doing that."

On the next pass of her thumb, his hips bucked against her. His arms trembled against her shoulders. His lips brushed her ear as she debated what she wanted to do with all that power that was in her control.

"Make a decision, Jenna."

In her. She wanted him in her. And to hell with who might see. She angled his cock up as he pulled back until he was nudging her pussy. With a pulse of his hips, he seated the head in the well of her vagina.

She braced herself for his thrust. It didn't come. Instead, he spread her slowly, giving her gentleness instead of possession, trapping her between seduction and expectation, making her burn and ache as her muscles parted to accept his breadth.

"Nice and easy, baby," he whispered against her ear, his breath wafting across her cheek. "Just relax and take me in." His hips pulsed against hers. "A little at a time. Just you and me and nothing else."

Yes. Just them. Here. Together. She pushed back, taking him deeper, the pleasure spiking higher as his cock pierced the tight confines of her pussy.

"Oh God!"

He froze, his hands on her hips, keeping her still. "Damn it, Jenna, did I hurt you?"

"No." Nothing he did could ever hurt her. "Don't stop."

He didn't even seem to breathe as he asked, "Do you want more?"

"Yes." She wanted everything he had to give her.

"Baby, how did I get so lucky as to marry you?"

"You asked?"

He laughed—a harsh tortured sound. "Now you chose to crack a joke?"

"I'm sorry."

He kissed her cheek. "Don't be sorry," he rasped as he wedged his cock deeper, "Just promise to do it again later when I can appreciate it."

Reason fled as he seated himself to the hilt and gave her everything he had.

Chapter Seventeen

"Are you sure you don't want me to come with you?"

Jenna shook her head as Clint helped her down from the buckboard, pulling her cloak around her and Brianna as the wind blew down the busy street.

"I'll be fine." In truth she was dreading the shopping trip. It was a safe bet that her marriage to Clint McKinnely was going to be the talk of the town. People would no doubt be curious. She'd just have to get through it.

Clint straightened her collar. She glanced up. He didn't bother to try to hide the concern in his eyes. She wasn't very good at keeping things from him.

"Sure?"

She ducked her head so he wouldn't see the nervousness she was sure was apparent in her eyes. Having to mingle in town was always dicey. In her restaurant she had control, but going from store to store meant exposure and risk.

"You have your meeting." She hefted Bri's weight to her hip.

His forefinger bumped up her chin. "I can reschedule."

"I'm just going to get some things."

"I have an account at the store. Get whatever you want."

"You told me that twice already."

His finger stroked her cheek as the wind blew his hair around his shoulders.

"I'll probably keep saying it until I believe you mean to spend it."

"We don't need much."

"Sunshine, I've got more money than you could spend on your most frivolous day. It's all just been sitting there, waiting for my wife to come along."

"I'll take good care of it." She rested her fingers on his arm, loving the way his muscles flexed under her touch.

His breath hissed out from between his teeth. "I don't want you to take care of it. I want you to run amok with it." He tipped her chin up again with his thumb. The brim of his hat blocked the sun as his head tilted. "If I don't come back to find this wagon loaded to the sides with every notion and knickknack that you need or fancy, I'm going to be pissed."

He punctuated the statement with a hard kiss. It was over before it began. She licked her lips, catching a lingering flicker of his taste. "I'll do my best."

"You sure you don't want to tell me what has your tail in a twist about a day of shopping?" He smoothed his thumb over her lips, the worry still lingering in his dark eyes.

"Yes." She was one hundred percent sure. If she had her way she'd go to her grave with the information.

He held her chin and her gaze. She tried not to flinch. She made it for as long as she could hold her breath before she had to lower hers. Before Clint, looking a man in the eye had always meant a severe beating. She felt his lips brush the top of her head.

"You're doing better, Sunshine."

"Thank you."

"If you need me I'll be at the bank or the saloon."

"The saloon?" It came out sharper than she intended. The bitter taste of jealousy filled her mouth. She clenched her fingers on her cloak. It wasn't her place to question Clint's movements.

"Jasper likes to talk business over a drink."

"You don't drink."

"Sure I do."

"Oh." A drink in his office wouldn't be the same as in the saloon where there were loose women available to pour.

"And Jenna?"

The thumb under her chin insisted she raise her face. She didn't want to. She knew he'd be able to see the truth. She didn't want another woman anywhere near him.

"Look at me, Jenna."

She did, blinking when wind whipped his hair across her face in a silken reprimand.

"You don't have to worry about me with other women."

"I wouldn't presume—"

His thumb stroked over her lower lip, pulling it away from her teeth as he drawled, "I want you to presume, baby. I want you to put your brand all over me."

She looked at him. There was no mockery in his gaze, no glimmer of humor. He was dead serious. She knew he meant that, but he didn't know everything about her, what she'd done. It was easy to make bold statements when a person didn't know everything.

"You're going to be late for your meeting."

His hand dropped from her face. "And you have a ton of shopping to do."

"I've got my list." The paper crinkled in her palm against Brianna's back as she tightened her grip.

"Let me see it." She handed it over without a qualm. She'd been very thorough in assessing their needs. Running a house was her one area of expertise. There was absolutely no reason for his frown.

"What?" Her tone brought a smile to the corners of his mouth. The man was pure contrary.

"You forgot something."

"What."

"I've got it." He pulled a pencil from his pocket and leaned the scrap of brown paper against the wagon. With every scratch of the pencil, her resentment grew. There was no way she'd forgotten all that. And still he kept writing. She tapped her toe impatiently. His smile broadened. "No sense tapping your foot and frowning. I'm not making another run into town until a week from Saturday. It's important the list be complete."

"It is complete."

"Now it's complete." With a last tap of the lead point on paper, he folded the list and handed it back to her.

She started to open it. He folded her hand around the paper and kissed her again, this time more softly and with an edge of humor. His tongue traced the seam of her lips—slow and easy—the way that he knew fractured her grasp on propriety until, right there in the street, in front of the mercantile, with her daughter in her arms, and the town no doubt watching, she leaned into him, needing more of his touch, his flavor, his heat.

"Ah Sunshine, you tempt me."

He didn't sound at all upset about it. Despite the blush that she knew made her cheeks cherry red, she smiled. "I'm doing my best."

The heat level in his gaze went from a spark to a flagrant roar. Against her thigh, his cock surged and thickened. Oh, he liked it when she was bold. And truth be told, with every attempt she was liking it more and more. She liked being a temptress. At least with Clint.

"You, Sunshine, could burn a man to cinders." He cupped her face in his callused palm. She hadn't recognized the slight hitch in his breath before, but now she knew it for what it was. Desire. For her. A desire he wasn't shy about showing her. She liked that, maybe best of all.

She fought to hold his gaze and admitted, "I'm glad you think so."

His low laugh surrounded her like a hug. "So am I, Sunshine. So am I."

He cupped her elbow. "I'll meet you at the bakery in about three hours?" he confirmed as he helped her up the wooden steps.

She nodded. "Mara said Lorie has it all under control."

"But I imagine you're anxious to see for yourself?"

"What makes you say that?"

"Because I would be."

In that case she didn't feel badly admitting the truth. "I am."

He opened the door to the mercantile. The little bell above the door jangled as she turned. He looked over her head into the shop, and a fleeting frown creased his forehead before he took her mouth with his, kissing her hard and passionately, like a man making a point. When she was gasping for breath, he pulled back, smoothing the moisture from her lips with his thumb. He gently flicked Bri's nose, his hard face softening as she screwed up her face in responses.

"I'll catch up with you later." With a tip of his hat to the occupants of the shop behind her, he was off. She watched him head down the wooden walk, his long legs eating up distance with that smooth, effortless grace that spoke of power. He was a fine figure of a man— broad shouldered, lean hipped, and all hers. She didn't know if she'd ever get used to it.

Bri squirmed and she shifted her up on her hip. The paper in her hand rustled. Bracing Bri on her forearm, she opened the list and read his additions. He wanted her to have a muff for her hands, fancy dresses, new boots, the rose powder she liked, chocolate, cooking utensils, clothes for her and Brianna, chocolate.

The repeat of chocolate made her smile. He didn't have to look too deeply to see her liking for that, but it was what he added last that brought tears to her eyes. She brushed the pad of her thumb over the hastily written list. There, in his bold masculine scrawl were the words, *Anything your heart desires.*

She was beginning to think he meant it.

* * * * *

An hour later both Jenna and Brianna were played out. The mail order catalogue was filled with every conceivable item a human could want. And at prices that made her gasp. Like how much they wanted for that fancy new dress she kept coming back to over and over.

"Everything all right, Mrs. McKinnely?" Eloise Fawcett asked.

Jenna winced. She must have gasped aloud again. She glanced between the stacks of new denims until she located Eloise. She was behind the counter portioning sugar into small bags.

"I'm fine."

"Do you need some help?" Eloise's eyes were a warm blue under her raised brows.

"Oh no. There are just so many options…"

"It's amazing, all the things they come up with back East, isn't it?" she asked without breaking her rhythm.

It was more than amazing. It was mind-staggering. "Yes."

"Do you need more paper?" She tucked a pencil into her soft brown hair.

"Gracious no." Jenna didn't know how she was going to sort through everything she'd already put down as a possible.

"That Clint can be an impatient one, can't he?" Eloise didn't wait for a response, just launched into the rest of what she wanted to say. "Imagine giving a new bride only one day to make all of her purchases."

Jenna didn't correct Eloise's assumption. It was better that the pushy shopkeeper think this was a one-shot deal instead of the open invitation she had a feeling Clint intended to extend. Bri began to fuss again. She jostled her on her hip while trying desperately to add the impossibly long row of numbers. No matter what Clint had said, there was no way he could want her to spend this much.

"Why I remember when he bought Elijah's place. He wanted everything *now*, without a thought to the expense, not to mention how difficult it is to get items freighted."

"It was nice of you to accommodate him." She looked down at her list. She hadn't realized it would cost money to freight the items on top of paying for them.

"We were happy to do it. Fawcett Mercantile prides itself on meeting all its patrons' needs with the utmost efficiency." Eloise grabbed up the small bags, disappearing from sight for a second as she turned to put them on the shelf behind her.

"I'm sure Clint appreciated it." And they made a hefty profit, but being a businesswoman herself, Jenna couldn't begrudge Eloise the success.

Eloise popped back into view, smoothing her apron and then her hair. "We are the ones who appreciate the business."

Jenna ignored the "we". Technically, Eloise co-owned the mercantile with her brother, but the one who did the work and made it a viable business was Eloise. Her brother Mark merely pocketed his half of the profits and wandered through every gambling saloon in the west losing it as fast as she sent it. He only came back into town when he needed more money. Thank God it had been a year since his last visit.

Bri's fidgeting escalated to fussing. "I'm afraid I'm going to have to finish this later. Bri needs attention."

"Do you want to use the back room?"

Her "no" was probably a bit hasty to be polite, but there was no way Jenna was going back there. Even if Mark was hundreds of miles away. "I need to check out things at Sweet Thyme anyway."

Eloise nodded, a frown marring her pleasant features. "Lorie seems to be doing a good job, but you can never be too careful. It's not the same as you being there."

No, it wasn't. But she seriously didn't know how she was going to manage running a home, being a mother, and running the bakery. Right now she was baking a lot at Clint's home and having one of the hands drive the goods in, but even that was getting difficult. It would be ideal if Lorie was a great baker, but while she did phenomenal bread, her other baked goods were lackluster, though getting better.

Laying Bri on the counter, Jenna folded her list and tucked it into her pocket as she reached for her cloak. She swung it around her shoulders. As it flared behind her, there was a huge crash. She froze. Oh heavens! What had she broken?

A flash of movement caught her eyes. A blur of black and brown before Eloise's husband Dan leapt out of the back room and pulled the blur to a halt.

"Got you!" It was a boy. A wild-haired, wild-eyed, filthy boy. His dark skin and darker eyes proclaimed him Indian. The torn clothes and rail-thin frame proclaimed him homeless. Dan pulled him up short by a handful of shirt and hair.

The boy swung around with his fist, threats tumbling from his mouth in an incomprehensible torrent of sound. The blow glanced off of Dan's groin. Dan's curses joined the melee as he raised his fist. His fist was huge, a grown man against a gangly boy. Jenna caught her breath and released it on a protest, "Don't!"

Dan ignored her cry, punching the boy in the stomach, letting him drop as he doubled over and heaved. "Damn thieving Indian!"

With a quick glance to make sure Bri was secure, Jenna raced around the counter and between the aisles. She got there just in time to hear Dan order Eloise to go get the sheriff, and to see the boy whip a knife out of his threadbare moccasin.

"No!"

She grabbed for his wrist. She missed. The knife slashed past her skirts. She screamed for Clint as loud as she could as Dan kicked the knife out of the boy's hand, bringing his foot back again.

She did the only thing she could think to do. She threw herself over the boy, wrapping herself around his scrawny, writhing body, and yelled, "Don't. Don't."

She closed her eyes and braced herself to take the kick. It glanced off her shoulder, much of the force gone.

"Goddamn it, Mrs. McKinnely, get the hell away from that filthy Indian."

The boy lay still beneath her. His bones so prominent they poked her through her clothes. She could feel the chill of his flesh against her hands. She opened her eyes. He was staring back at her, his eyes such a deep brown that they were almost black. There was anger and hatred in his gaze, and somewhere way down deep beneath the negative, a flicker of hope.

"Get off me." At least he spoke English. Bri screamed, scared and alone, across the room. The boy frowned at her. In that instant he looked so familiar, she knew, knew who he was. Everything in her went hard with determination.

"No." She turned her head so she could meet Dan's eyes, pressing hard with her bad leg over the boy's thighs. She ignored the cramping pain that immediately commenced. "Don't touch my son."

"I know you got a soft heart and all, Mrs. McKinnely, but saying it doesn't make it so." Dan said.

"Yes it does." If she had to call in the McKinnely muscle, she was making it so.

Beneath her the boy froze, as if her words stole his ability to breathe. Across the room, Bri let loose with the full power of her lungs. Jenna didn't know what to do beyond what she was doing, so she held on and waited for inspiration to occur.

"That's one lowlife piece of scum you don't want to be laying claim to. He's been stealing from me for weeks." Dan reached down to help her up.

"Don't touch me and don't touch my son." Jenna hunched her shoulder away from his hand.

Again, Dan ignored her as if she hadn't spoken. His fingers curled around her upper arm, and the boy sprang to life, heaving her off. He was incredibly strong. As Dan lifted her, the boy struck, kicking him hard in the groin, and shoving her behind him. His filthy hair slapped her in the face as a string of threats fell from his mouth. She didn't know what he was saying, but she knew they were threats from the way he stood, ready to take on all comers, defending her. Dan got to his feet, his face red, murder in his eyes.

"Run!" Jenna pushed the boy aside.

He stumbled two steps and then pushed back, trying to get between her and Dan. She needed help. She needed Clint. She screamed for him as Dan lunged, reaching around her for the boy who was leaping forward to meet him.

She bit Dan's arm, pushing him back with all her might. Behind her the boy pressed forward, shoving Dan's hands away. Bri's screams mingled with hers as Dan grabbed her jaw.

"Dan, I'm trying to think real hard on why I shouldn't slit your throat, but I'm fast running out of reasons."

Jenna turned. Clint stood in the aisle, dwarfing the room, his black eyes flat and hard, his hand on the hilt of his big knife.

"Don't let him hurt my son, Clint," she begged, grabbing for the boy's arm. She caught the edge of his sleeve as he jumped at the sight of Clint. She couldn't blame him. Clint in a snit was as cold and as scary as it got.

Only by an arch of his brow did Clint register his surprise that she'd claimed the boy.

"The boy isn't her son," Dan growled. "He's a damned thief. Been stealing from me for weeks."

Clint's second eyebrow joined the first. "Did Jenna say the boy's our son?"

"Yes."

He looked over at Jenna. Nothing in his expression gave away what he was thinking. She clutched the boy's arm harder, her stomach sinking. As if he sensed her fear, the boy edged in front of her. Another quick arch of Clint's brow, a quirk of his lips, and maybe a hint of approval? He turned to Dan and shrugged. "Then it's so."

The boy broke free from her grip. Clint caught him as he sped by.

"Be careful!" Jenna cried, biting her lip as her leg gave, catching herself on the counter. "He's hurt."

Clint held him away from his body, letting him swing and curse, feet dangling off the floor. He glanced at Jenna. "Hurt?"

"Dan punched him in the stomach!"

"Stay." Clint lowered the boy's feet to the floor. The boy didn't move. Clint caught Jenna's hand and steadied her as he asked Dan, "You punched a kid in the stomach? My kid?"

"He tried to kick him, too," Jenna added.

"Tried?" Clint pushed Jenna behind him, keeping his eye on Dan.

"The kid pulled a damned knife," Dan interjected, as if that made a difference.

"Can't imagine why, when a grown man starts whaling on him."

"Jesus Christ, McKinnely." Dan glanced over his shoulder before stepping back. "He's a goddamn thief."

Behind him, Clint heard Jenna's outraged gasp. Her hands touched the small of his back. If she asked him to kill the guy he would, but she just stood there, her hands pressing into him, letting him make the decision, her anxiety surrounding him like a cloud.

"He's my son," Clint said, letting the cold calm that came with fury encase him. "There's no way he can be a thief."

"How the hell do you figure that?"

"Because he can have any goddamn thing he wants."

Clint turned, caught Jenna's hand, and pointed her toward the door. A smudge on the shoulder of her cloak caught his eye. He knew a boot print when he saw one. The rage flashed bright and hot through his calm.

"You son of a bitch." He spun around, the room dissolving out of focus, his being concentrated on the only thing that mattered.

"It was an accident, Clint." Dan threw up his hands and took another step back.

"I don't care." Clint took two steps forward.

"She threw herself over the boy." Dan backed up against the counter. "I couldn't pull back."

"I don't care." Clint closed the gap between them.

Dan threw the first punch. Clint blocked it easily and sank his fist deep into the son of a bitch's stomach, in his mind picturing Jenna on the floor, her body shielding the boy, and the hulking bastard kicking her. Them. Using his size against a small woman and a half-starved boy. Against his family.

He hit him again, and again, easily dodging the other man's attempts to fight back, knocking him back over the counter, following him over with an easy leap. The man didn't get up, just lay there hands up, admitting defeat. The urge to put a bullet in his brain was almost irresistible.

"Clint." Jenna's voice seeped through the anger.

"Go wait outside."

There was a pause and then, "No."

He turned, his hair whipping over his shoulder. "No?"

She stood there, her hands clenched before her, her lip between her teeth, visibly pale and shaking, and defied him again.

"No."

"Why not?"

"Because it's enough. I want to go home. Our daughter and son are hungry and I refuse to let them suffer while you amuse yourself."

"Amuse myself?" He straightened. "I'm avenging you."

"No. You're angry and taking it out on others. Avenging me would stop at a punch or taking your business elsewhere."

"And how would you know?"

"Because that would be fair." Fair? The woman hadn't known a day of fair in her whole life, and suddenly she was an expert?

"What are you telling me, Sunshine?"

"I want to go home, Clint. I want to take my children and my husband, and I want to go home." Her big blue eyes shimmered with fear and a need that tore a hole in his chest.

Where she felt safe. He understood. Damn, he'd wanted this trip into town to be good for her. He glanced down at Dan. "If you touch my wife or kids again, I'll gut you. And I'll take my time about it, too."

"Jesus, Clint, it was an accident."

"There are no accidents when it comes to my family."

"I didn't know the kid belonged to you."

The man actually believed that made a difference. That there was ever an excuse for a grown man to beat on a kid. He glanced over at the skinny excuse for a boy who was holding Bri. The boy who'd done his best to put himself between Jenna and Dan. The family resemblance between Bri and the boy was strong.

"He was just hungry, Dan."

"It's not my job to feed the world."

"No, it's not." Clint settled his Stetson back on his head. "You can send the final settlement of my accounts to my house."

He walked around the counter. Jenna reached him as he rounded the corner, her arms going aground him. She hugged him as if he were hurt and needed soothing. The softness of her breasts pressed into his stomach as her cheek rested against his chest. He cupped her head in his hand and pulled her closer. Let the softness of her ease over him, soothing the beast that prowled within, filling the dark hole that housed his rage.

"I'm sorry, baby."

"How did you know to come?" Her hands stroked his back.

"Eloise."

"Dan sent her for the sheriff."

"She fetched me instead."

"Oh."

"Did he hurt you?" He touched her shoulder lightly over the smudge, probing gently.

"No, but I think Bri's brother is hurt."

"We'll take him to Doc's. Dorothy will fix him a good meal."

"He needs it." She propped her chin on his chest, much more comfortable with his nearness now. "He's so skinny."

He could tell that offended her personally. "He'll fill out with a few square meals under his belt."

"I hope so." A pause and then, "Do you mind?"

He kissed her lips. "No. But I do mind you getting hurt."

"I couldn't let him kick him."

"You could have waited."

"Would you?"

"No. But I'm a man."

"And I'm a woman."

"My woman."

"Yes." She leaned back, "I know he was stealing but he obviously doesn't have anyone to care for him."

"I said I didn't mind." He kissed her again, longer this time, breathing in her scent and her generous spirit as he did.

The boy stared at them across the aisle, suspicion, aggression, and challenge in his dark gaze. He looked so much like Cougar had when he'd blown into town almost twenty years ago that Clint couldn't help but smile.

"I think the boy and I will get along just fine."

Chapter Eighteen

"Nice-looking boy you've got there," Asa said, joining Clint on Doc's porch, his collar turned up against the evening chill.

Clint looked through the window to where Dorothy was forcing another piece of pie on the kid. Nothing offended Dorothy more than an underfed male. "For all the fuss he made about taking that bath, he did clean up well."

Asa touched the bruise on his cheek which he'd gotten while escorting Gray to the tub. "A fighter to the bone, that one."

The door opened and light spilled onto the small porch before being blocked by Cougar's big frame. "Talking about Gray?"

"Hell of a name to pin on the kid."

Clint shrugged. "The kid chose it."

"I'm thinking that was more self-defense," Asa offered, leaning against a porch support. "No offense, Clint, but Jenna doesn't have an ear for languages."

Clint smiled. "If the kid hadn't conceded, I was considering begging. It was pure torture listening to her butcher his Indian name."

Cougar leaned back against the log wall, melting naturally into the shadow. "She's not one for giving up, that's for sure."

"No, she isn't."

"And you like that about her."

Clint smiled. "Yes, I do."

Cougar's teeth gleamed white in the sudden flash of a sulfur striking.

He held out the cigarette he'd just lit. Clint shook his head.

"Since when aren't you partial to an after dinner smoke?" Asa asked, the amusement in his tone indicating that he had a fair idea.

"Since I got married." The only time Jenna had pulled away from his kiss was right after he'd had a cigarette. She'd recovered, but he liked her better when she was leaning into him rather than away.

"Pussy whipped already?" Cougar asked.

"No more than you."

"I'm safe tonight," Cougar said, taking a deep drag on his cigarette, his eyes narrowing with satisfaction. "Mara can't mess with my dessert if she catches a whiff of smoke seeing as how Dorothy's cooking."

"You could just lay down the law to her," Asa suggested.

"The same way you laid down the law to Elizabeth about breaking horses?" Cougar asked, smiling.

Clint echoed the grin. It was the worst kept secret in the territory that Asa indulged his headstrong wife.

"Along those lines," Asa admitted. "I might just be getting soft, but all that woman has to do is turn those pretty green eyes on me, and I forget my point."

"Yeah. Same here." Cougar took another drag. "The only difference is that Mara's eyes are brown."

"Elizabeth's prettier too," Asa said with a perfectly straight face.

Clint rolled his eyes, knowing what was coming. Cougar was a keg of dynamite when it came to Mara.

"In your dreams." Cougar flicked the cigarette into the dirt beyond the porch.

"I'm not saying Mara isn't sweet and smart, but when it comes to looks, Mara can't hold a candle to my Elizabeth."

Cougar pushed off the wall, stepping into the light. Clint shook his head and entered the fray.

"Hell, you're both sucking dust when it comes to my Jenna. There isn't a prettier, softer woman in the territory."

"I'll give you that," Asa drawled. "She has to be pretty damned soft in the head to take up with you."

"You got that right," Cougar agreed, laughter in his eyes.

Clint shrugged. "You might be right there."

"Ah hell, you're still not thinking you're not right for the girl, are you?" Cougar growled.

"She deserves someone who can love her."

"She needs someone she can depend on," Asa countered, his tone serious for once. "Someone she can trust to lead her without abusing her."

"She doesn't need a leader."

"Christ, Clint," Cougar scoffed. "The girl's been trained to do nothing but follow. And I suspect, been beaten into accepting it, and you want her to just up and take charge?"

"Shit, no wonder she's having nightmares," Asa murmured.

"She's not having nightmares anymore." Clint reached for his makings.

"Well, that's a blessing," Cougar cut into the argument. "Any word on who raped her?"

"No." Clint untied the pouch.

"Damn. I'd rest a lot easier if we knew that."

"We'd all rest easier." Asa paused, caught Clint's eye and nodded to the pouch in his hand. "Sure you want that cigarette tonight?"

Clint sighed. He wanted it but he wanted Jenna more. Especially as Dorothy was hinting that Gray should stay with her and Doc tonight while dropping additional hints that the boy shouldn't be separated from his sister so soon after their reunion. He put the pouch back in his pocket.

The door opened and Gray Fox Searching and Doc came out. Doc took a seat in the bentwood rocker and took out his pipe. Cleaned and dressed in clothes Dorothy had dredged up for him, Gray almost looked civilized, except for the wariness in his gaze and the slight curl to his full lips.

"Evening, son."

Gray cut him a glare and nodded. Clint considered it a victory that he didn't deny the relationship. Then again, being Indian, the boy understood kinship by claim. And by his own words, he really had nowhere else to go. The Indian wars had seen to that.

"You're packing a lot of attitude for an eleven-year-old," Cougar pointed out conversationally.

"I am not a child."

"You're not a man either, and until you learn to fight, you'd better rein in that challenge."

"I fight just fine."

"That why your mother got kicked while protecting you?" Clint asked.

Before the boy could open his mouth, Asa was shaking his head. "A man protects his women, Gray. He never endangers them."

A shadow passed over the kid's face, and Clint swore, knowing he wasn't thinking of Jenna right then. The boy's mother had been forced into prostitution and then murdered when she had refused to continue after her daughter was born.

"You couldn't help what happened to your mother, son. Some things are out of our control. It's the ones we can control that we need to be aware of."

The boys jaw set in a line that said clearer than words that it wasn't over as far as he was concerned.

"In a few years," Clint told him, understanding, making a place for him at the rail, "if you want to hunt down the man who killed your mother, I'll ride with you."

That earned him a startled glance.

"You're a McKinnely now," Cougar cut in with a shrug. "You're not alone."

"However, between now and then," Clint continued, "you've got to get ready."

"Ready?"

"You need to learn to handle yourself."

"I can handle myself."

"That's pride talking," Asa interrupted. "Pride will get you killed. Common sense will get you to your goal."

"I'll teach you to handle a knife," Cougar offered.

"And who are you to teach me?" Gray demanded.

Clint had to hand it to the kid for gall. Even when Cougar's face went hard and his eyes went dead cold, the kid held his ground.

"I am your uncle."

Doc shook his head at Gray. "The first thing you need to learn is when to bite your tongue."

"Why?" Head thrown back, the kid was a picture of arrogance.

Asa rolled his makings into a cigarette. "Because you just went and told 'Gut 'em McKinnely' to fuck off."

The kid swallowed hard and went pale. To his credit, he didn't hand out excuses and try to cover. Instead, he squared his shoulders and remained silent. The kid had some real likable qualities.

Gray swallowed again, and looked at Cougar, Asa, and then Clint. Clint started counting in his head as he passed a match to Asa. In the orange flare, the boy's distress was easy to see. Gray took a step back away from the rail. His mouth set belligerently, but not before Clint saw the hint of a tremble. If Cougar didn't cut this short, he sure as shit was going to.

Cougar glanced at the boy from the corner of his eye.

"Lucky for you Gray, I've got a rule against holding grudges on family."

For an instant, Gray wavered, and then he stood tall. He looked so alone in that moment that Clint put this hand on his shoulder. The kid's bones poked his palm, but there was the promise of future strength in their width. He didn't flinch away so Clint didn't pull away.

"I was disrespectful."

"It's been a hell of a day, so I'll cut you some slack," Cougar allowed. "Plus, I'm grateful for your stepping in for Jenna."

The boy frowned. "She shouldn't have done that."

"No," Clint agreed, "she shouldn't have."

"What'd you expect her to do, let Dan beat the boy to a smudge?" Doc asked, his grizzled brows raised.

"She should have called for help."

"And let the boy be hurt? You don't know your wife, Clint, if you think she'd ever regard that as an option."

"She is too soft," Gray agreed.

"She's all heart, that's for sure." He turned the kid toward him. "That why you picked her for Bri?"

He nodded. "Her real name is Hope on the Mist."

Asa laughed. "I bet that's a humdinger of a name to pronounce in Cheyenne."

Gray nodded, glanced through the window, and then shrugged.

"Maybe it is best she be called Bri." He looked through the window again. Clint followed the trajectory of his gaze to where the women sat, Bri in their midst, her arms waving and a happy smile on her face.

"She has grown." He sounded almost resentful.

"Good food and care will do that to a baby," Doc said, the smoke from his pipe scenting the cold night air.

"It is good."

"The way the women were feeding you, we'll soon have to roll you in and out of the door," Asa teased.

"They are good cooks," Gray agreed noncommittally.

"Soon we'll all be as fat as pigs ready for slaughter," Cougar added with a slap to his stomach. He didn't sound at all upset with the prospect. Probably because he was in no danger of it ever happening, but he sure shocked the kid.

"You are a warrior."

"That I am, but there are real pleasures to being a married man."

"And yet you just have the one wife." Gray looked confused.

"Mara's more than enough woman for me," Cougar laughed, the sternness of his features dissolving into pleasure.

"They say she is too small to bear you sons."

Cougar's smile faded and his expression grew serious. "Then I'll find my children elsewhere."

"Another wife would be an easier solution," Gray countered with irrefutable logic.

"So you would think," Cougar smiled, his face hidden from view as he looked toward his wife. "But I've always been contrary."

"Now that," Asa agreed, "is the truth."

Gray turned to Clint and said, "Your woman cannot bear you children."

"No."

"That's not for sure, Clint," Doc countered.

"I've made my peace with it." He shrugged and the smile came from inside. "Besides, I can't see Jenna being happy with another woman under foot."

"You will not take another wife because it would hurt her?" Gray asked, surprise lifting his tone.

"That, and I don't want another wife."

He frowned. "Many white men have other women."

"What other men do is neither here nor there."

"You have grown soft." The kid scowled as if keeping his word to Jenna were a crime.

"So it's been said."

"I will never grow soft." Gray stared into the night, his thin, handsome face hardening to a razor edge of determination.

Clint squeezed his shoulders. "You may resent me for saying this, but I hope you're wrong."

"Amen to that," Asa murmured while Doc and Cougar nodded.

Clint wasn't leaving his son's future up to God. If he had anything to say about it—and he intended to have a lot to say—his son would never grow up to know aching emptiness that could never be filled. That hollow echo in a man's soul that came from too much purpose, too much killing. No matter how good the reason the boy thought he had.

* * * * *

It was late when they pulled up in front of their home. The temperature dropped with every turn of the buggy's wheels. Clint took his rifle out of his lap and jumped down. Ice crunched under his feet, and his breath frosted in the lantern light. As he held out his hand, his black eyes glittered with that strange emotion that had been there since the disaster in the mercantile.

Jenna placed her palm in his. His fingers closed around hers, their strength banked. She loved the way he touched her. Controlled, but with the promise of all the passion she could handle. Which was becoming more and more as each day passed.

"I wish Bri and Gray had come home with us," she said as he swung her down.

"And deprive Dorothy of a chance to mother them?" he asked, his voice neutral and his eyes hidden by the shadow of his hat.

"She's a nice woman."

"The best." His hands lingered on her waist as she got her balance. It was so dark she couldn't see the hem of her cloak.

"She's in her glory with two kids to fuss over," he added as he grabbed his rifle and High Stepper's reins. "Besides, it'll give us time to set up a room for Gray so he'll have a place here, and feel wanted."

"You don't think he'll take Bri and run do you?"

"If I did, I wouldn't have left them there."

She rubbed her arms and stomped her feet against the seeping cold.

"He's just so angry…" She bit her lip, remembering the boy's eyes, their haunted depths. "So alone."

"Give him time Jenna, and he'll be fine. Dorothy knows how to handle kids."

Jenna knew Dorothy could handle Bri, but Gray Fox Searching was a whole different story.

"So you think Gray will be okay?"

"His stomach's full," Clint answered. "He's got a warm bed to lie in, and his sister's near." He started moving. She moved with him, but the lantern cast shadows she couldn't see into and she fell behind.

"Watch, there's a hole right there." He stopped so suddenly that she almost ran into him. His arm slid around her waist, the reins dangling down the side of her cloak as he pulled her up against him. His grip on her waist tightened to the point that it didn't matter if she saw the hole or not. Clint wouldn't let her fall.

The trust she felt in his company was novel. In her youth she'd dreamed of a hero who'd like her for herself, take the good with the bad, and stand by her. With maturity, she'd accepted a good man was one who didn't use his wife as a resting place for his fist, and now Clint was causing her to reevaluate her assessments once again, taking her back to the dreams of a child. Was it any wonder that she waffled between caution and hope when it came to him?

"Stay there." He led her to the right of the door, his hand staying at her hip until he was sure she was steady. Just another of the considerations she was learning to handle. Worse yet, expect.

"Okay."

The wagon creaked as he opened the door and led the horse and buggy through. She was alone in the dark for a heart-stopping moment and then he was there, his hand touching her arm, making her jump.

"Easy, Sunshine. I'm right here."

It was pathetic, but ever since *that night* she couldn't stand the dark and the memories that stalked it. As if he sensed her need, his big, capable hand slid up her arm and across her back, pulling her into him.

"I've got you, Jenna."

"Hold me for a minute?" She felt his start. "I'm sorry." She pulled back. She got as far as his palm.

"That's the first time you've asked me to hold you," he murmured, pulling her into his chest. He smelled of leather, smoke, and man.

"Is it?" It seemed like she had been asking him to touch her forever.

"Yes."

"I must seem like such a baby to you."

"I've already told you how I see you."

She snuggled into his embrace, grabbed her daring, and plunged forward. "Tell me again."

Beneath her cheek, his chest jerked. She'd surprised him. Good.

"Getting bold?" he asked, his drawl deeper, neutrality gone.

"I'm trying it out." No reason not to admit the truth.

"I like it." The last was said against her hair. His lips moved across her head in a gentle caress. "Are you scared, Jenna?"

She shook her head. He would have left it there, but she couldn't. He never hid himself from her. He gave all he was, all the time. She liked how that made her feel. She'd like to make him feel the same. She wondered if he could feel her blush through his coat as she pushed herself down the path she was setting.

"I just wanted to be close to you." She buried her face in his coat. Of all the unsophisticated ways to phrase things. She sounded scared and whiny when she wanted to sound strong and seductive. His hand came up to cup her head. His fingertips rasped her hot cheek.

"Are you blushing?"

"Could you pretend not to notice?"

"Depends on why."

"I don't want to be someone you feel sorry for."

His fingers stilled. "What makes you think I feel sorry for you?"

"Please don't treat me like I'm stupid."

"I wasn't aware that I was."

"You're always fussing over me."

"That's because you're sweet to spoil." His big body leaned into her. She leaned back against the barn wall, bearing his weight and his expectations.

"I am?"

"Yeah. I've never had a wife before. I find I like making you smile." He kissed her ear as his hair fell against her.

"Sigh," he whispered against the side of her neck. He nibbled on the cord beneath her ear. She didn't contain her groan as shivers raced down her spine and his smile spread.

"Moan." He took her earlobe between his teeth and bit lightly. "Moan for me some more, baby."

She did, helpless to do otherwise as he sucked at the flesh under his mouth, pulling her hips into his.

She licked her lips, swallowed twice, and asked him, "Why?"

Again that start. She felt his smile spread against her neck. "I like you bold, and to answer your question, because it makes me hard."

She tucked her chin, trying to see his face, but it was too dark, and his hat brim was in her way. But his lips were hot on her neck, scorching her with the intensity of his want.

"I'm glad you like me." He drew back and his gaze was as unfathomable as the night around them. She clutched at his coat. "I mean the way I look. I'm glad you find me attractive."

"Good." His smile was slow coming, but when it did, it was beautiful. She wanted to taste his smile, experience his pleasure. See herself through his senses. She tugged on his lapel.

"What?"

"Bend down."

He cocked an eyebrow at her. "Why?"

"I want to kiss you." Her voice wasn't nearly as confident as she wanted. Her cheeks burned so hot that she thought her tongue would burn off.

"What's wrong, Jenna?" His eyes narrowed. He didn't bend down and his smile disappeared.

"Nothing." She ducked her head, embarrassment eating her alive. Her breath rose up to mist her face in a mockery of her hopes. He tipped her chin up. His finger held her in place for his scrutiny.

"You don't have to be something you're not for me. If you want or need something, just ask."

"Who says I'm being something I'm not?" she muttered.

The arch of his brow said more than enough. He could never understand if she didn't tell him. She braced her fingers on his chest, flattening the tips one by one against the soft leather of his coat as she took a slow, deep breath.

"My whole life men have been telling me I'm sinful." His chest expanded under her hands as he took a breath to argue. She shook her head, and focused on the pale blur of the collar of his shearling coat. "Don't say anything, please." She risked a quick glance. "Just let me get this out."

His chest lowered as he released a slow breath. She heard the rustle and saw the sway of his hair as he nodded.

"That when I look at a man, I tempt him to sin. That my body is the Devil's playground and that when men look at me, I tempt them to amoral thoughts and acts. That the Devil acts through me."

She'd never understood how, but she'd been beaten black and blue more times than she could count for those thoughts in men's heads.

"Sunshine…"

She shook her head, not looking at him. He didn't say anything more, just pulled her closer, as if his big arms could shelter her from her memories. "You don't see me like that."

"Hell, no."

"You like me." His hand stroked over her hair, sliding into the contained strands.

"Yes."

"I mean the way you feel with me."

"That, too." His hand pulled away and her hair fell down her back.

"I'm not used to it."

"I gathered that."

"But I like it." If she didn't burst into flames in the next minute, it would be a miracle. "It's just…sometimes I forget, and I fret."

"I know."

"It makes it hard sometimes."

"Makes what hard?" His fingers threaded through her hair, lifting it to the faint moonlight, working his fingers through the tangles.

"Finding out who I am…" His hand stopped moving. "With you," she finished in a breathless rush.

"You need to be something different with me?" He gathered her hair into his fist. He didn't sound happy. She was messing this up so badly.

"Not different, but maybe, for once, me. Does that make sense?"

"Maybe." His hand moved and there were a couple tugs at the back of her head that tilted it up. The shadows hid his expression from her view while she was sure he could see every nuance of hers. "How did your husband make love to you, Jenna?"

The blush drained from her cheeks so fast that she felt lightheaded. She tried to turn away, but he'd wrapped her hair around his hand, and she couldn't move. She had to stand there, open and vulnerable as he asked her to bare her soul.

"Don't hide from me now, Jenna. He's been standing between us long enough."

"He's dead."

"He lives in your mind where I can't see him, hurting you in ways that I can't protect you from."

"Please."

"Draw me a picture of him, Jenna. Show me the son of a bitch so that I can make him go away."

"I can't." She closed her eyes.

"Goddamn it, you will. I won't have the bastard hurting you from the grave." He shook her lightly. The shaking stopped and then his lips were on hers, hard, possessive, desperate. She didn't fight him, just opened her mouth for the thrust of his tongue. She was his. Always had been. Even while she was married to another man. God spare her soul. Clint drew back slightly, his breath hitting her moist lips in uneven puffs. "Tell me, baby. Let's make him go away together."

"Here?"

"Here. Now." He kissed the corner of her mouth. He turned and took three steps to the left, taking her with him with his arm around her waist. He kept his hand at her waist as he sat. He tugged her down to sit across his lap. "Out here where God can hear every word, let's send that son of a bitch to hell where he belongs."

She remembered the beatings, the humiliation, the pain, the confusion of never knowing what she was supposed to do, what she'd done wrong. The unrelenting knowledge that she was tainted. She buried her face in his throat.

"I don't want you to see me that way," she admitted, inhaling his familiar scent, hugging it to her.

"What way?"

"Worthless. Dirty."

She was breaking him in two.

"I could never see you as dirty, Sunshine." Clint wrapped his arms around Jenna, gathering her softness into him, feeling whole the way he did only when he was touching her, wishing he could protect her from the memories.

Against his chest she shook her head. "You don't know how I was."

"I know you were sweet and trusting and did your best to please." She stiffened in his arms as if surprised. Didn't she know how long she'd fascinated him? "I've been watching you a long time, Sunshine."

"I was married." She sounded shocked, as if a piece of paper had anything to do with how he felt about her.

"And I kept my distance."

"I never knew."

"There was no reason you should."

"How could I not know?"

"Would it have made a difference?" She didn't breathe for the span of a heartbeat and then she nodded. "Then I'm sorry."

She was shaking her head before he finished speaking. "I couldn't have borne it if I'd known."

"All you would have had to do was say the word and there wouldn't have been anything to bear."

"You would have fought him?" He couldn't have meant what she thought he meant. Try as she would, Jenna couldn't make out his expression in the dark and his body gave her no indication. He was relaxed and calm beneath her.

"I would have killed him." The finality in his tone was shocking.

"You can't kill a man for how he treats his wife."

"It's been done a time or two."

"By you?"

"Once." There wasn't an ounce of remorse in his tone. She pondered all she knew of Clint, what she'd heard, what she'd seen.

"You're not a murderer."

"Depends on how you define it." He wasn't apologizing, just stating the facts.

"If you killed a man over how he treated his wife, he deserved it." She felt that certainty to the soles of her feet. She touched the indentation where his collarbones met.

"He did." His fingertips on her cheek were incredibly gentle. Tender. He traced her jaw, the pad of his index finger coming to rest on the point of her chin. It lingered there, stroking as if he couldn't get enough of the feel of her skin. "Tell me about how it was, Jenna."

"It was awful."

"How?"

"There were so many rules."

"Name some."

"I couldn't look a man in the face. Couldn't question an order any man gave. Couldn't speak unless spoken to."

His curse echoed above her. "And in the bedroom?"

"I just had to do what I was told, exactly how I was told, no resistance and no complaints." Nausea welled. She buried her face in his throat, breathing deeply of his scent, his strength.

"What happened if you didn't?"

"I got hurt."

"How."

"I can't tell you that." Shame burned deep into her soul, and spread outward.

"I want him gone, Jenna, so you'll tell me because you know it won't change the way I feel about you." His hand cupped her stomach beneath her cloak. Big and warm, it soothed her. She burrowed deeper, wishing she could climb inside him in that moment, know everything there was to know about him, let him know all there was to know about her. All without having to say a word.

"It has to."

He forced her chin up, tapped her lips with his thumb until she raised her eyes. "It can't."

"I didn't have any choice…" He held her so hard, she thought her ribs would crack.

"I know, baby. I know." He tucked her head into his neck with his chin, bundling her into his heat, his strength. "But you have a choice now and it's time to lance that boil and let the poison out."

He was right. She had choices, and one of them was to stop being a coward. She took a breath, and gathered her courage. Paused. Faltered. Caught herself and his hand in the same breath. She brought his hand to her breast.

"Remember how you held me the first night we fed Brianna?"

"Yes." His breath hissed out from between his teeth.

"Hold me like that while I tell you. Touch me that way so I remember where I am, who I'm with, and I'll tell you."

He calmly unbuttoned her shirt. A glance at his expression showed the same control. His big hand slid inside her camisole above her corset, and cupped her breast with incredible gentleness. She closed her eyes and sank into the feeling.

"I love the way you touch me."

"I'll always be gentle with you," he whispered, his drawl more pronounced. "You don't have to worry about that."

"It isn't your gentleness." His eyebrows rose and his fingers nudged her nipple in inquiry. "You touch me like I matter. Like I'm a person." She stroked his hair as it lay on his coat, the strands coarser than hers, cool with the night chill. "As long as you touch me like that, you don't need to always be gentle."

"You might be jumping the gun." His black eyes burned with sudden heat. His grip on her breast tightened.

She shook her head. "I can't be afraid of you Clint. No matter what, I know you won't hurt me."

His fingers on her breast paused, and then began the soft stroking motion, from base to tip. Over and over. When he reached her nipple on the forth pass, he skimmed the areola until he captured the nipple, squeezing gently. The pleasure poured through her in a soft surge. She leaned her head back against his shoulder. She couldn't see his face.

"Could you take off your hat?"

He did, revealing the intentness of his expression and the worry in his eyes. Worry for her. She placed her hand over his, holding him and the pleasure he brought her close to her heart.

And told him what he needed to know.

Chapter Nineteen

The bedroom door opened. Jenna's heart pounded and her throat went dry. Her hand went to the sliding sleeve of her nightdress. This had been a really stupid idea.

"Son of a bitch, Jenna."

"I thought you'd like it." The heat in her cheeks went to scorching. It was the short nightdress she'd worn the first night, except she'd left the robe off and unbuttoned the first three buttons of the top to expose more cleavage.

"I like it." The door clicked shut behind Clint.

From the other side of the door she heard Danny whine. Clint crossed to the bed, his boots making solid thuds on the hardwood floor until he reached the braided rug at the side of the bed. She didn't have the guts to meet his eyes. Not because she was afraid, but because being brazen was a little too new to be nonchalant about.

His hand touched the top of her head, hesitated, and then lifted a strand of hair, rubbing it between his fingers. She waited in vain for him to do more.

She looked up and caught him staring down at her. For the first time, with indecision. She put her hand over his, curling her fingers around two of his. "What's wrong?"

"Believe it or not," he admitted in a tight voice, "I'm afraid to touch you."

"Because of what I told you?"

"Baby, I don't know how you survived." He brought her hand to his lips, his eyes hot and sad.

"But I did."

"Yes." His tongue touched the center of her palm in a flickering caress. "How the hell can you stand for anyone to touch you?"

"I can't." She shrugged, comfortable with this truth. "Just you."

"Remind me to start taking up church-going again." He pushed the hair off her face.

She touched his jaw. "I'm glad I listened to the voice inside that wouldn't let me give up."

"If you had told me what he was doing there would have been no need for listening." His jaw clenched and a muscle twitched under her finger.

"There's nothing you could have done. I was married."

"Like hell." His eyes narrowed and under her left palm, his pectorals bunched with tension.

"If you'd killed him, you'd be in jail. And I wouldn't have you. This way is better." She rasped her finger over the shadow of stubble on his jaw. She knew that look. That promise of retribution. It used to terrify her. Now it just made her feel safe.

He was shaking his head before she was done, catching her finger between his strong teeth, nipping it gently before saying, "Sunshine, we are never going to see eye to eye on that, and if you don't think I know how to kill a man without leaving evidence, you need another think."

Maybe she did, but it didn't change the truth.

"It's better for me, Clint."

His hand touched the side of her breast. It wasn't a caress so much as a reaffirmation of a memory. She held her breath, afraid he was going to press her for the one piece of her past that she hadn't revealed. But he didn't. Just shook his head and stroked her gently with hands that always pleasured, and said, "You are an amazingly stubborn woman."

"But you like me." She smiled. This was her man. The one person in this world who saw her for what she was.

"Yes." Just one word, but it was said with a hunger that made her burn.

She waited for the smile that curved his lips to reach his eyes before she asked, "And you're going to let me play tonight?"

This time his "yes" was slower, deeper, as if his mind was already going down the path where she wanted to lead him. The hand on her breast clenched with carnal hunger. The other brought her palm back to his mouth. He nipped the base of her thumb. Her knees buckled as her womb clenched.

"Good," she breathed, letting her own hunger burgeon and flow. "Because I'm asking favors this time." Clint froze, his lips on her palm, his melting black eyes locked with hers. She pulled her hand free and stepped back. She licked her dry lips and pressed on.

"I've been punished many times for tempting a man, but I've never actually done it. I'd like to try…" Oh God, she was going to die if he said no. She licked her lips again. "To tempt you."

For a split second he did nothing. Said nothing. Then his eyes seemed to burn from within and a smile—a real smile—spread across his face.

"Come here." That drawl, low and deep, slid along her desire, stoking inner fires to flickering life. He caught her hands in his big ones and pulled her to her feet with an ease that still amazed her. He placed her palms on his chest on either side of the button placket, holding her for a second while she steadied. He was always taking care of her.

"So you want to play with me?" he asked in that same deep, need-spiking baritone.

"Yes." She slid her hands up to thread her fingers through the blue-black strands of his hair.

"Then come play." The left corner of his sensual mouth lifted higher than the right.

Such an invitation, given in that raspy tone, backed by that sexy smile and that challenging look encouraged a woman to boldness. And for once, Jenna didn't back away from the dare. This was her man. Her house. Her marriage, and she wanted joy in all three. She slid her hands to the buttons on his shirt, feeling the increase in his heart rate shaking her palms.

"You like me like this," she said as she undid the second button.

"No lie, Sunshine, this is about my favorite fantasy." He settled his hands on her shoulders.

"You've had fantasies about me?"

"For as long as I've known you."

She'd known him for three years. "Even when I was married?"

"Yeah." He nudged the edge of her nightdress so that it slid off her shoulder. She left it there. "But those tended to end as a nightmare."

The rules preached into her from childhood chose that moment to pop forward. "It's a sin to covet another man's wife."

"You were never meant to be anyone's wife but mine."

She touched the scars over his breastbone.

"No. I wasn't." She might have been imagining it, but he seemed to relax slightly with her agreement. She tugged his shirt free of his pants. His heat and scent surrounded her in a potent embrace. She leaned into it, and traced the edge of one of his scars with her tongue. His big body shook. The smile started way down deep inside.

"I like that," she whispered, after tracing the scar to the end, just below his nipple.

"What?" His thumb edged her night rail off her other shoulder. Goose bumps chased the soft slither of material over her skin.

"The way you react to my touch."

"Sunshine, you make me burn just by being in the room."

"Good." She slid her arms out of the nightdress, leaving the top caught on the hard peaks of her breasts.

"I'd be obliged if you could just wiggle the slightest bit," he hinted.

She knew why. She could feel his eyes like a touch, heavy on her breasts, making them swell and the nipples bead harder.

"I bet you would," she said as she pushed his shirt off his broad shoulders. It didn't slide off his arms like hers did. There was too much muscle on the man for that. She had to stand on tiptoe to nudge the fabric off his biceps, trailing her fingers along the crease in his upper arm, dipping her finger into the dent of an old bullet wound. So many scars on his hard body. So many times he might have been killed.

When she settled back down, her nightdress fell to the floor. She was naked before him. There was a heartbeat when she wanted to cover up, but then she looked into his face, drawn tight with desire for her, his nostrils flaring as if he were scenting her arousal, and she did the opposite. She stepped back and squared her shoulders.

His response was immediate. "Son of a bitch."

She'd never heard a curse said with such reverence. The blush she couldn't control seared her skin. His dark gaze followed the path from her stomach, over her breasts up to her cheeks and then back down to her breasts, where it lingered. His tongue dampened his lower lip.

"Come here, Sunshine, and let me ease some of that heat."

She shook her head, feeling very daring, very feminine. "No. This is my time to play and if I come over there, you'll take over."

"No I won't, but I can see how hard your nipples are. Wouldn't you like me to take them in my mouth? Suck them a little? Tease them?" Her knees almost buckled at the thought. He pressed his advantage. "I can make them feel so good. Bring them here, baby, and let me nibble."

Need arced out from the hard tips, shooting through her body before rebounding to her breasts, flaring outward at the tips, creating a searing ache that only he could soothe. She cupped her breasts in her hands to contain the demand.

His curse echoed through the room. Surprise had her attention flying to his face. His gaze was locked on her hands. His fingers were on the fly of his denims, working the buttons over the bulge of his cock, the shirtsleeves caught on his wrist hampering the effort.

"Do you like it when I touch myself, Clint?"

His "yes" was a guttural expression of hunger.

"How?" She slid her fingers along the underside of her breasts toward the tips. Her hands weren't as big as his and didn't give the satisfaction of his, but his open sensuality and the heat coming from his heavy-lidded gaze fueled her passion.

"Touch those pretty nipples, baby." He kicked off his boots.

She did, pinching them lightly, watching his tongue flick over his lips as she did and his lids drop lower over his eyes.

With a simple flex of his arm the shirt ripped up the back. He tore his arms free, before shoving his pants impatiently down over his hips. The material caught on the thrust of his shaft. He swore as she pinched her nipples again, harder this time, moaning a little as the shot of pleasure took her by surprise.

"Did that feel good?" His smile grew broader. His gaze hotter.

She nodded, her breath coming in short bursts as she watched him lever the long thick length of his cock free of his pants. Even from here she could see that he was full to bursting, his heavy balls drawn tight to his body, the broad head of his cock dark and glistening with his seed.

She forgot to move, to breathe as he cupped his shaft in his hand, dragging his palm up the heavily veined length, lifting it to her gaze, letting her see how it jerked beneath his touch.

Her palms itched to touch him, to hold all that power in her hands. She took a step toward him. He kicked free of his pants, standing before her, unselfconscious in his nudity. The shadows from the lamp highlighted the dense cuts of muscle across his big frame, the power inherent in his touch and the sexuality he radiated so effortlessly. With his hair swinging freely around his face, shadowing his eyes and emphasizing his cheekbones, he looked every inch the dangerous, sexual man that he was.

Everything inside of her thrilled to the knowledge that he was hers. She pinched her nipples again, holding them the way he did, drawing them away from her body, lifting them toward his mouth.

His cock leapt at the sight. His tongue ran over those delicious lips and he moaned. For her. Juices flooded her pussy along with the knowledge that she did this to him. He saw her as something he couldn't resist. She took a step closer, lifting her breasts higher.

He frowned. "Gently, baby."

She didn't want gentle. "I like this."

"Damn it, come here." His fingers twitched on his cock. He stared at her mouth, her breasts, her pussy, like a man starved. Clear fluid spilled over the tip of his cock, dribbling down the wide shaft.

For the first time in her life, she refused an order from a man. She stood where she was and pinched harder, lifted higher. He gritted his teeth and shuttled his cock though his fist, fluid coming in a steady stream, easing his way as he watched her.

"This is not a good time to be teasing me, Jenna," he warned in a deep, dark voice.

She disregarded the warning. There was nothing he could do to her that she wouldn't welcome. The way he handled his cock enthralled her, fascinated her with what it revealed. He wasn't nearly as careful with himself as he was with her. There was an expediency to his touch when he handled his flesh. Not at all the way he touched her. On her, his hands had a tendency to linger, to savor. To pleasure. The way she wanted to touch him.

He stroked the length of his cock again and grimaced. She knew his touch, knew how his calluses scraped deliciously against sensitive skin. Knew the pleasure he was giving himself. And wanted it for herself. She slid one hand down her stomach, moving gently on the soft flesh, inching toward her pulsing clit.

"Son of a bitch, you're tempting me," he growled in the back of his throat.

Yes, she was. And enjoying it. Her pleasure must have shown in her smile, because with one last muttered curse, he was on her, lifting her against him, one hard, muscled arm hitching under her buttocks, anchoring her hips to his as he strode to the bed. He fell with her onto the mattress, laughing when she squealed, catching himself on his hands, his lips still aligned with hers, his cock edging the cleft of her pussy, sliding easily along her lubricated flesh, teasing her clit with a slow, gliding pressure.

This time she was the one who moaned. And he smiled that wickedly dark smile and dipped his head, his hair stroking her breasts in a silken caress as his lips hovered above hers.

"You shouldn't tease a starving man, Sunshine."

"Why not?" she whispered into his mouth, the last syllable ending on a moan as he pumped his cock along her labia again.

"Because you might get more than you bargained for."

"How much more?" She bit her lip and arched her neck as the pleasure whipped through her.

He paused. "You're in a strange mood tonight."

Yes. She was. For the first time in her life she was free and she was in a rush to try everything, but how could she explain that to Clint, who'd probably never felt trapped in his life? She slid her hands over his shoulders, running her nails along the swell of muscle, arching her back into his shiver.

"It's like there's been something weighing me down my whole life and suddenly, it's not there anymore."

"Are you trying to tell me you're ready to fly?" He kissed her mouth, the right corner, the left, and then the end of her nose.

"Yes."

"It's dangerous to tell me that now." He rested his forehead against hers.

"Why?" She titled her head back to facilitate the kisses he was spreading down the line of her jaw. She loved his mouth. His kisses. Firm yet soft, each kiss accented by the prickle of his beard. That edge of danger heightening her excitement.

"I'm holding on by a thread, Sunshine."

"Holding onto what?" Oh God, when he sucked on her neck she could barely hold a thought.

"Control, baby, control."

"Do you need it?"

His laugh buffeted the curve of her shoulder. "Sunshine, I'm a hair's breadth from either fucking your ass or paddling it."

That did not sound good. "Why?"

"Because you could have been hurt today." He plumped her breast into his callused palm. "Because I could have lost you."

"But you didn't."

"The near miss is driving me crazy."

His hot mouth closed over her turgid nipple searing her with the heat of his need. Against her, his body was taut with the same desire. She pushed his hair back, watching his cheeks flex as he suckled her. She traced the arch of his brow. She remembered back to their wedding night. His excitement. His kindness. She traced the line of his right eyebrow. He looked up at her, for a split second his soul bare in his eyes. She'd never seen such emptiness in a man's eyes before. She'd do anything to remove it from Clint's.

"I don't think I'd like to be paddled," she whispered, taking a leap of faith.

He froze, releasing her nipple with an audible pop, hitching himself up so he could see her face. "Excuse me?"

It was harder to say with all of his attention on her. "I don't think I'd like to be paddled."

He cupped her burning cheeks in his palms, forcing her gaze to his. "Baby, are you telling me that you want me to fuck your ass?"

"I don't know." She caught his wrists in her hands, holding tight to him. She just didn't want him to look so empty. Against her pussy his cock throbbed. Against her chest, his ribs expanded with the effort it took him to breathe. Oh God, he wanted this.

"Will it hurt?" she asked, hating the quaver in her voice.

He kissed her hard. "Not in any way you'll mind."

She didn't find that reassuring. "Will I like it?"

"I'll make sure you like it."

"How will you fit?" She flexed her hips against him. He was huge.

"Nice and easy." He drew his hips back. His cock slid down her slit, brushing her anus in a soft kiss before nestling into the crease. A forbidden pulse of excitement crept into her desire. "Just a little bit at a time."

Her bottom cheeks spasmed against his cock, hugging it to her as if trying to tempt him.

"You like the thought of that." There was a wealth of satisfaction in his tone. He pressed against her. She sank her nails into his wrists as the pulse spread to an ache. He moved a little and the sharp flare of desire took her breath. "Damn, you're as sensitive there as you are in your breasts."

"That's good?"

He kissed her then, his tongue thrusting into her mouth, twining with hers, taking possession. He pushed harder, settling his cock more firmly against her. She couldn't breathe, couldn't do anything but press back and try to understand the gamut of emotions tearing at her control. When he allowed her to breathe, he said, "Very good."

"I'll need my cream." It was half question, half statement of fact.

He shook his head, his hair swishing against her cheeks. "I have something better."

"Better?" She trusted her cream.

"Yes. Better."

She followed his hand with her eyes as he reached for the bedstand drawer and pulled out a jar. It was white and plain and not the least impressive.

She bit her lip. "I'd rather use my cream."

"Trust me, baby, you want this." He nudged his cock against her anus, her muscles contracted with pleasure and fear. He propped himself on his elbows and opened the jar. She sniffed. It didn't smell nice like hers.

"Are you sure you wouldn't rather use my cream?"

"I'm sure." His grin was sin personified. He put the lid on the bed. She caught her breath and closed her eyes as he scooped out a dollop of cream. He kissed her softly as his fingers replaced his cock with a smooth coolness. "This is going to make you feel good, Sunshine."

She thought he meant the act, but as his fingers parted her that first stubborn bit, a strange warmth began. She twisted her hips, arching up into it, impaling herself just that much more.

"Can you feel that?"

"Yes."

"It's going to get warm and then you're going to want to move."

"I am?"

"Yes. Just go with it. Move against my fingers."

"Fingers?" The one he had in her stretched her to the point of pain.

"I need to stretch you, baby." He pushed his finger in deeper. Her muscles tensed around the knuckle. It burned. She would have cried out except the warmth from the inside burst into a tingling itch.

"Oh, heavens."

"Shh, don't tense. Just relax."

She couldn't help but tense. His finger was in her and the heel of his hand pressed against her clit and that itch was demanding she scratch it. Oh God, she needed him to move. He did, but not in a way she wanted. He removed his finger from her rectum, dragging exquisitely along the sensitive inner tissue, temporarily soothing the maddening itch.

"Clint, please."

He scooped out another dollop of cream. She caught his hand as the hot, maddening itch began again.

"No more."

"We'll need a lot more." He slipped her grip. She twisted her fingers into the comforter by her head as he pressed his fingers against her ass. "Relax now."

His finger touched her. Oh God, it felt so good. She bent her knees and braced her feet against the mattress.

"Right there, Jenna?" He circled the rim of her anus with his finger, soothing her itch, but spiking her need. She bit her lip and nodded. "Don't hold it in, baby. I want to hear what you feel."

He pressed in slightly, still circling her anus, opening her. A second finger joined the first. One big hand splayed over her stomach, down low.

"Hold still now." A sense of fullness invaded her rectum. There was a bite of pain that quickly blended to pleasure as he seated his fingers to the first knuckle. He began to fuck her slowly, in and out, rubbing and stretching her, keeping her between heaven and hell until with a hard push, he seated his fingers to the base, sending mixed signals of pleasure and pain to her brain, which seemed only interested in the pleasure and its need for more.

"Please." She arched her neck and screamed. It felt so good, but she needed more. So much more.

"What is it?"

"I need you to move."

"Not yet."

"Give me more."

"In a minute."

"Now!" She fought the restraint of his hand, her very womb aching for him.

He shook his head, lashing her abdomen with the thick dark silk of his hair as he kissed her stomach, her hipbone, her pubic mound, and lastly, her clit. The pleasure shot like pain outward, sensitizing all her nerves to the potential for more. She hung with breathless anticipation on the hot wash of his tongue over that straining nubbin, her pussy clenching in an agony of need, her breath suspending in her lungs.

She grabbed his shoulders, seeking purchase against the sensations destroying her world as she groaned, "Oh God. You're torturing me."

He nipped her clit with his lips, restraining her jump with his hand, keeping her in place for the light scrape of his teeth. "I'm making you feel good."

And he was. Every word whispered against her clit stoked her passion, every brush of his breath held her hostage to the need for more. He gave it to her, scissoring his fingers in her ass, the agony and relief driving her hips up into the descent of his mouth.

"Clint!"

"Right here," he murmured against her, the soft folds between her thighs muffling his drawl, but not his impact on her senses. He was her husband, her lover. He was everything to her, made her want to give everything to him, but he wouldn't take it. Wouldn't let her go. He just kept lapping at her pussy, drinking in her juices, swirling figure eight patterns on her most sensitive spots with that wickedly agile tongue, nudging her passion higher but not high enough. Seemingly content to feast on her forever, while his fingers worked her ass.

Oh heavens, his fingers! She needed more, so much more than he was giving her. More than the throbbing combination of burn and relief. She needed his cock. Driving deep, filling her full, soothing the agony of unfulfilled desire he was feeding. She needed him.

"Please." She arched her neck, her back, striving to break the restraints of his hand, wanting to shove her whole pussy into the hot cavern of his mouth. "Help me, Clint."

She'd never felt this way before. As if with just a little more, a little something more, she'd disappear onto the swirling hunger that consumed her. It scared her. Even as she wrapped her fingers in Clint's hair and dragged his mouth harder into her pussy, moaning when she felt the pressure of his teeth, she was pulling back mentally. Afraid of this pleasure, so intense that it had to be a sin.

"Please."

There was no mistaking the fractured knot of fear in Jenna's high-pitched plea. Clint stilled his fingers and mouth. Her juices spilled over his tongue as she moaned and shifted. He traced a path from her clit to her ass with his index finger.

"It's okay, baby," Clint soothed, spreading her sweet cream around her tightly stretched anus. Damn, she was so small she was going to have trouble taking him. He touched the taut flesh with his tongue. She gasped and jerked, no doubt shocked, and then more of her sweet juices spilled to coat his hands and his tongue. He let them flow around his fingers. If he were a less selfish man, he'd use one of the smaller toys in his collection to stretch her, but he wasn't, and he wouldn't. Not with her. Not this first time. This time it had to be him. And her. And nothing else.

He adjusted their position so her hips were on the edge of the bed. "Bend your leg, Sunshine."

He guided her with his hand on her left ankle. She wasn't a tiny woman, but she felt tiny in his hands. Amazingly fragile. Infinitely vulnerable. He geared her foot to a spot near her hip, exposing the deep pink of her swollen labia as he took her right leg and bent it carefully, knowing the scar tissue and twisted muscle wouldn't cooperate as easily.

"Let your legs fall open, Jenna."

She did. Slowly. Cautiously. He looked up the length of her body, over the opulent curve of her stomach. Her lush breasts shivered with the force of her breathing. Their tips were engorged to a bright red, and by looking between, he could see her expression. Her delicate features sharpened with desire, her eyes luminous with pleasure and uncertainty.

He shifted up until his shoulders supported her thighs and he could rest his chin on her pubic bone. Her ass milked his fingers, straining to get more sensation.

"You don't have to be afraid, Jenna. It's just you and me, Sunshine, and you know I'll take care of you."

"I can't control it," she gasped as if it were a problem.

"You don't need to control anything, you just need to let go." He worked his fingers out. Her muscles clamped down, trying to keep him in her. He worked them back and forth, easing them free for a heartbeat "Give yourself over to me, Jenna. Just let go and trust me to catch you."

He thrust his fingers back in, not as easily, pressing his mouth to her stomach as she shuddered and screamed, arching into him, thrusting against his hands, kissing her stomach as she shuddered and strained up for more.

"Son of a bitch, Jenna, you're hell on my control."

"Really?" She braced her torso up on her elbows. She didn't look upset. He smiled and prodded her tight ass with a third finger.

"Yes." She clamped down, denying him entry. "Relax baby. Let me in."

"Sorry." A new blush raced over the first. Her lip slipped between her teeth as she asked, "Do I excite you as much as some of your other women?"

It was such a revealing question to ask, exposing so much of her soul that he didn't need to hear the catch in her voice to know how vulnerable she felt. He rubbed her engorged clit with his thumb as he met her gaze.

"There's never been another woman like you."

She parted for the slow intrusion of his third finger, her head arching back and a long, drawn out scream of pleasure tearing from her throat as he screwed his fingers into the hot, willing depths of her ass. He waited until her scream faded to eager pants. Beneath his thumb her clit pulsed. She was very close to climax.

"Look at me, Jenna." She did, albeit with difficulty, struggling to lift her lids, struggling to focus past the agony of holding back. "There won't ever be another woman for me."

She blinked. He held her gaze, pulling back, letting her see his tongue before he sank his mouth into the hot fluid warmth of her pussy, lapping at her, staying longer than he meant to, caught up in her heat, her taste. Her whimper brought him back to himself. He drew back, licking her taste from his lips.

"No other woman could ever taste like you." He fucked her with his fingers, spreading them as he pulled out.

"No woman could ever feel like you." He thrust them hard and deep, taking her faster than before, knowing she was aroused enough to enjoy the bite of pain with her pleasure. Her scream scraped the edges of his control. "Sound like you," he finished.

She threw her hips up, taking a fraction more, her face twisting into a grimace of agonized pleasure. His cock leaked pulses of hot seed, wanting to be buried where his fingers were, wanting to fill her with his come.

"No other woman could ever make me feel like you do, Sunshine."

He turned her over, letting her legs dangle off the bed, its height keeping her feet off the floor, perfectly poised for what he wanted. He stepped between her thighs, spreading them so they rested on the outside of his. He stroked the full curves of her buttocks, kneading them, smiling when she gasped and her back muscles tightened in an effort to increase the pressure.

"Easy, Sunshine." He stepped forward bringing the wide head of his cock in alignment with the shiny, reddened opening of her ass, using just enough pressure to keep the head in place. He aligned his thumbs at the base of her spine, sliding them slowly up her back, over her shoulders, along her arms until he could enfold her hands in his. He lowered his head, relishing the softness of her skin along his torso. Everything about her was so soft, lush, giving.

His black-as-night hair tangled with her blonde waves, pooling in sharp contrast as he whispered in her ear, "Until the day I die, you're the only woman I'll have."

"Oh God!" She shuddered beneath him. He pressed against her, absorbing her heat and the promise of pleasure beyond.

"That being the case, you need to take care."

He eased his hips forward, his cock wedging against her soft flesh, filling the well left from the pressure. His cock jerked and swelled. He gritted his teeth as his balls drew up tight. A spurt of come leaked past his control. She whimpered as it flowed around the point of their joining.

"No taking chances." He grunted, reinforcing his point. "No risking yourself."

Beneath the pressure of his shaft, her muscles began to part. Her hands clenched in his as her nails dug into the comforter.

"You're mine, Jenna," he whispered in her ear, feeling the truth deep in his words, shaken by the reality. "From now on, no matter what, you've got me."

He pushed her control with pulses of his hips. "Relax and let me in, baby. Accept me."

She shook her head. The soft denial ripped the veneer of civilization off his soul. Possession, primitive and wild, surged to the fore, demanding her compliance. He brought his determination to bear on that critical connection.

"Yes." His voice was as guttural as his emotions. The shake of her head only increased his resolve. She would not deny him in this. "Accept me."

"Can't," she gasped. She shook her head harder, her fingers wrapping around his, her back pressing against his chest in rapid pulses of distress.

He worked his lips to the side on her neck. "I'm not leaving you a choice."

The soft muscles of her ass were no match for the force of his determination.

Her "You'll leave" was a high-pitched wail of surrender as her anus spread over the tip of his cock, pulsing and tempting him with the promise of what could be.

You'll leave.

He held himself still inside her. The rage ebbed as the cry echoed in his head. She wasn't denying him, she was denying herself. He kissed her cheek, her hair, the side of her mouth.

"Jesus, God, baby. Wild horses couldn't drag me away from you."

"Why?"

"Because you're everything I've always wanted."

"I don't understand," she whispered into the comforter, her voice tight with pain, both physical and mental.

He fought back the need to plunge inside her and gave her the truth instead. "I don't either, but that's the way it is."

It was a damned weak reason to give a woman, but surprisingly, Jenna relaxed beneath him. Her voice was soft as her skin as she whispered, "For me, too."

The confession exploded through him, reaching deep to that wild primitive part, blocking out all other emotions. One word chanted over and over in his mind as he surged into her, past her resistance, making reality of what had only been a supposition. "Mine. Mine."

He didn't realize that he was saying it aloud as he tunneled in and out of the hot, slick grip of her ass until Jenna arched beneath him as he freed one hand and reached for her swollen clit, pinching it in time with his thrusts. Her scream of "Yes" battered his ears, and shattered his defenses as the last of her resistance faded. He surged deep into her body, pumping harder, longer—striving to reach that part of her that she kept hidden. His balls slapped against the soaking wet pad of her cunt as he increased the power of his thrusts, deepened the angle of his penetration, arching into her shudders, knowing he'd found his mark as she screamed and fought, her body convulsing…

She screamed his name as her ass clamped down on his cock, choking off his own climax. She shuddered and cried beneath him as her body milked his. He wrapped his arms around her, pulling her back into his chest, holding her close. Her tears soaked his arm as he powered to his own release. She turned her head, her lips brushing his cheek, accepting his wildness, his need.

"I love you," she whispered.

He heard her over the shaking of the bed, the protest of the mattress, and the thundering of his heart. She whispered it again, the last of her tension fading from her muscles, leaving her wide open to his thrusts, to him. He came in a rush, his seed boiling up from his balls, bursting into her tight channel and filling her to overflowing. His seed mingling with her juices to coat his balls and her pussy until there was nothing left in him. Just an aching emptiness. He sucked in a deep breath. The scent of roses, sex, and satisfied woman filled his lungs, spreading through his being, drifting into the void.

And then as her ass spasmed one last time around his cock, she whispered it again, those three little words that filled him with peace.

"I love you."

Chapter Twenty

By the time Jenna rode up to the front of Mara's home, she was bathed in sweat. Not just because Clint was going to be furious that she'd ridden out alone. Not because she was so new to horseback riding that every time the placid roan Clint had given her slipped, she went into a panic. No. She was in a lather because of what she was going to do. What she needed to do to protect her home. Her children. She shifted in the saddle, wincing as her posterior protested.

The last week had been difficult. Clint had been insatiable in his demands. He'd taken her over and over, his big body driving hers to climax like a man possessed, needing her surrender, forcing her to give him the words he wanted. Afterwards, he held her as if he wanted to pull her into his body, easing her through her tears, kissing her gently, tenderly, but he never said the words back. Never let her in.

So she'd pulled back, not giving him the words he wanted. Trying to be more like him. But it never worked. Clint took charge at night, taking her however he needed to break down the walls she built, not resting until he had what he wanted. Her total surrender.

She shifted again as her pussy pulsed with remembered pleasure. Last night, she'd held out longer than usual. He'd arched above her, muscles glistening with sweat, eyes burning with passion, face tight with resolution as she bit her lip against the declaration wanting to spill forth—and then he'd flipped her over. He hadn't taken her ass since that that first time, waiting for her to recover. But last night he'd taken her over and over, not content with hearing the words "I love you" once. She'd lost track of how many times she'd screamed her love as he took her, staking his claim, as if he wanted to imprint himself into her very soul.

This morning he'd woken her with a soft apology as he'd eased his big cock into her sore rectum, kissing her gently, fucking her gently, relentlessly until she'd surrendered, holding his hand against her cheek and giving him the words he needed.

He'd moaned and then had come immediately, the tension seeping from his hard muscles as she convulsed around him. He'd held her for a long time afterward, rubbing her back, kissing her cheek, calming her as she cried. But he still hadn't said what she needed to hear.

And it wasn't hard to figure out why.

She pulled the roan to a halt at the hitching post in front of Mara's big house. As usual, just looking at the place made her feel inferior, but that was just another thing she was going to have to get over. She was a McKinnely now, and McKinnelys bowed to no one.

She squared her shoulders. If she wanted Clint to love her, she was going to have to learn to be a woman he could rely on. A woman he could see as being strong enough to trust with his heart. Which was going to take a lot of toughening up. She looked up as a big, tall man came out of the barn, then raised her hand and waved.

Cougar broke into a run. His long hair flying out behind him as his legs ate up the distance between them.

She tried to swing her leg over the horse's back, but her tortured muscles screamed a protest. The roan shifted and she quickly settled back in the saddle.

"What's wrong," Cougar barked as he got close enough to be heard.

She smoothed her hair and straightened her skirt. "I came for a visit."

He stopped a foot away. His hair settled around his shoulders in a wild tangle that was as primitive as the man himself. He looked down the road, then at her dress, and frowned.

"Alone?"

"Yes."

"Dressed like that?"

"I didn't want to get my good clothes horsy smelling." It wasn't her best dress but it wasn't her worst either.

"I repeat, what's wrong?" He crossed his arms over his chest.

"I just want to see Mara."

"So you cut across the territory on a horse you barely know how to ride, unescorted, without Clint's permission?"

"How do you know I don't have Clint's permission?"

His right brow went up in an expression reminiscent of Clint. "Because you're here alone on a horse you barely know how to ride, in clothes more fit for cleaning than visiting, and if I'm not mistaken, without all the proper undergarments."

How could he tell *that*?

"So," Cougar continued with intimidating calm, "don't tell me nothing's wrong. Tell me the truth."

"I need to talk to you," she managed through her embarrassment.

"Why?" His eyes were flat and cold.

"I need your help."

His expression didn't soften. "If you're looking for help leaving him, you came to the wrong place."

She blinked. "Leave who?"

"Clint."

"I don't want to leave him."

The front door opened and Mara came flying out. "Jenna! I wasn't expecting you." She looked around. "Where are Clint and the children?"

"They're home."

"Uh-oh." The same guarded expression came over Mara's face that had been on Cougar's.

"Why does everyone assume that there's some sort of problem just because I came out for a visit?"

"Because Clint wouldn't leave you unprotected," Mara answered as Cougar tucked her into his side.

"For heavens sake, I'm not a child."

"Of course not," Mara said, rubbing her arms as Cougar stepped away. "And we're thrilled you came to visit, aren't we Cougar?"

"Thrilled," Cougar echoed, coming toward Jenna, his eyes narrowed in speculation. He patted the horse's neck as his gaze met hers, the eyes she'd thought cold a moment before now warm with concern. He really was a handsome man when he wasn't looking so scary.

"Whatever it is, Jenna, we will help you."

"I don't know if you can."

"Then maybe we should get you off this horse so we can talk."

She bit her lip and confessed yet another humiliating moment. "I'm stuck."

"So I figured." As if she were a feather, he lifted her off the horse, steadying her as her leg cramped and gave out. He frowned down at her. "You shouldn't be riding."

"I had to." She shifted her weight to her good leg and held to her purpose.

His thumb brushed her cheek. "If you tell Clint what's bothering you, he'll fix it."

"He can't."

"But you think I can?"

"Yes." She was counting on it.

"What do you need?"

"I need for you to teach me to fight."

* * * * *

"I don't think I've ever seen quite that expression on Cougar's face before," Mara commented as she poured the tea.

Jenna rubbed her thigh where it rested up on the hassock, easing the cramping muscles. "He did seem surprised."

"You flat-out shocked him to the soles of his moccasins." Mara laughed, her elfin face lighting from within.

"I need to know how to defend myself."

"Why?"

"I need to be strong."

"Why?" Mara dropped a sugar chunk into her cup.

"I just do." She couldn't just blurt out "so Clint will love me".

"Are you in danger, Jenna?" Mara asked, growing serious.

"No."

"Do you think Clint wants a sparring partner?" Cougar asked from the kitchen door, a hot brick wrapped in a towel in his hand.

"I just want him to respect me." She took a sip of her tea.

"And you think fighting will make that happen?" he asked, handing her the brick. She laid it on her thigh, her breath hissing out as the warmth seeped into the twisted muscles. Cougar squatted beside her, watching her face as the heat seeped in.

"Clint respects strength."

Cougar sighed. "He respects his wife."

No, he didn't. But he would.

"He'll respect me more if he always doesn't have to worry about me."

Cougar shook his head. "Learning to fight won't change how he feels about you."

"I disagree." It had to. She couldn't live the rest of her life loving Clint when he didn't love her.

"It won't hurt for her to learn to fight," Mara pointed out. "You did say it was important for every woman to know how to defend herself."

"I did." Cougar stood.

"So you'll teach her?" Mara asked, her hand on his thigh looked small against the long expanse of muscle.

"Without telling Clint?" Jenna added, knowing Clint would forbid it.

Cougar's big hand engulfed Mara's where it rested on his thigh. He stared at Jenna, his golden gaze so intent that she immediately dropped her eyes, remembered her vow, and brought her gaze back up to meet his. She might have imagined the slight nod of Cougar's head, but she was so desperate, she interpreted it as approval to shore up her resolve. He made her hold his gaze for two heartbeats before a slight smile turned up the corner of his mouth.

"As I owe the man one, I'll teach you."

Jenna closed her eyes as relief swept through her. When she opened them, all she could see was the back of Cougar's head and the long fall of his hair as he leaned over Mara.

She'd never seen a man kiss a woman. Watching Cougar kiss Mara was a revelation. For a man who made her think in terms of danger and unpredictability, he was incredibly careful with his wife. From where she sat, Jenna could see the play of muscles under his shirt as he shifted his angle. He was a powerful man. As powerful as Clint, but whereas she was a big woman with meat on her bones to take a blow, Mara was tiny and slender. Cougar could break her neck with a slap.

Jenna thought she heard Cougar groan and then Mara's hands crept over his shoulders, the tips curling into his shoulder as if she would pull him to her. Cougar seemed to lean into her grasp. By shifting just the slightest to the right, she could see his hand cupping Mara's head. She expected to see his fingers fisted in her hair, holding her for his pleasure, but the hand that engulfed her head was open, supporting, not demanding. The dark thumb resting against the white of her cheek caressed the skin with incredible gentleness.

"Damn, Angel, you go to my head," she heard him murmur, and she knew the rumors were true. Cougar McKinnely may have found his wife in a notorious bordello, but he loved her.

She pulled her gaze away from the two and moved the brick down on her thigh. If Cougar could love Mara despite her past, then maybe Clint could love her. Maybe she'd go to his head the way Mara went to Cougar's, and maybe he'd hold her the way Cougar held Mara—as though she was everything precious that made up his world.

The floor creaked as Cougar straightened. He was still looking at Mara, concern on his face. "You take care, today."

Mara shook her head at him. "You tell me that every day."

He touched her cheek with the backs of his fingers. His skin was very dark against hers. "I have hopes that one day you'll listen."

"I listen."

"Uh-huh." The smile that tilted his wide mouth was as soft as down. He flicked her nose. "And leave the furniture upstairs alone, until I get back."

Mara merely rolled her eyes. "Don't you have work to do?"

"Yes."

"Then why don't you do it?"

"When I have your promise."

"Can I clean house?" Mara blew her hair off her forehead.

"Yes."

"Figures you'd agree to that."

"I'll have your promise on the other." Cougar touched her cheek again.

"Soon as you're out the door, I could break my word."

"But you won't." The faintest of smiles crinkled the corner of the eye Jenna could see. He kissed Mara on her head. "You two come on down to the barn when Jenna's feeling better."

"Thank you."

He left the room. Mara's gaze clung to his broad back as he left, her heart in her eyes.

"I want that," Jenna said. The declaration landed hard in the sudden silence.

"My husband?" Mara turned, her expression amused.

"I want Clint to look at me like Cougar looks at you." Jenna knew she was blushing from the heat in her cheeks. Not to mention the laughter in the other woman's gaze.

"You want Clint to love you."

"Yes." It sounded so stark when said aloud.

"And you don't think he does?"

"No."

"Do you love him?"

"Yes."

"Have you told him?"

"Yes." Her blush turned to scorching.

"And?"

"He's kind to me, but he never says it back." She shrugged, feeling the emptiness of that "and" to the bottom of her soul.

"That's not good."

"No."

"It will have to be fixed."

"That's what I'm trying to do." With a wave of her hand, Mara dismissed Jenna's efforts.

"We'll need help." She walked over to the small desk and pulled out paper and a pencil.

"You think Cougar can't teach me?" Jenna asked, putting the towel-wrapped brick carefully on the gleaming floor. That was not what she wanted to hear.

"Cougar would be hopeless at this," Mara snorted, and not in a ladylike manner. She scribbled on the paper. With a sharp flourish, she finished writing and folded the paper in half. Mara glanced up from the desk and the smile on her face promised ill for someone. "I'm calling in reinforcements."

* * * * *

"Damn it woman, do it like you mean it."

Jenna flinched at Cougar's growl and once again let her body drop while bringing the stick she was pretending was a knife into Cougar's knee. And once again, at the last moment, instinctively pulled back.

Cougar hauled her back up, his breath hissing between his teeth with impatience. "That wouldn't have even broken the skin."

"I know." She'd tried six times, and every time, given in to the sick feeling in her stomach at the last minute.

"If you can't take out the knee, how are you going to hamstring them?" The question growled past her ear as Cougar tightened his arm around her stomach.

"I don't know." She had absolutely no idea. She did know, however, if she couldn't master this, she was never going to succeed in her plan.

"Goddamn it, you'd better not be crying." Cougar took a step back so fast she stumbled.

"I'm not." She blinked the moisture out of her eyes.

He caught her arm and turned her around. Sunlight dappled the barn floor. A stray beam shot through the room and struck her across the eyes, blinding her. She shifted to the left in time to see Cougar fold his arms across his chest.

"You asked me to teach you."

"I know." She waved her hand helplessly. "I just didn't expect…" How could she say she hadn't expected it to be so violent?

"What?"

She pushed her hair off her face, forgetting about the stick and tangling it in her hair.

"It seems so mean," she admitted, unwrapping a strand of hair from the branch bud.

She flinched when Cougar swore and shoved his hair back over his shoulder. "Did you think you could just ask an attacker to let you go?"

"No, but do I have to stab them?" She lifted her chin as she yanked at the stick.

"What the he-eck else are you going to do? You're no match for a man in a fistfight, you can't run, and you're too soft for other things."

The calm listing of her negatives just made them seem so much bigger.

"Maybe I could knee them in sensitive places?" Cougar was shaking his head before she finished.

"That's not reliable and you have to be too close." He stepped forward into her shadowed area, his expression a combination of amusement and exasperation. She flinched as he brushed her hands aside and took the stick.

"Your best bet is to use what they know about you," he said as he went to work on the snarled mess, showing none of her impatience, gently untangling the strands.

"Do you really think it'll work?"

His hands stilled. "Don't take this wrong, Jenna, but for years you've taken whatever anyone dished out to you, not saying a word. If push comes to shove, you can bet everyone will be expecting you to surrender."

"They'll probably be right." It wasn't a very pretty picture he painted. She sighed. The stick came free.

"I'm counting on them selling you short." He said that in that deep drawl that reminded her of Clint. He handed her the stick. "And when they do, you'll use that to your advantage."

"I will?" She rubbed her fingers down the rough surface.

"Yes." He motioned for her to turn around. She didn't immediately.

"What makes you so sure?"

"Because you're a mother now, and anyone who harms you, harms your children."

She hadn't thought of that.

"And you really think I'll be able to do this?"

"I think if push comes to shove and someone you love is in trouble, you'll surprise yourself."

"I'm not so sure if it's Gray."

"The boy giving you problems?" His smile flashed across his face.

"He's so cold and angry."

"Scared, too, I'll bet."

She shook her head, remembering the determination that settled in Gray's eyes and the resentment that curled his mouth. "He doesn't have time to be scared. If he's not working with Clint, he's here with you or over at Asa's earning that horse he fell in love with."

"The boy's got a goal, that's for sure."

"I don't think it's a good one."

"Probably not, but he'll work through it and be glad for his family when he gets to the other side."

She shrugged. "I think he just doesn't think much of me."

"I'd say he thinks the world of you," Cougar contradicted, turning her around.

"What makes you say that?" She twisted against his hand to see his face.

"He gave his sister to you." With a simple push, he finished turning her around. She stood where he placed her, staring at the dust motes floating through the air.

Gray had given his sister to her.

"He didn't argue when I claimed him," she mused aloud.

"He's not dumb. He knows a good thing when he sees it." His arm settled around her waist. "Like Clint."

She slipped the stick of wood in the slit pocket of her skirt, biting her lip against the urge to ask him how he knew Clint saw her as a good thing.

"This time," Cougar said, spreading his legs, his hard body a solid wall behind her, "let's just do it all the way, no matter what. You drop hard on that one side, bring the knife around."

"Okay."

"And try to picture someone hurting Tidbit while you're at it."

She did, but as always she pulled back, tapping his knee, rolling when she hit the ground to lightly hit the back of his ankles. He grabbed her skirt. Remembering what he'd told her, she brought the stick down on his hand, closing her eyes as she did so, missing. He sighed as she scooted back.

Cougar got to his feet holding his hand out to her. She bit her lip as he helped her up.

"Maybe I'll do better if it's the real thing."

"Maybe." He didn't sound any more convinced than she, and his "Let's try it again" had a resigned note she didn't find comforting. Brushing off her skirt, she stepped into his arm, and vowed to do better.

* * * * *

An hour later her leg was aching, she had bruises on her hips, and she still hadn't mastered the art of being vicious. It was a relief when the sound of a fast approaching horse interrupted yet another attempt.

"That, I expect, will be Clint," Cougar said as he walked to the entry, left open for light. He glanced out then back at her. "You left word where you were, didn't you?"

"I told Gray." She pushed the tumble of her hair out of her face, grimacing as a piece of hay stabbed her palm.

"Hmm."

That was not a comforting "Hmmm".

Twisting her hair into a braid behind her head, she walked to the door. Sunlight poured over her, unnaturally bright after the dimness of the barn. She blinked against the sting, and the sight of Clint tearing into the yard atop his big buckskin, Danny close behind. The way he leaned over the horse's neck, urging it to more speed, sent her heart into her throat. Something must he wrong.

"Clint!" She let go of her hair and started running toward him. Her leg gave out on the second step. She went down, only to be snapped back up again as Cougar snagged her arm. Clint's head whipped around, and as if horse and rider were one, the big buckskin pivoted and without a break in stride, came charging at her.

"You okay?" Cougar asked.

"Yes," She didn't have time to say more. Four strides and the horse was on them, so close she could see the pink in the flare of his nostrils. So close she flinched, expecting to be run over, but in another of those moves that was more like poetry than riding, the horse sat back on its haunches and slid to a halt while Clint, in a graceful flow of muscle, launched out of the saddle, hitting the ground on a run. His eyes black as pitch, his mouth set in a grim line.

"Son of a bitch," he growled as he snatched her out of Cougar's grip and up against his hard chest. "I'm going to beat you black and blue." A hard squeeze nearly cracked her ribs, and then he held her away. His lips thinned to a flat line as his gaze paused at her hair, her dirty skirt, and the smudges on her cheeks. "What in hell happened to you?"

"I was practicing."

"What?"

"Fighting."

He blinked. His fingers on her arms tightened. "You weren't hurt?"

"No."

"Son of a bitch." His lips slammed down on hers, his hand in her hair pulling her head back further as his mouth opened over hers. His tongue filled her mouth along with his groan.

She didn't know what to do, what was wrong, so she dug her nails into the hard muscle of his arms and hung on, while he fucked her mouth with brutal intensity, hunting for a response that she didn't know how to give. Twisting her head to the right as if he wanted to permanently mate their mouths, their breath, their souls.

"You might want to take that into the barn." The amused drawl from the right was like a dash of cold water.

Against her, Clint froze. His black eyes unreadable, he stared at her. With a brief nod and a curt "I think I might" he bent and put his shoulder to her stomach. In the next instant she was upside down, Cougar's moccasins swinging in and out of view with the swish of her hair across the ground.

"I'll cool Ornery down while you're occupied."

"I'd appreciate it if you could keep Danny with you, too."

Cougar grunted a "You owe me" before his moccasins faded from view.

Clint's first step drove the air from her lungs. His second a protest. The third a scream as the flat of his hand came down on her sore rear.

"Quiet, Jenna."

Sunlight changed to shadow as they entered the barn. Shadow turned to darkness as the barn door creaked closed. She groaned as he set her on her feet and pain shot up her leg. His "Don't try to get around me with a play for sympathy" was as mean as a snakebite, but his hands were gentle as they probed her thigh, and became tender as he felt the spasming muscle.

"Well hell." He lifted her and then sat. His thighs were hard beneath her hips. "How am I supposed to beat you when you're hurting?"

If he didn't know, she wasn't going to tell him. Try as she might she couldn't see his expression in the gloom. "Why do you have to beat me at all?"

"You scared the shit out of me woman." His callused palm slid up her thigh beneath her skirt.

"It's not that far over here."

"One foot beyond the porch is too far." He began to knead the tight muscle. "Especially when I didn't know where you were going."

"I told Gray."

"Must be he thought I'd hurt you when I found you because all he did was shrug when I asked."

Or maybe he was trying to start trouble. The unwelcome thought slipped through the pain to prod Jenna.

"I don't know what I'm going to do with him," she whispered, the last syllable coming out high as another spasm wrenched her leg.

"Give him some room to sort things out and he'll be fine," Clint countered.

"Will he sort it out?" She felt his nod in the brush of his hair against her cheek. "Good."

"Leg still hurt?"

She bit her lip and nodded, unable to do anything else as the muscle contorted excruciatingly. At her whimper, Clint cupped her cheek and pulled her head against his chest. "Shh, baby. Just relax into me and let me take care of this."

She did, turning her face into his neck, breathing deeply of his scent, riding the soothing notes of his baritone as he reprimanded her for riding, for scaring him, for hurting herself, for tricking Jackson. By the time he got the muscle to relax and the pain to a manageable ache, he was pretty much condemning her for getting up in the morning.

"It wasn't that bad."

His finger tipped her chin up. She could barely make out the whites of his eyes as he corrected her.

"It's as bad as it gets, and if you don't believe me, imagine coming downstairs a year from now and not being able to find Bri. Not knowing if she was taken or if she just walked out the door and into trouble. And while you're looking for her, you just keep imagining all the trouble she can get into, knowing damned well exactly what can happen."

Nausea mixed with pain. She'd die if that ever happened.

"Exactly." His finger touched her cheek. She'd forgotten he could see where she couldn't. His hand scooted up her thigh, not flinching as his fingers hit the dips and ridges of the scars. "You scared the shit out of me. Again."

His palm came to rest on the bulge of her hipbone, his fingers dangling in the crease of her thigh, the thin cotton of her pantaloons doing nothing to diminish the searing heat of his touch. Deep inside, her body sprang to life. She turned deeper into his embrace.

"I'm sorry I worried you."

"You're going to be." The hard edge to his voice sent a shiver of worry sneaking through her.

"When?"

"Just as soon as you're up to it."

"I don't think you should beat me." She'd never be up to it. She tested the give in his biceps. There was none. She opened her fingers measuring their depth. She couldn't even get her hands around the upper curve.

"Tough." He set her on her feet, the rustle of his denims and the shift of his grip telling her that he stood also. "When you married me you took the good with the bad."

Chapter Twenty-One

She had to take the good with the bad. The thought plagued Jenna as she rode behind Clint, her arms wrapped around his waist, her cheek pressed against his broad back. His coat kept her from feeling the heat of his body, but if she closed her eyes she could imagine it. How warm he always was. How caring.

She had to take the good with the bad. She pressed a little closer, the back of the saddle pressing into her stomach, the scent of his cigarette drifting over his shoulder. There wasn't an ounce of bad in the man. She'd bet on that when she'd joined this marriage, and she hadn't seen a thing to change her mind since.

The saddle creaked as he half-turned, "Something wrong?"

"My hands are cold."

"If you'd asked before leaving, I would have made sure you had the right clothes." He flicked the half finished cigarette to the ground.

Again that reference to the fact that she needed looking after, as though she were a child. She slid her hands up under his coat and rested them against his belly, just above the waistband of his denims. He jerked. He was clearly still angry. She needed to do something about that.

She gently stroked his stomach through his shirt. The muscles under her fingers knotted on the upstroke. On the downstroke her knuckle slid beneath the waistband of his denims. His flesh burned hotter there. Her fingers lingered. His breathing grew rapid. The gap between material and flesh widened.

"Clint?" she asked softly, her daring rising to conquer her modesty.

"What?" His drawl was a growl.

"If you don't want me to touch you, you need to tell me now."

"Son of a bitch!"

"Is that a yes or a no?"

"This isn't going to change my feelings, Jenna."

"I know. You're going to beat me when I'm up to it." She kissed his back through his coat. He leaned back, giving her better access.

"Damned straight."

"But can I touch you now the way I want?" She worked his shirt up, sighing as her fingers reached the heat of his flesh. His stomach muscles leapt under her touch.

"How do you want?" His hand caught hers.

"Intimately." She wanted to touch him with the same generosity with which he always touched her, releasing his fear and tension into a storm of passion that carried him away.

"Yes." His fingers jerked on hers and then opened, freeing her.

"Good." She smiled against his back. Who did he think he was fooling with his snapping? She could feel the excited jump of his breathing against her palms as she snuggled closer.

She tried to unbutton his pants with one hand while stroking his stomach with the other, dipping her finger into his navel while she tugged at the stubborn flap. When her nail bent back she acknowledged the truth. This was going to be a two-handed job. She got the fly of his pants open before running into another problem.

"I want to touch you," she whispered.

"Who's stopping you?"

She stroked the thick length of his cock through his denims, pressing her forehead against his back as the heat of embarrassment washed her face.

"I can't get to you."

"That, Sunshine, I can fix." He stood in the saddle, raising his hips and straightening the line from thigh to hip. She reached into the open fly of his denims, very carefully cupping his hard flesh, easing him up. The head caught and she had to stop. Just when she thought he was stuck forever, he pushed the waistband down. On a soft sigh, she lifted him into her grasp.

She couldn't see him, but she didn't need to. The sheer weight was impressive. His cock rested on her hands, jerking and twitching with need. Every inch of his heavy shaft burned into her memory. The roping of veins under the silky smooth flesh. The hardness covered with velvet, ending in the flared head with its cushiony resistance. She ran a fingertip around that intriguing softness. He pulsed with life and promise. And if he was to be believed, only for her.

"You feel good in my hands."

"Sunshine, I can't begin to describe how good your soft little hands feel on me." His laugh was choked.

"Do you like it when I do this?" "This" was a gentle pumping motion. His hips bucked, giving her a little more to play with.

"Yes."

"Then I'll do it again."

"What happened to my shy little sunbeam?" He asked over his shoulder, strands of his hair brushing her face.

"She's coming out of her shell."

"About damned time."

Even though he couldn't feel it, she kissed his back. He made her feel so special.

"Twist a little on the upstroke baby," he ordered.

"Like this?" she asked, setting the suggestion to action. He jerked as if shot, his head arched back and then fell forward. His hands came down on the pommel, gripping hard.

"Son of a bitch, just...like...that." She did it again and again, picking up speed as moisture leaked down the shaft, smoothing it back into his flesh as she planed his mood though the surface of his cock. Smoothing out his rough edges, taking away the hardness and giving him what she could. "Baby, I'm going to come."

"Not yet."

"It's not like you're giving me much choice."

"Oh." She hadn't realized she could control the pace. She gentled her approach, matching her rhythm to the slow, easy gait of the horse, drawing his cock up and out on the forward stroke, bringing it down and back on the downstroke. He fought her, punching up in short jabs, trying to get the speed back, but she snuggled into his back and kept to her own pace. This was her gift. She'd deliver it how she wanted.

"Are you trying to kill me?"

"I'm trying to pleasure you." This time on the upstroke she cupped the tip in her palm. It overflowed the center like a big juicy plum, ripe to bursting. Moisture pooled in the well of her palm. She rubbed back onto the head in easy circles. He groaned and shuddered. His cock surged against her palm. More silky moisture replaced the first. She scooped it up on her middle finger.

"Don't look," she whispered and she brought her hand back.

"At what?"

Before he could turn and see, she slipped her finger into her mouth, sucking it clean, letting his salty flavor spread through her mouth. Wanting this small part of him. When it was gone, she wanted more. More of his taste. His compliance. His acceptance. Heavens, she wanted him.

He turned in the saddle, catching her with her finger in her mouth, his eyes dropping to the sight, pausing before burning like black fire as they met hers.

"Did you like that little taste, Sunshine?"

With her cheeks so hot that she felt sure they'd catch fire, she whispered, "You weren't supposed to see."

He unbuttoned his coat and pushed it back. "Did you like it?"

She nodded. Her gaze locked on his cock as it rose from the V of his fly. Dark, throbbing, powerful, hungry. Her pussy swelled and clenched with anticipation. She took her finger out of her mouth and touched it to the tip, smiling as his cock danced.

"I like that." She ran her finger down the side, tracing the curve of the vein to the base.

"You do?"

"Oh yes." She wiggled her finger under the tight material of his pants, reaching the soft skin at the top of his scrotum before the material cut off access. He grunted as she scraped gently with the edge of her nail.

"I like touching you, too."

"I know." She pulled her finger free, retracing her path back to the moist tip. "It's one of my favorite things about you."

"All men want to touch a beautiful woman. It's not a reason for finding favor." He cocked an eyebrow at her in that half-play, half-serious way that made her want to smile.

"I know." She leaned her cheek against his arm. That he found her beautiful was a miracle she couldn't get over. She closed her fist around him. He arched into her touch. She tested his readiness with a squeeze. He bucked and pre-come dribbled over her hand. She opened her fingers, letting the silken fluid pool on the edge of her palm. "But I like being able to give to you."

"Look at me, Sunshine." He caught her hand in his, holding her tight against him. She did. All play was gone from his face. He was still aroused, but he was serious too. "Be careful that you don't give me more than you can spare."

"You're always taking care of me."

"I'm warning you." He shook his head, his hair rustling across his coat. When it comes to you, I'm a starving man."

"I'm not afraid of you."

"You should be."

"I can't be." She pumped him through her fist, knowing he was close to coming from the way his cock hardened to steel and throbbed. She squeezed him until his breath hissed between his teeth and his cock jerked in her grip before whispering, "I love you."

She watched his face as her words threw him over the edge, his teeth gritted against the agony of sensation jerking his body. His eyes closed as he moaned deep in his throat, and in her hand, his big cock pulsed jet after jet of his hot come. She let it spill over her fingers, washing her in his seed, his pleasure, marking her as his. She pulled a handkerchief from her pocket, catching the excess. She milked him gently, watching as another spurt welled, feeling his shudder all the way to her soul. Oh, she liked him like this. Open to her, nothing held back, letting her in further than he ever had before, seemingly vulnerable. Though no man as tough as Clint could ever truly be vulnerable, she enjoyed the illusion.

A bead of fluid lingered on the broad head. She curled her finger around it. His moan as she stole that bit of seed sent a thrill of hot desire to her womb. She looked straight into his slitted eyes as she lapped it off her finger. His body jerked again and his lip lifted as a growl emanated from deep in his chest.

"Come here." His arm curved behind her shoulders pulling her around until she sat across his thighs.

Clint turned her face up and kissed her hard, nipping her lower lip when she didn't immediately open for him. Kissing her deeply when she did as always, opening herself to his needs. Goddamn, she was too generous. She'd give him everything if he asked for it, no holds barred. A man who had a woman like that had a treasure, but he'd have to guard her very carefully, place the limits for her that she couldn't. He hugged her tightly.

"I'm not like this with anyone else." The confession floated upwards on a puff of frosted breath. Though he probably wasn't meant to hear the hint of fear in her voice, he did. She worried way too much.

He shifted her higher in his arms, resting his chin on the top of her head, breathing deeply of the scent of roses and contentment.

"I know you, Sunshine. I may not know where you've been, but I know who you are, and you're mine. You've always been mine." He accepted that now. He didn't know why, but he wasn't fighting it anymore.

Danny growled beside him. He followed the dog's lead, looking across the field. A lone rider approached. He reached for his rifle.

"Sunshine, button me back up. We've got company."

He held the rifle clear as she knifed upright, her breath coming in short gasps, her hands soft and shaking as she eased his semi-hard cock back under his coat. She couldn't get him back in his pants, and her breathing grew almost desperate.

"That's fine. Leave it like that." The rider was too far away to make out features, but he didn't recognize the horse. He kicked his foot free of the stirrup. Clint kept his voice calm, as he urged Jenna around. "Now turn and put your foot in the stirrup and get back up behind me."

"But—"

"No buts. Just do it." If it came to a confrontation he wanted his body between her and any bullets. As soon as she was settled he motioned to his side. "Take the revolver out of my holster." There was a long hesitation in which she didn't move. "Now, Jenna."

She took it, following his orders, shaking so badly he was afraid she'd fall off.

"You're not going to need it. It's just a precaution."

"I don't know how to shoot."

"Nothing to it. Cock the hammer, aim for the chest, and pull the trigger." The rider came closer. He wasn't getting any more familiar.

"I can't."

"If I go down, you start firing and don't stop until the chambers are empty. Danny growled again. Clint levered a round into the Spencer's chamber, the barrel resting on his thigh, pointing at the stranger."

"Oh God, you can't go down." She spread her palms over his chest as if to shield him. The muzzle of the revolver pressed up into his chin.

He moved it aside. "It's not in my plans for the evening."

"You have plans?"

"Big plans." He squinted against the sun. There was something familiar about the rider now. "They start with stripping you naked and end with my tongue buried in your pussy."

"How can you think about that at a time like this?"

"With you for a wife, it's a wonder I think of anything else." If he wasn't mistaken that lump boring into his spine was her forehead and she was grinding it back and forth.

"Please be careful."

"I won't let anything happen to you."

"I don't want anything to happen to you." The fierce whisper sent his heart to pounding and slipped beneath the familiar cold anticipation of battle.

"Then I guess we'll just have to keep this encounter friendly." Which might be easier than he thought as he recognized the rider. Mark Dougherty wasn't his favorite person, but he didn't think their meeting would come to a killing event. Nevertheless, he didn't lower the rifle. "You can probably relax. It's Eloise's brother. He's not anyone's favorite, but I don't think he's a danger."

If a body discounted the rumors that he'd taken up with a gang of no-goods and started down a bad road. Jenna didn't relax at his assurance. After a brief pause, her shaking grew worse. Dougherty drew up alongside.

"Evening McKinnely."

"Evening." Jenna all but buried herself in his back.

"That one of the Emporium's girls?" Dougherty jerked his chin in Jenna's direction.

"The Emporium burned down a year ago."

"For sure someone took it over."

They had but he wasn't going to get into that discussion with his wife behind him.

"You heading back to your sister's?"

"Yeah, I thought I'd visit a bit."

Which probably meant he'd run out of money. Clint eyed him. The man seemed to have aged ten years in the year and a half he'd been gone, his blond good looks dissipating under the influence of too much alcohol and too little exercise.

"I'm sure she'd appreciate the help." Not that Clint thought Mark would be much help. The man was shiftless to the bone, but Eloise seemed to love having him around. There was no accounting for taste.

Mark moved his horse closer. Danny growled. Behind him Jenna stiffened. The shaking stopped, and beneath his arm, the muzzle of the revolver lifted and pointed. For a woman who said she couldn't shoot at someone, Jenna was taking damned careful aim. Clint tipped his hat down over his eyes, absorbing the information.

"That's close enough."

"You're not being very neighborly." Mark pulled his horse up.

"Can't help it. My dog doesn't like you."

"And you let your dog do your thinking?"

"He hasn't failed me yet." Clint shrugged.

"They said you'd turned strange after you quit marshaling. Soft even." Mark's bark of laughter was forced. He palmed his coat away from his belt. Clint wasn't impressed with the move or the stomach that overhung the other man's buckle.

"They say a lot of things." He smiled. He clamped his elbow down on the muzzle of the revolver Jenna was trying to shove forward.

"You going to introduce me to your companion?" Mark asked.

"No." Clint kept his answer short and to the point. Jenna relaxed infinitesimally.

"You didn't use to be so unsociable." Mark's thin mouth disappeared under the lash of the slight.

"Your memory might be failing. I've always been damned unsociable."

"Butter wouldn't melt in your mouth when you were courting my sister."

"Walking her home when she worked too late at the store isn't courting."

"It damned well better be, seeing as how you were out alone with her after dark."

"If you were that worried you could have walked her home yourself."

"I was busy."

Busy only if you counted gambling and whoring.

Clint shrugged. "Seeing as she's married, I'd say it's all water under the bridge."

"I suppose so." Mark frowned, but he didn't have any argument for the truth.

The smile he put on his face was forced. "Mind if I ride in with you?"

"Yes."

"Planning on a little horse sport?" Mark's smile turned lecherous. He tried to peer around Clint's shoulder.

Clint kneed Ornery to keep Jenna hidden, while observing, "You always were an ill-mannered son of a bitch."

"And you always were a selfish bastard, keeping all the good whores to yourself."

Clint wanted to bury his fist in the other man's smirk. As if sensing his mood, Danny snarled and lunged at the chestnut's hooves.

"Goddamn it!" Mark cursed, trying to rein in the terrified horse. "Call off your dog, or I'll shoot him."

"I wouldn't." Clint raised the muzzle of his rifle. Behind him, Jenna tensed. She was afraid of the son of a bitch. He didn't know why, but he would. And then, if necessary, he'd gut him like the pig he was. "However, if you move it along, Danny might see fit to leave you be."

Mark hauled back on the reins, causing the bit to cut into the horse's mouth. The chestnut reared and spun. Clint wasn't surprised when the horse took off under a gouge of spurs. Dougherty had always been a bully. When Mark was a blur in the distance, Jenna relaxed, slumping against his spine.

"For a woman who couldn't shoot, you sure were ready to plug Mark." Clint removed the revolver from her hand, and eased the hammer back into place.

"I don't like him."

"So I gathered."

"You can't trust him."

"I never have, but I'm more interested in why he terrifies you."

"He doesn't terrify me."

"Worries you, then."

"He's a bully."

"Has he ever bullied you?" There was a little too much lag before her "no" to be believable. "C'mon back up here, Sunshine."

He felt the shake of her head rather than saw it.

"Are you telling me no?" Her nod was emphatic. "It's only ten minutes to the house, Sunshine."

"I know."

"You're only adding to that beating you've got coming." He pried her fingers loose from the folds of his jacket. Her hand jerked in his. He kissed her fingers.

"I can't talk about it."

"You will."

"Not tonight."

"Why not?"

"Because you promised me something better."

"So I did." He smiled, tickling her palm with his tongue, enjoying the press of her breasts on his back as she took a steadying breath. He waited until she rested in relief against him, before adding, "But I'm not going to forget the other."

He hadn't earned his reputation by giving up.

Chapter Twenty-Two

Jenna ladled stew into the last bowl. The tension in the small kitchen was thick enough to cut with a knife. When she turned, Gray was glaring at Clint, who was bouncing Bri on his knee and ignoring the boy in that complete way that added sparks to Gray's resentment. Her stomach churned. She had to do something about this.

She held out the bowl. "Gray, could you please take this."

The boy sat and stared at his utensils as if he hadn't heard. Clint frowned. She quickly brought it to the table and set it in front of him.

Gray centered it with a shove. Broth sloshed over the side. Jenna wiped up the spill with the towel, but Gray didn't even glance her way.

Jenna angled her body so that she blocked Clint's view.

"I'm sorry, Gray." She took his grunt as a response.

"You don't have anything to apologize for," Clint pointed out from behind her.

She ignored him and focused on Gray. "I had no right to put you in the middle like that."

"You didn't put him anywhere. The boy made his own choices." The tightness in his tone indicated that he wasn't pleased with either of them.

Gray had made those choices to protect her. Jenna understood that even if Clint couldn't. She kept talking to Gray as if Clint wasn't behind her putting in his two cents.

"In the future, I don't want you to ever go against your father. Even to protect me." She touched Gray's shoulder. He glared at her and jumped up, knocking over his chair. She flinched from the disgust in his eyes. Bri started to cry.

Clint hushed her with soft talk and a knuckle to chew on.

"He hates me." Jenna sighed as the door slammed behind Gray.

"He doesn't hate you, Sunshine. Clint sighed. "He's just mad because he can't go over and work toward that horse he wants."

"You were too hard on him."

"He risked your life."

"He thought he was protecting me."

"He thought wrong."

"Couldn't you just —"

"No." He patted Bri's back with the softest of touches, but his eyes were hard as they met hers. "He can't come between us, Jenna, and he can't endanger you, Bri, or himself by being a wild card."

"But he's new here, Clint."

"The sooner he learns, the sooner he'll settle."

"His supper is getting cold." Jenna touched Gray's bowl. He was so thin.

"He'll come in when he's hungry."

"He's too proud." Jenna looked out the window. All she could see was the reflection of the oil lamp. Gray didn't even have his coat.

"Doesn't the Bible say something about pride going before the fall?"

"Pride is all he has."

"Would it make you feel better if I went and talked to him?"

"Yes." She had great faith that Clint's heart would soften if he spent time with the boy.

"Take Bri then." Jenna eased Bri off his shoulder. As always, it didn't matter how careful she was, Clint was Bri's favorite person in the whole world and she never left him willingly. Clint kissed her lips as Bri wailed in her ear. "The boy isn't going to thank me for this."

She found her voice. "But I will."

"I'm counting on it." He nodded and shrugged into his coat, grabbing Gray's off the adjoining hook.

* * * * *

Gray hadn't gone far. He was sitting on the far corner of the porch. In the light spilling out from the window, Clint could see him rubbing his arms. Clint made his next step heavy, giving the boy warning. Gray immediately sat up straight and dropped his hands.

"Your mother's worried about you." He handed the boy his coat.

"She's not my mother," he growled, shrugging into the heavy wool.

"Do me a favor son, and don't ever say that to her directly. Even if you feel it." Clint pulled his makings out of his pocket.

"Or you'll beat me?"

"Worse son, she'll cry." He sprinkled tobacco onto the paper.

"Women always cry."

"Not my woman." Clint had to give the boy credit. He had his sneer down to an art form. Still, he was going to have to debate the point. He licked the side edge of the paper to seal it before twisting the ends. "I like my woman happy and content."

"A man should not fear a woman's tears."

"He shouldn't go courting them either." Clint struck the sulfur.

The boy had the grace to flinch and looked through the window. Clint followed the trajectory of his gaze. It led straight to where Jenna sat at the table, toying with the rim of a plate, her expression heavy with worry. As he watched, she bit her lip, and a tear slid down her cheek. He took a drag on his cigarette, his insides twisting at the sight. Damn he liked her smile better.

"I want to thank you for bringing Bri to her."

"I knew she would not turn her away."

"No, she wouldn't." Clint took another drag, blowing the smoke out in a lazy stream. "I also want to thank you for not kicking up a fuss when she claimed you, too."

"It wasn't necessary." Clint looked the boy over, from his lean frame to his too-old eyes. If anyone needed Jenna's warmth, it was this hard-edged boy.

"I know that, just like I know her fussing annoys you, but she has her heart set on you being her son, and she's just treating you the way she would her own."

"It's not bad when she's cooking me something." Gray shoved his hands into his pockets.

"She does know her way around an oven," Clint chuckled.

"I didn't ask her to talk to you." Gray cut him a glance.

Now there was a loaded opening.

"I never thought you did." He flicked the half smoked cigarette into the dirt. He was doing better with his quitting.

"She shouldn't have done it," Gray muttered.

"Son, she can't help wanting to protect you anymore than you could help wanting to protect her."

"You won't beat her?" Gray rubbed Danny's ear as if the answer didn't interest him much.

"I hadn't planned on it. Especially now that I've got you and Danny dead-set against the idea." Clint figured it wasn't a good plan to let the boy know he'd threatened her with it. For all his nonchalance, the kid was a keg of dynamite ready to explode.

"It would break her spirit if you beat her."

"She's stronger than you know."

Gray shook his head. "She would shatter under your hand." He turned those too-old, too-wise eyes on Clint, suddenly looking all man. "She loves you."

"She thinks she does."

It was an unsettling experience to be pitied by a kid, even if it was only with a look.

"If you are ever so foolish as to hurt her, I will kill you."

He believed him. "If I ever sink so low, you have my blessing."

"You need to stop her tears." Gray nodded toward the window. Clint looked. That single tear had burgeoned into a torrent.

"The only thing that's going to do that is if you and I come back in smiling."

"Some things were easier when I was alone." Gray sighed and glanced through the window again.

"Yeah, but I bet the grub wasn't nearly as good."

"That is very true. Gray pushed to his feet." He wiped his hands of the seat of his pants. "What will you tell her?"

"The truth. Things are settled between us, and instead of a week of being ranch-bound, you've got two days and extra barn chores until Sunday—when you get back from Asa's."

"Thank you." Gray stood there and suddenly he was all uncertain kid, faced with an emotion he didn't know how to handle. He rubbed his hand on his skinny hips.

"Don't be thanking me until you see the shitload of crap I've been putting off getting to."

"It won't matter."

Clint knew it wouldn't. The boy had integrity and drive. And he loved that horse.

"I'm going to need a promise from you, too."

The wariness returned immediately to Gray's eyes. As if he knew that there had to be a catch to anything good that happened in his life. That wariness tore at Clint's insides as much as Jenna's tears. Maybe he really was going soft. He put his hands on the kid's shoulders, amazed at how lacking in muscle they were. Gray just gave the impression of mass.

"Don't withhold information from me again. Not when it concerns Jenna, Bri, or yourself." Gray shrugged out from under his hand and grunted. "Is that a promise or your stomach acting up?"

"I promise."

"Good, because McKinnelys work together, not against each other." Gray didn't have anything to say to that. Clint mentally sighed. Getting Gray settled into the family would take time and patience. He glanced through the window. Jenna had stopped crying, but she still looked worried.

That, he could do something about.

"You ready to go make Jenna smile again?" he asked.

He thought the kid would balk when he opened the door, but he didn't. He walked straight through, and when Jenna caught his eye, Clint answered with a nod. Gray didn't flinch away from her hug. He even patted her awkwardly on the back, which had Jenna promptly bursting into tears. Gray stepped back in horror.

"I'm sorry."

Clint shook his head and tucked Jenna into his side. "These are happy tears, son. Nothing to do but ride them out."

Gray didn't look any less appalled with the explanation.

"If you could see to Bri and eat your dinner, I'll take care of this."

Gray bolted for the table.

Against his chest, Jenna sniffed. "I don't think he could get out of here fast enough."

"McKinnely men don't tolerate tears well."

"I'll try to toughen up." She wiped her nose on her sleeve.

"How many times do I have to tell you? I like you just the way you are." He wiped her face with the towel that was sitting on the edge of the Hoosier cabinet. He had to use his finger to wipe off the smear of flour the towel left. She turned fully into his arms.

"Even though I cry at the worst times?"

"I've gotten used to it."

Her laugh choked on a sniff. "Thank you for talking to Gray."

"I gotta tell you, Jenna. That's a hell of a boy you brought into the family." He kissed the top of her head.

"You like him?"

He nodded, brushing a hair off her face. "He's going to be a hell of a man." And a hell of an enemy for someone. He didn't tell Jenna that though. She had enough to deal with, and she wouldn't understand the drive a boy felt to avenge the death of his mother. He also didn't tell her the boy had threatened to kill him. She wouldn't understand that, either. Another hiccough shook her.

"C'mon, Sunshine. Don't cry." He kissed her hair, wiping at her damp cheeks with his thumb. "It tears me up."

"The McKinnely weakness?"

"Yes." He looked at her red eyes, tear-wet cheeks, and mussed hair. He tilted her face and brushed the tears from her lashes with his lips, the salty flavor spreading through his mouth. She was beautiful through and through. "Damn, I'm going to have to beat the men off with a stick next Saturday at the social."

"We're going to a social?" Her lashes fluttered against his lips.

"That's not supposed to scare you."

"I've never been to one."

"Then it'll be my pleasure to take you to your first."

"I don't know how to dance."

"Another first for us to share."

"I'm not good in crowds." She plucked at a button on his shirt.

"You just have to be good with me." Her fingers slid under the flap, soft and warm on his chest.

"I could say or do something stupid and embarrass you." Her nails dug in, teasing his senses.

"I could behave like an ass and embarrass you." Her fingers were still on his chest, just inches from his nipple. She looked up, her eyes wide.

"You never embarrass me."

"And you never embarrass me, so I guess that means we're set for the night." He turned them slightly so that the boy couldn't see.

"I don't have a dress."

"Guess you'll have to spend my money then."

"There isn't time to get one made up."

"Then throw more money at the problem." He kissed her nose. He ran his fingers down the prim row of buttons on her dress, pressing in as he went so that the deep valley between her breasts was revealed. Son of a bitch, he'd love the privacy to rip that dress open and bury his face between those soft mounds. "Just don't make it too low-cut. I don't want to spend the night beating awestruck men over the head with chairs."

"You think men are going to be interested in me?" Her chuckle was as soft as her touch.

He smiled at the wheedle in her voice. He considered it a real step up in their relationship that she felt comfortable enough with him to fish so obviously.

"There's going to be a line out the door waiting to dance with you. But," he didn't have to work to find a frown, "I don't want anyone but me shining their belt buckle with you so you practice saying 'no' every way you can between now and then."

The thought of another man anywhere near her drove him nuts.

She patted his hand comfortingly. "I'll practice, but I don't think you need to worry."

He touched the shining length of her bright gold hair. He'd had a hard enough time keeping men away from her before they married, but now that she was beginning to find her feet, that inner light that so warmed him was shining brighter and brighter, drawing more and more attention to her gentle beauty. He touched the strand of hair to her full pink lips. She was all shiny light and deep heat, his Jenna.

"Ah baby, if you think that, you've got one hell of a surprise coming."

He tugged the strand of hair, tilting her head back. As she looked at him, a question in her light blue eyes, he took her mouth deep and hard, thrusting his tongue past her surprised gasp, tasting her sweetness. Her willingness. The truth.

It didn't matter how many men came at her. At the end of the night and every other night she'd be going home with him. And no other.

* * * * *

Jenna didn't have to wait until the social to be surprised. Walking into Pearl's Dressmaking Shop with Mara three days later took care of that for her. If seeing Lorie, Elizabeth, Millicent, and Dorothy crammed into the small parlor wasn't disorienting enough, when Pearl reached behind her and locked the door, flicking the sign to closed, the deal was sealed.

"What's going on?"

"I sent them a note," Mara answered, weaving through the women.

"In regard to what?" Jenna squeezed to the left past Millicent's bulk, Bri in her arms complicating the maneuver.

"In regard to Clint being an ass," Millicent answered, frowning impatiently toward the back of the small shop.

"He's not an ass," Jenna protested.

"Sounds to me like he's being a perfect one," Lorie interjected.

"You don't know him." Clint was wonderful. Good to her in all ways. It wasn't his fault he couldn't love her.

"I do. I know that boy inside and out and I'd say about now he's being an ass." Dorothy looked up from the lace she was admiring.

"I don't want to fight. I just need a dress." How was she supposed to argue with Clint's? She patted Brianna's back.

"Oh honey, don't you worry," Pearl said, coming forward, a measuring tape around her neck and a pincushion tied to her wrist. "We can do more than one thing at a time."

That's what Jenna was afraid of.

"But we might want to get the fitting done before the reverend gets here," Lorie offered.

"That's a good point," Millie added in her husky siren voice that was so at odds with her flamboyant red hair and clothes. "Won't be any good for business for Jenna to be sporting a dress with uneven seams."

"Isn't that the truth!" Pearl grabbed Jenna's hand. For such a petite, ladylike woman she was amazingly strong. She yanked Jenna past Elizabeth. Jenna mouthed a "Help". Elizabeth smiled, shrugged, and held her hands out for Bri.

Jenna had just a moment to pass Bri off before she was tugged through the gold velvet curtain to the dim interior. The room smelled like dye, paper, and…sugar cookies?

"C'mon in everyone, we might as well get settled," Pearl called, motioning Jenna to go behind the curtain and change into the shimmering sky-blue dress that was hanging there. Jenna slid out of her dress. Surely Pearl didn't expect her to wear this?

"Pearl which dress am I supposed to wear?"

"The only one back there, honey."

The smooth satin slipped through her fingers. Oh heavens, this was way too nice. What if she spilled punch on it?

"Do you have something less…?" How could she say less fine, and not sound stupid?

Pearl popped her head through the curtain. Jenna clasped the dress to her chest.

"Clint came by and picked out the material for that dress himself dear. Said it was his favorite shade of blue."

Dorothy peeked through the curtain, looked at the roughed out dress and Jenna's face. "Easy to see why. It's the same color as your eyes."

The curtain flew open as Millicent stepped through. "The boy always was partial to blue."

Jenna wanted to sink through the floor. She inched the dress a little higher. Millicent whistled through her teeth as she looked at the dress Jenna held against her.

"He also has excellent taste."

The next face to appear was Mara's. She looked at Jenna, the dress, and the women. "The dress is gorgeous. Clint is an ass with excellent taste, and Jenna might appreciate a little privacy."

"Whatever for?" Pearl asked, taking the dress out of Jenna's hands and gathering it up before dropping it over her head. Her "We're all women here" was slightly obscured by the swish of satin as the slippery material poured over her head. Jenna shoved her arms into the sleeves.

"Watch out for the—"

"Pins," Jenna hissed as one stabbed her in the underarm.

"Did one get you?" Pearl asked moving the material around.

"It's all right."

"You're not bleeding on the fabric are you?" Millicent asked.

Jenna pulled the sleeve down. "No."

"Good." Elizabeth made a face at Brianna. "It'd be a shame to ruin such a beautiful dress, wouldn't it, sweetie pie?"

"What's going to be ruined is this meeting," Millicent muttered as Pearl motioned Jenna to the box in the middle of the floor. "Where the heck is the reverend?"

"Why does the reverend need to be at my fitting?" Jenna asked as she stepped onto the wide box. She certainly didn't want a man there, least of all that too-handsome reverend.

No one answered. She tugged at the bodice, managing to get the buttons done up through sheer force of will. The dress was definitely going to have to be let out in the bust. She was about to point that out when a knock at the back door interrupted the proceedings. The other women turned as one, varying degrees of anticipation reflected on their faces.

"Thank goodness!" Pearl exclaimed, grabbing a basket and hurrying to the door.

The door opened far enough to reveal a tall, broad-shouldered silhouette backlit by streaming sunlight before Pearl reached through and yanked the man in, swinging the door shut.

Jenna smoothed her skirts and then looking down, crossed her arms over her very exposed chest. The reverend's gaze fell on her and his frown dissolved into a slow grin that made her distinctly uncomfortable.

"If I wasn't afraid word would get back to Clint, who'd for sure be feeding me my teeth for noticing, I'd tell you that you are a fine-looking woman, Mrs. McKinnely."

Jenna managed to choke a "Thank you" past her embarrassment, which only had that unholy reverend smiling broader. He unbuttoned his coat and tipped his hat at the ladies in general.

"So Clint's the reason this latest meeting had to be called?" he asked with an arch of his brow.

"He's being a bit of a pain," Mara said as picked up a bunch of pins and eyed the hem of Jenna's dress.

"In the ass," Millicent elaborated.

"McKinnelys excel at that kind of thing." The reverend smiled, obviously very comfortable in a room full of women.

"Clint is not being an...a pain," Jenna gritted out

"Don't you worry Jenna," Mara muttered around a mouthful of pins as she bent to tug the hem down in front. "The women of W.O.M.B. are geniuses at getting a man's head on straight."

"I'd hardly rate fixing Cougar's idiocy as a matter of genius," Millicent retorted as Jenna clutched the bodice in the wake of Mara's tugging.

Lorie laughed. "He was rather easy once you got him tied down."

"It was the tying down that was a challenge," Mara agreed, the blush on her cheeks rivaling one of Jenna's.

"I don't understand," Jenna muttered through her embarrassment. And she wasn't sure she wanted to, but she was curious. Like everyone else, she'd heard stories about Mara and Cougar's courtship.

"You will." The reverend outright laughed, his teeth flashing white in his suntanned face, and pulled a wrapped bundle from under his coat.

Jenna looked at Lorie. "W.O.M.B.?"

"Women overcoming male bullheadedness," Lorie whispered as the reverend swapped his parcel for Pearl's basket.

He swung the basket on his fingers and sighed, "Don't know what I'm going to do for snacks once you women get the men in this town straightened out."

"You could settle down with a nice young woman," Pearl suggested.

"What would I do with a nice woman?" He leaned down and kissed Pearl's cheek. "If you've got to hook me up with someone, you'd be better served finding me one who's well acquainted with the rough side of bad."

Jenna blinked because for that one brief second she thought the man was totally serious. Which was ridiculous. A reverend's wife was always a woman above reproach.

"Ain't that the truth? For a reverend, you sure are a wild one." Millicent laughed and gathered an assortment of glassware from the sideboard.

"Just earning my way to redemption, Millie. Just earning my way." A lock of his sun-streaked blond hair fell over his brow as he opened the door.

"Straight to hell is where that boy's going," Pearl muttered as he left the room, taking his laughter and the scent of sugar cookies with him.

"If he is, we're probably helping him on the way," Millie added handing out the glasses. "Sending the preacher to the saloon to get our libation is sure to get the Almighty's attention."

"You sent the Reverend Swanson to a saloon?" Jenna took a glass, feeling more than a little foolish, standing on a box trying to figure out what was going on.

Lorie yawned and nodded. "He's the only one we can trust."

"You trust a reverend who drinks?" Jenna didn't know whether to be shocked or amused.

"If you can't trust a reverend, who can you trust?" Lorie shrugged.

Jenna wasn't sure, but she also wasn't sure they should be putting all their trust in a man of God who so clearly didn't look or act the part.

Lorie smothered another yawn, and Jenna felt a pang of guilt. Even though she'd made Lorie a partner in Sweet Thyme and gave her three-fourths of the profit, it was an awful lot of work for one person.

"Is the bakery too much for you?"

"Oh, no. I love it. I just didn't get to bed on time last night." Jenna knew how that was.

"Have you been feeding Harry?" As hard as it had been to let go of the bakery, it had been doubly hard to let go of caring for those who depended on her. To her surprise, Lorie flushed bright red.

"Yes."

"Who's Harry?" Elizabeth asked as she played peekaboo with Bri.

"One of Jenna's strays," Lorie answered before Jenna could.

"Well, if he's eating from your bakery, Jenna, he's eating darned good," Millicent said as Pearl filled Jenna's glass. Even from a foot away, Jenna's nose wrinkled at the smell of spirits.

"That new line of herbed breads you introduced is wonderful. I need to talk to you later about ordering some for the restaurant."

"That's a high compliment." Jenna grabbed the bodice again as Mara continued tugging at the hem. Millie was the best cook in the whole territory. Fights were known to break out as patrons waited to get into her restaurant. She didn't praise others' cooking often, and certainly didn't bring it into her establishment.

"Thank you." Lori's blush deepened.

"No need to be thanking her," Pearl said as she rapidly filled the other glasses. "The woman knows a good thing when she tastes it, and I'm sure she means to make a pretty penny off the deal."

"That's the God's honest truth." Millie raised her glass to Jenna. She paused, her eyes dropping to Jenna's chest before widening. "Pearl, did you get a description off Clint before making up this dress?"

"Of course!"

"Well," Millie took a sip of her whiskey and frowned, "I've never known a man to underdescribe that aspect of a woman's body."

Pearl looked up, frowned, and took a quick sip of her drink before setting it on the floor. She whipped her tape measure from around her neck, crossing the room in four steps.

"Clint's no different than any other man," she grumbled, wrapping the tape around Jenna's chest before letting it drop to tug at the tight material under Jenna's armpit. "Which is why I took his assessment with a grain of salt."

"More than a grain," Mara murmured, glancing up. "Sure you can't spare of bit of that Jenna?" she asked with a rueful glance at her flat chest.

"You can have all you want."

"Like she needs it," Lorie snorted. "Cougar already looks at her like the frosting on his favorite cake, and she's looking for more incentive?"

"Can't help thinking about the women he knew before me." Mara shrugged, took a sip of her liquor, and shuddered.

"Doesn't matter who came before," Millie tossed back the rest of her drink. "All that matters is that none come after, and Mara honey, that man of yours is a one-woman man."

"Yes, he is." Mara's smile reflected her satisfaction with that fact.

"And," Elizabeth tossed in after covering Brianna's ears, "I heard through Asa that Cougar finds your measurements exactly to his liking."

Jenna closed her eyes, feeling more like a cow with every word. Mara was delicate and dainty and everything men liked about a woman, while she was a woman whose curves overflowed even a dressmaker's expectations.

"Maybe we could find something that would," she brushed her hands over her breasts, "flatten me?"

Her whisper landed in the conversation like a rock in a pond, disturbing the equanimity with ripples of surprise.

Pearl's "Why on earth would we want to do that?" was almost overwhelmed by Millicent's "Honey, with a chest like that you need to think in terms of flaunting, not hiding".

"She's got a point," Lorie put in. "If you lowered that neckline just a little, there isn't a man in the territory who wouldn't drop to a heel."

Lower the neckline? She was already showing her collarbones and three inches of cleavage. "I don't want men panting over me."

"Just Clint," Dorothy said, her voice sympathetic.

"Yes." She would love for Clint to feel about her the way Cougar felt about Mara, as if even her flaws were something to celebrate. But for that to happen, he'd have to love her.

"Well, just having Clint notice you is not going to solve your problem," Pearl muttered as she adjusted the dress with efficient movements. She whipped small scissors out of her belt and two snips later the darts in the left bodice relaxed with startling swiftness.

"I don't have a problem." Jenna grabbed for the bodice, almost spilled her drink, and settled for standing absolutely still.

"I heard you don't feel Clint loves you."

"Clint's a good husband." She closed her eyes briefly and took a deep breath as Pearl snipped the darts on the other side. She let her breath out slowly. At least she could take a regular breath.

"Huh." Dorothy set her glass on the small wooden table with a decisive click. "Not if he hasn't told you he loves you."

"Especially if you told him you loved him."

"Selfish bastard, playing it safe."

Jenna closed her fist on the impulse to yell. "Don't you call him that. He's a wonderful man. Much better than I deserve."

"Hell, with an attitude like that, no wonder you need our help." Pearl picked her glass up and drained the last drop.

"I don't need your help."

"The rest of the fit is just fine, but the top is going to be an issue." Pearl eyed the loosened bodice. She shook her head. "And of course you need our help, otherwise you wouldn't be making excuses for your man."

"He can't help that he doesn't love me."

"Jenna, don't take this the wrong way," Elizabeth ventured as Bri began to fuss, her little fist working against her gums, "but you are plain nuts if you don't think Clint loves you."

"That man can't breathe straight for want of you," Mara added.

"He cares about me and feels protective, but that's not the same as loving." Even she wasn't naive enough to think wanting had anything to do with love. And Jenna couldn't blame him. She wasn't strong yet. But she would be.

"I tell you," Millie said, pouring another glass all around, stopping when she got to Jenna, "emotion is wasted on the young."

"Isn't that the truth," Pearl agreed around the pins she was tucking into her mouth as she tugged the bodice down. Jenna edged it back up with her free hand as Pearl reached for her glass. She might as well have saved her time as the minute Pearl finished her drink, she was back to tugging it down.

"I think if I lower the bodice, I can get the fall right." She stepped back the length of her arm. "And you certainly have the stature to carry it off." This time Pearl didn't let go when Jenna tugged.

"Clint said not to get anything too low-cut." Pearl still didn't let go.

"Clint isn't wearing it."

"Pearl's got a point," Elizabeth said with a matter-of-factness that had Jenna looking at her twice.

"Is your dress this low?" She couldn't believe Asa would allow Elizabeth to wear anything that low. He was known to be a very possessive man.

"Lower. I've got to take advantage of this baby bounty while it lasts." Elizabeth grinned, squared her shoulders, and thrust out her chest.

"Wonderful," Mara laughed, "there's hope for me yet. Just need to get a baby for me to feed, and I'll be one of the bountiful."

"Bountiful?" Millicent raised her eyebrows.

"No harm in dreaming big." Mara shrugged and took Bri from Elizabeth.

"As if that husband of yours isn't bounty enough," Pearl muttered around the pins. Jenna could only blink at the way the women talked, as if their husband' opinions were not paramount.

"Asa will allow you to wear a dress like that?" she asked Elizabeth.

"He's not going to be happy, but by the time he finds out, we'll be at the social and it will be too late."

"What will he do?"

"He'll whisper threats in my ear about what he'll do when he gets me home and then he'll spend all night drooling over my new breasts and glaring at the men who'd like a peek." Elizabeth shrugged, unbuttoning her jacket.

"And when you get home?"

"He'll take me upstairs to the bedroom and show me how much he appreciates my charms." Elizabeth smiled widely.

"Won't he be jealous?"

"I'm counting on it," Elizabeth laughed.

Her expression gave Jenna pause. Elizabeth was looking forward to her night with her husband, to tempting him and teasing him and reaping the results. Jenna couldn't imagine teasing Clint like that, testing the edge of his patience while tempting his desire. But Mara obviously could. She held Bri above her head, laughing with the child as she kicked her feet and waved her hands.

"You know, Pearl. I'm thinking my dress is a bit too modest."

"And going to stay that way too," Pearl muttered. "Cougar about tore the head off that boy he decided was dancing too close last summer."

"He didn't really hurt him."

"Scared him out of town, though, and my Evie was just getting around to settling on him."

"Wishful thinking on your part that Evie has plans on settling down. She reminds me too much of you," Millicent joked.

Pearl pulled herself to her full height. "I am the soul of propriety."

"Which doesn't mean you didn't kick over a few traces in your day." Millie finished off her second glass of drink. "And it looks like Evie intends to follow in her mother's footsteps."

"Heaven forbid."

For all of her eye-rolling, Pearl didn't seem that upset with the situation.

"How old is Evie?" Jenna sucked in her breath when Pearl looked up. She didn't want to be stabbed.

"She's twenty." Pearl shook her head as she folded the loose bodice under and pinned it in place. "And not in any hurry to provide me with grandchildren."

Jenna was afraid to glance down but a kind of morbid fascination had her looking, and promptly had her hand flying up to cover her chest.

"I can't wear a dress like this!"

Pearl's answer was an arch of her brow. "Why not?"

"My bosom is showing."

"I prefer to think of it as being showcased."

"Clint would kill me."

Lorie choked on her drink. "I may be the only maiden here, but even I know the last thing on his mind if he saw you in that dress would be murder. You're beautiful, Jenna."

Beautiful? She took her hands away from her chest and turned to the mirror while murmuring, "He told me not to make it too low."

"It's low, but not too low," Elizabeth offered, coming up behind her and taking the glass from her hand.

When she faced the mirror fully, she looked up. It was beautiful. She'd never seen anything like it. Her whole life she'd worn baggy gray or brown high-necked dresses. Dresses designed to diminish a woman's looks, to lower her ability to tempt a man from the straight and narrow. But if Clint saw her in this dress...

Oh heavens, she wanted him to see her in this dress that seemed to capture the light and reflect it in flattering shimmers over her skin. This dress that fit her like a glove and made her look sensuously curved rather than fat. This dress that made her hair blonder, her eyes bluer. This dress that made her look like a woman who should be on his arm.

"It's beautiful," she whispered. Pearl shook her head and handed Jenna back her glass.

"A dress can only enhance what's already there." She adjusted the seam under her left arm. "And you've always had a lot to work with."

"I'm not beautiful."

"Clint told Asa you were," Elizabeth pointed out.

"When?"

"The first time he saw you outside the mercantile."

"That was a long time ago. How would you know?"

"Because he's been watching you ever since, and Asa never lies."

You were always meant to be mine.

She tried to get used to the expanse of neckline, tracing it with her finger, imagining Clint's reaction if she did it in front of him. He would love it if it were in the privacy of their bedroom, but at a social?

"I can't wear this."

"You have to wear that," Dorothy countered. "You have to wear that dress to the social, and you have to smile and dance and have the time of your life with every man who asks you to dance."

"Why?"

"Because the only way to get a man to face what he's feeling is to give him a taste of what he might lose."

"You want me to trick Clint?"

"New brides," Millicent muttered.

"Think of it more as opening his eyes," Pearl suggested.

Jenna recalled the honesty and emotion in Clint's dark eyes as he held her through her fears. The tenderness of his touch. The surety in his voice as he said, "I see you, Sunshine." And she saw him too. His pride. His honor. His need.

"No."

"It's the quickest means to an end," Elizabeth pointed out.

"That doesn't make it right." Hurting Clint would never be right.

"Doesn't make it wrong, either," Millicent put in. "Just another path to where you want to go."

"It would upset him." Jenna had had a belly full of people taking her down paths that her instincts said were wrong.

"Won't be the first time he's been upset," Mara offered. "And it would only be for a minute."

"I won't do that to him." A minute would be too long to inflict that type of pain on someone.

"Well damn," Millicent muttered. "Now we'll have to use the boring backup plan."

"What's that?"

"Just walk up and flat-out ask the man if he loves you."

Jenna took a sip of the foul whiskey, shuddering as the taste filled her mouth. Maybe wearing the dress wasn't such a bad idea.

Chapter Twenty-Three

Jenna blinked as she stepped out of the dress shop into the bright sunlight.

Bri turned her face into her neck and whimpered. Jenna pulled the little one's bonnet down to shield her eyes even as she pulled the thick blanket up higher over her head against the biting cold.

"I think winter will be cold this year," Mara said, waiting by the edge of the wooden walk so they could head over to the bakery.

"It sure feels like it," Jenna hurried to catch up, "but no matter what, Clint's house will be a lot warmer than my previous ones."

"Clint had that place sealed six ways to Sunday after he bought it."

Jenna patted Bri's back. She was overdue for her nap and beginning to fuss.

"He's like that."

Mara cast her a sidelong glance. "I think it was more than that."

"Oh."

"Said he didn't like the thought of his wife freezing."

"I forgot about the great wife hunt."

She'd deliberately put it as far from her mind as possible.

"I think he had someone specific in mind."

"Oh."

Mara gave her a shove on her arm. "You silly."

"I was married!"

"We were all painfully aware of that. Especially whenever Clint would see you shivering about town in that old cloak, and Hennesey would be in that saloon gambling and drinking. There were times when Cougar worried that Clint would lose it."

"Clint hates injustice."

"Clint hated not having the right to protect you," Mara said, pulling up short as the barber/dentist shop door swung opened. A man stumbled out, holding his jaw. He nodded to them both, winced, and stepped off the walkway.

"I'm so glad my teeth are good." Jenna followed his uneven walk as he crossed the frozen, rutted street.

"You and me both," Mara echoed her shudder. "But if that was an attempt to change the subject, it's not working."

"I wasn't trying to change the subject."

"Uh-huh."

"Frankly," Mara continued down the walk, rubbing her hands together against the chill, "we were all surprised when Clint didn't start courting you the day after Hennesey died."

"That wouldn't have been proper."

"I've never known Clint to be overly concerned with propriety when he wanted something." Mara held her hair out of her face.

Neither had Jenna, truth be told.

Mara reached over and tucked the blanket under Bri's shoulder, making a face at the little girl as she did. When she straightened, her expression was completely serious.

"And he wanted you, Jenna. Don't ever doubt that."

He wanted you. The words echoed in Jenna's head, giving birth to that hope that battled common sense.

"Wanting isn't loving."

"To a McKinnely it is," Mara said that with the certainty of a preacher declaring sin.

"There are things you don't know that affect Clint's feelings."

"Bullshit." Mara stopped and turned, her fingers on Jenna's cloak, catching her arm, forcing her to stop and look at her.

"Clint and Cougar are as close as brothers, share the same values, and have that McKinnely tenacity to a fault so I know, absolutely know, there is nothing in your past, present, or future that can ever turn that man from your side."

"Cougar loves you."

"And Clint loves you." There wasn't a smidgeon of doubt in her tone. "I know everyone's been giving you well-meaning advice and I'm probably no more welcome than the rest, but my guess is that whatever kept Clint from claiming you immediately, is the same thing holding him back from saying that he loves you."

An interesting theory but so damned unlikely.

"He could just not love me." Jenna stepped to the left as the mercantile door jangled a warning. Mara stepped right with her, chin coming up in a way that screamed stubborn.

"He loves you."

She wanted to believe that so damned much.

"Mrs. Hennesey," a woman's voice interrupted. "Could I have a moment?"

Jenna had heard that cold, controlled voice too many times not to tense as it came from behind her. Meetings with the mayor's wife were never pleasant. Today, when her nerves were stretched tight and her stomach nauseated, promised to be worse than usual.

"Good afternoon, Mrs. Salisbury." She turned, nodding to the taller, well-dressed woman standing just outside the mercantile door.

"Afternoon Shirley." Mara nodded, demonstrating none of Jenna's instinctive deference. "And that would be Mrs. McKinnely now."

"So I heard." With a nod so slight it didn't even disturb the garish bird perched in the turned-up brim of her lavish hat, Shirley acknowledged Mara. The sniff that punctuated the remark conveyed as strongly as the bitter lines beside her thin mouth just how she felt about Jenna's marriage. "I hope you don't expect to immediately become part of our community just because you married Clint McKinnely."

Jenna's stomach churned acid. She hated confrontations like this. Bri, sensing her tension began to whimper. Her "Of course not" was drowned out by Mara's "She's already part of our community".

"Hardly." The look Shirley shot Mara contained more venom than politeness. "And if you continue to be seen in her company, you may find your own tenuous position threatened."

Jenna closed her eyes briefly against the waves of hostility battering them. She tried to edge between Mara and the woman, to deflect some of her anger. It was a waste of effort. While she'd heard tell of Mara's temper, she'd never actually believed the tiny woman capable of even a harsh word. She'd been wrong.

With an "Excuse me" that had Jenna blinking twice at its coldness, Mara stepped in front of her. She didn't stop there, either. She went two steps further, until the hem of her fashionable green dress pushed aside the hem of Shirley's matronly navy blue one.

"Did you just threaten me?" The question was asked in a flat monotone that was eerily calm for all the energy it contained. Jenna wasn't surprised when Shirley inched toward the edge of the walk. Mara was a very scary woman when riled. And she was riled. Her cinnamon colored eyes seemed to glow in her tight face as she matched Shirley step for step. "Did you?"

"I merely pointed out the facts."

"Mara, it's okay." Jenna touched Mara's arm while trying to gently bounce Bri from her own bad mood.

"Like hell it is." Mara's chin came up and her shoulders squared. She never took her eyes off of Shirley. "Let me point out a few facts of my own, Mrs. Salisbury. Jenna is a McKinnely. We are thrilled to have her in the family and any slight against her is a slight against us all."

"All, meaning you?" Shirley sneered, disdain dripping from every pore. "A whore from the most notorious whorehouse in the territory? I'm supposed to worry about offending you?"

The twitch in Mara's fingers gave away the fact that the shot had found its mark, and the panic in Jenna's stomach solidified to a hard knot of anger that exploded outward in violent driving waves.

"How dare you say something so filthy?"

"It's the truth and no amount of whitewashing will remove the stench." Shirley didn't even blink.

Mara leapt forward. Jenna caught her arm and shoved her behind her, advancing on Shirley, fury battling with reason.

"You vindictive, evil woman. You are so twisted with jealousy that you think you're entitled to spew your venom everywhere." Jenna stepped closer, forcing the woman back, for once glad of her size. "But you're not. It's not okay at all. I've let you spew on me for years because I felt sorry for you, always trying to put the best face forward when you had to be so unhappy the way your husband treated you, and because, quite frankly, I thought I was somehow deserving. But you will not," she shoved her face in Shirley's, so close that she could see the fine grains of powder she used on her complexion, "ever say a word against me or mine again."

"Or what?" Shirley snapped, not totally backing down.

She was never so glad for her years with Jack. One thing she knew was how to deliver a threat. She lowered her voice, settled her weight onto her feet, and smiled the coldest smile she knew how to imitate. "Or I'll use every evil, twisted, painful torture my dead husband taught me to make you scream with regret."

"You wouldn't dare!" Shirley took another step back.

"She's daring all kinds of things lately, Shirley," Mara offered, "so I wouldn't bet your health on that."

Bri's whimpers turned to wails. Shirley cut the baby a hate-filled glance.

"It shouldn't have been you," she whispered.

"What?"

"If you hadn't interfered, whored your way into his bed, played on his sympathy, Clint would have married my Rebecca."

"Is that what this is all about? You thought Clint was interested in Rebecca?" Jenna blinked, pulling back a step as the pieces fell into place.

"You stole him from her."

"It wouldn't have worked," she said over Bri's wails. "They never would have been happy." Jenna shook her head, the anger draining from her as understanding took its place.

"At least she wouldn't have stuck him with that filthy brat."

The rage surged free from deep inside Jenna, welling out of nowhere, years of swallowing it back just giving it more force, coloring her vision red, and giving her strength that she didn't know she had. With a hard push, Jenna sent the woman toppling backward off the raised walk straight into the horse trough. The cracking of ice punctuated Shirley's shriek as water splashed over the sides of the rough wood and closed over her head.

Mara's "Damn" drifted through the red haze surrounding her as Jenna stepped down to the trough where Shirley floundered on her back, her teeth already chattering from the frigid cold. With her free hand, she pulled the older woman's face clear of the dirty water. Powder ran off her face in pale streaks as Jenna held her suspended.

"If you ever say a word against my children again, I'll hunt you down and kill you."

"And when she gets done with you, it'll be my turn." The swish of Mara's skirts preceded her step into view. Sunlight glinted off the knife she held in her hand.

Shirley tore her gaze from Jenna's to the knife in Mara's hand and back to Jenna's face. Her pale face grew paler, blue mixing with the white. Her mouth opened and closed twice, and then she started to scream. Loud, earsplitting shrieks that grated. Jenna let her drop back into the water, and turned away, feeling shaky as the fury slowly subsided. Looking around, she noted townsperson after townsperson staring, their expressions in various stages of shock.

Her knees grew weak, and she started to shake.

"Well, one thing's for sure, we're going to be either heroes or villains in everyone's eyes by the end of the day," Mara muttered as she grabbed Jenna's elbow and hurried her out of the crowd.

"Heroes?"

"Don't you fall apart on me now," Mara ordered as Jenna stumbled. "There are a lot of people who would love to have the courage to dunk that old bitch."

"Oh God, I pushed the mayor's wife into the horse trough!" The realization of what she'd done began to sink in.

"Yes. You did."

"I need to sit down." She pushed a strand of hair out of her eyes. Her hand was shaking. Her whole body was shaking with the enormity of the potential consequences.

"Not right now you don't," Mara said, casting a glance over her shoulder.

"Oh God, Clint is going to hate me." Jenna followed the trajectory of her gaze. A crowd was gathered in front of the mercantile and from the gesturing, it was an angry one.

"Considering the woman called your daughter filthy and a brat, you're not the one he's going to hate."

"I'd better go apologize." Jenna tugged against Mara's grip. Mara dug in her heels and hauled Jenna along.

"What we'd better do is get ourselves to the livery and then home to our husbands."

"Is Cougar going to be mad at you because of me?" Jenna didn't need another person suffering because of her.

Mara shook her head and laughed. "He'll probably want to know why we didn't hold her under longer."

"I didn't even know I had a temper."

"Well, you do, and as a witness to what you're like when you get going, I'd say a pretty fierce one."

"I don't know what to tell Clint." Pain in her leg took her breath. She had to work to get the words even.

"The truth is good." Mara steadied her as she tripped in a rut.

"He'll be angry."

"And that's a damn impressive man to get riled. The mayor is going to wish he'd sent his wife back East like he planned last spring."

"He's not going to be happy with me either."

"No doubt we'll both get the full lecture about not endangering ourselves," Mara said as they darted around a wagon. She tugged harder on Jenna's arm, jostling Bri, who hiccupped mid-cry and then paused to see if she liked the new sensation.

"I'll give you a hint," Mara grunted as she hopped a frozen puddle. "If you start undoing buttons about halfway through, they lose steam fast."

Jenna smiled. She couldn't help it. She could just see the irrepressible Mara using feminine wiles against her big husband to get out of a lecture.

"I might try that."

The glance Mara cut her was wry. "Since you've got a heck of a lot more ammunition in your pack than I do, you might get away with only having to listen to a quarter of the lecture."

Jenna wasn't sure about that. Her foot twisted in a rut and her leg gave out. She fell, pulling Mara off balance as she did. Bri, contrary as always, gurgled with laughter as they landed in a pile of skirts.

"You ladies ought to learn to take advantage of the alleys."

Jenna froze. She knew that voice…that tone. She slowly looked up. Sunlight flashing off Mark's badge streaked her vision.

"Jenna Hennesey, you need to come with me."

Every nightmare she'd suppressed suddenly screamed for recognition, stealing her breath and her strength until all she could do was sit there on the ground in a cold sweat, pinned by memories that were no longer willing to be denied.

Mara scrambled to her feet, and glared at Mark. "That's Jenna McKinnely and she's not going anywhere with you."

"The mayor appointed me deputy while the sheriff is gone, so that pretty much means she goes where I say."

It wasn't what Mark said, but more the way he said it that sent chills down Jenna's spine. Mark could be very unpredictable—to the point that she'd often questioned his sanity. It wasn't wise to provoke him the way Mara was doing.

"It's okay, Mara," Jenna said, getting her good leg under her and standing slowly. She was Clint McKinnely's wife. Mark wouldn't dare touch her. "I'll be fine."

"You're darned right you will because you're going home to your husband." Mara reached for her hand. Mark grabbed Jenna's upper arm and with a bruising yank, lifted her up and back, out of Mara's reach.

"If Clint wants to see his wife, he can look for her over in the jail." He jerked his chin in the direction of the small, windowless structure set back in the alley beside the livery. "She'll be staying there waiting for a trial."

"Trial?" Jenna stared at the dark, square building. They were going to try her?

"For what?" Mara demanded.

"Mrs. Salisbury is charging her with attempted murder."

"I just pushed her in a horse trough."

"And in this weather, she could have died."

"But she didn't, and there's no way in heck those charges will stick," Mara growled, her hands on her slender hips, looking dainty and fragile and feminine, throwing the kind of challenges Mark lived to squash.

"That's for the judge to determine." Mark took a step back, Jenna stumbled after him, clutching Bri tightly, her weight on the wrong leg throwing her off balance.

"Like hell," Mara shot back.

Against her back, Jenna felt Mark's fury at being questioned by a woman coalesce into interest as he asked, "You looking to end up in jail yourself for blocking justice, little lady?"

"You're calling this justice?" Jenna felt Mark's breath catch as Mara ended the challenge with a sneer. Oh God, Mara had no idea what she was inviting.

"Mara," Jenna said, forcing the words past her tight lips, "you need to take Brianna home for me." Mara hesitated and for one split second, Jenna thought she'd cooperate, but then her chin came up and her shoulders squared.

"If he wants to arrest you, then he has to arrest me too."

"No!"

"I was just as much a part of it as you," she insisted, daring Mark to do it.

"Be more than happy to." Quick as a snake, Mark grabbed Mara's arm. He pulled Mara's face up close to his, lifting her up on tiptoes with ease. "Taming you could be fun."

Mara blanched, but being Mara, she didn't back down. Instead she spat in his face. Mark didn't even flinch, but he laughed that low satisfied laugh that haunted Jenna's nightmares. Through the roaring in her ears she heard the approach of multiple footsteps, a murmur of voices, and then one voice rose above the others, clearly triumphant.

"Oh good, you've got them."

"And they're not going anywhere either," Mark promised, turning them so that they faced Shirley. She was wrapped in a wool blanket, her lips still blue, the occasional shudder still running through her. She didn't look anywhere near dead. "At least not until the judge makes a determination."

"I'll take the baby," Shirley said.

"No." Jenna twisted away, ignoring the wrench Mark gave her arm. There was no way she would let this woman who'd called her precious Bri filthy, take her. Shirley stepped in, her intent clear.

"Keep your filthy hands off Brianna." Mara struck out with her foot, catching the other woman in the stomach.

"That's assault, Mrs. McKinnely," Mark offered.

"If she tries to touch Bri again it's going to be murder," Mara promised while Jenna searched the crowd for a sympathetic face. She didn't find one, only bored cowhands looking for a show, and townfolk who didn't know what to make of the situation.

"A word of advice, Deputy. I wouldn't mess with the McKinnely women," a cowhand, who looked to be straight off the range offered.

"The McKinnnelys are no more above the law than anyone else," Mark snapped.

"Mister, in case it escaped your notice, the McKinnelys *are* the law in these parts." There was a murmur of agreement from the crowd. Mark's only reaction was to tighten his grip on Jenna's arm and bark out another order.

"One of you men come get this baby."

"If you want to piss off the McKinnelys that's your problem." The cowhand stepped back, hands raised. "But I don't want any part of it."

As if pushed by an unseen hand the crowd took a step back, shaking their heads and murmuring uncomfortably until there was only Shirley, Mark, and a wrangler Jenna didn't recognize standing in the middle of the street with them. The man came forward, his eyes never leaving Brianna. His hands were cut and dirty, his eyes were haunted, yet kind as he took Bri from Jenna's arms.

"No," she whispered. His gaze flickered to hers. She didn't see any meanness in his eyes, only a soul-deep sadness that had no end.

"I'll be careful with her, ma'am."

"Give her to me," Shirley demanded immediately.

"Take her to my husband, Clint McKinnely," Jenna begged, holding the man's gaze. She thought she saw a flare of recognition in his eyes at her husband's name. "Don't give her to anyone else. Please, just him."

"I'll keep her safe ma'am. Don't you worry." The man tucked Brianna into his arm with that same reluctant sadness with which he'd reached for her.

"Let's go you two," Mark ordered, turning them toward the jail. "We've provided enough entertainment for the evening."

"Remember," Jenna yelled, straining to make eye contact with the stranger who had her baby, "don't give her to anyone but Clint." Jenna twisted to see what was happening with Bri. Shirley intercepted her glance and the cruelty in the other woman's gaze terrified her.

Shirley gave her a nod and smiled, stepping toward the stranger as Mark dragged her along, away from her baby. He shoved her into the alley and she could no longer see anything, but she could hear Shirley's satisfied "I'll take her now" and it struck terror into her soul. Her baby was alone and unprotected with a woman who saw her as an obstacle to what she wanted.

Oh God, this was her worst nightmare come to life.

* * * * *

"Just like old times, isn't it pretty girl?"

Jenna struggled to block out the reality of being locked in a jail, her arms tied together and then tied with a separate rope to the bars. Tied with enough give that she could turn but not escape. Mark's bloated body pressed into her back as he whispered her nightmare into reality.

"Remember the fun we had? Remember how you learned to obey under my hand?"

She remembered the pain. The futility of resistance. The agony of being helpless before his torture. "Go to hell."

"Let her go you bastard!" Mara hollered from inside the gloomy jail's only cell.

"It's all right, Mara." Jenna forced her eyes open, forced herself to connect with the here and now long enough to warn Mara. She had to stay quiet, to stop challenging Mark before she drew his attention.

"You keep telling me that like you expect me to believe it." Mara jerked at her bound hands.

"But it is all right, isn't it, Jenna?" he asked loud enough to carry. Mark rubbed his crotch along Jenna's buttocks, rapping her skirt with the quirt he held in his hand, a reminder of what to expect. He nuzzled her hair aside and kissed her ear in a gross parody of tenderness. "We've played this game before. Remember that night, Jenna? Remember how your husband gave you to me? How you spread your legs to pay his debts. How you danced for my lash."

Mara's eyes widened with shock and for a heartbeat, she stopped struggling. Jenna met her gaze, saw the understanding sink in, and felt the shame to the bottom of her soul.

"I told you there were reasons," she whispered.

The quirt came down hard on her hip. Hard enough to bite through the layers of cloth. Hard enough to bring a strangled scream from her throat as Mark laughed and pushed his erection against her. She'd forgotten how much it hurt, how much he enjoyed hurting.

"I didn't tell you to speak," he grunted, lashing her again.

Tears leaked from her eyes as she shuddered under the blow, the stays of her corset absorbing most of the force.

"McKinnely must be soft. You've forgotten all the rules I taught you."

Oh God, Clint. This was going to kill him. Kill them.

"He's going to kill you for this, you know," Mara said, echoing Jenna's thoughts, her voice unnaturally calm. "He'll hunt you down, stake you out, and skin you alive. And while you're screaming for relief, he'll cut off your balls, shove them down your throat, and leave you for the buzzards to eat."

Mark laughed as if she didn't have a care in the world.

"Clint's never going to know about this, though is he?" He ran the quirt over Jenna's cheek. She had to either accept the caress or lean into Mark's face. She held perfectly still. "Jenna won't want her precious husband to know she's just a filthy little whore who likes it rough."

"I'll tell him."

"No you won't, because you care too much about my little slut here to risk her marriage." Mark tilted his head back. From the corner of her eye, Jenna could see Mark's smile. Its cold, sinister edge sent a shudder down her spine.

"You don't know me too well." Mara tossed her head back.

"I know you well enough to know that if you were willing to prove Jenna to the world as the slut she is, you would have screamed blue murder by now."

"You said you'd kill her if I did."

"So I did, but you should have risked it to save yourself."

"I don't need to." Again that unnaturally calm voice.

"Why?"

"Cougar is coming." She said it as if it were a given.

"McKinnely is miles from here."

"Somebody has gone for him, and when he gets here, he'll tear you to pieces." Mara shifted on the wood bench that served as bed and seat.

"I'll be gone long before he gets here."

"Running won't save a pathetic worm like you."

Mark tensed in that way Jenna recognized. He was turning his focus on Mara. She'd never survive five minutes of his attention.

"Mara," she croaked, "shut up."

Mark stepped away from Jenna. The coolness of the air on her sweaty back was not a comfort. Not when it meant Mara was becoming a target. Mark stepped to the left. The quirt slapped against his boot.

"Awful brave talk for a woman who'll be greeting her husband with my seed dripping from her cunt."

"Is that the best you've got? Rape?" Unbelievably, Mara smiled. She tossed her head again in that way that had Mark's nostrils flaring. "Cougar will want me no matter what. Long after your corpse has rotted, he'll still be loving me."

Mara was serious. She had every faith that her husband was coming for her and that he'd want her no matter what. Jenna could only envy her that confidence.

"That only holds if there's anything left of you to love," Mark returned just as calmly.

"I'll hold on until he gets here." The promise drifted on the stale air, unfazed by Mark's threats.

In a blur of motion, Mark brought the quirt down in a vicious slice that caught Jenna across the shoulders. She fell to her knees and a scream tore from her throat as waves of agony clawed at her back. The ropes on her wrist halted her descent, jerking her forward against the bars, smashing her cheek into the metal as lights exploded behind her eyes. With the tip of the quirt, Mark traced the first tear as it escaped Jenna's control.

"What makes you think I'll let you?" he asked Mara conversationally.

Jenna opened her eyes. There were tears in Mara's eyes, but her expression didn't change.

"Because I promised Cougar I would." She moved back in the seat, and her smile rivaled Cougar's for feral coldness. "And because I want to watch Clint tear you apart, inch by inch."

"I'm going to enjoy our time together, Mara McKinnely," Mark said as he hauled Jenna to her feet. He grabbed her by the bun at the base of her neck and twisted her face to his, "And you'll get to watch. Every beautiful second."

Like hell. Mark let her go. Jenna waited until he took one step away, grabbed the bars for support, and then with every ounce of muscle she could muster, kicked him between the legs, driving the hard pointed toe of her brand-new boots into the softness of his groin.

Grinding it deeper as he dropped, kicking out again as he retched and doubled over. She got two more kicks in before his hand struck with the speed of a rattler, grabbing her ankle, yanking her off balance.

"Jenna!" Mara cried, the bench rocking as she lurched forward. Jenna shook her head at her as she fell, knowing the landing was going to be hard, mentally trying to prepare herself, but nothing could have prepared her for the wrenching agony of her bound wrists taking the sudden force of her drop.

Mark didn't relax his grip even though she was down, partially suspended on the bars. Instead he climbed her body, and held on as she moaned, not relaxing his grip as her bound wrists took her full weight and part of his, dragging his way up her body one inch at a time.

"So you went and got some spirit since I last saw you," he grunted as he pulled even with her face, his foul breath striking her like another blow. "I like it."

"It's going to make our next little game lots of fun." He pinned her legs with his and braced his arms on the bars beside her head.

If she'd had the spit to do it, she would have spit in his face, but her mouth was bone-dry with the fear shaking her from head to toe. Mark had been horrible before, but this close, she couldn't miss the insanity in his light grey eyes. She could only offer up a prayer of thanksgiving that he'd forgotten about Mara.

With a grunt he lurched to his feet, grabbed her by the front of her dress and dragged her up. Buttons popped and seams tore as he wrestled her around until she was once again bent over at the waist, facing the bars, her buttocks sticking out.

His hands on her skirts were efficient as he gathered them up, dropping the heavy weight to the middle of her back as he leaned over and whispered in her ear, "If you scream once, I'll snap the little bitch's neck."

He looked at Mara as he placed the quirt against Jenna's neck. The leather was as cold and as flat as his voice as he said, "If you make a sound, I'll strangle her."

Mara met Jenna's gaze, bit her lip, and nodded.

"Glad we understand each other."

The quirt left her throat. She felt Mark's hands on her hips. The soft rip of cotton being torn rent the silence and her pantalets fell to the floor. And then there was only her panting breath and the slight grind of her teeth before the quirt whistled though the air. The force of the blow sent her forward into the bars. Her mind registered the sharpness of the snap before her thigh exploded in agony. She caught the scream in her throat, fighting it back, biting her cheek until blood flowed to keep the agony contained.

The pain swelled and built, expanding through her body. Before it could ebb, Mark leaned over her, his breath hot in her ear, "Oh, that was very good. Got me hard. Let's see if we can up the ante. You last until I come and I'll let the little bitch go." He kissed her cheek. "Understand?"

Jenna gritted her teeth so hard she thought they'd crack. She didn't know if Mark could still come after the way she'd kicked him. Didn't know if he'd really let Mara go if he could. He was insane. Anything was possible, but it was worth a try. And their best bet was still to buy time, so she nodded.

He stroked her tear-wet cheek with the quirt. The leather was hot and wet against her flesh. Had he cut her?

"Good girl," he murmured again as if they were lovers on a tryst. She felt the muscles in his chest stretch as he raised the quirt. She sucked in a breath as she felt them tense and his weight come down.

The blow she braced for never came. Instead, Mark jerked, threw his head back, and swore. She looked up. Mara was on the other side of the bars, looking like a virago, one hand clenched in Mark's hair as she stabbed at his back with the knife, her lips drawn back from her teeth in a feral snarl, equally feral growls coming from between her lips.

Sparks flew as the blade hit the bars. Above Jenna, Mark twisted. She tried to throw him off by heaving up but her legs gave out. She went down, taking him with her, but not soon enough. As she twisted she saw Mark's ham-like fist connect with Mara's jaw and the tiny woman went sailing across the dirt floor, landing in a puff of dust. She didn't get up.

The little bit of hope Jenna had been holding onto left her, along with it her grasp on reason. Arching her head back she screamed loud and long, crying for Clint, for their daughter, for what might have been if her life hadn't been tainted by her father's belief, her husband's weakness, and Mark's insanity. She screamed, clawed, and bit when Mark tried to haul her up. She kept screaming when the rush of cold air added to the agony in her buttocks. She screamed louder when Mark's heavy weight suddenly left her back and a strange thumping and groaning began.

She stopped screaming when the words that blended with the odd pounding reached her consciousness.

"You worthless piece of shit!" She opened her eyes. Reverend Swanson had Mark up against the wall. He was holding him there with nothing more than the speed and force of the blows he was raining into his midsection, seemingly heedless of the blood and vomit Mark was coughing all over him.

With a last punch that Jenna fully expected to see come out his spine, Brad let Mark drop. He turned. There was nothing civilized about his face. His lips were white with fury and his eyes burned with the fires of hell. If he was one of God's angels, he was an archangel. One with a thirst for justice. He snatched the quirt off the floor.

Mark held up his hand. Dirt and blood covered the surface. "Please," he moaned as blood slid down his face. "No more."

With two vicious slashes, Brad laid opened the man's cheeks.

Mark screamed and sobbed, rolling into a ball on his side, his bloody hands covering his face. Jenna closed her eyes, unable to watch anymore. She heard the quirt whistle, that peculiar slapping sound it made as it landed, Mark's pitiful moan.

"Reverend," she whispered, "enough."

She sensed the change in the room. The stillness coming over Reverend Swanson, the control seeping back into his breathing. Something snapped and then fell to the floor beside her. She opened her eyes and saw the quirt in pieces.

The faintest of touches on her skin and then her dress was carefully lowered over her legs. Just the brush of the fabric was agony and she whimpered.

"I'm sorry."

"Mara," she managed to croak through her scream-torn throat. "He hit Mara."

The ache in her head blossomed again and she had to close her eyes against the pinpoints of light stabbing at her.

She traced the reverend's movements through sound, hearing the rattle of the door as he tested it, the jingle of keys as he took them off the hook, the clank as the lock gave, and mostly his soft "bastard" as he reached Mara.

The door creaked again and then she was surrounded by the scent of bay rum and the sensation of power. She opened her eyes. The reverend was squatting before her, reaching for his boot.

She licked her dry lips. "Mara?"

"I think she's just knocked out." He touched her forehead, where it throbbed. His fingers came away red.

"Bleeding?"

His smile was a weak shadow of his normal grin. "Just a little."

He wiped his hand on his pants. Metal scraped on leather. She caught a glint of steel and then her arms were free. She dropped into the reverend's arms, leaning into his strength because she had none of her own left.

She looked over at the bloody pulp that was Mark. Reverends were supposed to be peaceable, which could only mean one thing. "You're not a reverend?"

"Yes, I'm a reverend." He looked over at Mark. "Just a little more Old Testament than most." He shifted his grip. His arm brushed the welt on her back, she moaned, then cut off the sound, and asked the one thing she needed to know more than anything.

"Brianna?"

"She's safe at the rectory."

She wanted to ask why she wasn't with Clint but all that came out was a broken, "Clint?"

"He's coming, Jenna." The reverend eased her down to her side on the floor. "Elijah went for him."

She moaned again, this time unable to keep it back. It was over then. Clint would come, find out what had happened — and what had happened to her before — and it would all be over. The gentle touches, soft teasing, the comforting arms. All gone. Tears trickled down her cheek to puddle in the cold dirt.

"Are you all right?"

Jenna stared across the dirt floor at Mara, lying unconscious. She thought of her baby girl, of what could have happened. Of what did happen.

She shook her head. She didn't know if she was ever going to be all right again.

Chapter Twenty-Four

"Son of a bitch, as soon as you can get out of this bed, I'm going to beat you black and blue."

"Okay." Jenna sank deeper into the pillow under her cheek, relaxing into its softness as she relaxed into the gentleness of Clint's touch as he spread ointment over the welt on her back.

"Okay. Is that all you have to say?" Clint eased the sheet up over her back. It stuck to the ointment, sealing off the burn of air. "You go and damned near get yourself and Mara killed and the only thing you have to say is, 'Okay'?"

"Would you prefer please?" A tug at the foot of the mattress jostled her. The cool air of the bedroom slid up her legs with the sheet.

"What I goddamn well would prefer is my wife letting me know when there's trouble afoot." His teeth snapped closed on the last word as the sheet pooled at the base of her spine.

"I didn't know the mayor had appointed Mark deputy in the Sheriff's absence."

"Jesus Christ, Sunshine." The growl dropped from his drawl. His fingers shook as they grazed the edge of her right hip.

"I'm sure it looks worse than it is," she offered, trying not to wince from even that light touch.

"Shut up and hold still."

She did, not liking the new note that had entered his drawl. It was hard, mean, and unforgiving. He'd been waffling between the two extremes ever since he'd picked her and Bri up at the rectory. He'd spoken with the Reverend Swanson, then picked her up, and carried her to the buggy he'd rented, laying her down on a mattress in the back, not saying a word as he'd placed Bri beside her.

As they'd pulled away, she'd seen Cougar carrying Mara in his arms. She'd looked so tiny, so defenseless, and Cougar so wildly, primitively furious.

The small group that had formed outside the rectory when word had spread that the McKinnely women had been abused, parted as Clint and Cougar urged the horses forward. The look the men exchanged chilled her to her bones. Both men were hanging onto control by a thread. Both men looked capable of anything.

A fiery shaft of agony ripped outward from her buttock as the softest of cotton pressed against her welt. She bit the pillow and curled her fingers into the sheet, smothering her whimper in her throat.

Another harsh "Son of a bitch" rent the silence. Jenna bit back a sob. The silk of Clint's hair brushed her left buttock before the softness of his lips.

"Go ahead and scream, Sunshine." A string of equally soft kisses were trailed over the rise of her ass and up onto the hollow of her spine as Clint held the compress to her. "I know it hurts, baby, so go ahead and scream. Do whatever you need to do but let me make you feel better."

The kindness in his tone broke the dam she'd been backing her emotions behind. Her "I'm sorry" was a puddle of tears. The mattress shifted as Clint eased his big body up beside hers.

"Ah shit, baby. You don't have anything to be sorry for."

"I thought it was over when Jack died."

He propped himself up on his elbow beside her. His hair fell in a curtain, limiting her vision to the expanse of his chest and the powerful muscles of his arms. If she lifted her gaze just the slightest bit she'd be able to see his beautiful face. She kept her gaze locked on the too-fast pulse in his throat.

"Did he rape you, Sunshine?" Clint's fingertips slipped between the pillow and her cheek, pressing gently.

"What makes you ask that?" Her breath froze in her lungs.

"Brad said he found you tied and naked." His thumb stroked over her mouth. "It's a natural assumption."

He hadn't raped her today, but he'd raped her before, and the memories she'd buried for so long were clawing their way out of the grave she'd made for them, screaming and wailing to be recognized. "Clint?"

"What?"

"I know you're angry but please, please…"

"I'll give you whatever you need, Sunshine. Just tell me what it is." He tipped up her chin, forcing her to look at him, to see the anger in his face, the primitive rage blending with concern.

"Please just hold me like it doesn't matter. Just for a few minutes." She wanted what she could never have, but for now she was ready to pretend.

"Son of a bitch!" He lifted her and slid beneath her, taking her moans of pain into his throat, not stopping until she was lying on top of his big warm body. His arm on her waist held her firmly in place, his other hand cradled her head to his chest while he brushed kisses over the top of her head. "It doesn't matter, Sunshine. Doesn't matter at all."

"It has to matter." Beneath her cheek she could feel the tension vibrating through his muscles, feel the throb of his heart as it raced to keep pace with his emotions.

"Why?"

"Men care about that."

His thumb tipped her chin up as his mouth met hers in a kiss that defined tender.

"I care that I wasn't able to protect you," he whispered against her lips, the edges of his moving hers with every syllable. "I care that you were hurt. I care that you keep secrets that endanger your life. But Sunshine, nothing anyone does to you can change how I feel about you."

"And how is that?"

"You're sweet and special and you're mine."

Which wasn't the same as saying he loved her.

"Mark didn't think I was sweet."

"I heard you kicked his balls up into his teeth."

"I had to. Mara wouldn't stop challenging him."

"Jenna baby, I'm not complaining."

No. He wouldn't. He pushed her hair out of her face. "Mara said you stopped fighting."

Was that disappointment in his voice? "I had to."

"Why?"

She couldn't tell him. Couldn't. It was too dirty.

"I already know he's a perverted son of a bitch, but you will tell me exactly what he put you through."

"Why?"

"Because he's not leaving you with any more nightmares."

Oh God, he knew. He knew. She shivered.

He shifted and swore. "I want to hold you so badly, Sunshine, but there's just not that much of you in holding condition."

"This is good." She turned her mouth to his throat and kissed him.

"Then tell me what I need to know." He tucked her hair behind her ear.

"He said if I didn't scream for as long as it took him to come, he'd let her go."

"While he cut you with that quirt?" The calmness of his tone was scarier than his anger.

"Yes. I knew it wasn't likely. He's crazy, but there was a chance…"

"He's done that to you before?" Clint's fingers moved up to the side of her breast, to the old scars.

She couldn't get her "Yes" past her throat, so she nodded instead.

"And your husband let him?"

"They made a deal."

"He sold you?"

"He had debts. It was his right."

"Like hell!"

"They had different beliefs." And she'd gone along with them because she hadn't known any better. Jenna stroked Clint's chest, petting the tight muscle, trying to calm him. To no avail.

"I should have taken you from him when I first saw you."

"I was his wife."

"You were mine."

"I know." Ignoring the pain in her back she arched so that she could kiss the underside of his chin.

"Stay put or I won't cuddle you." He pressed her back down. It was a toothless threat, considering that his big hands were coasting over her body, touching her everywhere he could as if reassuring himself that she was really there. As if he couldn't get enough of her. Still, because he worried, she settled her cheek back against his chest.

"So what happened when you said no?" His hands went to the muscles knotting in her back, gently massaging away the tension.

"What makes you think I said no?" The question was more of a groan than a statement. He had wonderful hands. Her scalp tickled as Clint brushed his lips across her hair.

"I know you, Sunshine." It was the softest of whispers, carrying the utmost of confidence. As Jenna listened to his heartbeat and felt the determination carefully couched in his gentleness, she realized he really did. He knew everything about her, and it didn't matter. He wanted her anyway. She started to cry again. Big fat tears of relief.

"Tears are not going to sway me, Jenna. I want to know everything."

"I know." She sniffed. The second and third tear came hard on the first. "You don't hate me," she whispered.

"Ah hell, is that what has you crying?" He squeezed her carefully. "Sunshine, I could never hate you."

"You don't think I'm weak."

"You're the strongest person I know."

"You don't want me tougher."

"Baby, I want you happy and safe, in my home, loving me, our kids."

He kept answering her statements like they were questions.

"You really do care about me."

"Yes."

"And it really doesn't matter."

"No."

"I love you." She worked her arms around his neck. Moaning and crying at the same time as pain and joy lanced through her. He held her while she cried, steadying her so she didn't have to until, finally, he understood.

"These are happy tears, aren't they?"

"Very happy." She nodded and wiped at the pool collecting in the hollow of his throat. His sigh blew her hair off her face.

"Sunshine, I'm never going to understand you."

"But that's okay."

"Yes." He took a corner of the blanket and wiped her face. "But I still want to know."

She took a breath and gave him the last of her trust.

"They locked me in a grain bin full of rats until I agreed to do what they wanted." She shuddered. "The rats were everywhere. On my face, my legs, under my skirts. I thought I'd go crazy.

"Instead you did what you needed to survive," Clint provided in that deep baritone that soothed.

"Mark raped me then." She ducked her head.

"And he'll die for it." It was a calm statement of fact that brought her face up.

"You can't kill him!"

"I can do whatever I want." He cocked an eyebrow at her.

"But that would be murder and we... I need you."

"A man doesn't let an animal like that loose in the world."

"Let the law take care of it."

"He touched you." He cradled her cheek in his palm. His fingers brushed the bruise on her forehead while his thumbs stroked her lip. "Hurt you. There's no way in hell he's seeing another sunrise."

His eyes were the cold, deadly eyes of a stranger. She didn't have any doubt that Mark would not make it to trial if left to Clint.

"Does Cougar feel the same way you do?"

"Yes."

"You've talked to him?"

"No."

"Then how do you know?"

"The man laid hands on his wife. I don't need to know any more than that."

"Oh God, you're going to get yourself killed."

"I'm just going to put a rabid animal out of its misery." His kiss was cool, not the least comforting, his mind clearly on revenge.

"You are going to have to hunt him first," Gray interrupted from the door.

Jenna squealed, knowing she was bare to Gray's gaze. Clint pulled the covers over her body, carefully settling them over her injuries as he slid out from under her.

"You have reason to come barging in, son?"

"I thought you would be caring for her, not doing…other things."

"I *was* caring for her."

Jenna peeked out from under her lashes. Gray was staring at her, a brooding expression on his face.

"Mark escaped the jail."

"How?" Clint asked, reaching for his gun belt.

"Someone let him out."

"When?"

"A couple hours ago."

"Who brought the news?"

"Jackson."

"Does Cougar know?"

"He told Jackson he'd meet up with you at the river."

"Is Jackson still downstairs?"

"Yes. He said to tell you that the reverend is staying with Mara and he'll stay with Jenna."

"Good."

Jenna caught the pocket of Clint's pants.

"Don't do this."

He buckled his gun belt low in his hips. His hand was gentle on her wrist as he removed her hand. He smoothed the hair off her face, his expression solemn.

"You can ask just about anything of me, Sunshine, except for me to let Mark live."

She bit her lip against the protest that leapt forward. This was her husband. She knew him the way he knew her. It would be impossible for him to leave Mark free to hurt another woman. She swallowed her selfishness and fear. Nodding her agreement was the hardest thing she'd ever done.

The slightest of smiles lit the cold depths of Clint's black eyes.

Gray broke the silence from the door.

"I am riding with you."

"No." Clint's hair swung forward as he grabbed his black hat off the chair.

"He used to beat my mother like that. Many times. Many marks." Gray met Jenna's gaze and she wanted to cry for the too-old eyes in such a young face.

Clint settled his Stetson on his head. "He'll never beat another woman."

Gray nodded with the purpose of a much older person. "This is true."

"Clint will handle it, Gray," Jenna whispered, scared by the cold-blooded determination in the boy's face.

"It is my debt."

"I need you here." She pushed herself onto her side. Oh God, Clint had to do something.

"I have not been a child for many years." Gray's eyes softened with pity. "You must stop thinking of me as one."

"Clint." He was her son. Brianna's brother. Despite what he said, he was still just a child.

"Easy, Jenna," Clint said, "I've got this." In two strides he was at the boy's side. "You're my son now, Gray. That makes your debts mine and I promise you, before the son of a bitch dies, he'll know exactly who's killing him and why."

"Yes."

"Tell him he can't go, Clint." Jenna didn't for one second think he was agreeing to let Clint handle his revenge.

Clint stared at the boy. In that moment they looked so alike, both of their faces drawn tight with fury, their eyes hard with the call for revenge as they took each other's measure. And she knew. She knew before a word came out of either of their mouths that the decision had been made.

"No."

Gray stepped forward and touched the bruise on her head. She felt his pain and his determination in the brief connection.

"If the gods will it, I will be back and be proud to be your son."

"And if it goes wrong?"

"Then I will die a man for you to be proud of." His hand dropped to his side. He stepped back. He turned for the door.

"This isn't necessary." She couldn't lose him.

"It is." He didn't pause or flinch. Clint ushered the boy out the door before turning back to her. He filled the doorframe the way he filled her heart to the brim, a big powerful man who always did right.

"I know you don't agree, Jenna, but Gray is right. He's not a kid, and he's got a bellyful of hate he needs to let loose. If I leave him here, he'll just light out on his own."

"You don't know that." The sheets tightened painfully around her fingers as she twisted them.

"Yes. I do."

"How?"

"Because that's what I'd do."

The reality sank past her fears and her denials. If their places were switched, he would. Which meant Gray would, and if Gray had to go at all, it would be better if he was with Clint.

"You'll take care of him?"

"Yes."

She caught his hand, and using his strength, pulled herself up. Clint's arm around her waist helped her the last painful thirty degrees to upright.

"And take care of yourself. Promise me you'll take care of yourself. No matter what. Promise me you'll come back to me." She dug her fingers into his upper arms. "*No matter what.*"

"I'll take care of myself." He kissed her slowly—hot and sweet— his tongue rubbing hers in an easy rhythm. As if they had all day, as if he wasn't riding out with her son to chase down a madman. He pulled back a hair's breadth. "No matter what."

The shift of his weight told her he was leaving. Despite her resolve to be brave, her hands clung to his as he stood. She was clinging to him when he needed her to be strong.

"I'm sorry."

"If you tell me worrying makes you a lousy wife, I'll beat you." He bent down and kissed the backs of her hands.

The laugh caught her by surprise. "You're always threatening me with that."

"And one of these days I will, too." His eyebrow arched up.

She touched the back of his hand, running her finger along an old scar, before looking up.

"But not today."

"No." His gaze softened with emotion as he looked at her, studying her features as if he were memorizing them one last time. "Not today, Sunshine."

One last kiss on her hand and he headed for the door. She held back the words she wanted to say, the pleas she wanted to make until he reached the door. The instant his hand touched the knob, she lost her grip and one slipped past her guard.

"Clint?"

She knew from the set of his shoulders that he was ready to fend off her tears. Under his arm she could see Gray waiting, rifle in hand, expression solemn.

"Remember, I love you."

"That's not something a man forgets."

Jenna waited until she heard the horses leave the yard and then swung her legs over the side of the bed. There was a demon out there. He'd haunted her nightmares, and almost ruined her future. She couldn't leaving her son and husband to face him alone.

* * * * *

She couldn't believe what she was seeing. Just to be sure, she crept closer to the edge of the rock ledge, squinting against the gloom to find the edge.

Below her, in the glow of a large encampment were seven men. Four of them she recognized. Clint, Asa, Cougar, and Mark. Three were strangers, but from their unkempt appearances, she had to assume that they were acquaintances of Mark.

Mark himself was leaning face-first up against a tree, hands above his head, his fingers digging into the bark. Cougar stood beside him. From the reflection winking off of something in his hand, Jenna assumed that he was keeping him there with that wicked blade of his against Mark's neck. Cougar's face was hard as stone. A little to his left stood Asa, a rifle in his hands, his face impassive as he pointed the barrel at the three men she didn't recognize, his easy smile giving the impression that all he needed to make his night was for someone to twitch toward one of the guns tossed at the men's feet.

And Clint. Her Clint, the gentlest man she'd ever known, was methodically laying into Mark with a whip, his expression cold as he brought the lash down across Mark's shoulders, leaving a bloody welt that cut diagonally across his back. From what she'd seen in the mirror, pretty much a duplicate of the wound Mark had left on her, which explained the satisfied smile on Clint's lips. The sound of leather meeting flesh reached her ears a split second before Mark's agonized cry.

Beside her, Danny growled.

"Quiet," she whispered as her stomach roiled at the sight and sounds of the ongoing whipping. She knew her husband was a dangerous man, knew he could be single-minded in his revenge, but it disturbed her to witness the reality. From the determination on Clint's face, it didn't look like he intended to stop until the man was dead. Killing a man that way would leave a scar, no matter how well deserved. Clint had enough scars. She didn't want him to have even one more because of her.

"Stay," she told Danny, not trusting him to remain calm amidst the violence.

He whined, his attention on the scene below, but he lay down. She searched the scene again. Where was Gray? She sincerely hoped that Clint had left him someplace where he couldn't see this. He was too young for such things. She crawled back from the ledge. The whip cracked again and another scream filled the night. She redefined her thought. No one was old enough for such cold-blooded revenge. She had to put a stop to it. For Clint's sake as well as her own. She couldn't live with a man being whipped to death in her name.

Her body aching, her leg screaming in protest, she worked her way down the small hill, the sounds of the whipping a rhythmic accompaniment to her uneven steps. She stumbled several times, the descending night obliterating her ability to see the uneven ground. She made it to the edge of the clearing, close enough to smell the sweat and blood when a hand clamped across her mouth, dragging her back into a foul-smelling embrace.

"Don't even breathe," the man holding her ordered. The hard rap of metal against her temple sent stars shooting across her vision.

His knee in her thigh urged her forward. "Walk."

She did, guilt and failure swamping her in a debilitating rush.

The man made no effort to mask their approach. As he pushed her into the circle of light from the campfire, she looked up to see the barrels of three guns trained on them, and three equally disapproving frowns.

"Son of a bitch, Jenna" Clint groaned while Asa and Cougar muttered things she couldn't make out.

"Put down the guns or I'll put a hole in her pretty little head," the man behind her ordered, the gloating in his voice as offensive as his breath.

She caught Clint's eye. "Don't" she whispered, as the muzzle of his revolver dipped.

"Not much choice, Sunshine." The gun fell to his feet.

Similar thuds punctuated Asa's and Cougar's acquiescence with the order.

She closed her eyes as the man behind her shoved her forward. She'd thought it was safe. She'd only meant to stop the whipping, not to leave them all defenseless.

"Good job, Simon," Mark wheezed. She opened her eyes to see him limping toward her, his gun trained on Cougar and Clint as he shrugged his coat over one bloody shoulder. "You guys have these three covered?"

"They aren't going anywhere."

"Good." Mark reached her side, shrugged his other arm into his heavy duster, his breath hissing through his teeth as the material made contact with his lacerated flesh. "Go tie those three up," he ordered the man beside her.

A quick glance revealed him to be filthy, potbellied, and just generally ugly, with lank brown hair and a pockmarked face. She shuddered as Mark yanked her toward him. Her leg gave out. Her fall took them both by surprise, freeing her from his grasp.

"Son of bitch, Sunshine, I'm going to beat you!" Clint swore as she hit the ground, and this time he sounded like he really meant it.

"You're going to have to get in line," Mark grunted in a distortion of his normal voice.

Jenna cracked her right eye. Through her lashes she saw his face. It wasn't a pretty sight. His mouth and cheeks were grotesquely swollen.

His nose was plastered halfway across his face. She didn't know how he even spoke, let alone issued threats.

"You are a very ugly man," she whispered on the first breath she could take after the pain faded.

"And you are a very stupid woman."

"Who's going to get her ass beat as soon as I get her home," Clint growled from across the fire.

Mark nudged her with his foot when she'd been expecting him to kick. "Get up."

Look for weakness. You never know when an advantage will come your way.

As if he stood beside her, Jenna could hear Cougar's instructions. At the time it had seemed inconceivable that she'd ever have the advantage, but it just went to show how little she really knew about how things worked. Mark was clearly favoring his ribs, moving slowly, staying hunched over. He prodded her again.

"Get up, bitch."

She stayed where she was. A bullet hit the ground beside her cheek, sending a spray of dirt into her eyes. The report came from just above her head, making her ears ring.

"Do as he says, Sunshine," Clint ordered calmly as she blinked and rubbed the dirt from her eyes.

"I'm trying," she called, imitating his calm as best she could, groaning as every muscle in her body screamed against movement.

"If you'd stayed home where you belong," Clint offered conversationally, as if they all weren't within seconds of dying, "you wouldn't be in worse shape than when you started."

"Lord grant me patience, I married a told-you-so man," Jenna muttered as she rolled to her side. The knife she'd stashed in the sheath dug into her hip.

"A soon-to-be-dead man," Mark corrected, with too much satisfaction for her peace of mind.

"No!"

Mark laughed at her outcry and kicked her in the side. "Get up."

Between her back, her ribs, and the new bruising from the kick, getting up was easier said then done.

"Do as he says, Jenna," Clint told her again.

She jerked to her side. Pain speared through her back. She moaned.

"Nice and easy, Jenna," Clint admonished when she gathered her strength. "Take your time."

She did exactly as Clint ordered, drawing out the process as long as possible. She only got her knees under her before Mark lost patience.

"Boy, get over here and get her up."

Boy? Oh God, not Gray. She turned her head, wishing she knew better curse words as Gray came toward her, except he didn't look like the Gray she knew. His shoulders were hunched, his gaze downcast, and his steps hesitant.

"What did you do to him?" She pushed to her hands and knees.

"Fox and I are old friends."

The hair, knocked free of her bun when she fell, covered her face, obscuring her view. "I'll kill you if you hurt him."

"Jenna, shut up."

She ignored Clint's order. She was never shutting up again. "Stay away Gray!"

"Get over here, Fox." Mark motioned Gray forward. He went.

"Oh Gray," she sighed, the last of her hope gone.

In no way did the boy acknowledge her, keeping his face hidden from her gaze as he tugged her up. And while Clint swore when she moaned, Gray didn't even flinch.

"Look at me, Gray." He raised his head. She reached for him when he let go of her arm.

Mark backhanded him across the face. She had a quick impression of Gray's shock before he went down hard. Mark's "You know better than to pander to a woman" followed him to the ground in a disgusted snarl.

Everything within Jenna froze as she stared at her son as he tried to get up, drops of blood spattering the hand he braced under himself. She looked at the gun in Mark's hands, at the malice in his eyes, at the scene before her, the good men now hostage because of her impulsive decision. The cold ball of emotion in her stomach gathered tighter and tighter, compressing into a hard knot even as it sent equally cold tendrils of energy through her extremities.

"I'm going to kill you for that," she whispered to Mark.

"You aren't going to do shit." Mark's body shifted against hers as he raised his revolver. Jenna followed the trajectory of the smooth back barrel. He was aiming at Clint.

"I'm going to enjoy this," he told Clint, the words distorted as he forced them through his swollen lips. His finger tightened on the trigger. The cold knot in Jenna's gut exploded outward into a hot ball of fury.

Jenna launched herself at the gun, grabbing it in both hands, throwing her weight on Mark's arm, hanging on with everything she had as he beat at her, pulling the gun down and away. A bullet tore a hole in the dirt between her feet. She held on harder. Only five bullets left.

Clint's "Let go" barely penetrated the red haze blurring her vision as she fought Mark for the gun. This man had taken everything from her. Her pride, her respect, her peace. She'd be damned to hell before she let him take her husband and son. Another shot went wild. Mark swore. Clint hollered.

She blocked his voice, blocked everything but the need to get the gun. She screamed in frustration when her leg gave out and her hands slipped. Before she hit the ground, Mark had her by the hair, dragging her up, dangling her for a spilt second before he wrapped his arm around her stomach and yanked her back against his chest.

"You goddamn bitch," he panted, his voice loud in her ear. "I've changed my mind. You're going first."

The muzzle of the gun touched her temple as she reached in her pocket. Across the way, Gray's head jerked up, his eyes wide over his swollen cheek. As he jumped to his feet, a fresh drop of blood welled and pooled in the corner of his lip.

Jenna screamed and threw herself back. As Mark stumbled she let her weight fall, driving the knife down and back, exactly as Cougar had taught her, but with all the strength she could muster. She felt it slice through skin, bite through muscle, and bounce off bone as Mark's body jerked in shock.

Gunshots and cries echoed all around her as she fell. When she hit the ground, she slashed at his ankles, missing but not caring. She didn't want to get away. She wanted to kill the son of a bitch. She rolled over, diving for Mark's heart, uncaring of the gun pointed at her face. Uncaring of anything except making sure that he never hurt her son again. Ever.

A flash of light ruined her aim while a deafening explosion and splash of red obscured her vision. A hand caught hers as she tried to bring the knife down again. As much as she tugged, she couldn't move. Beneath her Mark was still. Unnaturally so.

She wiped her eyes with her shoulder and looked up the length of her arm. Gray stood staring down at her, a smoking revolver still in his hand, the other wrapped around her wrist. As she gazed at him uncomprehendingly, he shrugged.

"I did not want to lose another mother."

She didn't want to lose her son.

"He's why you don't want to be called Fox, isn't he?"

"Yes." In a fair imitation of Clint he arched his right brow, "You are unhurt?"

She wasn't sure. As she did a mental inventory the cacophony of noise filling the clearing pushed through the perimeters of her mind. She became vividly aware of men hollering, and a dog snarling. A high-pitched scream was suddenly cut short, followed by three gunshots in rapid succession.

"Is she okay?" Clint called, sounding strained, but alive. So very alive.

Gray lifted his brows in inquiry. She swallowed and nodded, more and more sure the body she was lying on was dead.

"Yes," Gray called.

"Keep her there."

Jenna did not like that note in Clint's voice. She tugged her wrist. Gray didn't let go, just shook his head when she tried again.

"Pa said to keep you here."

She froze. "You called Clint pa."

"What else would I call my father?"

"And me, mother."

He shrugged again. "What else would I call my mother?"

The bruising made his smile lopsided, but it was the first one she'd ever seen on his face and it was beautiful. So beautiful that she forgave him for for holding her for Clint.

The clearing dropped to quiet.

Two seconds later, Clint dropped to his knees beside her. His expression was pure fury. "What in hell did you think you were doing?" He rubbed at her face with his sleeve. "I've never seen such pure foolishness in all my born days."

She pushed his hand away. He swept her resistance aside with a curse and renewed his efforts.

"Clint?"

"What?"

"Please tell me I'm not lying on a dead man." The horror of it was beginning to get to her.

His "son of a bitch" told her all she needed to know. He scooped her up and just as quickly turned her over as her stomach heaved. He held her head and supported her as he swore at her, calling her foolish, impulsive, rash, and yelling at her for messing up their plan, yelling at her for almost getting herself killed and quite a few other things that she thankfully missed due to retching.

When the last of her heaves faded to lurching hiccoughs, Clint scooped her up and carried her over to the rocks, as far away from Mark's body as they could get. She wiped at her mouth with her sleeve.

"Here." A canteen was shoved in her face. She took it gratefully, smiling up into Cougar's stern face as she first rinsed out her mouth and then took a long drink of the cool water.

"You were right," she said. "I did have it in me."

"I'm rarely wrong." A hint of a smile crinkled the corners of his fascinating eyes.

"Do not encourage her." Clint glared at them both as he ran his hands over her body, unmindful of their audience as he lifted her dress to check her legs, her hip, her back. When his hand slid over her buttock she shrieked and pulled away. Clint's response was a curt, "Don't push me, Jenna."

He hauled her against his chest, swearing when she flinched away from his gentlest touch. Over his shoulder she saw the wicked twinkle in Cougar's eyes and his smile spread from a hint to full-blown.

"If I were you Clint, I'd watch what you say. The little lady has a hair trigger temper."

Clint wasn't impressed.

"The little lady is going to have a sore ass."

He probed down her thigh, and she moaned as pain flared. Now that the excitement was over, her body was making her aware of every bruise. She looped her arms around his neck and buried her face in his throat, breathing deeply of his wonderful scent.

"I already do."

"You've got no one but yourself to blame," he growled, fingering the knot in her thigh and massaging it, his touch incredibly light in direct contrast to his biting words.

"If I start unbuttoning my blouse, will you stop yelling?"

The jerk of Clint's body could have been laughter or irritation. Before she could find out, Asa came up, holding Danny's ruff. She didn't look too closely at the stain around the big dog's mouth.

"Now there's a woman knows how to sweet-talk a man."

This hadn't been his fight, but he'd come, backing her husband, risking his life. She only had one thing to say to him. "Thank you."

He shrugged. "McKinnelys stick together."

"You're a MacIntyre."

"He wore us down with that damned perverse sense of humor of his," Cougar admitted in a disgusted tone. "We claimed him out of sheer self-preservation."

Asa smiled and tipped his hat, leaving it a little lower over his brow as he said dryly, "I was flat-out honored."

Clint grunted. "Did you get the others?"

"They're all wrapped up nice and tidy. Mark doesn't run with a bright group." He motioned to the center of the clearing where two men were lying face-down in the dirt, their hands tied behind their backs. The other bodies weren't tied and didn't move.

"Who got Mark?" Asa asked.

"Gray." Clint shot the boy a concerned glance. "He saved Jenna's life."

None of the men said anything for a moment. Then Cougar spoke up.

"Good job." Gray nodded, his expression tight.

Clint ran his hand over the welt on her hip. Jenna couldn't help wincing.

Asa's eyes narrowed. "She doesn't look in any shape to ride."

"She's not." Clint pushed the hair off her cheek, his eyes searching every inch of her face.

"You two want to wait for us to come back with a wagon?" Cougar asked.

Before Clint could weigh in, Jenna shook her head. She didn't want to stay here. "I want to go home."

"Baby, you're too busted up."

"I got here, I can get home." She was not staying here.

"Speaking of which, how did you find us?" Asa asked.

"Danny."

"I thought you had better sense." Clint glared at the dog.

Danny merely sat and cocked his head, the dog equivalent of a shrug.

"I for one am glad that he came. Took out one of the bastards who had the drop on me." Asa patted Danny's big head. "Think I'll have Old Sam whip him up a steak when I go back to get the wagon."

"I'm not staying here," Jenna repeated. If she could have she would have folded her arms across her chest. "I'm going home."

Clint sighed. "You're so weak now, you're shaking. You'll never sit a horse."

She was. In the aftermath of the violence, she felt totally drained, buffeted by so many emotions that she couldn't make sense of any but one. "I'm going home."

"Goddamn it, Jenna." Clint tucked her tighter against him. "You are in no shape to ride."

"Fine. She could tell he was working up to yelling at her again so she headed him off. Then get my pillow and let me ride in front of you."

"What?"

"I used a pillow to get up here. I can use one to get back."

"*A pillow?*"

"The saddle hurt, so I used a pillow," she muttered into his shoulder. The look he sent her questioned her sanity. "It worked fine until the pillow slipped. Bucky didn't like that—"

Around her there was the stifled sound of laughter. Against her, Clint's muscles tightened to hard ridges of disbelief.

"You rode one of my testiest cow ponies on a pillow?"

"Yes."

"And he waited to balk until you got here?"

"Yes."

"Son of a bitch, somebody upstairs must hate me." He dropped his forehead against hers.

"Maybe the good Lord wanted to make sure you'd be able to find me when I got bucked off."

"That must be it," He said in a resigned tone.

He touched her forehead, her cheek, her lip, all the places she knew she had marks and then pulled her hard against him, asking in a weary voice, "What am I going to do with you Jenna McKinnely?"

She only had one answer for him.

"You could try loving me."

Chapter Twenty-Five

You could try loving me.

Clint leaned his shoulder against the door, popped the bottle in Bri's mouth, and watched the soft glow of moonlight play over Jenna's gentle face as she slept.

How could she not know he loved her? Since the day he'd first seen her, he'd been a goner. He'd fought it, tried to rise above his selfish need, but there hadn't been any true hope that he'd escape. He was too far from a saint, and she was just too much temptation with her shy smile, sweet softness, and hot, giving nature. Son of a bitch, he loved her.

As he watched, she turned, reaching out to his side of the bed before frowning and rolling back. He'd have to take her back to see Doc tomorrow. That'd require some sort of clever excuse as Jenna would balk at another examination, but damn it, she worried him. She'd been listless ever since that night. Not eating well, not smiling, and generally withdrawn. Part of it was her wounds—any movement at all the first day was agony—but even when that let up, her listlessness didn't. Son of a bitch, he wasn't going to lose her.

The baby kicked her feet and turned away from the bottle.

"What's the matter, Button? Suck too much wind?" he whispered, taking the bottle from her mouth. She gave him one milky little smile, no doubt delighted with her ability to disturb the adult world, and then proceeded to pout.

"Oh no, you don't. No waking up Mommy."

He shifted her to his shoulder. She'd doubled in size since the first time he'd seen her, but she was still the tiniest bit of humanity, her back barely stretching his palm and for all her spirit, felt as fragile as the china tea cups Dorothy pulled out on special occasions. With the tip of one finger, he rubbed her back, feeling the delicate ladder of her baby spine. And frowned. Maybe he'd have Doc look at her again tomorrow, too. He didn't care what the women said about her being fine. She needed more meat on her bones.

He sighed. Jenna would have something to say about that, no doubt. She was always riding his case about worrying too much, but he'd gone from nothing to everything and those kinds of changes had a man thinking in terms of the cost of losing. Especially with the scare Jenna and Gray had just given him. He frowned as Jenna turned and the blanket fell off her shoulder revealing the head to toe nightgown she'd taken to wearing.

He sighed once more and kissed the top of Bri's head. Jenna's taking to wearing smothering nightclothes was his fault, too. Every time he'd seen her cuts and bruises over the last four days, he'd lost his temper. He couldn't help it. It scared the shit out of him that that sick son of a bitch had gotten his hands on Jenna. And it would take at least five lifetimes to forget the sight of her facing down the barrel of a gun, uncaring of her own safety as she defended her son.

"Your mother has a bit of a wildcat in her, Button," he whispered, a smile working past his worry. Bri bobbed her head on his shoulder, belched, and tangled her fist in his hair. "If you're lucky, some of it will wear off on you."

"I don't think that will be a concern," Gray said, touching his sister's cheek. "She has quite a temper."

"Couldn't sleep?" Clint turned, not surprised to find the boy up, or Danny by his side. The two had taken to each other and patrolled the halls nightly.

Gray shook his head, his long braids swinging with the motion.

"Killing a man is hard, even if he deserved it."

"It is already getting easier."

"Then why are you up?"

Gray's gaze skirted his to touch on Jenna as she lay on the bed. He tickled Bri's cheek with one hand while the other clenched in Danny's rough fur. A sure sign he was working up to something big. Clint rubbed Bri's back, waiting him out. Finally, the boy raised his face, his jaw clinched and his shoulders set for battle.

"She is not happy."

"She had a tough time of it out there." So he wasn't the only one who'd noticed the change in Jenna.

"I do not want to lose another mother." The boy's mouth was set in the same determined line as his jaw.

"Jenna's not going anywhere."

"She is an easy person to love." The boy's expression went from stubborn to mutinous.

"I know." That was the truth. Falling in love with Jenna was as easy and as natural as breathing.

"Then why doesn't she know you love her?"

"Because I haven't told her."

"I will take Hope on the Mist, and you will tell her." The look of disgust the boy gave him said more than words. Gray reached for Bri. Bri went to him willingly. Clint untangled her fist from his hair while she dangled sleepily between them.

"I was planning on telling her at the social." He'd come up with the plan after Mara had let slip what that bitch Shirley had said about his reasons for marrying Jenna. Saturday's social was going to be a territory-wide party, celebrating his marriage to Jenna, and right in the middle of it he was going to work up the courage to get down on one knee before God and the territory and ask Jenna to marry him again. It was going to be the granddaddy all of romantic gestures. It would embarrass the hell out of him, but he'd do it for Jenna. Dorothy and Elizabeth were handling the arrangements. Lorie and Patricia were helping. After the social, there wouldn't be any doubt in anyone's mind that Clint McKinnely was head over heels in love with his wife, and he'd married her for love and nothing else.

"Three days is too long to wait," Gray countered, stubbornly clinging to his point.

Jenna moaned. Clint glanced over. She was trying to turn onto her back. One hand reached for him. Her fingers splayed over the empty side of the bed. Her fingers closed, her arm relaxed, and that sad resigned expression he'd come to hate took up residence on her face.

He sighed and shook his head. The kid was right. He'd have the party, and he'd make Jenna a legend with how she'd brought Clint McKinnely to his knees, but he wouldn't make her wait any longer for that last piece she needed from him.

"I suppose it is." He cupped Gray's shoulder and kissed Bri's head. "Do you think you and Bri might want to spend a couple days visiting with Uncle Asa and Aunt Elizabeth?"

"You will tell her?"

"Yes." It was a measure of how much the boy loved Jenna that he even hesitated, seeing as being with Asa meant being with his horse. The boy's smile flashed brighter than sunshine off a mirror.

"We will leave in the morning."

"Take Jackson with you."

"I can handle myself."

"I know you can," Clint handed Gray the bottle and the burping rag, "but a baby limits a man's ability to react, and it's better not to take chances." He expected the boy to argue, but instead he nodded, his eyes taking on that too-old look.

"I will not take chances. You do not have need to worry."

"I'm not worried, son, just naturally cautious."

Before Gray could cite stories to the contrary, Clint turned him by the shoulders and pointed him down the hall.

"If you want me to be making peace with your mother, I suggest you give me space to do it in."

In two seconds, he had all the space he needed.

* * * * *

Clint shucked his denims and sat on the side of the bed, turning sideways as he carefully eased the thick rope of Jenna's braid from behind her. He loved the way she looked bathed in moonlight. Her skin taking on the color of cream and roses. Her hair shining with an ethereal light. She looked like one of those angels from the paintings. Plump, sweet, and as tempting as sin itself.

He tugged the tie from her braid and worked the silken strands free. He arranged them around her face, smiling as the waves fell where they would despite his plans. He leaned over, bracing his hands on either side of her torso. He brushed her ear with his lips, his smile broadening as she shivered in her sleep and goose bumps sprang up on the one arm he could see.

"Wake up, Sunshine."

She stirred. "Clint?"

He braced his palm on her spine before she could roll back and hurt herself.

"Easy, baby."

Her right eye cracked open and she nuzzled into his thigh. Lord help him, he even loved the way she came awake in stages like a plump, sleepy little kitten, cuddling up to the warmth of his body.

"What's wrong?" She cupped his knee and stroked her thumb over the ridge of bone.

"Nothing."

He hitched his hip higher on the bed, urging her closer until her cheek rested high on his thigh and the soft silk of her hair fell across his groin.

"It's still night," she yawned. "Did Bri wake up?"

"Yes. Gray has her."

"He couldn't sleep?"

"No."

"But he's okay?"

"Yes." Her other eye cracked open.

"So there's no need for me to be up?"

"There's a need." He took a handful of her hair in his hand and rubbed it over his aching cock simply because it felt so damned good.

"You want to make love?"

"You're still too banged up." He couldn't tell how she felt about the idea from her tone of voice.

"So you did wake me up for no reason." She tipped her head back, her smile as soft as her skin.

"No." He eased his thumb between her lips, letting the moisture inside her mouth coat his flesh before sliding his thumb along the full curve of her lower lip, pulling it away from her teeth, teasing himself with the heat of her mouth. "I woke you up to tell you I love you."

Air hissed past his thumb, bathing it in a wash of moist warmth as she blinked at him. Both eyes were totally open now, shining deep blue in the dim lamplight. She didn't say a word, didn't move, didn't breathe for three seconds. Then she blinked again, sucked in a staccato breath, and those beautiful eyes began to fill with tears.

"Ah baby, those had better be happy tears."

"I've waited so long for you to say that." Her tongue touched the pad of his finger, sending streaks of need shooting up his arm.

"I know." He caught a teardrop as it shimmered on her cheek. "Too long."

"But why now?" She asked, as she shook her head, letting her hair flow erotically down over his balls.

"Because I realized even if you wanted an out, I'm never going to give it to you." She was his own little piece of heaven, his personal treasure, and he could no more give her up than he could give up his soul. "I can't let you go, Sunshine."

"I don't want to go."

"I'm beginning to believe that now." He slid his fingers across her cheek, behind her head, keeping his thumb against her lips, needing the contact.

She tucked her elbow under her torso and pushed up. Her flinch cut him to the bone. He'd have to take much better care of her. He supported as much of her weight as he could as she pulled herself higher against him.

"Hold me," she ordered. He did, groaning as the smooth skin of her inner arm slid over his thigh. Son of a bitch, she tempted him.

"You thought I'd want to leave?" she asked on a sigh of satisfaction as he gave her weight back to her gradually. She made it sound as if it was the most ludicrous idea that could ever cross a man's mind.

"Sunshine, as much as you like to think otherwise, beyond a hefty bank account, I'm not much of a prize."

"I decided long ago that you are no judge of people."

"I beg your pardon?" He was known far and wide for his ability to scent a lie before it was spoken.

"You should beg for it, making me wait so long for your heart." She trailed the backs of her fingers up the inside of his thigh.

"You've always had my heart." He tilted his hips forward a bit, giving her better access. "I just didn't tell you about it."

"Why?" She clasped his cock through the blanket of her hair, closing her fingers with that delicacy that was so much a part of her.

"I'm not the man you think I am." He looked down at her plump white hand wrapped in the moonlight-gilded blonde of her hair as it encompassed his cock. She was so pure compared to him. So innocent. He fought back the selfish lust that raced through him. She didn't look shocked or upset, just patient as she waited for him to elaborate.

"Jack Hennesey didn't die in that fire."

Her "I know" was a bare whisper.

"You do?"

"He slammed the door behind him when he left." She shuddered and he cupped her cheek, helpless to remove the memory that terrified her. "I knew he wouldn't be coming back."

"I killed him." The stark statement landed hard in the silence. He couldn't read anything in her slow blink, her stillness.

"How?" she finally asked.

"I was coming up to check on you—"

"Check on me?"

"Hennesey had been spouting a bunch of nonsense in the saloon." She didn't need to know that the man had suggested that anyone willing to lay out a gold piece could have her.

"And?"

"When I got there, the shack was on fire. Hennesey was outside. There was blood all over him, but not much damage."

"I told him I was leaving him. He went crazy."

"Not as crazy as I went when he told me I was too late. That you were dead." He covered the shaking in his hand by stroking her hair. "I snapped his worthless neck when he tried to stop me and went in after you."

"He told you I was dead?"

"Yes." The light had gone out of his world in that second. Even Cougar hadn't been able to hold him back. He'd needed to see for himself, to touch her one last time, wanting to howl right along with Danny at the thought of her loss.

"And you still came in after me?"

He gave up trying to cover the trembling. He cupped her cheek in his hand, rubbing his thumb over her lips, holding her close, remembering the agony, the searing heat, the despair when he'd entered that inferno, knowing no one could survive that heat, but unable to bear the thought of her soft body turning to ash.

"I couldn't let you burn."

"You could have been killed."

"I wasn't leaving without you." He hadn't thought he'd be leaving at all until Cougar had chopped through the back wall providing an escape route. He hadn't cared either. He wasn't letting her leave this world scared and alone.

"I love you." Jenna's eyes filled with tears. She touched the scars on his chest.

"Does this mean you might work up to forgiving me?" He hugged her to him carefully, everything inside of him strained to the breaking point with the most fragile of hopes.

"There's nothing to forgive."

There was — a hell of a lot, — and he knew it.

"I murdered your first husband." A God-fearing woman like Jenna couldn't just forget about that.

"I know. And he tried to murder me. It might make me a bad person, but I'm glad you came, glad you got me out, but mostly, I'm very, very glad that you took me for yourself." Her hand on his chest was infinitely soothing.

As if it had only been waiting for this moment, all the emotion he'd ever denied welled in a surge for freedom. He choked it back as Jenna stoked his chest, took a breath and then whispered, "I used to pray to God to give me the strength to get through every day." She touched the middle of the scar on his chest. "Sometimes, when it was really bad, I'd pray that He'd send an angel to take me away.

"He sent me you." Her finger followed a scar up over his collarbone to press against the pulse in the hollow of his throat.

He pulled back, took a shuddering breath and stroked her temple. "You think I'm an answer to a prayer?"

She shook her head, her hair rustling against his thigh.

"I think you're a dream come true. A man who sees me for what I am, and loves me anyway."

"It's not hard to love perfect." He traced the blue vein showing through her pale white skin. She was so fragile and yet so strong. Beautiful and sweet. Everything a man could ever desire. And she loved him. To his dying day, he'd never get over the miracle of that.

"I agree." She shifted up on his thigh so that her breath misted his cock, her gaze meeting his. "Which is why you shouldn't have any trouble understanding why I love you."

"You're a wonder, Jenna." He'd never understand why she loved him, but he'd go to his grave humbled by it.

She wrapped her hand back around him, and shook her head, amusement and patience in her gaze, as she corrected him, "We're wonderful together."

"I don't deserve you." He touched the corner of her mouth.

"But you'll take me anyway?" Her smile was a lush mix of gentleness and passion.

"Hell, yes!" He was grateful, not stupid

She blew a stream of air across the tip of his cock. He jerked as the flickering sensation traveled to his balls, pulling them tight before joining the white-hot bolts of need blazing out from the base of his spine. His drawl was a rough parody of what he wanted as he said, "Sunshine, you're playing with fire."

She laughed, flashing those dimples at him, laughing longer when his cock jumped and grew in her hand, running her tongue over her lips as a bead of come welled.

"I like the way you want me," she whispered with that honesty of hers that drove him crazy. She pumped him gently in her hand, treating him to the silky glide of her hair interspersed with the teasing softness of her skin. "I like the way you let me touch you." She leaned forward and lapped the bead of moisture from the winking slit, taking a long time to accomplish the job. He knew that she knew what the sight of that delicate pink tongue of hers moving over his cock head did to his insides.

"Witch," he muttered.

"Wife," she corrected, before taking his seed inside her mouth, closing her eyes and tilting her head back, as if savoring his flavor, smiling as she swallowed.

His heart stopped, reconsidered and then charged to a gallop, thundering in his chest as she opened those eyes and leaned forward again, her expression one of impish determination.

"Sunshine, we agreed, no play tonight."

"I'm not playing." She pumped his cock through her hand, working it up and over as she did so until it lay across his thigh, pointing directly at her, throbbing in an agony of anticipation.

She rested her cheek on his thigh. He moved his hand down to the side of her neck so he could see her expression as she milked him in easy, lazy motions that teased and burned when he wanted to thrust and come. A tiny smile played on her lips as his cock twitched and stretched in a plea that echoed the fire searing under his skin. There was the slightest of tension around her eyes, which from experience he knew meant that she was unsure about something.

"What do you want, baby?"

She blinked and the skin on her cheeks stained dark.

"Haven't you learned by now that there isn't anything you could tell me that I don't want to hear?" He tested the heat in her cheek with his thumb. She was hot, flushed, and hungry. Just the way he liked her. He just didn't know for what.

"I want to love you," she whispered, still staring at his cock with that hungry longing.

"How?"

"Slowly." She touched the tip of her finger to the tip of his shaft. "With my heart."

"Son of a bitch!" He was in danger of coming from her touch.

"You won't mind?" Her eyes flashed at him.

"Try me and see."

She took him at his word, delicately testing him with her tongue. Easing her lips around the tip, she sipped at him as if this were a moment she longed to draw out. Savor. As if loving him was the best thing in life. Exactly the way he felt when he had her under him, listening to her whimper in pleasure, knowing no one gave her what he did.

Against the heel of his hand, her jaw pushed as she worked the sensitive head past her teeth, bathing him in liquid heat, welcoming him home.

"Sunshine?" She looked up, her expression one of loving contentment and passion. He traced her lips as they stretched around him, the smile starting way down deep inside. "I'm still not forgetting I owe you a beating."

Her answering smile showed in her eyes. And then, slowly—so slowly that he didn't know what was going on at first—she turned on his lap, tucked her knees under her, and called his bluff.

He laughed through his lust, remembering when she would have cowered at the threat, and brought his hand gently down on the right cheek, just under the bruise from Mark's abuse.

Jenna smiled around the thick wedge of his cock before working him free, and catching his throbbing cock in her hand as she arched into his touch. "If you beat me, I won't wear my new dress to the social," she warned.

"You won't?" He arched his brow at her.

"Nope, and it's scandalously low-cut. Shows off everything I've got." Her smile was butter soft as she said it. His mouth went dry and a spurt of come slipped past his control. Her everything was damned impressive. She caught the small spill on her palm, smoothing it back into his skin with a purr. It took him two shuddering breaths to find his voice.

"What makes you think I want you wearing a dress like that?"

"Because," her tongue stroked over his cock in a slow, burning pass. Her smile was pure womanly confidence. "I'll let you," she paused to suck delicately at the little slit, dragging another drop of come past his control, "*only you*...take it off when we get home."

Love laced with desire trapped his laugh in his throat. He wanted to see her like that, dancing at the social, head up, shoulders back, teasing him with those gorgeous breasts and his own desire, confident in herself and her power. He cupped her cheek in his palm, holding her gaze with his, smoothing his thumb over her dimples, letting her love pour over him, filling all those empty places he'd thought forever barren—catching it, magnifying it, and reflecting it back, loving her beyond sense and reason. Needing her more than he needed his next breath.

"Guess I'll be holding off on that beating for awhile."

Her "I thought you might" rolled over his passion in a hot breath of laughter.

She was light to his dark. Sweet to his bitter. Soft to his hard. He traced her smile. She was his complete opposite. Open and honest. She held nothing back, giving him all that she was, expecting nothing in return. Just hoping.

It was that hope that was doing him in. Had been since the day he'd met her. It had steadily hammered at the wall around his emotions until all it would take was one word from her, and he'd be defenseless.

He pulled her up carefully, settling her across his lap, only to discover that she didn't need a word. She just needed to wrap her arms around his neck, offering herself, her comfort, her unquestioning acceptance of whatever he needed.

He buried his face in the curve of her neck, breathing in the faint scent of roses and woman, not recognizing the sting in his eyes for what it was until her whispered "I love you" slammed through the barricade around his emotions, tearing it down with one unguarded truth until there was nothing left to hide behind. Nothing left to shield either of them.

Emotion poured over him in an unfamiliar wave—relief, fear, joy—and love welled out of the dark place where he'd buried it so long ago. So much love that it swamped him in a shattering revelation of everything he'd tried to deny. He tugged her closer when she would have arched away, holding her tightly as the reality of what loving Jenna really meant crashed through his carefully formed plans. As long as Jenna was his wife, he'd never experience the peace that came from containing emotion. Jenna would demand everything from him, every thought, every feeling. With her, he'd experience life in all its highs and lows. He'd be vulnerable in ways he had yet to comprehend, and that scared the shit out of him.

But nothing scared him as much as the thought of living without her. His sweet, giving Jenna who even now was pushing back to see his face, ready to take on his demons, armed with nothing more than the strength of her love. Son of a bitch, she had such courage.

"What is it Clint?"

He shook his head, not trusting his voice.

As if she sensed how close he was to breaking, Jenna's hand paused over his heart, pressing reassuringly, steadying him with her touch alone, quelling the desperate flood of emotion that was drowning him, seeming to take it into herself until he could breathe again.

"Whatever it is Clint," she said, her soft blue eyes meeting his, "I can handle it."

She was a living, breathing miracle. And she loved him. He rested his forehead against hers, easing her chest into his, letting their breath mingle as he said, "I know you can."

He cupped her head in his hands and tilted her face for the descent of his mouth, brushing his lips over hers once, twice before smiling into her eyes as he gave her what he'd never give another—his heart, his trust, and his faith.

"I love you, Sunshine."

About the author:

Sarah has traveled extensively throughout her life, living in other cultures, sometimes in areas where electricity was a concept awaiting fruition and a book was an extreme luxury. While she could easily adjust to the lack of electricity, living without the comfort of a good book was intolerable. To fill the void, she bought pencil and paper and sketched out her own story, and in the process, discovered the joy of writing. She's been at it ever since.

Sarah welcomes mail from readers. You can write to her c/o Ellora's Cave Publishing at 1056 Home Avenue, Akron OH 44310-3502.

Why an electronic book?

We live in the Information Age—an exciting time in the history of human civilization in which technology rules supreme and continues to progress in leaps and bounds every minute of every hour of every day. For a multitude of reasons, more and more avid literary fans are opting to purchase e-books instead of paperbacks. The question to those not yet initiated to the world of electronic reading is simply: *why?*

1. *Price.* An electronic title at Ellora's Cave Publishing and Cerridwen Press runs anywhere from 40-75% less than the cover price of the <u>exact same title</u> in paperback format. Why? Cold mathematics. It is less expensive to publish an e-book than it is to publish a paperback, so the savings are passed along to the consumer.

2. *Space.* Running out of room to house your paperback books? That is one worry you will never have with electronic novels. For a low one-time cost, you can purchase a handheld computer designed specifically for e-reading purposes. Many e-readers are larger than the average handheld, giving you plenty of screen room. Better yet, hundreds of titles can be stored within your new library—a single microchip. (Please note that Ellora's Cave and Cerridwen Press does not endorse any specific brands. You can check our website at www.ellorascave.com or

www.cerridwenpress.com for customer recommendations we make available to new consumers.)

3. *Mobility.* Because your new library now consists of only a microchip, your entire cache of books can be taken with you wherever you go.

4. *Personal preferences are accounted for.* Are the words you are currently reading too small? Too large? Too...**ANNOYING**? Paperback books cannot be modified according to personal preferences, but e-books can.

5. *Instant gratification.* Is it the middle of the night and all the bookstores are closed? Are you tired of waiting days—sometimes weeks—for online and offline bookstores to ship the novels you bought? Ellora's Cave Publishing sells instantaneous downloads 24 hours a day, 7 days a week, 365 days a year. Our e-book delivery system is 100% automated, meaning your order is filled as soon as you pay for it.

Those are a few of the top reasons why electronic novels are displacing paperbacks for many an avid reader. As always, Ellora's Cave and Cerridwen Press welcomes your questions and comments. We invite you to email us at service@ellorascave.com, service@cerridwenpress.com or write to us directly at: 1056 Home Ave. Akron OH 44310-3502.

NEED A MORE EXCITING WAY TO PLAN YOUR DAY?

ELLORA'S CAVEMEN

2006 CALENDAR

COMING THIS FALL

THE
ELLORA'S CAVE
LIBRARY

Stay up to date with Ellora's Cave Titles
in Print with our Quarterly Catalog.

To recieve a catalog,
send an email with your name
and mailing address to:

CATALOG@ELLORASCAVE.COM

or send a letter or postcard
with your mailing address to:
Catalog Request
c/o Ellora's Cave Publishing, Inc.
1337 Commerce Drive #13
Stow, OH 44224

Lady Jaided magazine is devoted to exploring the sexuality and sensuality of women. While there are many similarities between the sexual experiences of men and women, there are just as many if not more differences. Our focus is on the female experience and on giving voice and credence to it. Lady Jaided will include everything from trends, politics, science and history to gossip, humor and celebrity interviews, but our focus will remain on female sexuality and sensuality.

A Sneak Peek at Upcoming Stories

Clan of the Cave Woman
Women's sexuality throughout history.

The Sarandon Syndrome
What's behind the attraction between older women and younger men.

The Last Taboo
Why some women – even feminists – have bondage fantasies

Girls' Eyes for Queer Guys
An in-depth look at the attraction between straight women and gay men

Available Spring 2005

www.LadyJaided.com